Before becoming [illegible] s a research psycholo[illegible] ne mother and variou[illegible] en a frequent contributor to *The Times* and has been published in *The Guardian, The Observer* and *The Independent.* Her earlier novels are *Plotting for Beginners* (written with Jane Linfoot), *Zuzu's Petals,* and *But I Told You Last Year That I Loved You.* Sue lives with her husband in the Derbyshire Peak District. Her blog is at www.suehepworth.com

Plotting for Grown-ups

by

Sue Hepworth

in association with

Jane Linfoot

Also by Sue Hepworth and Jane Linfoot

Plotting for Beginners

And by Sue Hepworth

Zuzu's Petals

But I Told You Last Year That I Loved You

Plotting for Grown-ups

by

Sue Hepworth

in association with

Jane Linfoot

Delicately Nuanced
Derbyshire

First published in Great Britain in 2013 by
Delicately Nuanced
Wayside, Mires Lane
Rowland
Bakewell
Derbyshire, DE45 1NP
email: info@delicatelynuanced.com
www.delicatelynuanced.com
Cataloguing in Publication Data is available from the British Library
ISBN 978-0-9568457-2-6

Printed and bound in Great Britain by
CPI Group (UK) Croydon CR0 4YY

With all my love to

Tate, Gil, Lux and Cecilia

- bringers of joy

SH

SEPTEMBER

Thursday September 1st

Encounter

What a fantastic day. Not.

Pippa disturbed my morning by battering on the front door and saying when I opened it, "Good morning, Sally. I'm so sorry. Are you not well? I mean – you're still in your pyjamas. Yes you are."

"I'm fine, Pippa. I write in bed. What do you want?"

"You sound tense. Yes you do."

I must have been really snippy in my tone with her. She is not a perceptive woman.

"I've just had an email from my literary agent," I said. "Two *more* publishers have rejected my latest novel. That's what's up."

"Oh dear, I'm sorry. I am." She looked at her watch. "Oh my goodness, it's getting late. I have a hair appointment, and Richard has disappeared just when I need him to walk the dogs." She said this as if she is still Richard's girlfriend. How could a brother of mine possibly fall for someone with a pearl addiction? "Will you take them for me?" she said, pressing the leads into my hand. "Just watch the blue lead. It's rather unreliable. Yes it is. Wonky." And she scurried away before I could stop her. The outrageous cheek of the woman! I hadn't even a smidgeon of a chance to say, "No! Sort out your own wretched dogs! I'm busy writing!"

Actually, I hadn't done a lot of writing. I'd re-read the bit about the 'Cute Meet' in Billy Mernit's *Writing the Romantic Comedy* and then tweaked a couple of sentences in mine to make it perfect, and after that I'd been messing about in the form of:

- emailing Giovanna to ask if she'd managed to sort out the sagging middle of the romance novel she's writing, and to have a jolly good moan about the awful news about my rejections;
- Googling myself;
- checking my blog statistics to see how many readers I have.

And now Pippa's annoying dogs were barking and tugging at their leads, so I bundled them into the back of the car, rushed back in the house and pulled on some clothes, and then drove to Hassop Station, where two slobbering canine reasons helped me resist the double lure of the bookshop inside, and the sun-splashed cafe tables on the disused platform outside.

Soon I was walking up the Monsal Trail with the blessed hounds on their stupid extending leads, one of which had a catch that didn't hold the lead unless I gripped it tightly with my thumb.

And because the weather was balmy, the Trail was heaving. It's been like that since they souped it up and opened all the old tunnels. There were wappy tourists on tandems with tagalongs, five year olds with stabilisers cutting people up, and huge groups of hikers that sprawled across the carriageway.

I kept to the left hand side (which is what you're supposed to do) with the dogs on a short tight rein. I was in a haze, thinking how crap life is, and how it is that you're chugging along fairly happily, thinking everything's more or less in place, and then fate hurls a freezing cold tsunami over your dreams.

And how it's exactly three years ago today that Gus left for the last time. Hordes of women my age wish their other halves would bog off to another continent, but when it actually happens, it's another story. The first time he went – newly retired – it was empowering. The second time, it was tiresome. In the end it was...well, the end. And here I am, 60 next month, and what hope is there of sorting out my life before I die – a has-been writer and a washed-up wife?

Meanwhile, the dogs were tugging and sniffing and being annoying. I am not keen on dogs at the best of times. And these were Pippa's dogs, and it was not the best of times. But I was in control. I was in control until one of them decided to have a crap on the verge, and I was bending down to scoop it up in a bag, and as I fumbled with the bag while holding both leads, my thumb slipped on the dodgy lead catch and Maisie (or Millie – I don't know which is which) ran out across the Trail, and there was a squeal of brakes behind me and a male voice booming "Bloody hell!" down my neck and I swirled round and a guy was sprawled at my feet, with cycling accessories flying off in every direction. The man was still attached to his bike by those clippy pedals that I personally have always refused to entertain on my bike, even though Gus has flirted with them and every other man I know swears by the things.

"You should be shot!" the man shouted. "Your bloody dogs should be shot!" He couldn't get up because the bike was on top of him, and he couldn't get into a suitable position to get his feet unclipped from his pedals. And then the dogs circled round and started pawing him and licking his face, and the leads got tangled on his handlebars. Arrgghh!

He huffed and groaned and squirmed and wriggled and eventually I managed to pull the dogs clear, and he extricated himself from his own personal snarl up, and heaved himself to his feet, and said "For God's sake!"

And all the while I stood there useless, clutching a bag of shit, wanting to help but unable to do so because I was struggling to control the wretched dogs. He started to examine the gravel rash on his knees and the cut on his hand which was bleeding, and I pulled the dogs tightly in and said, "I am so sorry. Are you all right? These aren't my dogs and I have a dodgy extending lead and–"

"You shouldn't be allowed out. Why are you in charge of them if you don't know how to handle them?"

"Please let me help you. I think I've got a wet-wipe in my bag. Hang on, I–"

"You can stuff your wet-wipe up your…ouch!" he said as he tried to pick a piece of grit out of his knee.

"Please let me help. I've done a St John's Ambulance course so I'm not a complete dumbo. I–"

"Are you trying to drum up business? Just butt out. You've done enough damage already."

He was about my age and slim and tall and not bad looking (I couldn't help noticing, not for me, but for best-friend Wendy, who would want every detail) – but he was the rudest man I have ever had the misfortune to meet. As soon as he was on his feet and had gathered up the stuff that had been knocked off him or his bike – poncey water bottle, fast-boy sunglasses – he turned his back on me, and cycled away without a word, in the direction he'd come from.

I'd had enough. It was the first and last time I'd be doing a favour for Pippa. As I turned to go back to the car, I saw something shiny nestling in the grass verge. It was a slender, expensive looking, clip-on bike light. It must be his. Fast Boy's (aka Fast Pensioner's). I picked it up and brought it home and now I suppose I shall have to take it with me every time I go on the Trail, in case I see him and can give it back. What a pain.

Real life pretty much sucks – which is why, I suppose, I spend my days concocting alternatives.

Friday September 2nd

Fraternal update

Richard came round again. He is nicely settled in his new rented cottage between Main Street and the rec, but he still calls in here every single day. I had him here for three months when he was in recovery after splitting up with Pippa, and his homing habit is clearly hard to break. There I will be, sitting in bed, writing on my laptop, and he'll let himself in the front door and shout, "Are you there? I just want to have a look at *The Cupid Column* in your *Recorder*." Anyone else would buy their own paper to check the personal ads, but this is my brother we're talking about.

I suppose he's still getting used to being on his own again, so he pops in here for company. It's his birthday today so I didn't stay in bed and ignore him, I came downstairs and made him fresh coffee and pancakes. He was still deciding what he wanted as a present.

"Pippa's asked me to have the dogs for a fortnight while she goes on holiday," he said, picking up *The Recorder*. She's always asking him to do something – walk her dogs, pick her fruit, make her jam, hold the mirror while she touches up her roots, take the dogs' extending leads while she scratches her nose.

"She even dumped the wretched animals on me, yesterday! Why do you put up with it, Richard? Why are you always bailing her out?"

"It feels so mean not to help."

"But she has to get used to the idea that you two are no longer an item. Moving out of her house has obviously not done the trick."

"It took long enough for you – with Gus."

I swivelled round from the stove. "Gus was my husband. For 30 years! Not exactly the equivalent of your post-divorce fling with Pippa which dragged on for...how many years? Six? So do you want these pancakes or not?" I turned back to the frying pan and grabbed the ladle and sloshed in some batter, spilling a load of it down the outside edge of the pan.

"Keep your hair on," he said, absentmindedly. He was staring at a photo on the front page of the paper. "I'm rather worried about Kate Middleton's teeth."

"She's the Duchess of Cambridge now."

"Whoever she is, I'm concerned about her teeth. Look at them," he said, turning the paper round to show me. "They need some work. It looks as if she's brushing too vigorously. Her gums are receding – particularly her upper canines. That reminds me – I can't find my electric toothbrush. I haven't left it here, have I? And talking of tools, I think I've found what I'd like for my birthday. My new Screwfix catalogue arrived today and there's a very tasty dove-tail jig in there!"

And there was I, thinking he'd chugged on from his Screwfix phase.

Saturday September 3rd

Trying hard

Donna Pickett's latest email, received last night:

```
Hi Sally
All is not lost yet, so cheer up.
I'm sending your book to an editor I know at
Headline, and a new guy (who no-one seems to
know anything about) at Transworld.
Please consider Twitter again, Sally. It's all
part of being an author in 2011.
Will be in touch,
Best
Donna
p.s. please will you complete and return
attached questionnaire, so I can give it to a
publisher for press release info.
```

Press relief info? That sounds so authorly. That I can handle. But what a relief that *she* is touting around my book to publishers, not me. It took me an entire year to find a literary agent, so it's wonderful that finding a publisher (or not finding a publisher) requires zero emotional effort on my part. It's so nice to have even a tiny buffer between me and rejection. But I really don't like the sound of that "yet" in her first line.

I just wish she'd stop nagging me to tweet. I have a blog, and I write a new post every week, so why do I have to bother with Twitter? Lucky old Charlotte Bronte, not having to consider her web presence, not having to bother with blogging and tweeting, not having to justify to her agent why she wouldn't do Facebook. Never mind thinking up stupid tweets, it's hard enough to make myself keep working on the current novel, when my writing career hangs in the balance.

According to Donna, it's common for authors' second novels to bomb and I shouldn't let it put me off. Cheek! My second novel hasn't bombed. It hasn't had the chance to bomb.

Sunday September 4th

Racy

Wendy popped in at lunchtime, to sell me tickets for an event in the village hall next Saturday, and to flaunt – yet again – her latest peplum look. Today her nipped-in waist had all but disappeared. It is impossibly trying having a best friend who is slim and petite.

The village hall committee are trying to raise funds to update the kitchen, and Wendy says they're having one of those race nights where you show videos of horse races and everyone has to bet on them. I told her I'd go along with Richard, and bought two tickets. I can't see him actually putting his hand in his pocket and placing any bets, but it'll do him good to have an evening out, even if it is only in the village.

Monday September 5th

Twenty questions

I tried to fill in the Author Questionnaire that Donna sent and only managed 7 out of 20. Writers' block on a publicity questionnaire is not a good look for an all-but-remaindered novelist.

today's tweet from **@sallystoneymoor**
Do you believe everything you read in celebrity Q and A's...........?

There! I tweeted! I hope Donna noticed. No-one else will.

Ooh, she did:

tweet from **@donnapickett**
Well done **@sallystoneymoor**! Blogs and tweets are the icing on the modern author's cake.

Hmm, someone said yesterday that grandmothers are like mothers with icing. There are a whole lot of frosting metaphors flying around these days. I blame the current cupcake explosion.

Tuesday September 6th

Playing hooky

It was so sunny and warm this morning that I couldn't bear to be inside, so instead of settling down to write, I went for a bike ride on the Monsal Trail. What happened to my glory days when I followed a writer's routine and wrote every single morning? *Sic* something, *gloria mundi*.

When I got back, I made myself sit down and write a wretched blog post. I warbled on about the village horticultural show for a couple of paragraphs.

Then I tried to work on the novel. I flicked through the amazingly helpful *Writing the Romantic Comedy* and reminded myself about the next thing I need to tackle in the novel. I've done the 'The Chemical Equation: Setup,' a key scene where you have to introduce your main character (Jenny) and let the reader know about her interior conflicts, and what is lacking in her life. I've done the 'Cute Meet.' Now I need to work towards the 'Sexy Complication: Turning point.'

today's tweet from **@sallystoneymoor**
How does your garden grow? Here's a pic of mine right now...
View media

Whoop-di-doo! That time the tweet had a photo attached. Eat your heart out, Stephen Fry.

Friday September 9th

Am I my brother's keeper?

Richard called at lunchtime and I showed him a pair of jeans I'd bought in the Scouts jumble sale. They are just Richard's size, and they look quite hip to me.

He tried them on and said precisely what I expected: "The waist is far too low." Richard spends the entire day hitching whatever pair of trousers he is wearing up round his waist, and these wouldn't go high enough for his liking. They weren't the kind that exposes your pants, they were merely an inch lower than the M&S seconds he bought off Bakewell market five years ago. "I want something more robust," he said.

"They are robust!"

"I'm looking for something more workaday. I need something that genuflects less to fashion and more to safety and comfort."

"But you're trying to look attractive to women, aren't you?" I said.

He pulled up his sweatshirt and exposed the flesh above the waistband. "This low waistband is an outrageous ploy to dupe the consumer. Dickies don't skimp on material like this." (Richard worships Dickies work clothes because "they are commodious, they shrug off stains, and they have wonderful pocketry.")

"These jeans make you look ten years younger, Richard."

"I don't think I'll be wearing them," he said, vainly trying to hitch them up high again. "They look like a high risk trouser. Edgy."

I need to find him a woman. Despite the difficulties of having a putative sister-in-law who was mega-irritating, it was better when he was shacked up with Pippa – nice for him, peaceful for me.

today's tweet from **@sallystoneymoor**
Today's dilemma: waistbands – high or low?

Saturday September 10th
Cast-offs

What happened tonight…

We all trailed along to the village hall for the 'do.'

Richard got dressed up, I got dressed up, and Wendy got dressed up (no surprise there), and her husband Alan was looking impossibly smooth.

Richard had on a green and blue striped shirt and the 'edgy' jeans, and he looked rather dashing when he wasn't hitching up his waistband.

"Nice shirt, Richard!" Wendy said. "Let me see the label – ooh, Thomas Pink! Where did you get that from? A gift from Pippa?" We both knew full well that Richard would not, could not, have bought it for himself.

"It's from a load of stuff I took to the Oxfam shop for my twenty-something neighbour," he said. "Austerity Britain my foot. Kids today don't know they're born. If they'd been brought up in the 1950's they wouldn't be so come-day go-day about their resources."

I was wearing a secondhand polka dot dress, navy and white. And I had on a hat I'd bought for the first of Richard and Pippa's cancelled weddings. Or was it the third? Who knows which? We've all lost count.

Wendy had plumped for looking like the Queen on country pursuits.

"But why, Wendy?"

"Because I want to wear my new brogues. Why shouldn't I?"

"Maybe because the Queen is eighty-something, and dowdy is not a good look?"

"Oh pish, posh. Don't be so boring. Everyone will be doing it next summer for the Diamond Jubilee – just wait and see!"

She had on pearls, a disgusting tan twin set, a brown and green check tweed skirt, a belted khaki mac, pale tea tights, the brogues, and a horse-print headscarf. Oh, nearly forgot – she also had on a flat quilted waistcoat over her twin set.

When we eventually stepped inside the village hall we found no screen for the racing video, no serried ranks of chairs, and no-one else was wearing a hat. Why? Because it was not a faux racing and betting night. It was a Speed Dating social! Wendy had obviously misheard the chit-chat in the village shop and got confused with speeding and racing and oh, who knows?

There was a huge turnout, and the hall was divided into two. There was a singles side and a not-a-singles side. What I mean by that is that there was a side for people who were looking for a partner, and another side for people who were not on the market, but just wanted to get to know people in the village a bit better, to expand their social network. (Eat your heart out, Facebook.)

Richard walked over to the singles side, hitching up his trousers as he went, and Wendy said to me: "Why aren't you going over there?"

"Me? What are you talking about? I'm not looking for a date. I'm just here to boost the funds. I'm going with you, to the side for people in a relationship."

"But–" began Wendy and then shut up because at that moment Pippa left the group of dog-owners she'd been standing with, and bore down on us. "I'm so upset," she gushed. "Yes I am. Upset. Why is Richard over there, on the other side? Why do you suppose he is? I thought we were just having a little break from each other. A little break."

"But Pippa–" I started to say.

"He knows I love him," she interrupted. "And we were so happy until that woman came along and caught his eye. Yes we were. I am going to get a drink to calm my nerves. I will be back. I will." Oh goodie, Pippa.

Wendy and I watched her push her way through a knot of pensioners to get to the bar, and Wendy whispered, "She really doesn't get it, does she? I thought Richard had explained it was all over forever."

"He did. He did it on his own and it wasn't working. So I told him to bring her round to my house for a coffee and tell her again while I was in the hall listening behind the open door, to see if he was making himself clear, or saying it wrong, or something."

"And?" said Wendy.

"He could not have been clearer. He was explicit with a capital E. Some people just don't want to face the truth, and I'm afraid that Pippa is one of them. Denial is a wonderful strategy for dealing with life's difficulties, but–"

"Talking of which," said Wendy, "don't you think it's time you stopped doing the denial bit yourself? Saturn is coming up to conjunct your Sun and it's time to be realistic."

"Uh?"

"I mean, it's all very well talking about Pippa not accepting that things are over, but what about you with Gus? Moving on and all that? He's been gone for yonks, so when are you going to kick-start your social life? Tonight's the perfect opportunity!"

"But I'm not looking for…I don't want a…no, I couldn't possibly."

"Oh, never mind." She touched my arm. "We'll talk about it another time. Hey! What do you want from the bar? I'll go and get us some drinks." She hurried away, and I found a chair in a corner, away from the tables. I needed to sit down.

When she came back, her face was red and her hands were shaking so the wine was swirling around in the plastic glasses.

"That man," she seethed. "God, I'm sweating, and it's not a hot flush. It's real heat."

"Well look how many layers you've got on."

She handed me the drinks, and opened her mac and flapped it open and shut a few times. "OK." More flapping. "That bloody man!"

"Who?" I said.

"Alan. He is over there on the singles side of the room, flirting with everything in a skirt."

"*Your* Alan? Your *husband* Alan?"

"What other bloody Alan is there? I'll kill him. I'll bloody kill him."

And that was our evening out.

today's tweet from **@sallystoneymoor**
There are at least two sides to every story.

Sunday September 11th

The cold hard light of day

I was awake for most of the night. My brain was chuntering over annoying stuff about Gus, and about how sad it is that it fell apart after lasting so long, and then about my derailed writing career, and how that seems to be on the brink of falling apart as well. At 5 a.m. I gave up, switched on the light, and opened my laptop to look through my photos in the hopes of finding something to put on this week's blog. But then I got distracted by photos of the children and grandchildren. I wish they didn't all live so far away.

At 9 a.m. Wendy was on the doorstep, wearing Raybans and slouchy layers with an overdose of grey marl, including an unlikely (for her) pair of tracky bottoms. Her outfit suggested she was about to launch into a dance-off, but the way she was clinging to the door jamb suggested otherwise.

I was gobsmacked to see her and said: "Why are you here at this time? I didn't think you opened your eyes until 10. Why are you wearing sunglasses when it's raining?"

She stumbled over the doorstep and followed me into the kitchen. "I was so mad with Alan that I slept on the sofa last night, and it was bloody uncomfortable! Then I got up early to go to the loo and couldn't get back to sleep again. I was lying there thinking how I've had it up to here with him, and then about how lost *you* looked last night, and I realised we both need to make some changes. Oh God, my head hurts. The daylight is so bright. Oh God, I need a coffee. I shan't be trying this crack of dawn thing again." She went and filled up my kettle and switched it on.

Then she turned round and leaned against the worktop, and folded her arms. "Let's start with you, sweetie."

"What?"

"Well, the thing is…um…Do you think you might be just the tiniest bit stuck in a rut?"

"What are you talking about?"

"Gus."

"Come off it, Wendy!"

She reached out and stroked my arm. "So you've totally accepted that people don't apply for permanent US residence unless they're intending to stay for keeps?"

I shook myself free of her touch, and took a step back. "Of course! I told you when he left, we couldn't make it work, we wanted different things. I don't even miss him any more! Now, can we talk about something else?"

"Sally. Look at me." She grabbed my shoulders and turned me round to face her. "I can't see your eyes," she said.

"Take off your stupid Raybans then."

She moved them onto the top of her head.

"Phew. OK. Sally. Look at me."

"I am!"

"About Gus. He's gone. He is not coming back. OK?"

"Oh for goodness sake, shut up about Gus!"

"OK, but are you happy being single? I mean – do you want to stay that way?"

"Look. Just because I have accepted that my marriage is over, it doesn't automatically mean I am looking for someone else. I realise I need to get my life sorted out, but it's got nothing to do with finding a replacement for Gus. What I need to do, what I *want* to do – I've been turning it over in my head all night – is concentrate on my writing. Really make an effort. Take it seriously again like I did the very first time he went away to live in the cabin."

"But I thought you were."

"Hardly! There's been so much other stuff happening – my mother dying, helping Nina with the grandkids – but now I really am going to buckle down."

So tomorrow will be a new start. I'm going to keep to my writer's routine every morning, write my journal every day for practice, do daily writer's exercises from my Bodmyn Corner books, etc etc etc. My problem is not that I don't have a man, but that since *Fast Work* was published seven years ago, I have only managed to write one book, and that book has so far got no publisher. How can I call myself a blooming novelist?

today's tweet from **@sallystoneymoor**
Just read research that shows that times of doing nothing are vital to the creative process. Phew.

Monday September 12th

New start

I started again. My new routine is to write from 8 till 1, and then after a sandwich, I'm going to walk or cycle on the Trail to keep fit.

I opened Bodmyn Corner's *Successful Fiction* and chose this exercise:

Imagine you're pitching a proposal to a film producer in Los Angeles, and tell him about each of your main characters in just one sentence.

I started with my kids…

Nina, ex PR consultant for a multinational, metamorphosed into earth mother of three fantastic kids, and temporarily living in Munich.

Daniel, Denver-based, quiet, helpful brainbox, working for a US telecoms company in a job incomprehensible to mortals, no matter how many times he explains it.

Sam, lovable itinerant idealist whose commitment to making the world a better place is hugely uncomfortable for those he lives with.

After this, I wrote 1,000 words of the novel. Yay! Go me!

today's tweet from **@sallystoneymoor**
Reading Bridget Jones's Diary again. She spells Yuk like I do, when everyone else spells it Yuck. Is it a sign? Does bestsellerdom beckon?

Wednesday September 14th

Memories

I watched *Neighbours* at teatime. Karl and Susan are still living apart with little hope of reconciliation: another long-term marriage that's bitten the dust.

It's not as if Gus and I didn't get on well. It's not as if we were *unhappy*. But things changed after the kids left home and he took early retirement. I got into my writing. He got into Thoreau. Then he developed an obsession with simple living and remoteness and silence.

I keep remembering little snippets of things he said during the years we tried to make it work, after his first year away, when he came back and he seemed so pleased to be home. Huh! That honeymoon period lasted a month, and then he was yearning for the simple life again.

Once I found him looking at lecterns on eBay. I think it was just before he had the six month stint in the Alpine cowman's shack.

"The price of lecterns on here is ridiculous," he said. "They don't know what to charge!"

"Did you say *lecterns*?" I said. "What on earth do you want a lectern for?"

"Now I'm retired, I do far too much sitting around. I'm getting slack. I want a lectern so I can stand up to read. In the morning, I can read the paper at it. In the evening, when we're in the sitting room watching the news, I can stand at the lectern and do the crossword."

"But I'll miss having you on the sofa next to me."

"Don't worry," he said, "I'll wave."

He's never done much waving from the Rockies, has he?

today's tweet from **@sallystoneymoor**
A windowsill lined with green tomatoes – the up-side of a disappointing summer.

Thursday September 15th

Ghost-writer

Cracked on with the novel. It's going well.

The blog is not going well. It's tricky finding new things to put on there, to keep my blog readers interested. I missed a trick when Gus left. I should have written a blog about my husband preferring solitude to me. That's what some people do. They write a blog about really private stuff and get a huge following and then a publisher makes them an offer and before you know it they're at the top of the best-seller charts and they've got a column in *The Recorder on Saturday*.

But I am not that person. I wouldn't have wanted everyone in the cybersphere seeing into my soul, or thinking I am impossibly stupid, impossibly dull, and impossible to love.

He did love me once – more than his precious solitude. I know he did.

After doing the blog I tried to think up today's tweet, and failed. Then it struck me that the person who'd be brill at tweets is Kate Wensley (aka Giovanna) from writing group. I emailed and asked her if she fancied sending me a list of random tweets that I can use when my mind is a blank.

Bless her, she emailed back within an hour:

```
hi daise,
whoop whoop! just won another e bay auction - a
tenner for some hunter wellies - bargain or what
- the only down side is they have holes in
currently watching a velvet laura ashley sofa,
(why? it won't fit in the living room), a
tandem, a bench hooded parka, and a seat ibiza
cupro turbo -
e bay is soooooo much easier than battling with
my romance and its sagging middle
writing some tweets for you will not only be a
pleasure - it will a) save me from certain
bankruptcy due to buying ebay crap  b) help me
get my writing head back into gear
tweet list attached
best pay pals, love giovanna
```

I knew she wouldn't mind. She fancies herself as a wizard with one-liners and is desperate for exposure. I am trying to remember how and when we started to call each other Daise and Giovanna…?

today's (Giovanna-sourced) tweet from **@sallystoneymoor**
Black tulip bulbs....my kind of dark promise.

Friday September 16th

Discipline

The new routine is working well. And I think my exercise regime is depressing my appetite. Excellent.

Wendy called round this afternoon wearing a ragged white dress and Doc Marten boots.

"My Lana del Ray look," she explained. "A total nightmare sourcing the grey fishnets. How are you doing?"

"Yep. The writing's going well."

"Great!" she said. She straightened her miniscule cardy, which was so cropped it could be mistaken for two tiny arm-warmers. "Well, it's going to be exciting times all round. We've both got major transits coming up – Pluto is coming up to trine your Venus, and Uranus is smack on my Descendant. It's looking good! Drastic, admittedly, but you can't say it's not fruitful for relationship changes."

"I'm not interested, Wendy."

"Yay!" she said, not listening. "Richard is trying to hook up with someone, you'll be trying to hook up with someone, and I am on the lookout for a replacement for Alan. He's had his chips."

"What? Are you leaving him? Don't rush into anything. You–"

"You know what he's been like, he's been having a mid-life crisis for twenty years! Last Saturday night was the last straw. I'm going to find someone else and then I'm going to dump him."

"I don't think that's what usually happens when you're married, Wendy."

"Happens, schmappens. Who cares? I don't give a shit what people usually do. This is what I am doing. He has had three affairs to my certain knowledge. How many are there I've never found out about?

"Yes, but–"

"Look, if I left him now we'd have to sell up and split the money from the house, and share the pensions, and I'd be really poor. Haven't you seen all those sad divorcees in the Co-op with basic range rich teas in their trolleys? There's no way I'm going there. It would be awful! I need to know I have a new partner to share stuff with, before I dump Alan. Whatever, now *you're* single, we're going to have some fun – we're all in this together."

Why does she not cotton on? "I'm not sure I want to–"

"Course you do!" she blundered on. "You need to get stuck into finding someone else, before sex is just a distant memory."

Ah – sex. I do miss sex.

today's (Giovanna-sourced) tweet from **@sallystoneymoor**
Butterfly earrings: would they look too flighty?

Saturday September 17th
Solitude

I suppose that if Gus had been born in earlier times he would have been a hermit.

I remember when our Sam was planning his first road trip round Europe with his mates. He was thinking about the size of the group, and said: "I can't decide whether six is a good number or a bad number."

And Gus said: "What? Six is far too many."

"No, Dad, in terms of group dynamics," said Sam. "I'm not sure whether it's good for team work, or if it's a bit too big."

Gus said: "The best size for group dynamics is me."

That says it all.

today's (Giovanna-sourced) tweet from **@sallystoneymoor**
Just splashed out on snakeshead fritillary bulbs...the perfect impulse buy

Why do her tweets always involve shopping?

Sunday September 18th
The meeting of minds

I scratted around for something to put on the blog and eventually decided on a photo of some late blue cranesbill which I found still flowering on the Trail, with a line about global warming, and a link to Friends of the Earth. It will have to do.

Richard came to tea and afterwards we sauntered to the end of Goose Lane to look at the sunset. We leaned on the gate and looked at the sky and I said, "I wonder what Daniel is doing right now, in Denver, this very minute."

"There's no telling," said Richard, being someone with no imagination. He's like the man in the Thurber cartoon who doesn't know anything except facts.

"Well, *you* make the conversation," I said.

"I listened to a podcast while I was walking Pippa's dogs this morning," he said. "Melvyn Bragg on *In Our Time*. There was a fascinating discussion about the development of the scarf joint."

"No, talk about something else."

"OK. I've been making a list of potential income streams to boost my pension, and I think the one to crack is pet embalming. A cheap stuffing service would go down really well."

today's tweet from **@sallystoneymoor**
A wise man speaks because he has something to say; a fool because he has to say something. Plato.

Monday September 19th

Girl talk

Nina rang at seven o'clock this morning – eight o'clock her time, in Munich. She was treating herself to a late start because all three of my gorgeous grandchildren were still asleep. Oh, I do miss being able to pop down to London to see her and the kids. I know they'll be back next year, but children change so fast. I *must* book a flight soon.

We rattled on like nobody's business about everybody's business. It was the kind of chat after which Gus used to say "What did you talk about?" and I would say "Not very much."

We covered:

- the jumper Nina's currently knitting;
- the exact arrangement of the buttons on said jumper;
- whether Richard can be trusted not to tell anyone else in the family that Nina is trying to get pregnant again;
- how although I fancy Michael Fassbender something rotten, I will not be seeing his new film *Shame*, as it's an 18 and I have never felt grown up enough for 18s, and anyway, I am not looking for tips on *male* masturbation;

- how neither of us can stand Pippa, and oh what a dance she leads Richard;
- my so-called writing career;
- my tweeting – Nina (as ex-PR queen) thinks I need to have many more tweets than one a day. (OMG.)
- the exact whereabouts in Europe of our Sam;
- why Nina doesn't like reading fiction (her excuse for not reading mine);
- whether I think her Ma-in-law (who is visiting her next week) would like going to a Beergarten for lunch;
- and lastly, how she and Tim can only afford a camping holiday in Bavaria next year.

Camping…hmmm…reminds me of the dreadful three months I spent with Gus in his wretched cabin, 'giving it a go.' I knew I'd loathe it, but I really wanted to make things work.

In the end it was hopeless. People talk about compromise in marriage, but there are some things on which it's impossible to compromise. We couldn't compromise on Christmas – it was either ON or OFF – and we couldn't compromise on where to live and *how* to live. I wanted us both to live here. He wanted us to live in the wilds, and in the end he preferred my absence to my presence. What was that quote from Thoreau he liked so much? "I never found the companion that was so companionable as solitude."

today's tweet from **@sallystoneymoor**
@michaelfassbender, @michaelfassbender, where have you been all my life? Will you star in the film of my book?

Tuesday September 20th

Lost manuscript

I was sorting out the bottom drawer of my desk this morning (when I should have been writing) and came across some stuff I think I must have written about a year after Gus left. I'm past all this now, but it still makes interesting reading:

Final, definitive, ultimate and concluding evaluation of marriage breakdown

Losses:

- Gus is/was really good company. I loved talking to him. He was a bit weird, but he was always interesting.
- We have such a long shared backstory. We were at Uni together and all our cultural references were the same – when we were little, we both watched Rolf Harris on telly at Christmas visiting children in hospital; we both thought "Sparky's Magic Piano" on *Childrens' Favourites* was weird. We both watched *Ready Steady Go* on Friday nights when we were 15. When we met, we both had Bert Jansch's first LP. We went to the 1970 Isle of Wight Festival together and we both loved Leonard Cohen and Joni Mitchell and... ("Shut up, Sally. Don't drivel on," growls Spiky Pete in my head.)
- Losing Gus has meant goodbye to my sex life. But as there were so few occasions when Gus was ready, willing and even in the same country (never mind bedroom) in the last few years, this may be more of a perceived loss than an actual one.

- Gus is a walking encyclopaedia. You can ask him anything, and 99.9% of the time he comes up with a helpful answer. e.g. Me: *Do Buddhists believe in God?* Gus: *They believe in Buddha.* Me: *Who is Buddha? What does Buddha want?* Gus: *He wants the eight-fold way and he wants it now. Actually, he doesn't want it now. He wants it when it comes, whenever that might be.*
- It can be a heavy burden being a single parent, especially when Sam gets into trouble.
- I don't want to come from a broken home.
- With Gus gone for good, clearing out his shed is now up to me.

Gains:

- I've got used to having the bed to myself.
- I can get on with my so-called writing first thing in the morning undisturbed, while my mind is fresh and creative. (Really?)
- I shan't ever have to nag him to take his shoes off at the door to stop him bringing in mud.
- I will never again have a five minute tussle with the chain for the plug in the bathroom wash basin because he has knotted it round the stupid tap.
- There will never be a fridge full of half empty milk bottles, because he has taken the top of the milk from all of them to make his milky coffee.
- I can kiss goodbye to darning his 30-year-old cycling jersey.

- No more having the answering machine on all the time so he can screen every single call.
- I might possibly, just possibly, get to try sex with somebody else. (eeeeeeek!) Oh, no! Just remembered my mastectomy! Would it put a new man off?

If I'd known I was going to end up single, I'd have done it a whole lot sooner. Marriage can be such a hard slog, and you have to compromise on so many things, so *many* things, just to keep the peace. I feel cheated to be ending up alone at this age.

today's tweet from **@sallystoneymoor**
The Sixties. How did they swing in the Peak District?

Wednesday September 21st

Working hard

Writing. Monsal Trail. *Neighbours.*

Struggled to blog. I hope my readers will enjoy hearing how I have so many plums that I tried (unsuccessfully) to persuade the village shop to sell them, and I'm now giving them away at the gate.

today's tweet from **@sallystoneymoor**
I have the most wonderful harvest of plums this year.

Thursday September 22nd

Still at it

Writing. Monsal Trail. *Neighbours.*

today's tweet from **@sallystoneymoor**
What else can you make with plums besides plum crumbles, plum chutney and plum jam? Any suggestions? #plumrecipes

Friday September 23rd

Doubts

My jeans slipped on so easily this morning, with the waist so loose that I needed to ferret in the back of my sock drawer and find a belt. So I took the risky step of looking in a full length mirror. I am definitely looking trim: it's no wonder after so much exercise.

But my face looks horribly worn, and my hair looks terrible. My plait is limp, and the hair on my crown has that awful fluffy look. I grew my plait to make me look authorly. Gus encouraged me. He said: "It makes you stand out from the mass of menopausal crows." He has such a way with words.

I need to do something about my hair. But what?

It's crap having to pay so much attention to clothes and face and hair at this age – I never did it before – but unless I do, I look like a bag-lady.

today's tweet from **@sallystoneymoor**
Would I feel better if I got rid of all the mirrors in the house?

Friday September 24th

Enough is enough

This morning when I was getting dressed, I went to get a clean cardy out of the chest of drawers and opened the wrong drawer by mistake and saw all Gus's stuff.

Why didn't he clear it all out before he went, when he knew he wasn't coming back?

More to the point – why haven't I cleared it out before now, when I've known he's not coming back?

I went round the bedroom and yanked all his clothes out – from the chest and from the wardrobe and from the clothes basket in the corner – every darned jumper, every secondhand T shirt with frayed neckband, every last patched pair of jeans. What a scruff! Well, his ragbag of clothing no longer has a place in my bedroom. I stomped downstairs and fetched up a roll of bin bags. I stuffed it all in – five bags full – and slung them in the spare room. I'll dispose of them later.

Then I had some muesli and went in my study and Googled "Divorce in Derbyshire." It's time to make things final. I've been drifting for far too long.

I found the website of a woman solicitor in Chesterfield who offers conciliatory, non-contentious divorces, no-trouble separations. It sounded comfortable and non-threatening. In her photograph, the solicitor is leaning into the camera and simpering, in big trendy specs, trying to look friendly as well as intelligent. Her website is peppered with adverts for all kinds of things, including wedding dresses and jewellery shops. Weird. Are they trying to catch the second marriage market? Well, that's a route I shan't be taking.

I left her website and looked for someone else, but very quickly ran out of steam, so I went back to the woman in the over-sized specs. When I rang to make an appointment, her secretary said "Patching you through" and then there was a shriek "Oh, no! You found me through the website? I must get that photo changed. I don't look like that any more, I've changed my image. My friends all said I was turning into Dame Edna Everidge. My glasses are completely different."

?

She was available immediately, which was not surprising when she sounded such an airhead. She offered me an appointment for Monday, and although I did feel iffy about her (and about the whole damn enterprise by that time) I was desperate to get off the phone, and I agreed.

today's tweet from **@sallystoneymoor**
The cosmos in my garden is still going strong. It's so pretty and such good value, and the foliage is brilliant for flower arrangements.

Are my tweets becoming too floral?

Monday September 27th

The divorce lawyer

The divorce lawyer's office was in Chesterfield, in that row of Georgian houses, near the roundabout by the Co-op. In the reception area, things were not Georgian. Everything was polished – shiny green polished granite floor with mega sized pieces of granite strewn around, green granite walls, and an infinity water feature. It was a fabulously sunny day outside, but in there it was freezing. The running water made me wish I'd been to the loo before I left home, but I didn't go there: I might've got frostbite on my bum.

Thankfully the lawyer's office was cosy, even if it did have black and purple floral flock wallpaper and silver painted Louis Quatorze chairs with purple velvet seats. Her receptionist showed me in, and I sat there thinking that all this décor was going to add squillions to my bill, as fancy décor doesn't come cheap, even when it mixes its metaphors. I heard clicking heels on the granite floor outside and the door opened and I heard something else clicking. It was spectacle queen. The clicking was caused by her three strings of oversized pearls – huge ones like gobstoppers. She could have given Pippa a run for her money, although I couldn't see Pippa in four inch spike heels and a jacket with a peplum (what's this thing with peplums?) over a tight skirt.

"Ms Howe, how nice to meet you." She leaned over to shake my hand and looked as if she was going to topple off her heels and crash into her marble-topped Louis whatsit desk. Then the next thing she said – before even sitting down – was "Oooooh, I love your perfume. What is it?"

"Um, Chanel. Coco."

"I must get some!" she oozed.

Then she settled herself in her chair and straightened the papers on her desk and looked me straight in the eye, and said "This is a half hour free consultation – you know that, I hope – but after today, I'll be charging £250 an hour."

I gulped and made an involuntary turn to look at the door. Could I make a run for it?

"Now, now," she said, "relax. Tell me your story." And she sat back with her hands clasped behind her head and her elbows sticking up and pointing at the shimmering chandelier above her desk.

After my quick resumé of the situation, she picked up her Bic biro (at £250 an hour?) and started asking questions and making notes.

Her: When did you move in?... ooooo, good that you lived together before you got married, that might count, that might help… Me: but that was in 1975... Her: that really doesn't matter…ooooo, lots of children, and career abandonment – excellent…and going off and living in a shack – hmm, desertion.

Excellent. Ooooo, much better idea – unreasonable behaviour! – if living in a shack on a mountainside doesn't count as unreasonable behaviour, I don't know what does... Me: I'm not sure. I've never thought of him that way. Eccentric, perhaps, pursuing his dreams, perhaps, but behaving unreasonably?

And so it went on.

It all sounded very combative, and hearing this woman say nasty things about sweet old Gus in that evil conspiratorial tone made me want to stick up for him.

And then she found out I was living in the family home, and she leaned across the desk and narrowed her eyes, and said: "He may be about to take out a court order to restrict your claim on the family home, even though he is so far away."

What rot. "He isn't interested in the family home, and he would never be out-and-out nasty to me. He would want *me* to have the house."

"Deserting husbands all say things like that, to lure you into a false sense of security before they come back and Rottweiler you in court."

I'd had enough. I stood up. Yes – I, Sally Howe, took control and stood up. "Well, thank you. I think the half hour must be up now." I looked at my watch, which was a bluff, because my brain was addled and I couldn't for the life of me recall what time I'd arrived. "Thank you. I will give it all some thought and get back to you."

She was flummoxed. She had cast me in the role of submissive wife and thought she could dominate me too.

"Oh," she said, "I just need to ask you before you go if your husband might be coming back soon, because it's going to be a much more complex and expensive exercise to serve the papers on him if he's abroad."

I shook her hand and said, "He's not coming back." Stupid bint. Isn't that why I was there? "Goodbye. I'll be in touch."

She followed me out into the hall, talking all the time. "You have a lot to consider...but the most dangerous course of action is doing nothing...you need to protect yourself...and I can do that for you...I can do it right now..."

I was actually running by the time I made it to the exit to the street. What on earth was I doing talking about divorce? And talking to such an awful woman? I'm not the sort of person who gets a divorce. I am a family person, a steady person. I'm not the kind of woman who slices up their husband's suits and has her hair streaked and goes on singles holidays. I couldn't, anyway: Gus doesn't have any suits.

today's tweet from **@sallystoneymoor**
Water features in waiting rooms? No thank-you.

Tuesday September 28th

Advice

I was so churned up last night I couldn't sleep.

Even after I'd poured it all out to Wendy this morning, I felt the same. Then Richard came, but he just patted my hand and said, "Divorce is one of life's little trials. How we handle it tests our mettle. You'll come through it, just like I did, when Izzy and I split up."

"But what is the point of getting divorced? We're not fighting over anything and neither of us wants to get married again. The house is paid for. We both have our pensions. I have that bit of money my mother left me. Basically, money's not an issue. Neither of us have much, but we have enough if we're not extravagant. And we're NOT extravagant. How can Gus be? There is one shop, seven miles down the trail from his cabin and..."

I whittled on like this for half an hour, until Richard suggested we change the subject. Well actually, that's not true. It was just that I noticed he wasn't responding and wasn't looking at me. He had his nose stuck in *The Cupid Column* in my *Recorder*, and he was circling some of the ads.

"Richard," I said. "I want to talk to you about Pippa."

"Really? Must you?"

"I think you should distance yourself from her more, stop doing jobs for her, stop walking Millie and Maisie."

"They are a handful. They're even worse than Emmie and Ellie, God rest their souls." He said this last phrase with his hand clasped to his chest, in imitation of Pippa, and I laughed out loud. "I don't know why she had to get another pair of red setters. They're so horribly highly strung."

More like strung up, like their owner should be.

"Just tell her," I said, "next time she asks, just tell her…just say *no*."

"OK, Sis."

"And don't call me *Sis*. You sound like a character in *East Enders*. It doesn't suit your persona. Trust me on this. I'm a writer, and I know these things."

today's tweet from **@sallystoneymoor**
Repeat after me: "It's all right to say no."

Wednesday September 29th

Positively the very last time

I was in the middle of Chapter 3, when there was a tiny rapping on the front door. I hauled myself out of bed and went down to find a pale, dishevelled Pippa on the doorstep.

"What do you want?" I said. Then hurriedly, "Hello, Pippa. Are you OK?"

"You sound cross," she said. "Are you still upset about the solicitor?"

"How do you–?"

"Richard told me you'd been to see one about a divorce." Like hell he did. I'd be having words with that brother of mine. "I just saw him," she said. "He told me he couldn't walk the dogs this morning even though I am feeling unwell. I do wonder why he can't. Yes, I do. Did you go to a solicitor in Chesterfield? Near that nice builders centre? Jacksons? I do like them. They have a big car park, and it's not like a builders merchants at all. No it isn't. It's so tidy, and all the men wear matching dungarees with their names on, and the company logo. They even have their names on the back of the donkey jackets they wear when they go outside into the gorgeous fencing and decking and water feature part. Oh, I never mind when Richard sends me there to get bits and bobs for his little jobs. I don't."

"Personally, I prefer Midco in Bakewell," I said. "They're friendly and helpful and they don't patronize you." *What?* What was I doing responding to her stupid boring rubbishy conversation? I had some real dialogue, some quality dialogue, that I should be getting on with upstairs on my laptop. I folded my arms. For someone who was supposed to be feeling crook, she still had way too much to say for herself. "Just tell me why you're here, Pippa."

Yep – she wanted me to walk the wretched hounds.

"You remember what happened last time, Pippa! It was awful."

"But I've bought two brand new leads from Pets R Us and they come with a lifetime guarantee. Yes."

So I gave in to her again, and took the hounds for a walk on the Monsal Trail. I could have dumped them at Richard's house but what would be the point when I'd just told him to stop helping her, and for once in his life he'd done what I said? Also, she really did look ill, and I felt sorry for her.

This time, the dogs were strangely subdued. Were they sickening for something, too? I actually had a fairly pleasant walk until someone came up behind me on a bike and sounded an appalling klaxon and scared the bejeezus out of the dogs, and they barked and leapt about like crazy, and I had a job to control them as the cyclist sped past us, yelling: "Why don't you learn to control those bloody animals?"

Grrrh! It was that awful man again! I actually had his stupid poncey light in my pocket, but he can jolly well whistle for it, now!

today's tweet from **@sallystoneymoor**
Yet another of those days when I should have stayed in my pyjamas.

OCTOBER

Saturday October 1st

Going bananas

I need to do something about my image. When I look in the mirror, I can't believe how old I look. Aging isn't gradual. You trundle along not changing much for a couple of years and then suddenly – BAM! There are three more furrows in your forehead, your crow's feet have doubled in length and your entire face droops. It's like a banana in the fruit bowl – one day it's green and inedible but full of promise, and the next time you look, it's brown and inedible and past it.

today's tweet from **@sallystoneymoor**
I'm thinking a banana bag would be a good idea. Anyone tried one?

Sunday October 2nd

Going west

I dreamed that Gus was home. What the heck is that about? Gone for three years and now he's boomeranged back into my dreams. He was lying beside me in bed and we were chatting, and he was fiddling with the end of my plait, and he said: "Don't ever cut it off, will you? It makes you look wonderfully sensible and sturdy, and yet motherly, just like a homesteader. You know – like one of those pioneers travelling westwards across the plains in a covered wagon."

I woke up and switched on the light to get rid of the dream, but his words were still there. Did I look sturdy and sensible? I rushed to the bathroom and looked in the mirror. I was horrified by my reflection and forgot that no-one, not even Joanna Lumley, looks good in the middle of the night. And I fetched the kitchen scissors and chopped off my plait.

Is it a huge mistake? I've been growing it for years.

today's tweet from **@sallystoneymoor**
Just saw an ad for a "3 minute miracle hair reconstructor." Anyone know if it works?

Monday October 3rd

A new day dawns

Richard was sweet this morning when I was feeling iffy about my chopped-off hair. "Your plait did look very distinguished, as well as distinctive, but so what?" he said. "You have a nice face, apart from the wrinkles, and you're a lovely person – and that's what matters. Why don't you go to that expensive hairdresser in Sheffield that you like – what do you call it?"

"Pricey Paul's." Sniff.

"I'll treat you. Here's a tenner – get yourself a new lipstick as well." And he smiled. He really thought that £10 would cover it, and there'd be money for Smarties as well.

"But, it's thirty-five quid, just for a cut and blow." Sniff. "A re-style will be more."

He blanched. "Really? They don't know what to charge." Big sigh. "OK, well, if that's what it costs to cheer you up, shall we go halves?"

When I got back, he said, "You look like a computerised mock-up of an aging Cleopatra."

Wendy was more encouraging. "It's fantastic! It makes you look so much younger!" She was wearing all over black and white, and looked a little like a draughts board – enough to give me a migraine. "Single plaits are just not cool," she went on. "And I always thought yours dragged your face down, and made you look older and–"

"Now she tells me!"

"And anyway, a drastic change of your style, your aesthetics, so-o-o-o fits in with your transits – Pluto trine your Venus."

today's tweet from **@sallystoneymoor**
How I love having a hairdresser who never asks me if I'm off out tonight, or where I'm going for my holidays.

Tuesday October 4th

Making the best of it

It's smooth, it's sleek, it's sharp, it's trendy, but it's not my plait, which I started growing the day I decided to become a writer. Now where am I? A writer with a slightly lower than chin-length bob, whose career has stalled prematurely and who has this week been rejected by *Headline* and *Transworld*.

Donna Pickett emailed yesterday with that bit of news. She said she had got to the last one on her list, so fingers crossed for *Piatkus*. Oh hell! What am I going to do if *they* reject me?

Career crisis, image crisis, aging crisis (i.e. being 60 in a fortnight's time). Everything awful is happening at once.

If my life was a novel, there'd be too many plot points too close together, and if God (the writer) was in our writing group, Spiky Pete would be hauling Him over the coals. When I first started writing, my writers' bible was a book by Bodmyn Corner called *Plotting for Beginners*. Now, with the current dire status of my writing and my life, I could do with a book called *Plotting for Grown-ups*.

today's tweet from **@sallystoneymoor**
Just saw a florist's van slogan – "We deliver emotions." Please don't bring them to my house – we have more than enough already.

Wednesday October 5th
Time wasting

Writing went well until I was in the middle of Chapter 4 with my heroine Jenny, at an antiques fair in Newark, and I was just checking on Wikipedia to see how you tell real Crown Derby china from fake stuff, and somehow I found myself on Amazon, checking the sales ranking of *Fast Work*. I do try to restrict myself to twice a day – this laptop obviously has rat-runs.

The sales rank was even worse than yesterday. It was awful. It was so awful I am not recording it here for posterity for my literary executor to find. (I should be so lucky.)

To cheer myself up I had to Google myself to see if anyone anywhere was saying anything nice about *Fast Work*.

More bad news. Someone called Sheila Finnegan has had the cheek to give me a rating of 2 stars. There was a link to her own ebook on *Smashreads* and I had a look: absolutely hopeless. I got tangled up in a dodgy sentence construction in the first bloody paragraph. At least I can write. Let she who is without sin (and with faultless prose) cast the first stone, Ms Sheila Finnegan.

today's tweet from **@sallystoneymoor**
It's so much easier to criticise a piece of writing, than it is to write.

Thursday October 6th
Spam

```
Hello Mrs S C Howe, we have recommendations for
you
Hello Mrs S C Howe,
Are you looking for something in our Fiction
store? If so, you might be interested in these
items…
Fast Work
Sally Howe
RRP: £7.99
Price: £6.07
You Save: £1.92 (24%)
```

This is what happens when you check your Amazon ranking every day: they try to sell you your own book.

I could do it! I could buy a hundred copies in a day and my rank would rocket and look really impressive, and then I could take a screenshot and put it on my blog. That would stub out Spiky Pete at writing group.

today's tweet from **@sallystoneymoor**
Can anyone send me a link to a step by step guide to taking a screenshot?

Friday October 7th

Bad hair day

I washed my hair today, and now some of it looks like hay and the rest of it looks like wire. It is thinner than it was before the menopause, and has a tendency to frizz. This doesn't seem fair: but then not much about aging is fair. They make special shampoos for every possible life event, emotion and scenario – tired, fly away, thirsty, extra clean, curl defining, colour treated, hot styling, extra volume, extra gloss, etc etc – but no-one's thought about cashing in on the post-menopausal pound and making shampoo for hair starved of oestrogen.

This afternoon, I got out the secateurs to do a little light pruning, and when I stood back to admire my handiwork I saw that I'd butchered the whole damn border. What's got into me?

Then Pippa called.

"Coo-eee! Sall-leee!"

She was crunching on the gravel round the side of the house.

"Oh dear! What on earth have you done to the Spirea? I've come to see your new hairstyle. Yes I have. Down, girls!" she said to Maisie and Millie. "Ah, sweet! They want to see it, too. Yes they do." She appraised my hair. "Oh yes. That's so much better. So much better. You've got rid of that horrid bohemian look. It's much more sensible, yes it is. I never understood why you wanted a plait. Never understood. Now you've taken the first step, you can take it to its logical conclusion."

"Sorry?"

"Have it cut really short and have a perm, of course. Act your age. I'll tell you where I go for mine, shall I? It's a little place round the back of the Co-op. They have those nice helmet hairdryers on stands – none of that fancy blow-dry stuff – they make a wonderful cup of Tetley's, and they always have the latest edition of *Woman's Weekly*."

I was just thinking that quite apart from this being Pippa, it was impossible to take anyone seriously who preferred one-cup Tetley's to Yorkshire tea, when she said: "Won't Iain see a difference in you when he comes to stay? The last time he was here, you still had your plait, and not that...well...that funny kind of wavy bob."

I blanched and dropped my secateurs. "Iain?"

"Yes, didn't you know he was coming to stay with Richard next week? Oh well, must be going."

I rushed inside and rang Wendy and wailed down the phone about Iain and about my hair.

"You remember Iain! That guy who tried to whirl me off my flatties when Gus did his first disappearing trick?"

"Oh, him. But your hair – you need to do your hair again with conditioner," she said. "At our age you can't get away without it. Plus – you're going to have to get some hair straighteners. You can borrow mine for now."

She buzzed along to Goose Lane. Her look today: herbaceous border. (A cascade of floral pleats.) By the time she'd finished sorting out my hair, it was better than when I'd done it, but it still wasn't as sleek and classy as when I'd come home from Pricey Paul's. At least when I had a plait it saved me from the disappointment of not being able to recreate that fabulous just-come-out-of-the-salon look.

Richard popped in to check *The Cupid Column* while Wendy and I were still tweaking. Honestly, you'd think this place was a house in a cul-de-sac on a TV soap, the way everyone walks in and out the whole time.

He said, "What on earth has happened to your hair? It's changed. Today you look like Oliver Cromwell, just about to address the New Model Army."

"Sod off, Richard!" said Wendy. He grabbed *The Recorder* from the kitchen table and retreated to the dining room and Wendy said, "Don't take any notice of him, Sally. It looks fine."

"Fine? Fine? I know what *fine* means."

"I'm ravenous. Haven't you got anything better than these crumbly old custard creams?" she said, rootling around at the bottom of my biscuit barrel.

"You haven't told me what to do about Iain, yet."

"Are you going to see him, then? I mean – I don't see why you wouldn't. You're single now, and he did have the hots for you and–"

"I don't *know* if I'll see him!" Every time Wendy uses the word single and I remember that it applies to me, my stomach lurches and my heart beats really fast. I know I'm going to have to get over it, but right now I haven't. "I don't know what I'll do about Iain!" I yelped. "Richard might bring him round, I might bump into him at the post office, I might see him in Bakewell – the possibilities are endless. I have seven more years of wrinkles since last time I saw him. But I can't go into purdah for a week, can I?"

"But think how nearly you and he got it together when Gus was away in the Rockies that very first time. Don't you want to–"

“I'm not ready to – I don't know! Yes, he's yummy looking, but he's pretty dull, and remember how vain he is? Remember how he had all those hairdryers? And I look so...” I tailed off.

“So that's where you keep them," said Wendy. While we'd been talking, she'd been searching every receptacle in the kitchen, and now she'd alighted on my secret stash of chocolate digestives in the tin on the top shelf of the dresser.

“What are you two so animated about?” said Richard, who'd come back in. He helped himself to a chocolate biscuit from the tin.

Wendy improvised: “Sally is fretting about her image for book signing tours.”

“Your image? Who cares what you look like? You're old! I mean, it's your brilliant writing and your intelligence and your sparkling wit that matters, isn't it?”

What happened to “You have a nice face, apart from the wrinkles, and you're a lovely person”???

today's tweet from **@sallystoneymoor**
‘Twice a week I go to a beauty salon and have my hair blown dry. It's cheaper than psychoanalysis, and much more uplifting.’ Nora Ephron.

Saturday October 8th
The presenting problem

I was tussling with the Rom-Com plotline in my novel, when Wendy rang and begged to come over. “Go on, Sally. Alan's out playing golf, and I've had an idea about the Iain problem. And I've been reading this great book – *The Gods of*

Change: pain, crisis and the transits of Uranus, Neptune and Pluto. Plus, I have cake."

I was struggling. My two main characters, Jenny and Liam, had still not hooked up as a couple, so I was chapters away from the 'Sexy Complication' – and now Roland, the 'Bellamy,' (i.e. Mr Wrong, as opposed to Mr Right) had arrived on the scene.

"Oh go on then," I said to Wendy. Up till then, I'd resisted ringing her as a distraction, because she'd told me she was busy studying for her Astrological Counselling Diploma (Advanced).

"See," Wendy said, when we were ensconced in my kitchen with mugs of coffee and the tail end of a Cadbury's chocolate swiss roll, "this bit's all about Pluto transits to personal planets – which is what you've got at the moment – Pluto represents a force that tears down our ego-identities until we discover our essence, the trans-personal sense. Basically, you have to remember that our true and basic identity is not dependent on anything else – internal or external."

"You mean my hair? I know that, Wendy. Do you think it's really my hair I care about? Haven't you heard of the concept of a presenting problem? Good grief! I know more about counselling than you do. Yes, my hair is having an identity crisis, and yes I have more wrinkles than last time I saw him, but, well..."

The phone was ringing and I picked it up. Pippa. "Hello...No, Pippa... No, I'm sorry... No. I have a guest, it's not convenient....Well I'm sorry, you'll have to try someone else...OK, bye."

"Grrrh! That woman!" I said to Wendy. "You see. It's started already. Pippa is at Richard's house, alone, waiting for Iain to arrive – why is she there? And why is Richard *not* there? –

and she wants to know if she can bring Iain over here for afternoon tea."

"So tell me the *real* problem," said Wendy, as she gracelessly tugged at the waistband of her pencil skirt. (She was doing office wear today, probably because she'd been studying for her diploma, and was trying to get into a professional mindset.)

"The real problem?" I said. "Embarrassment, not knowing how I will feel when I see him, if I still fancy him, if he still fancies me, oh, I don't know – the whole excruciating situation. *I just don't want to see him.*"

today's tweet from **@sallystoneymoor**
Isn't it lovely when old friends that you haven't seen in years turn up out of the blue?

Sunday October 9th

In hiding

I lay awake from 1 a.m. till 4 a.m. last night, worrying about what I would do if Piatkus don't want to publish my book. Would I have the emotional energy to carry on? Would another agent do any better than Donna Pickett? Could I even be bothered to find another agent? Donna P was the twentieth one I approached. Trying to get an agent is the very worst thing about being a writer. But that is beside the point: if Donna P has approached all the main publishers with my book and nobody wants it, another agent isn't going to do any better, are they? By the time I woke up at seven o'clock, I had a stinking headache, and I felt sick and weak.

It's going to be a difficult few days. I am going to stay at home and stay locked in my study and do nothing but write –

just to avoid the possibility of bumping into Iain. But is it worth continuing with Jenny and Liam when the second book, *They Met on the Bridge,* is on its last ditch attempt to get a publisher? Is there any point in writing another novel?

It would be lovely to be out on the Trail enjoying all the autumn colours, except that I might see that horrible man and have to approach him and give him back his fancy-schmancy light. I feel a bit guilty about it. He probably needs it, though – the evenings are drawing in, and the clocks will be going back in a couple of weeks.

Meanwhile I am becoming addicted to junk TV. After a bad night, I sit down with my breakfast in front of the telly. I have never watched it in the morning before, mainly because of Gus's disapproval which was so vehement it resonates down the years (despite his absence). This morning I watched something called *The OC,* which is about a bunch of obscenely rich teenagers who live in California.

Richard called in while I was watching it. "Iain has been asking about you. He wants to see you," he said.

"Well it may not look like it, but I'm really busy this week. I'm only watching the telly as a short break between frenzied bouts of writing." Total rot. "I'm trying to figure out how to do the 'Sexy Complication' in the Rom-Com plotline. I'm trying to meet a deadline for my agent. I'd like to see Iain – of course – but you'll have to tell him I'm snowed under at the moment."

"That's a shame." He sat down on the sofa next to me. "What on earth is this rubbish? It's even worse than *Neighbours.*"

"I don't know if it's worse. It's aimed at teenagers, though."

"*Neighbours* is hardly for the adult mind," he said.

"*The OC* is much more glossy," I said. "I mean – there are ordinary people on *Neighbours*, but if ordinary people pop up on *The OC* they either become glossy, or they stay ordinary, as examples of some kind of underclass."

"Glossy!" said Richard. "I'd like to be glossy! Maybe I need to be glossy to get a woman."

"Those jeans with the low waist that you don't like – they're what a glossy person would wear. And that Pierre Cardin shirt I got you from the jumble sale – that's glossy, too. But your hair is a problem. It needs a decent cut. One that involves you shelling out more than £8."

"You can forget that!"

"And then there's your shoes."

"But these trainers are so comfortable," he said.

"Maybe you're not cut out to be glossy, Richard. Maybe you have other charms."

today's tweet from **@sallystoneymoor**
Everyone needs at least one junk TV programme they can relax to.

Monday October 10th

A torrent of worries

I went out on the Trail this morning on my bike. I went very early so as to avoid bumping into a/ Iain b/ hordes of tourists. I was thinking I would have just a gentle lady-like pedal up to the first tunnel and back and then come home and get on with a list of annoying little household jobs that have been waiting for attention (so much for my new writing routine.) But I got lost in a maelstrom of worry – *what will happen if there isn't a publisher in the world who wants my book? how will I manage old age alone, without a partner? will I ever make love to anyone again? where is Sam and what is he up to? will I be able to afford to keep the house going with all the price increases in Austerity Britain, etc, etc? how can I afford to keep going to Pricey Paul's to keep my hair looking half-way decent?* – and the next time I noticed, I was seven miles up the Trail from where I'd joined it, pedalling like fury into the mouth of a tunnel.

I turned to come home again, and now there were people about – a sprinkling of early-morning dog-walkers, several joggers, and one or two cyclists. I always say hello to cyclists and walkers coming in the opposite direction, and I had just said "Hello" to a man on a bike and whizzed past him, and then thought – *Hang on! It's him! Mr Nasty!* The rude rude man whose poncey bike light I'd been carrying around in my jacket pocket in case I should meet him. I circled round as quickly as I could and pedalled after him, all the time calling out in a ladylike way, "Excuse me! Hello! I need to speak to you!" But he was cycling way faster than me and I couldn't catch him. I tried ringing my bell – still no result. I yelled as loud as I could in an unladylike way: "Oi! Oi! You with the muddy stripe up your bum! Aren't you old enough to know about mudguards?" But it was no good. No good at all.

I turned back and came home and got in the bath and was so exhausted from the manic pedalling I stayed there until my skin was twice as wrinkly as it usually is.

today's tweet from **@sallystoneymoor**
Monsal Trail, Monday 8.am: 2 cyclists, 2 dog-walkers, 3 joggers, 1 power-walker & a ginger cat. Otherwise: scenery, sunshine, serenity.

Later:

It was so sunny and warm that I had the front door wedged open to waft some fresh air into the house. The writing was going OK, and Jenny was flirting with Liam, and then Nina rang to ask if I had the *Observer* from two Sundays ago because someone had told her there was an article in there about managing tantrums. Ah, it's come to this – once she was managing live feeds and satellite transmissions and celebrity interviews, and now she's managing tantrums. Just like her mother. Once I was in the national broadsheets with my pieces, on the local radio for constant phone-ins, had a debut novel (*Fast Work*) that sold 10,000 copies, and now I am waiting for the definitive rejection, the last rejection, the rejection that will end my career as a writer.

Anyway, I told Nina I'd look and ring her back, and I went in the cupboard under the stairs to search in the paper recycling box. So there I was with my head in the cupboard and my bum hanging out, when I heard a familiar voice – a male voice – a voice I have not heard for seven years – calling "Sally" from the direction of the front door.

Iain! Mercy me!

"Hello?" he said hesitantly.

There was obviously no way to escape, so I turned round to face him, and he gasped and said, "Sally! Is it Sally? Or are you her sister?"

"It's me, Iain." And I gave him a playful shove and he laughed.

"You look so young with your hair in a bob! Amazing! I mean, I did like your plait, but...well...now you have such a classic style, the epitome of streamline design."

We were standing there looking at each other – him smiling, me glowing – when Richard shouted from the front door and then strode down the hallway and said: "Come on, old man, we'd better be off if you want to get those posterity pics of the John Lewis building they're threatening to bulldoze. What did you call them? Iconic sixties white tile what?"

"Elevations," said Iain. "I suppose we should." He kissed me on the cheek and said, "Must dash, *lovely* to see you," and made to go, and then he turned round and said, "Would you like to come with us?"

"Oh, I have so much to do," I said. "I have a deadline to meet, and I've just lost half an hour by looking for something for Nina in the cupboard."

"Well, another time. We must catch up."

"That would be nice."

He followed Richard out of the front door, slowing down as he passed the mirror, in order to check his own impeccably tidy hair. Some things never change.

today's second tweet from **@sallystoneymoor**
From the recycling pile: Stray cow kills rickshaw puller. Sunday Times of India, April 1st 2007.

Tuesday October 11th

Submission

Well, of course I changed my mind about seeing Iain. I invited him out for a drink to catch up. Any man who looks like a male model (even a grey haired one), and who says I look younger than I did seven years ago, and who once wanted to whisk me off on a protracted Italian holiday, has got to be worth spending time with. I don't care if he has got a hair dryer fetish and is in the habit of giving people Christmas tree decorations shaped like Wallace and Gromit. Oh yes, just remembered! And who consults a Magic 8 Ball to make decisions about his relationships. Hmm. Did he come to see me because he wanted to, or was it just on the advice of his Magic 8 ball?

The evening turned out to be fun, a pleasant distraction. I'd forgotten how he loves Thurber cartoons as much as I do. I told him that Richard reminds me of the man in the cartoon who doesn't know anything except facts, and then we started to apply other Thurber cartoon captions to people we know.

He said: "Can't you just hear Pippa saying to Richard: *'It's our own story exactly! He bold as a hawk. She soft as the dawn.'"* and I collapsed in unseemly hoots of laughter, so everyone in the Derbyshire Heifer turned round and stared.

I said: "Yes! Yes! And Wendy is the woman who says *'Of course he's terribly nervous, but I'm sure he meant it as a pass at me.'"*

And then Iain said: "And are you the woman where they say *'She was crazy about him, but he interfered with her novel'*?"

And I didn't know what to say, so I gulped down my wine and jumped up and offered to buy him another drink.

I am not that woman. But I do like him. He's a nice guy. Why shouldn't I hang out with him while he's in Derbyshire? I need my ego boosting a bit, and he obviously likes my company, so where's the harm? He does look older than the last time I saw him. It's all that hanging out in the Italian sunshine – it may give you a sexy tan, but it also makes your face look like a piece of origami paper that's been folded and unfolded too many times.

I told him about the problem of trying to get the bike light back to Mr Nasty, and he said, "To be honest, I've never seen the attraction of cycling."

"So you wouldn't come for a ride with me on the Trail? You can hire bikes at Hassop Station, you know. And they have electric ones as well as the normal kind."

"Well, I do like the sound of the electric bikes. I like the concept, the true marrying of a man-powered machine with fuel-powered mechanical input, on a need for need basis – it's most ingenious...but..." he trailed off and touched his hair and I could tell he was thinking that there was no way anyone would get him into a cycling helmet. He'd rather die than have helmet hair.

I said: "If someone was with me, I wouldn't feel so iffy about approaching the guy with his light, assuming I saw him, of course."

"I'd love to go for a *walk* on the Trail with you. We can have a proper talk if we're walking. You can't do that on a bike, can you? What are you doing for your birthday next week? A party? A big night out? I hear from Richard that it's a significant one."

I told him I wasn't in the mood for a party. He nodded and said nothing. Very tactful.

today's tweet from **@sallystoneymoor**
Quote from Thurber: "Well if I rang the wrong number, why did you answer the phone?"

Wednesday October 12th
The End

Horrible, horrible news received today at 2.54 p.m.

```
Dear Sally
This is a very difficult email to write.
I am desperately sorry, but Piatkus have given
the thumbs down to 'They Met on the Bridge.'
```

They were the last on my list of possibles. We're at the end of the line. Five years ago I could have sold your book without a problem. Now with the current appalling state of publishing, scores of perfectly good novels are coming a cropper. I have been an agent for twenty years and have never known such a terrible climate. Publishers want a big-hitting novel that will appeal across the board. They are taking very few risks, and so a quiet, quirky, but thoughtful novel like yours just does not grab them, especially when it is aimed at a subgroup - women readers over 45. You and I know that this is the biggest novel-buying sector of the market, but publishers have yet to cotton on.

Take heart that it is not just happening to you. Writers with long and distinguished careers are also having to approach small indie presses to get their work out there.

Let's talk. Give me a ring.

Best

Donna

After I'd read it a second time, and stopped shaking, and had two mugs of Yorkshire tea with two spoonfuls of sugar in each, and walked to the end of Goose Lane and back, and changed the sheets and vacuumed the stairs, and then stretched out flat on the floor of my study for ten minutes deep breathing, I rang her up.

She was kind. She said there was nothing wrong with my writing. She said that this book was probably better than *Fast Work,* but the market was unrecognisable from five years ago. It's so tough. Publishers are buying fewer titles, and taking fewer risks, etc, etc, and she repeated everything she'd already said in her email. She said a small independent publisher might be interested in my book, but they would be unlikely to offer an advance and there would be no money in it for her, so it was not worth her while to continue. She was very happy to try to sell my work-in-progress, *Over to You,* so when the next draft is finished I should bung it over. In the meantime, I could approach small publishers myself with *They Met on the Bridge,* or self-publish it as an ebook.

I cannot write any more of this today. I am done.

I am gutted.

I am toast.

today's tweet from **@sallystoneymoor** is one of Giovanna's – *and incomprehensible*
wondering if a stuffed tiger would enhance my life…

Thursday October 13th
Despair

It's bad enough being a deserted wife, being unwanted.

Now, no-one wants what I write.

And my age: at 60 you're a dust bunny of society.

I watched yet more junk TV, then *Neighbours* at lunchtime and the repeat at teatime – anything to block up my brain and drown out the despair. I feel worse about the publishing thing right now than I do about the end of my marriage, which seems a bit out of proportion. But then, Gus and me splitting up for good was the end of a long road which had been petering out for some time, and I've had three whole years to get used to losing him. Just lately I've been investing everything in my writing, and I wasn't expecting that to fail.

I went to writing group tonight, and told them the news. Other writers are surely the people to hang out with when you've been rejected and don't have the heart to go on.

Everyone was sympathetic, even Spiky Pete; and they wanted the details. Then when they'd heard them, they spewed out optimism. They were upbeat and sunny-side-up, and told me how many times J K Rowling and William Golding (*The Lord of the Flies* man) were rejected and I felt like socking them all in the jaw. I am not best-seller potential (like Rowling) and I don't write literary fiction (like Golding). I am an ordinary mid-list novelist. Can't they see the difference? And anyway, don't people realise that it's actually better to go into the depths and say how awful things are and really get down in the mire with a person, and agree that the situation is totally crap, before you try to cheer them up and offer encouragement? It's all about acknowledging a person's feelings as real and valid, so they don't feel alone and misunderstood. I know how it works. It's *me* who should be doing a counselling course, not Wendy!

Spiky Pete started on about that ebook author who is a publishing sensation – Amanda Hocking. The woman writes books for teenagers about vampires and sirens and trolls. Her readers are all on Facebook and Twitter and they tweet about the books, with the result that she's sold millions and millions. (Why don't people tweet about mine? Maybe because most of my target readers – women over 45 – have got better things to do than tweet.) I don't do werewolves and I don't do trolls. I write novels about realistic people who do realistic things. I can't even stand magic realism, so Amanda Hocking and Spiky Pete can stuff their bloody vampires.

I was putting on my coat at the end of the evening when Kate Wensley (aka Giovanna) came up for a quiet chat. She reminded me that Jane Rogers, the literary novelist, couldn't find a publisher for her latest book and eventually found an independent publisher in Scotland, and next thing you know she was shortlisted for this year's Booker Prize.

"But I'm not a literary writer with an amazing reputation," I yelped, and she recoiled. I ranted on, "I have one book under my belt, quality commercial fiction, which sold 10,000 copies, a goodly number for a debut, but what the hell am I going to do now?" She took another step back. "I blame Tesco," I said. "If they didn't sell best-sellers cut-price, the publishers could make more of a profit and they wouldn't be strapped for cash, and...no! I blame the publishers! If they hadn't tugged their forelocks to the supermarkets and agreed to ridiculously low profit margins, they wouldn't be–"

"OK, OK, don't go ballistic. I'm not the enemy."

"Was I shouting? Oh, sorry, Kate. I don't know what's got into me. I'd better go. Email me!" I wailed, as I left to come home.

Good old Giovanna: she emailed me as promised:

hi daise

bummer about your book - sooooooooo not fair

but truly, before you hurl yourself off in front of a passing tractor you defo need to consider self publishing

why not do they met on the bridge as an e book and sell it on amazon?

you may not realise it, but the e book market is poised to explode

kindles and i pads are soooooooo easy to use now, and getting incredibly popular (outside stoneymoor) - they are truly about to become

HUGE - they're accessible to everyone now, not just geeks, and it's a snowball effect - a bit like the domestic white-goods market in china - the potential is mind-boggling - you sooooo should not miss out

take it from shopping page - every woman with even half a brain will have a kindle on their christmas list this year

in a very short time a kindle will be what every woman wants (after a night with hugh jackman obviously)

soooooo much easier to carry in your handbag than a stack of paperbacks - plus the best kept secret is that on a kindle you can make the typeface size as big as you want, so all us long-sighted over forties can read the text without our specs - blissful

the fact that e books let people read/buy books in private has already led to a mega-bulge in the steamy novel market (add some kinky knickers to they met on the bridge and you'll be onto a winner)

e books are a bit like internet dating - once the refuge of a dodgy minority, now everyone is doing it

plus you can make them instantly available world-wide

what the hell are you waiting for??? - get out there, get in there, and listen to the sound of cash registers ringing (or should that be sound of credit card transactions trans-acting?)

best global explosions and gravy trains,
love giovanna

Kate is always so encouraging, and talks good writing sense, and being a woman who always wanted to edit a shopping page, she knows much more than I do about what's going on in the big bad world of fashion, style and commerce.

But who on earth is Hugh Jackman?

And is it really true that even normal, sensible people are internet dating nowadays? What about people my age? Ooooh, I don't like it. I don't like it at all.

today's tweet from **@sallystoneymoor**
The Testament of Jesse Lamb. Rejection today. Booker tomorrow.

Friday October 14th

Character confusion

I need to make some decisions. Should I start submitting my book to small independent publishers, or should I forget about the crappy publishing establishment altogether, and check into the digital revolution?

I sat at my desk and wrote out pages of pros and cons for every possible option – the Jane Rogers indie publisher one, the Amanda Hocking self-published ebook option, or the self-published (real) book à la Jill Paton Walsh, *Knowledge of Angels*, which was shortlisted for the Booker in the nineties. I need to mull it over. I'll look at it again tomorrow.

This stage of life has nothing to recommend it, whereas being 50 was OK. I had a fancy dress party and people came dressed up as what they wanted to be when they grew up. I draped myself in scarves and wore two pairs of earrings and scraped my hair into my very first plait, and I carried a black Moleskine notebook (a la Hemingway) and a new black uni-ball micro pen around all evening, and noted down tasty bits of dialogue. Wendy wore fairy lights round her neck. They flashed on and off. People thought she wanted to be the Christmas fairy but she said she just wanted to be a little lighter.

Gus dressed up as a hermit. He wore a shaggy fur waistcoaty thing over his bare chest, and instead of trousers he wore a loin cloth. He spent the entire party alone in the kitchen, washing up. He is hopeless at birthdays. The last birthday of his that he spent at home he said he didn't want any presents from me or from anyone else.

"Tell people I am hungry for negation. The best present they could get me is nothing, because nothing is something, whereas accretion is subtraction. Tell people I am honing my essence."

And I said: "Please don't hone your essence any more. We couldn't take it in a stronger form."

Yes, being 50 was OK, because although I was going through the murderous menopause, I'd been bitten by the writing bug. I was launching into my first novel (which is now just a musty manuscript sitting on a shelf in the shed) and I had high hopes of the future. Ah, those were the days – my fifties, when *The Recorder* was printing just about everything I sent them and when Waterstones still had 3 for 2 tables and *Fast Work* was nestling up against Joanna Trollope and Katie Fforde.

today's tweet from **@sallystoneymoor**
e-opportunity: what the digital revolution has to offer women (writers)

Saturday October 15th

Safety Jacket

"Do you really want to go to this thing at the village hall tonight?" Iain said this morning.

"Don't you?"

"Truth be told, I'd rather spend the evening alone with you. A dinner à deux. Maybe at the Maazi in Matlock? Richard says their Arabian lamb is fabulous."

"Dinner à deux? What's happened to your Italian? I'm shocked." The man lives in Padua, not Paris.

He laughed. "You're changing the subject, Sally."

"I don't want to go to the village hall either, but it's a community thing and I don't do much for the village, so at least I can support the fund-raising events." And much as I love the Maazi, I'd rather not lead him on with dinners à deux.

"Well, can I take you out for dinner on your birthday?"

We settled on a birthday lunch – much safer – and he agreed to come round and call for me with Richard tonight and walk to the village hall.

At least there was no confusion about racing and betting and fancy dress. It was a speed dating social, with the non-singles option, as before. And going with Iain meant I did not have to venture onto the singles side, no matter how much Wendy nagged. Iain was my bulwark against the shark-infested seas of the dating inferno. (Oops, mixed my metaphors there. Good job Spiky Pete isn't reading this.)

Richard was an eager beaver. He left us as soon as we stepped over the threshold, didn't even have a drink with us first. He grabbed a beer from the bar and then joined the bunch of single men ready to make a bee-line for their first choice. Next to him were Billy Bathgate, unctuous village shopkeeper, and

Wendy's husband, Alan. I've always thought him suspect, well before he made that pass at me when Gus was away on one of his trips into solitude.

The "single" women were already sitting at the tables waiting, running their hands through their hair, crossing and uncrossing their legs, tweaking their skirts, etc, etc. I say "single" but Wendy was at the first table – what is she like? She was wearing a moss green satin dress with no sleeves. I went over to chat and asked her if she wasn't cold, and she said, "I'm freezing my butt off, so I hope people appreciate how good I look. I wish I had some tats on my arms, though. Hey – do you like my French pleat?" Her haircut is short and layered, but she'd added a hairpiece. I said "Um, very nice." Somehow I see French pleats as smooth and neat. Hers looked like a bird's nest.

Pippa was on the second table, on the third was a woman in some kind of space cadet uniform, and Mrs Mountain's twice-divorced daughter was on the fourth. I didn't recognize the women at the other tables. It looked like word had spread and there were loads of people from other villages, which was great for the village hall fund coffers. And great for me: I shan't feel I have to go along to make up the numbers at next month's event.

Mrs Mountain rang the first bell at 7.45. as advertised, and they were off.

Iain and I agreed we would sit the first round out and circulate down the socialising in-a-relationship side on the second round. This sounds more pleasant than it was. I was landed with Mr Mountain, a small, pale man with a pencil-thin moustache, who always wears a grey suit and too much Brylcreem. Although, let's face it, any Brylcreem is too much Brylcreem. And why are his trousers always so short, when he is so small? You'd think Mrs Mountain would sort him out. She attempts to sort out everything else in the village.

Then I got the curate, who is unable to talk about anything apart from his cactus collection. And then I was with Billy Bathgate, who had started on the singles side and moved over for the last round. I don't know if he had failed to score and was desperate, or if he thought it was his shopkeeperly duty (and good for PR) to come over and be friendly to the whole of the village.

I have no idea who Iain talked to – I was so exhausted by the end of the evening I didn't listen to what he said to me on the way home. Gosh, I hope he didn't ask me something that I agreed to and am going to regret.

Will just note here before I collapse into bed that Wendy disappeared in the middle of the evening with a tall, good-looking guy at least ten years younger than her. You have to hand it to her – she doesn't waste time.

today's tweet from **@sallystoneymoor**
Would you rather be mutton dressed as lamb, or mutton dressed as mutton?

Sunday October 16th

Feedback

I got a text from Wendy that was so long it came in two instalments.

```
Last night's news. Opportunity, luck n gorgeous
hunks in spades, or what? Pun intended, he is a
well fit gardener whoop whoop. Attracted 2 my
moss green satin ; ) Called gary. Ok, no-one can
b totally perfect, we need 2 keep our
```

```
expectations real.

Planets defo in house of swoon. Did u catch his
shorts?!!! He is blond adonis pond builder
currently at rowans. Amazin calves, pecs, abs
etc. Thighs 2 die 4. Reached 1st base!!! Snogged
like a dream  : - D  love wendy. Xxxx
```

She is one bad girl. I sometimes wonder if she is a rather iffy influence on me. Then I think about how much fun she is, how seeing her in all her crazy outfits cheers me up, how loyal she is, and how she'd do anything for me. Whoever gets her in the end will have a bargain. I hope she doesn't end up with a lunk-head, though.

Richard also enjoyed last night. He came round bright and early – ridiculous for a Sunday – because he wanted to tell me all about the woman he hit it off with. She was from the award-winning beauty salon in Matlock. She told him all about her job and how she does colonic irrigation. I guess this would have dried up the conversation for all the other (normal) men, but Richard was enthralled.

"Who would have thought a beauty salon person – do you say "beautician"? – who would think she'd be so interesting?" he burbled.

"Was it that space cadet woman? The fuchsia pink with the side-shoulder fastening and the matching pink trousers? Is that her work get-up?"

"Such sensible overalls – I wonder if she gets them from the Dickies women's range. She was fascinating! She explained the technicalities of the pumping system for colonic irrigation, and–"

"Don't tell me! I don't want to know!"

"Not even about–"

"Richard! Read my lips! I don't want to know! Tell me the important thing – did you get her number?"

"Yes. But what about you? Are you and Iain..."

"No. Let's talk about something else."

"Oh – OK. Your birthday! Are you absolutely sure you don't want to go out tomorrow night?"

"Tell me what there is there to celebrate! My marriage is over, I am finished as a writer, and I am going to be 60."

He patted my arm. "It's not so bad, you know. Being 60, I mean. I know the other two pretty much suck."

Thank God for Richard. He sees hardship for what it is. He understands the darker side of life. He does not try to pretend that horrible things that happen are anything other than horrible things that happen. He does not buff them up into shining opportunities, he doesn't frame them as transforming planetary transits which are for the ultimate good of the inner self, like Wendy does (heaven help her). Richard sees crap for what it is.

"What I would like, Richard, is for you to come and spend the evening with me – just you. We can play Scrabble. And we can drink champagne. Iain is insisting on taking me out for lunch, and I suppose that will pass a couple of hours fairly pleasantly, but it would be really nice to be with someone I don't have to make an effort for. All three kids will ring – they always do, they're good kids – and you won't mind if I interrupt the Scrabble game to talk to them, will you?"

"I'll bring my Screwfix catalogue to amuse myself in the interludes. I've conceived an unhealthy passion for a pair of trestles. I keep trying to stamp it down, but I'm constantly drawn back to them."

He got up from his chair (we were sitting in the kitchen) and tugged at the seat of his trousers. Then he sat down again and said, "Some of my underpants are terrible. It's as if they're alive – I can feel them creeping down my thighs. I need to cull them."

"What you need to do when you get home is get them all out of your drawer, and lay them all out on the bed and go through them, one by–"

"I am going through them! That's the trouble! But where can I get some decent ones? I have had it up to here with M&S Y-fronts. They're hopeless!"

What is it about men and their underpants?

"You need to get something that isn't a standard Y-front, something a bit more 2011-ish. Especially now you're on the pull. I mean – what would Ms Fuchsia Pink think of them?"

"This is where Dickies could pounce," he said. "They ought to be calling in their top designers, even as we speak."

"So what do you think the perfect underpant needs?"

"Security, material that shrugs off stains, adequate ventilation – possibly assisted – and a reliable fastening. It's about time persons of quality gave their attention to the comfort and protection of the nation's manhood. Paxman tried a few years ago – do you remember all that kerfuffle on the *Today* programme? Nothing happened. Next thing you know, Prince Charles will be muscling in with the Poundbury Pant and the Prince's Truss."

today's tweet from **@sallystoneymoor**
Screwfix catalogue. p.101. Amber 2 Gas Barrier, damp proof membrane preventing ingress of radon, methane & CO^2 gas. Fabric for underpants?

Monday October 17th

Birthday Blues

Text from Wendy:

```
Happy b'day 2 u! Taram! :-) Be sure 2 have a gd
1. Huge hugs 4 your best day, love wendy. Xxxx
```

Today's post: 15 birthday cards (a decent number), five presents, and a letter from the NHS, telling me that now I am 60, I am part of their bowel screening programme and they'll be sending me a home screening kit very soon. I really wish they wouldn't.

I got no card from Gus. Plus ça change. This year I'm not making excuses for him – we're finished.

10 a.m. I wanted a walk on my own this morning – a solitary time to reflect on my past and consider my future – so I drove to Stanton Moor and parked below the old quarry. The autumn colours in the trees and the sunshine and the blue sky were all so beautiful, it made my heart ache. I walked past the old quarry where the eco-warriors used to live in tree houses – ah – my glory days. I once stayed overnight in one of their tree houses and wrote a piece for *The Recorder* about it. I had to climb up a twelve foot rope ladder with rungs so spaced out I could only manage to heave my knees onto them, not my feet, and then I had to haul myself up to the next rung. I had unsightly bruises on my knees for weeks. The perils of being a writer. Just remembered! The editor spiked my piece: "Not one of your best."

10.20. a.m. Reached the top of the hill and the Nine Ladies Stone Circle. I sat on each of the nine stones in turn and made a resolution on each.

I will:

- Ring Pricey Paul and make an appointment to have him restyle my hair – this time to something that works when I wash it myself.

- Have six-weekly appointments with him to keep it looking good. You can't mess around when you're 60.

- Face up to the fact that I am single. I am single!

- Stop chewing everyone up. I've been a little bit hyper in the anger department lately.

- Exercise everyday so I am fit and slim.

- Clean the house once a week, and not just when visitors are expected.

- Be more patient with Sam when he comes home to see me.

- Begin somehow to think about meeting another man. Aarggh! Will my mastectomy be a problem? Maybe I'll join Friends Reunited and find my very first boyfriend, the sweet and funny Stuart Robinson?

- Get my book into print. I will publish it myself, as a paperback and as an ebook. Yay! Made a decision!

12 Noon

Iain picked me up in his Alfa Romeo and took me to lunch at the David Mellor cutlery factory's minimalist café near Hathersage. That's a mouthful. I was going to start off by looking round the chi-chi kitchen shop, where you're allowed to touch the merchandise as well as gawp at the prices, but Iain wanted to look round the factory first, which is built on the foundations of the old village gas cylinder.

Fortunately for me, it was closed. "Merda!" he said, when we saw the notice on the door. "But look at the building, Sally: it's a modern design icon. It delivers a thrillingly robust design solution in local materials which entirely avoids the neo-vernacular. What do you think?"

"Um, yes. I see what you mean." I'd forgotten how easily he slips into architect jargon.

He didn't stop: "The circle of the manufacturing process marries form with function and the antecedent homage is a joy. Sheer class."

We walked across the gravel forecourt to the kitchen shop, where he considered the cutlery. He picked up a knife and said, "Look at the design – a glorious amalgamation of simplicity, elegance and sophistication – you have to feel the balance in your hand to fully appreciate it – here – hold it." He passed the knife to me.

"Um, yes, I see what you mean."

"It's truly cutlery for connoisseurs. The quality of the manufacturing is second to none. This surely has to be living, breathing, working design at its best."

"Oh, yes." *???*

"Truth is, Serena and I were in love with Mellor cutlery. We bought a canteen of the 1953 design, Pride, in stainless steel with the black handles, and we had some Café for everyday use." He fondled a spoon.

Oh dear, it's ten years down the line, and one spoon is enough to spin Iain straight back to Serena. But that's what you get with widowers – the ever-present ghost of their wives.

I moved onto the saucepans. "Look at the prices! This pan is £195! And look! Tea towels for £12! At that price they need to dry up by themselves."

Iain wanted to buy me something for my birthday and I homed in on the cookie cutters which were suitably inexpensive. I was about to suggest this, when I noticed the heart shaped sets and had to steer him away at top speed. He offered me a designer apple corer. Why do I need one of those? What's wrong with the potato peeler with fake orange string wound round the handle that I got off Bakewell market for a quid?

"Oh, Sally, what about a pair of wine glasses? Look at these."

I liked the Spanish recycled glassware at £8 a glass, nice and chunky, which made them look robust. I couldn't imagine anything more fragile surviving in our house. But Iain insisted I had the Jerpoint version at four times the price. "If you must have a craft glass," he muttered with an unmistakable hint of disdain. "Or how about two cereal bowls instead? The curvature on these blue ones is perfection," he said.

Oh so much worse, cereal bowls for him and for her – implying together breakfasts...

"No, the glasses, please. Lovely. Thank you." I squeezed his arm, and he leaned over and kissed me on the cheek.

"We can toast each other with these," he said.

I made no comment.

The lunch was good. I had green minestrone soup and then a designer bread and butter pudding with cream. Yum.

In between courses, Iain asked me why I wasn't writing pieces for the papers any more. "I know the editor of *The Recorder* changed," he said, "and the new one didn't want your stuff – more fool her – but did you try other broadsheets?"

"It's only columnists who are given space for that kind of stuff these days. You've seen how the papers have shrunk in size in the last few years. There just isn't room for funny domestic pieces from freelances."

The café is unusual in that there's a display space on the wall opposite the window, showcasing some of David Mellor's designs, and in the space between that wall and the minimalist café tables, there are some real life examples of his larger classic design work, such as waste paper bins and Royal Mail pillar boxes and working traffic lights.

As I was licking the last traces of cream from my spoon, Iain pointed to the traffic lights and said, "I wish you were as easy to read as those. Truth be told, I can't tell if you're on amber, red or green."

I turned red with embarrassment – did he notice? – and was fumbling around in my brain for something to say, when Kate (aka Giovanna) from writing group walked in the door, bless her, and I called over, "Hi, Kate! Come and say hello. Thanks for my card."

Good old Kate. Perfect timing. She'd come to buy a pair of Pantone mugs for her son's new flat. I introduced her to Iain, and she asked me if I was having a nice birthday, and had I decided what to do about the book?

So I told her and Iain. Thank goodness she turned up when she did, because all the way back in the car I could chat to

Iain about self-publishing, and designing the cover, and of the importance of choosing the right font, and we could forget all about the colour of my traffic lights.

Is it very bad of me to let him think he might have a chance? Mightn't he be passing the time, as I am, just enjoying the company of an OK member of the opposite sex?

2.30 p.m. He dropped me off at home and I lay on my bed and listened to the last half hour of the afternoon play on Radio 4. There was a time when I thought about writing for radio, but it feels too late in the day to start that now, learning a new craft, finding out how you submit your work, waiting for rejection, etc etc, and all the while you're getting nearer to the time when there will be no rejection: death.

4.30 p.m. Wendy called in (wearing her frayed look) with a kiss and a card and a birthday pressie: hair straighteners. The card was not a standard birthday card, but a Solar Return card, which is some astrological thingy related to the position of the planets on your birthday. She did explain, but I can't remember it now.

After I'd thanked her and we'd dipped into the chocolates that came with Sam's Oxfam Unwrapped non-present of a goat, I said, "Tell me about the hunk!"

But she said "No. I don't want to jinx it. Anyway, there isn't time. I can't stop."

"Tell me!"

"There's so much to tell, and he's waiting outside. I have to be quick."

"OK, but give me some quick suggestions for my hair."

"Go for a short pixie cut," she said, getting up from her chair.

"Who do you think I am? Susan Kennedy on *Neighbours*?"

"Well, how about a short bob with blunt layers and a fringe? It would be really edgy." She was already half way out of the door.

"Those blunt layers don't work with naturally wavy hair! Something else!"

"You're being very negative, today," she said, leaning against the door jamb and looking twitchy.

"You try being sixty!"

"I know it's crap, sweetie. It'll be me next year." She came over and gave me a hug – a big thing for her. Then she left.

6.30 p.m. Richard arrived with fish and chips, and I opened the champagne.

7.30 p.m. Daniel rang from Denver in his lunch break. I thanked him for his card and asked what was happening at work, so I wouldn't be tempted to ask if he'd got a girlfriend yet, and then I asked if he was doing anything interesting this week. He said he's driving up from Denver with a couple of mates from work to go snowboarding in the Rockies, and on the way, they're going to take Gus his winter supplies from the British shop in Denver, namely, Heinz spaghetti hoops, pickled walnuts, and Yorkshire tea. They have to go this weekend, because by the end of the month they won't be able to make it through the snowdrifts on the track up to Gus's cabin.

8.30 p.m. Nina rang. She was too exhausted to talk for long, and she had to break off in the middle to make Ellie go back to bed. Oh, I wish they weren't so far away.

9.45 p.m. Sam rang. There was so much chatter in the background, I could hardly hear what he said, except that he'd be home very soon.

"But where are you, Sam?"

"London. Camping with some mates at the mo."

"What? Camping in London?"

I couldn't hear what he said next, because his voice was drowned out by ear-splitting emergency vehicle sirens, and he shouted above the racket: "Got to go. Love you, Ma. Don't forget – we are the 99%!"

Sweet boy.

today's tweet from **@sallystoneymoor**
Going out to lunch with a friend is lovely but oh how I hate to break off from working on the fast-boiling plotline in my new novel!

Tuesday October 18th

My glorious future

So that was it. My wonderful 60th birthday, portal to the next glorious phase of my life, which holds what?

- divorce
- the ignominy of self-publishing
- bowel screening every two years (courtesy of the NHS) involving small cardboard sticks and waterproof envelopes and various unglamorous procedures that Richard's new hottie would no doubt take in her stride.

today's (Giovanna sourced) tweet from **@sallystoneymoor**
I might need a Maine Coon. Correction. I definitely need a Maine Coon

This is beyond me – what does it mean?

Thursday October 20th

Smitten

I have heard nothing from Wendy for days. The sum total of what I know about her new man is contained in those ecstatic texts she sent me. I've tried ringing her and texting her, but I've had no reply. I hope she's all right.

today's tweet from **@sallystoneymoor**
Women's writing mag @Mslexia are still quoting me in their diary advert: "It felt like a special treat. How many diaries feel like that?"

Friday October 21st

Could do better

Still not seen hide nor hair of Wendy. (Oops! Cliché alert.) What is she up to? I'd have expected her to come round by now and spill the beans. Bother: cliché again. Maybe I need to take a writer's refresher course.

today's tweet from **@sallystoneymoor**
Even @anitashreve must have her off days...

Saturday October 22nd

Deconstruction

An email from my erstwhile husband sent from Daniel's phone:

```
Sally,
Daniel just reminded me I missed your big day.
Hope it was a good one,
take care, Gus

sent from my iPhone
```

Five days late! Sent from his son's phone and obviously prompted/leaned on by said son!

I thought (on my birthday) that it would be nice to hear from him. Now I wish he hadn't bothered.

Oh dear, oh dear, oh dear, when a one line email, sent under duress, is all I have left to get my teeth into, it really is the end of the game. But it's so frustrating. It's like trying to get cross with a vacuum.

Nineteen measly words, and nine of those an excuse.

And I hate that stupid phrase at the end – *sent from my iPhone*. It's like *sent from my iPad*. It makes me sick. It makes me want to put at the end of every email – *sent from my laptop*.

today's spam
your every night will be ultimate of passion

today's tweet from **@sallystoneymoor**
less than a week left of British Summer Time. Oh dear.

Monday October 24th

Character confusion

I downloaded a *Guide to Self-Publishing* from the Society of Authors website, and I am working my way through it.

The OC sucks. I shan't be watching it again. It is not only vacuous, it's dull. No-one ever does anything except float around in swimming pools or go to parties. You never see anyone reading a book, not even an ebook.

And there's something else. People from other TV programmes and films keep turning up in it and confusing me. I had got over the fact that one of the main characters is played by the ugly brother from that Rom-Com, *While You Were Sleeping*, and that another is an ex-boyfriend of Rachel's from *Friends,* when yesterday a dead character from *Neighbours* turned up. It was freakish.

today's tweet from **@sallystoneymoor**
Me: "Someone in Neighbours has been taken into protective custody." Friend: "They should all be taken into protective custody."

Tuesday October 25th
Deluded

I forgot to note here yesterday that I met Pippa in Bakewell and had the weirdest conversation with her.

Me: "Hi, Pippa! How are you? Did you enjoy the speed dating thingy at the village hall last week?"

Pippa: "No. I didn't. I really didn't. I don't like that kind of thing. I don't like it at all. I just went along to help Mrs Mountain behind the bar. I was doing the teas. Yes. The teas."

Me: "But hadn't you thought of the event as a way to meet someone new...you know...now that you and Richard are no longer...together?"

Pippa: "But Richard is just having a midlife crisis! I know that he'll tire of it soon and want to come home to me. There's no doubt about it. No, there isn't. I'm giving him a free rein, and while I wait for him to get it out of his system, I've taken up knitting socks. Mrs Mountain put me onto it. Have you seen that wool stall at the Farmers Market? They sell that wonderful variegated yarn that knits up into Fair Isle all on its own. I'm on my fourth pair. I'm knitting Richard a pair for Christmas in greens and blues. Yes I am."

Midlife crisis? He's 62!

Get it out of his system? With a beauty therapist girlfriend who does colonic irrigation, that's more than likely.

today's tweet from **@sallystoneymoor**
Now that baby-boomers are reaching their sixties, does middle age end at 70?

Wednesday October 26th

Straight talking

Iain took me out to Hassop Station Café for lunch (yum). I love the place since they chi-chi-fied it, and it's really handy having a bookshop and gift shop there as well as bike hire.

I started talking about my self-publishing plans, but instead of taking an interest – as he had seemed to do on my birthday – he took me by surprise and said: "Don't you ever think of taking things easy?"

"What do you mean?"

"I mean, how would you like to come back home to Italy with me for a holiday? Remember all those plans we made? All those years ago?"

My hands flew to my cheeks as I felt my face go horribly hot. Argghh! The embarrassing memory of what happened seven years ago when Iain and I spent a lot of time together, during Gus's first trip into Never-never-land! Iain fell for me and he thought that I felt the same and was ready to leave my marriage and go off into a Venetian sunset with him, walking hand-in-hand along the Riva degli Schiavoni, with the golden sun bouncing off the lagoon onto the walls of the Doges Palace. (Ooh it does sound nice. Maybe I could get into travel writing.)

"Iain. I'm really sorry about what happened before. How I led you on. You do know it was just stupid thoughtlessness, don't you? I mean, I wasn't trying to–"

"I know you're a sweet-natured person, Sally. Why do you think I like being with you? All that stuff from before is water under the Accademia Bridge. But let's be honest – things are different now. You're single. You're free."

I heaved a huge sigh. "Yes."

"So, would you consider it?"

It was time to be straightforward with him and stop shilly-shallying. It was time to be grown up and strong, and to act my age. The trouble is that I may look 60 on the outside, but inside I still feel about 43, and where men are concerned I feel 19 and a half (which is when I first met Gus). I took a deep breath. "I don't think I'm ready to think about another serious relationship. And maybe I never will be ready. I need to tell you that, Iain. But the other thing is my writing – it's really, really important to me. I'm not ready to throw in the towel. I've put so much into it. I've tried so hard. I'm not giving up on this book. I'm going to self-publish, which means I can't be taking time off. I don't know the first thing about publishing a book, so it's going to be a huge effort. And if I'm planning on bringing it out next May, I need to get on with it."

"So when *are* you going to retire, kick off your shoes and join the rest of us in the slow lane? Once the book is out?"

"I haven't thought about it. I mean – I'm in the middle of writing my *third* novel. All I know is, I want to write. When a book is going well, when I'm in the middle of a book, I just love it. As soon as I wake up in the morning, I can't wait to start writing. It's not been like that lately, because of...well...you know..."

"One of the things I love about you is your commitment and determination. I wish I had half as much. So truth be told, you don't surprise me. But can I still keep company with you?"

Keep company with me? Keep company with me? Who does he think he is? A hero in a rustic Victorian novel? I turned away and stifled a giggle under the pretence of sneezing. "It's nice to do things with you, Iain. I just don't want to make any kind of commitment."

today's tweet from **@sallystoneymoor**
I do wish people would always speak in character. Bad dialogue is one of life's vastly underrated irritations.

Thursday October 27th

Gob-smacking update

Still no news from Wendy, so I went round to see her. There was a filthy pick-up in the drive, parked behind Wendy's beat-up Beetle, and Alan's car was nowhere to be seen. The sitting room curtains were drawn. I knocked on the door, and saw the curtains twitch, and then Wendy came to the door in a silk kimono and a pair of vertiginous, red high heels. Demure geisha slippers have obviously passed her by. She pulled the kimono tightly around her body (was there nothing underneath?) and a side slit revealed the top of a white lacy stocking. I gawped.

"I think I'm in lurve!" she whispered.

I opened my mouth but nothing came out.

"It's Gary," she went on. "Look, I'll come and see you as soon as I can. I'm making the most of him while Alan is away on his so-called golf trip. I mean – it would be a bit weird bringing Gary back here if Alan was in residence, even if I have decided he's had his chips. See you, sweetie." And she pushed the door to, leaving me standing on the step like piffy on a rock bun.

today's tweet from **@sallystoneymoor**
I hate feeling like piffy on a rock bun.

October 31st

The return of the prodigal son

Sam is home!

today's tweet from **@sallystoneymoor**
Hooray! My son is home after 3 months away. How do you kill the fatted calf for a veggie?

NOVEMBER

November 1st
Wakey-wakey

It is so WONDERFUL to have Sam home! I didn't even mind him arriving in the middle of *Neighbours*.

I made him tea, and asked him three million questions about where he's been and what he's been doing, but he just kept saying "Sorry, Ma. I'm wasted. Can I tell you, tomorrow? Wasted."

He looks lean and hungry and tanned. It seems so long since he's been home, and every time I walk past him in the kitchen I pat his arm, or put my arm round his shoulders, or kiss his cheek. He hasn't started batting me off yet, but he will do soon.

After tea, he wanted a long hot bath, to remind himself what it felt like (he said) and that was the last I saw of him. I went upstairs two hours later to see if he was going to come down again, but he was still in the tub.

today's tweet from **@sallystoneymoor**
is it OK to wake up your 28 year old son when he's fallen asleep in the bath?

November 2nd

The voice

Sam was out of the bath and in bed by nine last night, and it's now noon, and he is *still* asleep.

I'll write my blog and hope he's woken up by the time I've finished.

OK. That is 45 minutes of my life I shall never see again. It didn't read well, so I scrapped the post. Sometimes I can think up something domestic to write about, such as my mice infestation, or something villagey, such as the well-dressing. Otherwise I have to do something weird, the sole purpose of which is to provide fodder for the blog e.g. learning to juggle fire clubs, sky-diving, swimming with sharks. Mercy me. At least readers like my photos of the Peak District. Today I could think of NOTHING. The best thing about self-publishing – apart from being able to choose my own book cover (yay!) is that it will give me something to blog about.

Later:

Fed up with waiting for Sam to surface, I went to Hassop Station Bookshop on the Trail, to look at the book-covers and fonts to help me decide what I want for mine. Stuff like that will make excellent copy for the blog.

So there I was, working my way along the shelves, when I overheard a conversation between two men on the other side of a bookstand.

The first bloke said: "Ey up, Kit, how's life in the world of printing?"

And the other one said, in the most amazingly attractive voice, deep and velvety with a tiny rasp – very male, utterly delicious, "It's tough. The printing is fine – plenty of work – it's the frigging bank that's the problem."

A printer? He had a voice that sounded familiar. It reminded me of someone, but I had no idea who. And I still have no idea who, but it was someone incredibly sexy. *Who was it?* I *had* to see what he looked like.

I crept to the end of the bookshelf where I was lurking, with a book open, held up to hide my face, and I lowered it for a second and peeped over the top.

My mouth fell open. It was the rude, obnoxious man from the Trail! Mr Nasty! I couldn't believe it. Why had I not noticed his voice on the Trail? Because it was shouting obscenities, that's why. Well maybe not obscenities, but certainly insults. Huh!

I ducked back behind the bookshelf as the other man said: "Who's minding the shop for you?"

"Gray. He can't get a job, and he's helping me out. Nice to have him around."

"He can look after things while you pursue your love-life, eh? Every time I see you, you've got a different woman on your arm."

"What? You're joking! Not happening, mate. Must dash. Just popped in for a bottle of water from the caff."

Fancy his being a printer. And wouldn't you just know that this afternoon was the one and only time in the last four weeks I'd been near the Trail without his stupid clip-on light?

When I was sure he'd gone, I emerged and went over to the till to talk to Lisa, the bookshop manager. She's sweet.

"Do you know who that man is – the one who's just left? The one in cycling gear?" I asked. "About my age. Slim. Tall. Brown hair, graying at the temples. A faint tan."

"Why? Do you fancy him?" she said, laughing.

"No, I-"

"Cos all the girls in the café do."

"He's twice their age!"

"And? He's fit. And so *nice*. Friendly, chatty, courteous."

Courteous? "I mean the man in cycling gear. Not the other one he was talking to. I think his first name is Kit…"

"Yes. Kit Wyatt."

I explained about the light, and asked if she knew how I could contact him, so I could give it him back. She said he owns Wyatt Printing, behind Caudwell Mill, at Rowsley.

"You could get a quote from him for printing your book, couldn't you?" she said.

What???

today's tweet from **@sallystoneymoor**
Eavesdropping can be very informative

today's tweet from **@sallystoneymoor**
Blogged about book covers and fonts on sallystoneymoor.com
What's your favourite font? Mine is Helvetica Neue UltraLight.
#fonts

Friday November 4th

Face to face with the voice

I found two printers in the phone book – one in Chesterfield and one in Ashbourne, but the guy in the village who publishes a lot of his own local history books said I should try his printer in Sheffield. All of which meant I had no need to consider Mr Kit Wyatt. All I needed to do was take him his light back.

But I didn't want to!

Richard told me not to be a baby, and just to get it over with. I would have asked Iain to ride shotgun, but he's back in Padua, having his house re-roofed. I am still cringing over our last conversation.

"This will be our last evening together," he said. "Till next time, of course. Unless someone has snapped you up by the time I get back."

"I have no intention of being snapped up."

I am sooo hoping he didn't think I meant I'd be saving myself for him, when all I meant was my priority is my book.

I went to Wyatt Printing at the end of the day on my own, on the way to the Derby Playhouse, where I was meeting Duncan and Alicia from writing group. We were going to see *Serial Killers*. No, it's not my usual type of gig, but I read a piece in *The Recorder* last week about learning to live on your own, and it said "Never ever turn down an invitation to a social engagement."

So there I was, all dressed up, hair newly washed, a smidge of eye make-up (to give me confidence), wearing my black ankle-length coat that I bought in a fit of optimism for imagined book signing tours, my translucent shimmery ear-rings, and my new scarf with the print of flying swallows that Nina gave me for my birthday.

An old lady emerged from the door as I went in, and I held the door open for her. There was no-one at reception and I guessed the staff had gone home. I heard someone talking at the end of a corridor to the left and walked in that direction, and as I got closer I recognised Mr Kit Wyatt's treacherously delicious voice.

I braced myself. I would apologise again for knocking him off his bike, and he would see how I had done the right thing, the awkward thing, by returning his light, and we'd be straight, and I could go off to the Playhouse and have a Bloody Mary in the bar while I waited for the others.

He was talking on the phone: "You call yourself the *friendly* bank?...Forget it!" And there was a bang and a growl of "Bloodsuckers!" followed by a string of expletives and a succession of short sharp thuds as if he might be kicking the desk. Then there was a miaow. *A miaow?*

And he said: "Sorry, Witty."

Then there was silence, and I felt it safe to knock on the door.

"Hello!" said the voice.

I pushed the door gently and peered round it and Kit Wyatt was sitting in an old oak swivel chair, with knees bent and his feet up on the edge of the desk in front of him. He was wearing a grey suit waistcoat and trousers and a white shirt, with sleeves rolled up. He looked up and then did a double take and thrust out his arm, pointing straight at me, and said, "*You're* the woman who derailed me! What do you want?"

There was a miaow, and I looked round. A massive black and white cat was sprawled in one of those fleecy cat-beds that you hang on a radiator. The cat turned its head to stare at me. Was the cat challenging me, too? I turned back to face Kit Wyatt, who now had his arms folded, but before I could speak, he said, "Well?"

Just like that. *"Well."* How incredibly rude!

I held out the light towards him. "You dropped this. I didn't know who you were, or I'd have returned it sooner. Anyway, I'm here now. And I wanted to say I'm–"

"I should think so too. It was the least you could do."

"What?" I was incensed by his attitude. I'd been going to tell him how sorry I was about the accident.

"You shouldn't have been on the trail with those dogs!"

"They weren't my dogs! And it wasn't my dodgy–"

"I don't care whose blasted dogs they were, and I don't want to hear any pathetic excuses. You were utterly irresponsible."

"But you weren't looking where you were going! Or were your yuppie-fied, trendy sunglasses too dark for your pensioner eyes? You realise, I suppose, that if it had been a road accident, you would have been liable? *You* ran into *me*!" Was this strictly true? Who had really been at fault? It was probably me and the blessed hounds, but there was no way I was admitting that now. He shouldn't have been so obnoxious.

"The dog ran out in front of me!" he protested. "I had no time to stop!"

"Crikey! I've done the decent thing and brought back your stupid poncey light and now you're abusing me again. Well, you can just bog off!" And I banged the light down on his desk and swept out. He was lucky I didn't throw the thing at his head.

I charged down the corridor and out to the car and jumped in and started it up and drove off without doing up my seat belt. My hands were shaking so much I could hardly hold the steering wheel, and I only remembered to turn on my lights when I was out of the car park and on the road.

Once I was down the lane, I pulled onto the grass verge. I switched off the ignition, and a wave of embarrassment swept over me. What was I thinking? It was the first time in my life that I'd shouted at a stranger. Thank God I didn't throw the light at him.

I gripped the driving wheel to steady myself. Why am I always losing my temper these days? Am I angry with Gus? Or am I angry at life and the way everything has crumbled at this late stage?

One crazy bout of hammering on the dashboard later, I realised what's going on: I'm furious with myself. I spent all that time, years, it's been, kidding myself about Gus and me and our marriage, hoping he'd come back, and then wasting valuable writing time on what? All that time wasted, time that is so much more precious now I've reached 60.

I sat there for several minutes, knuckles locked, resolving to sort myself out. I put on my CD of the *Out of Africa* soundtrack that I always find so calming and set off for Derby. Now *she* was a strong woman – Karen Blixen, the woman Meryl Streep portrayed. She never gave up. And I'm not giving up either.

today's tweet from **@sallystoneymoor**
(Bliss is) enjoying a Bloody Mary at the theatre bar before the performance of Serial Killers...

November 5th

Incendiary activities

I asked Sam if he'd go to the village bonfire with me tonight, but he refused.

"Why would I want to celebrate the death of someone who wanted to blow up Parliament? He was right!"

"It's not about that. It's a village event. A community activity."

"So was putting people in the stocks and throwing crap at them."

He said he was going to stay at home and do Facetime (whatever *that* is) on his iPad with a couple of his friends.

I was wondering who I could go to the bonfire with, when Wendy turned up on the doorstep with mascara running down her cheeks.

"What is it? What's up? Come in, you poor thing. Has Alan found out about Gary?"

"Alan hasn't found out. I bloody have! Oh God. Have you got a drink?"

I opened a bottle of Merlot that I bought from the nice man at John Hattersley Wines in Bakewell.

"Come into the sitting room, Wendy."

I threw a log on the fire and gave her some wine and she told me the tale. Gary has two wives – one in Sheldon and one in Middleton, and he also has another mistress, besides Wendy. A woman who lives in Youlgreave. Gosh. Fancy my describing Wendy as *a mistress*.

"But didn't you have an inkling about any of this?" I said, incredulous.

"Why would I? He's always rushing off to different places, but he said it was for jobs – you know – landscaping jobs."

"So how did you find out?"

"This woman came up to me in the Oxfam shop. I was just about to pounce on some denim shorts, just my size, and this horrible woman with bleached hair and black roots and a disgusting purple jacket walked up to me and slapped my face and called me a slut. It was awful..." poor Wendy burst into tears. "I had no idea," she said between blubs. "I didn't know he was married once, never mind twice. I wouldn't do that...It was really, really awful..."

I knew she wouldn't thank me for a hug, so I just topped up her wine glass.

"And Alan comes home from his holiday tonight. I had to get out of the house and calm down before he gets back. God! Alan! I thought he was bad enough! Gary makes Alan look like a monk!"

today's tweet from **@sallystoneymoor**
Confucius was right when he said life is simple, but we insist on making it complicated

Sunday November 6th

The perennial problem

Richard told me he's going on a third date next week with Ms Colonic Irrigation (aka Melanie.)

"But I'm so out of practise with this dating thing," he said. "I mean, I didn't really date Pippa, I just talked to her every time she walked past with the blessed hounds. Remember? When I was rebuilding your front wall?"

"You'll be fine, Richard."

"But I saw something on the telly the other night – American? – I don't know, and they were talking about the third date being – you know – where *it* happens. Is that right?"

"How would I know? The last time I was dating, string underpants were in fashion."

"That's it! I'm worried about my underwear!"

Again?

"Oh, Richard."

"Come on! Come on! I need a woman's angle on the underpant problem!"

I sighed. "Get some CK ones. That's Calvin Klein to you."

"Calvin Klein? I don't want poncey ones. And I don't want to feel as if I'm wearing cycling shorts. I'm very fond of ventilation. I want something that's up for the job without being intrusive. It's the difference between being affectionate and being clingy. Now if Dickies made underpants, they'd be worth some serious consideration."

He got up to go, and then he said "Oh, I've been meaning to ask you, do you know who that woman is who keeps riding up here on her horse? She's always hanging around your gate when I walk up in the morning. She says *Hello Richard,* and then she rides off, and I haven't the foggiest idea who she is."

"You've never mentioned her before."

"Haven't I?" he said insouciantly. "Well. Must be off."

Insouciantly! Now that's a good word!

today's tweet from **@sallystoneymoor**
I wish you could see the leaves on the beech trees at the end of my lane. They look golden in the autumn sunshine.

Monday November 7th

Photofit

I rang Wendy to see how she was, and also to ask a few questions about the woman on the horse, but as she was out, I left her a message on her answering machine. Then I had a shower and came out to find a message with questions from *her*: "Does this woman have unfeasibly long legs like that woman in the M&S advert for the shimmer jacket? And does she have a nose like that weird alien model in the Prada Eyewear ad? If she does, then I know who it is."

Wendy's brain has obviously been addled by too much sex and shopping at such a delicate age (i.e. menopausal.) Does she really expect that description to mean anything to Richard or me?

I asked Richard again what the woman looks like. "What colour hair does she have?"

"Medium."

"Is she fat or thin?"

"Medium."

"Does she have a weird nose?"

"Maybe."

Absolutely hopeless. It's a good job the woman isn't a criminal with Richard expected to give an eyewitness account to the police.

"Well what does the *horse* look like?" I said.

"How should I know? If she was carrying some kind of tool – a circular saw or an angle-grinder – I could give you a good description."

today's tweet from **@sallystoneymoor**
How best to describe someone – by the shimmer of their jacket or the contents of their tool bag?

Tuesday November 8th

4 colour process

I went to see the Sheffield printer, who was very nice, but basically not for me. Yippee, though, because it's fodder for another blog post.

Today I found out about bindings: the difference between perfect bound and limp sewn. Oooh, I love these technical terms. But I've forgotten which is which because I was so overloaded with other information. Though I do remember that the cover I described to him is called matt laminate.

I rang the printer in Chesterfield, who emailed me a quote immediately but it was even more expensive than the 4 colour printer. The Ashbourne printer said he'd post me a quote and a book he printed last year for another novelist, as an example of his work. Progress! Although he must be behind the door if he has to post me a quote and not email it.

I got back at lunchtime, when Sam usually surfaces. He spends all afternoon on the net on his iPad. Where did he get the money from for that? Can you earn enough for an iPad working in a coffee shop in Amsterdam? Or on an organic farm in Tuscany? Or picking olives in Palestine? Not the latter, certainly.

He says he's looking for jobs, but whenever I look over his shoulder, he's reading online news, anti-globalisation stuff, or checking Twitter. We have tea together and then watch the news and he rants about whichever politician he sees. e.g. "How can a bunch of millionaires possibly know what it's like for ordinary people? Osborne, and that fat cat Cameron with his smug round moon-face. At least Blair is looking satisfyingly wrecked these days. Bring on the war crimes tribunal."

today's tweet from @sallystoneymoor
Is ranting at the news an inherited gene carried on the Y chromosome?

today's tweet from **@sallystoneymoor**
My new blog post has the technical spec from my printer on it – check it out – sallystoneymoor.com

Wednesday November 9th

Distraction

Wendy came over to cry on my shoulder again – poor thing – and interrupted a row between Sam and me about green living. He'd thrown away every light bulb in the house, so I'd no option but to go to Bakewell for more, and nowadays it's impossible to get anything but those dreadful, dim, low-energy bulbs that take half an hour to emit what *seems* like 40 watts, so every room in the house feels like the cupboard under the stairs.

I took Wendy out to lunch at the café at Caudwell Mill. I thought it would be nicer for her than sitting moping in my dingy kitchen. And it did perk her up.

"Are you going to the speed-dating thing again this month?" I asked her, as we drained the last of the coffee from the cafétiere.

"I'm going to stick to window-shopping for a bit," she said. She took a sip of her coffee. "And talking of which, check out that guy over there. Yum."

I turned round to see who she was talking about and froze in my seat. Kit Wyatt was at the till, paying for a tray full of lunch.

"Oh God! Kit Wyatt!"

"You *know* him?" said Wendy. "Why don't I know that you know him?"

"It's the man who came off his bike on the Trail when I was minding Pippa's dogs – I told you about it. That's him. He's a printer. I took his light back last week."

"Why don't I know this? Why didn't you tell me? I could have come with you. Is he married?"

"You've been off the radar for a bit, haven't you? I wish you *had* come with me." And I told her about the row we'd had and how embarrassed I felt about it. "So come on. Let's get out of here, before he sees me."

"What a bummer," she said, getting up. "A gorgeous man crosses our path – a gorgeous local man – and you go and Rottweiler him. Hmmm, I wonder what we can do about it..." And I saw the expression change on her face, so I was pleased I'd taken her out and given her something else to think about.

today's tweet from **@sallystoneymoor**
Is anyone else mourning the demise of the 100 watt bulb?

Thursday November 10th

A rare sighting

I had never spotted Richard's equestrian stalker, though he says she is hanging around on Goose Lane every single day, but this afternoon I was driving home after doing the shopping in Bakewell, and I saw her as I rounded the bend just before our house. A rider on a large horse was peering up our drive. She heard the car and turned and saw me, and she galloped away. I couldn't see her face, but the horse was white.

"If the horse is white," Wendy texted later, "it can only be one person – Glenys Wallis. She's a virtual PA. She moved into that house next door to the Old Rectory in July."

"What's she like?" I texted back.

"Not a clue," texted Wendy, the woman who boasts she has her finger on the pulse of Stoneymoor.

today's tweet from **@sallystoneymoor**
You can take a White Horse anywhere..... remember those 80's whisky ads?

Saturday November 12th

The horror! The horror!

I was making a mug of tea this morning with the intention of sloping off back to bed with my laptop to do some research on designing book covers, when Richard banged on the kitchen window.

I unlocked the back door for him, and he stumbled in and slumped on a chair and groaned. "It's really scary out there."

"Have Baxter's bullocks got loose again?"

"I mean in the world of dating."

He looked pale, he had black marks under his eyes, and the wrinkles on his forehead were like crevasses. He looked even more gnarled than usual. And his hair was wild and weirdly lop-sided. Basically, he looked like Bog Man.

"What's up, chuck?" I said. "You don't look as if you've slept for days."

"Just one night."

Hmm, it's obvious that at our age, even one night without sleep is horribly aging.

"What on earth is the matter?" I said.

"My third date with Melanie. It was last night."

"So?" I sipped my tea. "Do you want a drink?"

He nodded and I filled up the kettle again, and switched it on.

"She invited me round to her house for a meal," he said, "and I bought a nice bottle of Oyster Bay Sauvignon Blanc from the Co-op – £9.99! They don't know what to charge!" He groaned again.

"And?"

"And I arrived at her house and she was looking lovely, with a really low-cut top and a soft silky skirt. And she ushered me in and gave me the most amazing kiss, pressing herself up against me in the most...oh...and she took my jacket and sat me down and went to her kitchen to get some wine glasses and a corkscrew and when she came back, I noticed she had *three* glasses and..."

"Yes?"

"And another woman."

"Oh, so she wasn't ready for what you were ready for! She wanted a chaperone."

"The other woman was dressed in something strapless, and shocking pink satin shorts!"

"So?"

"Oh, oh, I can't bear to think about it..." Another groan.

"What?"

"Do you know what a threesome is?"

"No! Really?" And I laughed so hard that my tea came down my nose.

"It's not funny!

I couldn't stop laughing. I was choking now.

"It's not funny!"

"There's you, worrying about your Y fronts, and there she is, thinking you are a swinging sixty-something."

"And she couldn't understand why I wasn't pleased! Pippa is looking rather more appealing than she was last week."

"Forget it, Richard! This is just one woman. There are plenty of women out there who want a normal monogamous relationship. Don't let it put you off." I put my arm round his shoulders and bent over and kissed his cheek. "Now. What can I do to cheer you up? Would you like a bacon sandwich? And would you like a new Screwfix catalogue? It arrived yesterday, addressed to you."

His eyes brightened. "That will stabilise me. Thanks, Sis."

"I've told you before! Don't call me *Sis*!"

today's tweet from **@sallystoneymoor**
For all those non-veggies out there: have you embraced the BLT or are you a bacon butty person?

Sunday November 13th

Number One Fan

I persuaded Richard to come for a walk along the Trail this afternoon. I wanted to encourage him to have another go at dating. The sun was shining and the autumn colours were out of this world. There hasn't been enough wind and rain yet to dispatch many leaves, and the beech trees are looking particularly lovely – those tall smooth silvery trunks, those arching branches, those stunning leaves. I do like living here.

"Isn't it a beautiful day?" I said.

"Yes," said Richard. "A far cry from the fleshpots of trendy London, or even the debaucheries of Matlock, come to that."

We'd been talking about the BBC radio presenter charged with seducing a male student with cocaine at a party, sedating him with temazepam and sexually assaulting him. The report in the paper had been detailed and graphic.

"I've never seen someone chopping lines of coke on a toilet lid. Have you?" I said. "Do you think they clean it first with Dettol? What a different world we live in."

"The man needs a decent hobby," said Richard. "He could be making cupboards."

He'd just said this when the woman on the white horse – Glenys Wallis – trotted up. And stopped. And dismounted. And I thought *– now's my chance to see what's going on.*

But holding the horse by its bridle, she walked over to me, not Richard.

"At last," she said. Then, "Oh, hello Richard," as an aside, as if Richard was a tiresome interloper "*at last,*" she said, turning back to me, "Sally. Ever since I moved to the village I've been wanting to meet you. I check your blog every day, I've read your book, and I've got all your articles from *The Recorder* in a ring binder, with that photo of you that the paper printed. Would you sign the photo for me? I am your NUMBER ONE FAN."

"I, I…" I spluttered.

"And do you teach creative writing?" she said. "I would love to be able to write like you."

"Actually, I'm still learning. I go to a–" but then I stopped. If I told her about the writing group she would probably want to come. Somehow I don't see her hitting it off with Spiky Pete.

"May I take you to lunch one day soon?"

"What did you say?" said Richard, aghast.

But GW ignored him: she had eyes and ears for me alone. "I was *so* hoping to get to know you properly. I can already see from all your *Recorder* articles that we have heaps in common."

Richard and I stood there flabbergasted and mute, and she took this as assent.

"I'll be in touch," she said, as she stuck her foot in the stirrup and swung her leg over the horse. "By-eee."

"Fancy her slobbering all over you like that!" Richard said, when she was out of earshot. "She hadn't even been properly introduced!"

"She hardly slobbered. She kissed me on the cheek."

"Both cheeks!"

I *was* rather taken aback, I have to admit. I choked a little on her Chanel No 5.

"Good grief! Why would she think I would want to go out to lunch with a perfect stranger?" I clutched his arm. "Richard, I have to move house."

today's tweet from **@sallystoneymoor**
Air-kissing-strangers has reached Derbyshire alert!

Monday November 14th

Behind the door

The Ashbourne printer's parcel arrived. The quote is only slightly less than the 4 colour printer's, he has quoted for a glossy cover, and the novel he sent as an example of his work is horrendous. It has a shiny cover in lurid colours, the typesetting is amateur (though that could be the author's fault) and the paper the text is printed on is a startling white. And it is really, really heavy! I was so surprised, that I checked it on my kitchen scales and it weighed twice as much as *Fast Work*. Apart from it feeling weird, it would really bump up my costs when I post out review copies.

I searched on the letter and the quote for an email address so I could email and check about the availability of different types of paper, and remind him about a matt cover – which I *had* specified! – but there wasn't one, and when I Googled the name of the firm, there wasn't a website. Hopeless. I don't want a printer who's even less computer-savvy than me. At least the huge disappointment will spice up my blog post.

I'll ask at writing group for suggestions. A couple of people have had things printed in the past.

today's tweet from **@sallystoneymoor**
Parcels are always exciting – until you open them and find you don't like what's inside :-(

Tuesday November 15th
Temporarily trounced

"But surely," said Wendy this morning, "it's nice to have someone who says they're your number one fan." I was telling her about the stalker, and she'd come round to show me her new outfit, assembled from a charity shop trawl in Sheffield – forties tea dress in pink and white, over seventies loon pants in emerald green.

"Of course it's wonderful when people say they like my writing. I *love* it. Even nicer these days, when Spiky Pete is continually ripping into me, and when no-one wants to publish my novel, and when I am old and alone."

"Come on, now, let's just enjoy the number one fan thing for a bit. We can talk about the other stuff later if you like. God, this dress wrinkles up all the time when it's over my jeans. How are you supposed to wear them?"

"But Wendy, this woman is a total stranger and she thought I'd be happy to go to lunch with her. That's really weird. Crikey, it makes my teeth chatter just to think about it."

Wendy laughed. "You'd be lapping it up if she was a journo! You've always wanted to be a famous writer. This is just the price of fame. Oops! Bad news!" she said, looking out of the dining room window in the direction of the gate. "GW is marching up your drive."

"For goodness sakes, Wendy, stay and give me moral support," I said as I got up to answer the front door.

GW was in full riding gear – jodhpurs, boots and crop hat.

"Hello, Sally! In full swing are you?" said GW, kissing me on both cheeks again, and lingering. Ugh! She smelled strongly of horse. "In mid-sentence, are you?" she went on. And with this, she barged past me and swept into the dining room where Wendy was sitting at the table, re-arranging her pants under her loons, under her tea dress.

"Oh," said GW, "you have someone with you."

"Yes, I'm in the middle of a meeting," I said. "Glenys, may I introduce Wendy Tennant? Wendy – Glenys Wallis. Wendy is my–" I was going to say *financial adviser*, or even *agent* but Wendy jumped in first.

"Stylist," she said, getting up and shaking GW's hand. "Personal stylist. And we have an awful lot to get through this morning."

"But I thought you'd be writing, and on your own," said GW to me, forlornly.

"The life of a writer isn't just about writing," said Wendy. *How the hell would she know?* "There's publicity, image, marketing – Sally, I really feel we should get on. If you'll excuse us...Glenda...was it?"

GW backed towards the door, perhaps because Wendy – who is petite, but who was wearing five inch heels and a menacing expression – was advancing towards her in an impressively assertive fashion.

"Oh well, perhaps another day," said GW. "I'll call tomorrow."

And she went.

Wendy and I scuttled into the kitchen (out of sight of the drive) and gave each other a high five.

"I think you owe me a huge favour," said Wendy.

today's tweet from **@sallystoneymoor**
Oh, how I would love to have a personal stylist…

Wednesday November 16th

Creepy

If I had a vivid imagination, or if I were paranoid, I'd say that someone who looks like GW is following me around. I had a busy day yesterday. I won't say I wrote yesterday, but I did sit in front of my laptop from 8 till 11, and then I had a list of errands to see to. I went to the Co-op to get stain remover for my jeans, Chatsworth Garden Centre to buy moss killer for the lawn, the vet's to get some flea stuff for Chewy, and Hassop Station to buy a birthday card for Alicia at writing group. Everywhere I went, there was a woman lurking in the background who had pink cheeks and a blonde pony tail and an expression that combined furtiveness with – well – drooling. But how could it have been the same woman in every place? And why would it be GW?

today's tweet from **@sallystoneymoor**
That's it. Last night's frost brought down the ash leaves. The oaks are clinging on.

Thursday November 17th

Inconvenient evidence

I asked around for printer recommendations at writing group, and Alicia and Duncan suggested Wyatt Printing! They both said that Kit Wyatt is very helpful, extremely professional, and not expensive. Duncan had a collection of poems printed a couple of years ago, which I had forgotten all about, and Alicia has written about her father's career as a diplomat and has approached Kit W and is considering his quote. She said it was cheaper than any other printers and she's seen some of his work and it looked very sleek and "just like books in Waterstones."

Hmph. Can I bring myself to ask him for a quote?

Could I work with him if I accepted his quote?

Would he even give me a quote, or would he just throw me out?

today's tweet from **@sallystoneymoor**
How does humble pie taste?

Friday November 18th

Too close for comfort

"Here I am, an ever-so-eager-beaver!" oozed GW on my doorstep this morning. "I just wanted to say that if you can't spare the time out for lunch, then perhaps we could just do coffee."

I was feeling bullish this morning. I actually slept last night and I'd woken up feeling really, really in charge, as in, *Mess with me at your peril*. So when GW turned up, my instinctive (if rude) reaction was to push the door shut immediately. Silly bint! I did push it to, but it jammed on the toe of her riding boot. Then my gentle nature unfortunately took over, and I opened the door wide and said, "Come in, Glenys. Come into the sitting room." Why do I let people use me like this? And why am I unable to be calm and cool and assertive and firm and polite, all at the same time, and say "NO"?

She followed me in and looked around the room and said "Oh, I so like the bohemian artsy look you've created in here." Did she mean the piles of books on the floor and the wine glass and empty crisp packet left on the coffee table from last night?

"I think we need to have a talk, Glenys."

"That doesn't sound very promising."

I offered her the armchair. I sat on the sofa. But she sat on the sofa next to me, so close that her jodhpured thighs touched mine. Did the woman like more than my writing??? Crikey, I hadn't even thought of *that*. I leapt up and went to the chair.

"How would you feel if someone you had never met introduced themselves and wanted to take you out to coffee?" I said.

She clapped her hand to her chest. "I'd be so flattered."

"Well, it's a kind suggestion, but I can't accept."

"But I want to introduce you to my friends!"

"I'm sorry, Glenys, this sounds mean, but I really have to get on with my writing." I got up from the chair and moved towards the door and she followed. I walked to the front door but she didn't follow.

"But Sally, as I'm here now, and I have already disturbed the creative flow, perhaps we could pop along to Hassop for a coffee? Or to my house? That would be quicker."

"It's a lovely suggestion, Glenys, but writing is a lot more time consuming than most people imagine – it doesn't leave much time for social engagements with individual fans. I try to meet my fans at events, like launches and readings. Otherwise, there wouldn't be any more books."

We were having a stand-off in the hall, when Richard knocked on the front door and came in. He realized immediately what was happening. *Stylish.*

"I understand you're a virtual PA," he said to GW. "You seem to have a lot of time away from the office." *Subtle.* What had got into him?

"As soon as I managed to track Sally down I – I mean – oh – is that your cat, Sally? Isn't she adorable?" and she bent down to stroke Chewy, who had just emerged from the kitchen. Chewy hissed and made a dash for the stairs.

"He's a tom," I said. A tom with unerring good taste.

"I suppose I'd better be going," she said, as she stood upright again, "I need to keep on top of things – check my emails, scan my faxes."

As soon as she'd gone I grabbed Richard's arm. "Thank goodness you came just then. Make me a cuppa. Tell me I'll manage to shake her off somehow. I think she fancies me!"

"Really?"

"All those pieces and photos in *The Recorder* – maybe I'm a gay icon."

Richard did not laugh. He was very sweet and said he'd give it some thought, and went in the kitchen and put the kettle on.

"I don't get it," he said. "Why can't you just tell her to get lost?"

"Because I have to be nice to my readers. I have a reputation – of sorts – to live up to."

"Really?"

"Well, maybe not. But if I am nasty to her, she could write all kinds of stuff about me on the net. I'm in a really vulnerable position."

"In that case, I think you should give her what she wants," he said, as we were drinking our tea. "Have a coffee with her and then tell her that's it."

"What? Won't that just encourage her?"

today's tweet from **@sallystoneymoor**
I'm a sucker for coffee-to-go.

Saturday November 19th

Different strokes for different folks

I woke up to find Sam packing a rucksack.

"Where are you going?"

"Occupy Sheffield."

"Uh?"

"Oh come on, Ma, catch up ! Occupy Wall Street? Occupy London? Occupy Sheffield? That's where I was camping in London: in front of St Paul's Cathedral."

"Oh, Sam."

"But *you're* one of the 99%!" he said.

"I know, I know. And I agree with their sentiments – the protest – but what are they actually asking for? And what are they actually achieving?"

"Do you know how many years it took to abolish slavery?"

At least I'll get a break from his music. All that passive listening to *Animal Collective,* his current favourite CD, makes me want to slit my wrists.

It was speed-dating night tonight at the Village Hall, but neither Wendy nor Richard had the heart for it, so I invited them round here for the evening. We had a Chinese take-away from Bakewell, and I suggested we watch Series 1 of *As Times Go By* on the DVD player – I *do* like Judi Dench. But Wendy said it was yawnsville and for some reason Richard loathes Judi Dench. We settled on *Strictly Come Dancing* followed by *Tootsie*. Wendy likes to criticise the weird dresses Dustin Hoffman wears and Richard is intrigued by the intricacies of his disguise as a woman. He was particularly interested in the pants he wears with inserts to round out his bum – oh blimey, I hope Richard hasn't got a secret yearning to be a transvestite. That's all we need.

Personally, I like the screenplay, specifically the plotting. It's especially masterful on the lead-up to the scene where Dustin H pulls off his wig and tells everyone he's a man. Gosh – don't I sound like a proper writer?

today's tweet from **@sallystoneymoor**
A film with a great screenplay is enjoyable on so many levels

Monday November 21st

Betrayed

I went to the village shop yesterday afternoon to pay the paper bill while it was quiet, before the school children came in to spend their pocket money. Billy Bathgate handed me my customary tube of Smarties (that I eat while watching *Neighbours*) and then grabbed my wrist. "Och, it's a relief to get you alone, Mrs Howe. Thank the Lord I have an empty shop."

Hell's bells, this is the man who once pinched my bum. Surely he's not going to start that caper again, is he? I pulled my hand away and swerved out of his reach and said, "Billy Bathgate! Really!" and made to go. Before I could reach for the door handle he had nipped round the counter and got between me and the door.

"No, no. You misunderstood me. I'm glad we're alone because I have something personal to say."

This was just as threatening as the hand-grabbing. Billy Bathgate has a reputation for personal, attentive service, but more attentive than you are really looking for. "Please let me out," I said. "I'm up to my eyes in errands. I'm expecting Nina and the children to arrive this afternoon." A total lie.

"But I have a confession. I fear, oh dear Mrs Howe, I fear I may have left you open to exploitation. Danger, even."

"What on earth are you talking about?"

"Has a Ms Wallis been to call on you?"

"Rather too often. Why?"

"A few weeks ago she came in here and asked if I knew where you lived. She said she admired your writing and wanted to tell you so in person. I was so proud at your success – at the thought of a famous writer being one of my customers – that without thinking I told her where your house was."

"So it's all your fault!"

"Och, I am sorry. I thought she was harmless. But since then she has been in the shop a lot, and every time she comes in she somehow steers the conversation round to you. I was beginning to feel uneasy, and then yesterday she came in and said: *I moved to the Peak District because of all the lovely photos on Sally's blog, and I especially chose Stoneymoor so I could get to know her in person.* And that's when the alarm bells started ringing in my head, and I knew I had to warn you. Tell me I didn't do wrong. Tell me you forgive me. Och, and please accept today's packet of Smarties on the house, as a goodwill gesture."

"Hmm," I said, my heart in my blue suede lace-ups. What he said has changed GW from annoying pest into sinister stalker. What am I going to do?

today's tweet from **@sallystoneymoor**
Blogging is a high risk activity – always wear a safety vest.

Tuesday November 22nd

Yesterday

I sat down to write this morning, and had only just opened up Chapter 8 when there was a knock on the front door. Stupidly, I went to answer it.

GW.

"I wondered if you were free for a coffee now."

I stood there holding the door, chewing my lip, thinking that maybe I should try what Richard had suggested.

"Glenys. I'm sorry, I know this sounds harsh, but I don't have the time for any new friends. My schedule is so tight. I am publishing one novel and writing another. I am snowed under with work. But I'm very flattered that you like my writing, and touched that you wanted to tell me..." (oh the guff I can come out with when I want to – but then I am a writer) "so how about we have a coffee and a chat this morning, your choice of café, my treat, and that will be that. And when the time comes, I will send you an invitation to my next book launch. What do you think?" *Book launch? Book launch?* I haven't even got a blooming printer sorted yet.

"Thank you, Sally," she said meekly. "May I come in to wait, while you get ready?"

So we went to Hassop and I went through the motions, and we parted – forever, I hope.

Finally, I'd been in a sticky and embarrassing situation and managed to keep my cool and deal with it. Go, me! No temper. No histrionics. Cool, calm and collected. (Yes, Spiky Pete. I know it's a cliché.)

today's tweet from **@sallystoneymoor**
I love the cappuccino bars at Hassop Station Cafe

Wednesday November 23rd

Chancing it

I was buoyed up with my success in dealing with GW, and decided that maybe I had the self-control and confidence to approach Kit Wyatt for a quote. It's not really what I wanted to do. Quite apart from anything else, he doesn't deserve my business, but time is ticking away and I need to get a printer chosen and instructed pronto.

Also, if I emailed the man, he might not even know who I was. He might not remember my name from before. There is no need to talk to him at this stage. Every time I interact with a printer I understand the lingo better, and I know now what are the deal-breakers in my specification. I mean, I hadn't even considered that paper choice was an issue until I saw that dreadful self-published novel from Ashbourne.

I emailed Wyatt Printing this morning and got a reply by teatime. Pretty efficient. He also said he had put some paper samples in the post and told me the titles of three books (local non-fiction titles) he's printed that Hassop Bookshop stock, so I could go and check them out.

Everything about the email and the quote was impressive. But the unit price was £3.25. Not cheap!

Is this what I am going to have to pay to get my books printed? And by Mr Kit bloody Wyatt, to boot?

today's tweet from **@sallystoneymoor**
Have you ever been in a situation where you didn't want to be recognised?

Thursday November 24th

D Day

I watched my *Out of Africa* DVD last night. It is so inspiring – as well as romantic and sad. Karen Blixen doggedly tries and tries with her business in the face of awful disasters, and at one point she even gets down on her knees and begs for something she wants.

I had no intention of getting down on my knees to Mr Kit Wyatt, but I did feel strong enough and determined enough to go to see him and ask if he would lower his quote.

Look at me! The new independent single woman! Managing her own life! Managing her own business!

I rang this morning and made an appointment, and I saw him this afternoon.

The receptionist directed me down the corridor, and as I approached the door to the office, I heard Kit Thingy arguing on the phone again, and...not that I listened or anything, but it sounded as if it was another bout with the bank.

I knocked, and he called, "Come in," but he was still talking as I rounded the door, with his back to me, and I felt rather awkward. The cat was there again in the fleecy bed, so I walked over to stroke it. I massaged the top of its head with one finger, and it started to drool. Not a pleasant habit. Chewy never drools.

Kit Wyatt finished his phone conversation and said to my back, "I don't like to interrupt your little love-fest with Witty, but would you like to sit down? Have you come to talk about the quote?"

Full marks for politeness. Was it his evil twin I'd tangled with on previous occasions?

I turned round to face him and he grimaced, his mouth tight, his eyebrows up, and said, "You, again!"

"Is that a problem?"

"Well, as long as you leave your dogs at home, I guess we can do business."

"For the last time, they're not my dogs!"

"Well...hmm...about this quote. Would you like to sit down?"

"Thanks."

I sat down.

"So," he said.

I took a deep breath. "Your quote was good – better than the other ones I've had. You seem to get what I want, to understand all the things that I think are important, plus – you're highly recommended," his face brightened, "but the price you've given me is higher than my budget allows." Gosh, that sounded professional.

"And?"

My heart started pounding now. Was he about to launch into another verbal onslaught?

"And," I said, pausing to summon up my courage, "and I've come to ask if you'll look at the figures again and reconsider."

"Hmm," he said. "Do you mind if I just look it up on the system?"

He swivelled his chair round to face his computer, and pressed a few keys. "Here we are. Sally Howe. You've been published already...I looked you up on the net. Why are you doing it yourself this time? Is it something to do with the recession? Are you one of those mid-list authors callously disposed of by the...hmm." He turned round to face me. "Is this book as good as your last?"

Had he read *Fast Work* and thought it good?! Things were turning out better than I'd hoped.

"Oh – you read it," I said.

"No, no. I don't have time to read novels. I skimmed your reviews. I was wondering why you couldn't get a publisher for this one – I mean – is it any good?"

I bridled. Was it any of his business? I was only asking him to print the thing. Then I reminded myself that I was asking him a favour.

I made myself relax: I pushed my shoulders down and visualised my happy place (signing books in Waterstones in Piccadilly, with the queue stretching through the shop, out of the door, and way along the pavement....), and I said "My agent says it's better than my last – which was published in the conventional way. But she can't find a publisher. She says it's the horrible economic climate. So it's self-publish, or stick it in the drawer."

He leaned back in his chair. "I know how it is. It's the thing you care most about, the thing you've poured all your energy and passion into, and the market and the wretched bankers are putting the mockers on it."

I nodded. It sounded as if the recession was doing him over too.

"Let's do a deal," he said.

I smiled.

And he smiled.

And I understood why Wendy thought he was gorgeous.

today's tweet from **@sallystoneymoor**
At last I've found a printer who measures up!

DECEMBER

Thursday December 1st
Hospitality by stealth

It was a very Decemberish day: cold, grey, bleak, and with the sky full of snow.

Richard sat in my kitchen all afternoon, wanting sympathy about his non-existent love-life. He looked washed out, and I didn't have the heart to boot him out, just because I had lots of publishing stuff to do. I invited him to stay for tea, but I needn't have bothered because he barely picked at his shepherd's pie. Then when we went to sit by the fire, he slumped against the sofa cushions, moaned, and closed his eyes. I put *Downton Abbey* on the iPlayer and he moaned every five minutes, all the way through. I exaggerate not.

"I feel awful. I feel really awful."

"What are your symptoms, chuck?"

"My throat hurts, my head hurts, everything hurts."

"Poor thing. It sounds like flu," I said. "You ought to be in bed. Shall I drive you home?" It's only a five minute walk down the village to his little rented house but he didn't look robust enough even to put his coat on unaided.

"Can I just stay here for a bit?"

So yes, he ended up going to bed in the spare room. He looks appalling. He is bright red with fever. I just went in to see him, and he was delirious.

"Do puffins have flags?" he was saying to himself. "Sometimes puffins have flags, sometimes they don't."

One of the advantages of not having a husband is surely not having to put up with a man when he's ill, and here I am with just such a man. At least Richard stays in bed. Gus used to get dressed and sit around downstairs and moan and groan all day, asking me if he'd ever feel better, while sweeping away all suggestions as to how to deal with his symptoms. I don't mind looking after people when they're ill as long as they keep their moans to themselves, appreciate my offerings of care and nourishment, and do as they're told.

today's tweet from **@sallystoneymoor**
People with flu should know their place – in bed and out of the way

Friday December 2nd

Bad news

I was calculating on Richard being here for a week, but it's *so* much worse than that because today when I collected his post for him, there was a letter from his landlord. He is coming back early from his trip to Australia, and wants the house, and Richard has to move out by the end of the month. This is the problem with casual tenancies.

"Can I come back and live with you?" he said pathetically, between coughs and sniffs. "We get along pretty well, don't we?"

"Let's just concentrate on getting you well again. I'm sure there'll be somewhere else we can find for you."

But it's looking grim. I have scoured the *Peak Advertiser*, and I've rung all the estate agents, and the prospects are dire. As far as the village goes, there's that large house near the pre-school, that's being rented out over the winter to stag parties and such-like, but it's massive, and mega-seedy. And there's also a chi-chi one-bedroom *Country Living*-esque cottage with a Belfast sink, stone flagged floors, and a humungous TV with surround sound Blu-Ray, but it will be three times Richard's budget. I love him. But I don't want him back. I don't. I don't.

today's tweet from **@sallystoneymoor**
Why do women complain about an empty nest? It is one of life's unregarded joys.

Monday December 5th

Narrative drive

I cracked on really well with my list of what's to do on the self-publishing front and in doing so, cobbled together another blog post – yay!

Then I read through it and actually thought about it and it scared the pants off me:

My to-do list

There is so much to think about and I'm not talking about Christmas. My (lovely) regular readers will know I mean self-publishing.

- Design:
    - Book design – font, layout of text.
    - Cover image and layout; choice of font.
- Content:
    - Getting the book ready: proof reading, copy-editing, typesetting.
    - Who can I get to help with this?
- Review copies:
    - Make a list people to whom I am going to send copies for review, in the hope of getting endorsements to put on the back cover.
- Ebook:
    - Organise formatting and production and selling. Find out about Amazon – how do I get in touch with a real person at Amazon and sort it out?
- Storage and distribution:
    - Thank goodness for my helpful printer. As well as printing the book, he is going to store the books, and package and send them to wholesalers as and when necessary.
    - I must contact local shops and enquire about sales direct from me.
- Official legal stuff:
    - Apply for an ISBN.
    - Get permission to quote from the poem quoted in the book, and from Ally McBeal, also quoted.

- Send a copy of the published book to the British Library.
- Selling:
  - Selling on the net?
  - Selling through wholesalers – find out how this works and arrange it.
  - How do I get Amazon to sell my paperback?
- Launch:
  - Where, when, who to invite; budget; media coverage.
- Marketing:
  - Media – newspapers, local and national radio, my blog, Twitter
  - Events, e.g. signings at bookshops, and talks at local festivals
- Barcode for the back cover ???? Aarghh
- V.A.T.
  - There is no VAT on books but there is on ebooks. How does this work? Do I have to collect it? Aarghh again.

Crikey me!

Richard came downstairs at teatime in his dressing gown just as *Neighbours* was beginning, so he watched it with me.

"I just don't get why you like it. Atchoo! Atchoo!"

"Look," I said. "I like to watch a soap, and *East Enders* is too miserable. A soap helps me unwind, and I like the continuing story. I could watch a comedy series on DVD every teatime, but I need something with narrative drive. Don't you?"

"The narrative drive of life is sufficiently taxing for me. Atchoo!"

today's tweet from **@sallystoneymoor**
Beechams Powders in tablet form? Wouldn't work for me.

Tuesday December 6th

Fretting

That list that I put on the blog is long and worrying. There is so much that's new that I have to find out about. All the stuff goes round and round in my head and I can't calm down enough to work out where to start. But I do know I need to get the product – the actual book – designed and ready to print. That much is clear.

Giovanna has offered to copy-edit and proof-read the manuscript, but I need another pair of picky eyes. Richard was thanking me effusively for being so nice to him while he's been ill, and he asked me what he could do to repay me. (I suspect he was also trying to soften me up so I'll let him move back here at New Year.) The upshot is that he's going to proof-read the book – the perfect occupation for someone who is convalescing, n'est-ce pas?

Wendy called late morning, and tried to persuade me to go Christmas shopping with her. When I said no, I was far too busy with book stuff, she made herself a coffee and ignored what I'd said about being busy and proceeded to ask my opinion on shorts. *Shorts?*

"Shorts are fine in the right place," I said. "Knee length shorts are really practical for hiking. And popular. Not for me, but you'd be OK. And *The Recorder* fashion woman – Janina Lemon, who's been demoted from having her own column, because of the cuts, I'm guessing – she was talking about shorts with city suits. But why are you asking now? Are you going somewhere hot for Christmas?"

"Get up to speed, Sal. I'm talking about short denim shorts over black tights."

"Hot-pants? For you?"

"Why not? Don't you think that by the time teenage stuff is hitting the charity shops, it's worked its way up the fashion food chain and it's fine for us to wear it?"

I pulled a face. "Oooh, Wendy. I don't think denim hot pants would ever be OK for the post-menopausal."

"You're just as bad as all those putrid fashion editors, who run their fashion pages showing fashions for different ages! The twenties get the nice stuff, and the suggestions get increasingly watered down and boring, so that the over-fifties idea is always slacks and a jacket, and the only concession to fashion is a trashy string of beads. These flippin' adolescent fashion editors have no idea that we can do see-through blouses with fabulous bras – you know, underwear that's designed to be seen – or that we can carry off a mini skirt and a strapless T."

"I think we do have to be careful," I said. "I mean, I would love to dress like a rock chick and have my hair in a bleached urchin cut, but..."

"Well, no-one's going to cramp my style! I'm going to re-cycle my latest strapless T, which OK, is a look that's a *little bit* tricky to pull off, into an over-jeggings skirt. What do you think, Richard?" she asked, as said brother appeared in the doorway looking droopy.

"Don't ask me," he said, shivering and retying the belt of his dressing-gown. "I'm still having an underwear crisis."

"Didn't you get some Calvin Kleins, like I suggested?" I said.

"I don't want to talk about it."

today's tweet from **@sallystoneymoor**
If underwear is on show this season, here in Stoneymoor we're all in big trouble...

Wednesday December 7th

Christmas shopping

I went to Sheffield with Wendy, on the grounds that self-publishing or no self-publishing, there are still Christmas presents to be bought for all the family.

I did really well. I managed to get something for everyone (the grandchildren are the easiest and the most fun, of course) except presents for Sam and Richard. Men are impossible. On the way out of town, Wendy and I dropped in at Oxfam in Broomhill. She wanted to look at the clothes, and I thought I'd get a load of little things for Sam, as he'd appreciate the fact that they all came from Oxfam, even if he disdained the items themselves.

Wendy took forever trying on shorts, so I looked at the books for cover ideas. *English Correspondence* by Janet Davey had a photo cover that was attractive but intelligent-looking, the blurb was promising, and it had plaudits on the back like this: "A beguiling and beautiful novel whose quietly intelligent surface conceals dramatic depths"– Doris Lessing. "Delicate, subtle, entirely lacking in brashness...I purred over its sheer intelligence, its quiet wit" – Margaret Forster.

I bought it, and I've been reading it this evening. I have reached page 50 and I have not been able to get below its quietly intelligent surface. Frankly, I think it's dull. I am obviously ineluctably, intellectually shallow – a cultural low-life. I'd have been better off buying shorts, like Wendy.

today's tweet from **@sallystoneymoor**
However hard I try, the ethical presents I buy never sparkle quite like the decadent ones

Thursday December 8th

Kit Wyatt wants a date

I was sitting at my desk pulling at my hair, nervously sipping hot strong Yorkshire tea laced with sugar and scanning my publishing to-do list, and thinking *OH HELP*, when Kit Wyatt phoned.

"We didn't talk about a date," he said in a bossy, officious tone.

What?

"A date?" I said, uncertainly.

"Your publication day," he said impatiently, and he continued at the speed of a horse-racing commentary, "and working back from that, when you want the books in your hot little hands, and working back from that, when you hope to have your pre-release copies to send out for review. What are your *dates*, Ms Howe?"

"Oh…um… I want to publish at the end of May, but I haven't got round to working the rest of it out in detail."

I'm finding the whole thing mega-daunting and wondering if I've bitten off more than I can chew (cliché alert) but I wasn't going to admit that to *him*. His manner was so off-putting, and that was quite separate from my memories of the imbroglio on the Trail.

"Would you mind terribly calling me *Sally*?" I said. "The only person who calls me Ms Howe is the dentist, and I am terrified of the dentist, and it's a bit, you know…"

"Gordon Bennet! *Sally*, then." He said my name in a voice like thick hot chocolate.

"I'm sorry not to be more specific about the dates. I'm still trying to work out every detail in the plan and how exactly it all fits together – what has to be done when, and…"

"Yep. It's a big undertaking. Most people these days just go for the ebook option, which is a piece of cake. There's so much more to consider and plan for when you're dealing with hard copies. When d'you think you'll have yourself sorted out?" He paused. "*Sally*."

Was he being a prick, saying *Sally* like that? I asked him a perfectly reasonable favour – a tiny thing – and he was making a whole big deal out of it. Honestly!

"Um…" I said, while I was thinking what to say next.

"Look," he said. "Do you need some help? I've got a window right now. It might not be the case after Christmas."

I hesitated. I could ask him about one specific thing without looking like a total twit, couldn't I? "Well, with the cover, I think I know what I want, but I need some technical help."

So it's arranged. I am going to see him tomorrow. He's a good printer, I know he is. Other people have told me so since I took him on, but why does he have to be so *off*, so up himself, so utterly obnoxious?

today's tweet from **@sallystoneymoor**
Do you have a telephone voice?

Friday December 9th

Fonts in common

Kit Wyatt was helpful today. Though I would not go as far as to say that he was normal and nice.

His receptionist, a lovely young man (*listen to me! "young man" – I sound about 103*) who is about Sam's age, showed me down to KW's office, as if I hadn't been there before, and asked me what I'd like to drink – tea or coffee – and I could swear that Kit Wyatt breathed down his nose in something approaching a snort, as if the receptionist had over-stepped the hospitality mark.

I took off my coat and sat down, and KW said, "Right, Sally," and I saw the tiniest hint of a smile, but then it disappeared, and he turned back into the man I don't like.

I told him about my cover ideas – a photo of a couple (Sophie and Greg) on an old stone bridge, with a background of hills. I explained that I wanted it to look modern and clean and with my name in Helvetica Neue UltraLight.

"No Comic Sans for you!" he said.

"Am I being too picky?"

"On the contrary! It's refreshing to have a customer who knows what they're talking about. And with impeccable taste, too. That's one of my favourite fonts."

"Could you point me in the direction of a graphic design person who's not going to be horrendously pricey?"

"I've got one in my pocket. My son Gray – who's covering on reception – is a whizz with graphics and layout. He's got a really good eye for visuals. He gets it from his mother. I'll ask him to come down."

Gray was pleasant, and listened well, and although he obviously wasn't smitten with my cover idea, he said he'd play around with it and see what he could do, and did I have any photographs I could email him? Or should he use stock photos and play with those?

As soon as he'd gone, Kit Wyatt said, "Now let's get these dates agreed, can we? Proofs, pre-release copies, and main batch."

And once he'd explained his turnaround times, we agreed them speedily.

Immediately he'd noted the dates in his planning diary, he stood up and said, "OK, good," and stuck out his hand across the desk, and it was all too easy to read the non-verbal cues: he had done what he'd agreed to do and now it was time for me to go, so he could turn his attention to far more important things.

If he'd been more approachable I would have asked him about the other stuff that's worrying me. Self-publishing would be so much more agreeable an experience if I'd found a printer who knew what he was doing AND who was even the teensiest bit warm and fluffy. Or is a warm and fluffy printer an oxymoron?

Oxymoron – now that's a good word. I've never heard Spiky Pete use *oxymoron*.

today's tweet from **@sallystoneymoor**
What's your favourite word?

Saturday December 10th
Intruders

I was in the kitchen at about half past four, stirring a panful of home-made celery and stilton soup and looking in the freezer to see if I had any garlic bread and cursing because I didn't, when I heard a commotion in the garden.

I pressed my face against the windowpane and peered out into the murky dusk, and saw people climbing over the stone wall that separates my garden from the field. They were staggering and stumbling, and knocking stones off the wall, and then there was the sound of shattering glass! One of them must have stepped on my cold frame and smashed it! And I saw a trail of something pale going across my central flower bed, down the path and across the near lawn, and round to the side path and the rose arch.

I pulled on my coat and wellies and rushed out and followed as they went round the side of the house. By the time I reached the front, most of them were tottering down my drive towards the gate, but two young men in fancy dress were stuck in my rose arch, caught up in my Paul's Himalayan musk, and yelping. That rose has got seriously out of hand this year.

One of them, dressed up in a yellow ankle-length dress, was gasping and saying "Ouch" and "Ow" and "Bugger" and trying to pull himself free of the thorny branches.

"What the hell are you doing?" I yelled. "Look – you've knocked down my wall and it sounds as if you've smashed my cold frame! You've trampled my plants! And what's all this straw about? What's going on?"

"I'm really sorry. I don't know why that idiot laid the trail over someone's garden – *your* garden – he's obviously – ow! – plastered. I'm sorry."

"Hmph!"

"We're sorry about the damage. We'll pay for it. We'll clear it up. We'll sort it out." He was trying to pull himself free of the rampant rose but without success.

"And now you're wrecking my rose!"

"We're *really* sorry. We'll pick up the straw once we get free of this."

"But what's it all *for*?"

"A straw trail. We're part of a stag party – staying in a house in the village. They stole our clothes – Jason, who's the groom, doesn't usually wear tights, do you Jase? He's supposed to be Prince Charming."

"I'm fed up with the whole blo—sorry – the whole thing," said Prince Charming. "And I feel awful about your garden."

"Who are you supposed to be?" I said to the boy who'd been apologising.

"The best man."

I pointed to his dress. "And?" I said.

He hung his head. "Oh, God. Cinderella."

I burst out laughing. I was fuming, but I couldn't help it. "I'll go and get my secateurs and my gardening gloves and cut you free. Honestly!"

Cinderella (who said his name was Brick) held my torch while I snipped. They were very sweet boys: they took full blame. I told them to come to the front of the garage, under the security light, so I could pull out the stray thorny fronds that were stuck on their clothes at the back, and I was attending to that when a man called from the road, "Brick? Is that you?"

"Oh no," said Brick. "It's Dad. Now we're for it."

The man trudged up the drive, and when he got under the light I saw it was the printer, Kit Wyatt! An ultra-glum Kit Wyatt. When he recognised me, his face fell even further.

"Is this your house?" he said in horrified tones. "Oh, hell! Look at the mess! What have they done?" Then he said to Brick: "Why the hell has that bozo laid the trail over someone's private garden?" Then to me: "This is dreadful. Have they done much damage? We'll clear it up. I'm so sorry."

"The lads have apologised," I said. "They've offered to clear it up. It's probably not their fault – I would say it's the idiot who laid the trail. And of course, their following it when it's getting dark."

Kit Wyatt said to Brick: "You two had better get off, and rein in the others. Go on – scoot!" They rushed off and he said, "I'm mortified! It's good of you to be so understanding."

"And why are you…?"

"I was walking up the lane checking for stragglers – trying to avert any trouble – trouble such as this!" He waved his arm, indicating the trail of straw. "Oh my God!"

"That's the least of it," I said, very calmly and pleasantly – maybe because he was obviously so appalled. "Let me show you."

We went to look at the back garden in the fading light, and saw the broken-down wall and the smashed glass, and a clematis trellis that had been knocked askew, and he said, "What an awful mess! It's terrible! Thank you *so* much for freeing…for helping the boys. It's amazing you can be so chilled about it." He obviously hadn't heard my initial rant. "My wife would have been horrified at the behaviour of her son."

Her son? *Would* have been? Is she dead? "Do you think you could spare a bin liner," he went on, "and I'll clear up the straw now, this minute. And tomorrow, when it's light, I'll come back and repair the damage."

So that's what happened. When he was done, he came to the back door, straw-filled bin-bag in hand, and apologised again.

"Would you like to come in for a hot drink? Sit by the fire and thaw out? You must be frozen."

"I'm very tempted, it would be respite from this horrific weekend, and it's very kind of you, but we've disturbed your evening enough as it is. I'll be off."

today's tweet from **@sallystoneymoor**
My holly has loads of berries on it this year. Does that mean it's going to be a bitter winter?

Sunday December 11th

Follow-through

KW was as good as his word.

He came back this morning just as I was turning on the radio to listen to the *Archers Omnibus*. Men have impeccable timing. He was wearing jeans with a rip below one knee, a thick fisherman's sweater in olive green, and a soft woollen scarf in a subtle plaid. He looks as good in civvies as he does at work. He could certainly give Iain (male model manqué) a run for his money.

He righted and stabilised the trellis, swept up all the broken glass, and then set to, mending the wall.

I took him out a mug of tea and some shortbread mid-morning, and admired his handiwork (men so like to have their handiwork admired) and he said he knew all about stone walling because of the extensive dry stone wall boundary at his house in Froggatt, which he has to keep patching because he never has the time to set aside to sort it out definitively.

I was heating up some soup for lunch, when he knocked on the door to say he'd finished.

"I've taken the measurements for replacement glass," he said. "I'll ring Matlock Glass first thing tomorrow and get that sorted. Mmm, that smells good."

"Come in, come in out of the cold."

"I wasn't hinting!"

"Oh don't be daft! Come in." I persuaded him to come in and have some soup and some fresh walnut bread that Richard had made for me, as yet another persuasive ploy in the pursuit of moving back in.

We sat in the kitchen because KW insisted I shouldn't go to any trouble, and I persuaded him to stop apologising for the mess: "You are sorting it out – that's all that's necessary. *Really*."

We chatted tentatively, in a careful, measured, verbal dance. We covered how long we'd lived in our houses, the therapeutic nature of gardening, and the current (stupid) fashion for over-the-top weddings with all the associated extravagant spin-offs. Then it got more personal, and I found out that his wife died of viral pneumonia ten years ago leaving him with four teenagers, poor man; and he found out that I have three children and am single and defending an empty nest.

"So how are your self-publishing plans coming on? And everything that needs to be done that is *on* the plan."

"So, so," I said, noncommittally. I didn't want him to snap back into officious printer-mode. I like him better outside of his work persona: he is so much more sympathetic and there's a hint of vulnerability about him.

"Is there anything at all I can do to help?" he said. "This is a quiet time – this run up to Christmas. Have you considered applying critical path planning to your project? I'm sure you'd find it helpful, Sally." When he said my name, he didn't say it in that snide tone he used on the phone last week. He said *Sally* softly in that amazing hot chocolate voice of his, and I melted.

I said: "The trouble is, I don't know where to start."

"Let me help. Come to the office this week! I owe you!"

I smiled. "Help would be good. Thank you."

I am going to see him next Wednesday so he can help me with my planning: an interesting development. What do you know? The erstwhile obnoxious, irascible Kit Wyatt has a helpful streak, as well as being pretty yummy.

today's tweet from **@sallystoneymoor**
It's always interesting to see someone in a completely new light, n'est-ce pas?

Monday December 12th

Your presence is requested…

I got a call from *SWISH Radio* (*SWISH* stands for South-West in Sheffield) who are a bit short on guest interviewees tomorrow, they said because of Christmas. They have a local author going in, but they want me to go as well, to beef up the programme a bit. It's not really the right time to be talking about my book, but I want to be as amenable as possible and keep in with them, and then in May I can ring them up and ask to go on the prog again.

It seems like a life-time ago that I first went on local radio to talk about Gus's crazy idea of the ON/OFF Christmas and Christmas in the Shed, which the local radio stations and the BBC4 *Today* programme got wind of from my article in *Hearth and Home*. Everyone wanted an interview. It was wild.

After that died down, I went back on *SWISH* for a phone-in on creative writing, and I am still on their books all these years later, and every now and then they invite me in for a chat show or a phone-in, like now.

today's tweet from **@sallystoneymoor**
Catch me on SWISH Radio tomorrow morning, 11 a.m.
www.swish.co.uk

Tuesday December 13th

Committed

I turned up half an hour early at *SWISH,* as requested, and told the woman at the reception desk my name, and which programme I was going to be on.

"Bowels, OK?" she said.

"Pardon?"

"You're the GP doing the phone-in on bowels, right?"

"No, I'm a writer. Johnny Hazlewood is interviewing me about my new book."

"Didn't you know? Johnny is in the Northern General, seriously ill. Beattie Castleby is filling in for him." She searched for my name on her visitors list, and as she ticked me off, she said under her breath, "That woman is a waste of space."

She directed me to the waiting area upstairs, outside the studio, and there I sat on an IKEA chair, across from another woman who looked vaguely familiar, but no matter how hard I tried, I couldn't place her. I smiled, and she smiled back. Then Johnny Hazlewood's researcher came out and ushered us into the ops room.

The producer was sitting in the ops room wearing a head-set. She looked up from her console and waved to us from behind her desk, and then went back to fiddling with the controls in front of her computer screens, and the other guest and I sat silently in the corner on two plastic chairs, waiting for a break in the proceedings. After a few minutes, the news bulletin came on, and the researcher ushered us into the studio and sat us down and Beattie Castleby introduced herself. She had a really plummy accent.

"And whom do I have the pleasure of interviewing today?" she said.

Didn't she bloody know?

"I'm Sally Howe," I said. "I'm a local author and my next book comes out next May." There was no way I was going to say it was self-published. People who aren't writers just don't understand how the world of publishing works.

"And I'm Jean Shardlow," said the other woman. "My first book comes out next week."

Beattie C fussed with the papers on her desk. "Now let me see what the researcher's prepared for me. Oh dear, oh dear, the news has finished, they're on the weather now, we'll be back on air very – oh dear, oh dear – I've just snagged my nail." She stopped rifling through her papers, reached down to the floor for her handbag and plonked it on her desk on top of her papers. She peered inside it, took out an emery board and started to file her nail.

"So that's the outlook for the rest of the day – better bring your washing in," said a voice on the speakers. "Now back to Beattie."

There was silence, just the sound of Beattie filing her nail. Then there was banging on the glass screen between us and the ops room. It was the researcher. Beattie Castleby looked up and said "Damnation." She threw down her emery board, and switched on her mike and said, "And now, I have two local authors in the studio. They are-"

She pointed to me, and I said "Sally Howe," into my mike and she pointed to Jean and Jean said her name into her mike.

Beattie then said, "It's widely believed that everyone has at least one book in them. I wonder if that is true. Certainly I think I have a book inside me. But tell us what you think, Sandra. How did you manage to get the book inside you onto the page? How did you start?"

Sally, I wanted to scream at her – *Sally's my name!* But once I started talking and she asked me more questions, it all went well. I feel really happy talking into a microphone. When you're in a radio station studio being interviewed, it very soon feels like an ordinary conversation, and you're not aware that there are other people outside the building listening in. I always enjoy it.

"And how can people get hold of your book?" said Beattie C. "Do they write to you, or–"

What on earth was she on about? I interrupted: "They will be able to buy it in all local bookshops, and on Amazon, as a paperback or an ebook," I said. Blimey, I was committed now.

"Really?" said Beattie C. "That's most impressive. Thank you, Sandra."

"Sally," I interrupted. "Sally Howe."

"Whatever," said Beattie C. "Now over to our other debut novelist, um…"

"Jean Shardlow," said Jean, who was sitting beside me. I turned to look at her more closely, and it suddenly clicked – I'd seen her photo in the *Peak Advertiser* as an eminent member of the local history society.

"Tell us what your story's about, Jean."

"It's not a story, it's not a novel, it's-"

"You said you were a writer, didn't you?" barked Beattie into her mike.

"It's a local history book," said Jean, rather taken aback.

"Oh, 1066 and all that."

"No not really, it's about-"

"It's a historical novel! Of course! Like *The Other Boleyn Girl.*"

I felt so sorry for Jean having to tussle with this stupid bint that I interrupted with "I believe Jean's book is about the local history of Bakewell. It's about famous people who were born or who lived in Bakewell. Is that right, Jean?"

Jean needed no further encouragement to talk. She launched into a polished and articulate description of her book. I asked her how long it had taken her to do the research and how long the writing had taken, and she responded.

"The book sounds really interesting," I said. "And what's your favourite story?"

"Oh, the history of how the Bakewell pudding was invented – by mistake – by an inexperienced kitchen assistant at the White Horse Inn," said Jean. She went on to describe in detail how to make Bakewell pudding, speculated on what the mystery ingredient could be, and explained clearly that the pudding is the traditional dish and that Bakewell tart is a Johnny-come-lately impostor.

Jean and I had been talking into our mikes for several minutes. The interview was going really well – with me as the interviewer, by default – and I glanced over at Beattie whose over-lipsticked mouth was pursed in a tight ugly pout. She was seething. Jean finished what she was saying and I didn't follow it up with another question, and Beattie seized the space and launched in with "Oh, yes, but I'm afraid I can't eat Bakewell tart. I'm allergic to cherries," which showed that she hadn't even been following what Jean had said, that the pudding is made from eggs and sugar and almonds and jam, and cherries don't come into it.

There was knocking on the glass screen again and I turned round to see Kathryn Henderson prodding her watch energetically and then making a slicing movement with her hand across her neck.

Beattie said into her mike, "And now it's time for the traffic report," and slumped back in her chair.

The researcher came into the studio, then, and ushered Jean and me out of the room.

Jean had gone through the ops room into the corridor, and I was just leaving too, when the producer placed her hand on my arm and said: "Thanks, Sally. That stupid woman has been foisted on us by the powers that be to fill in while Johnny's …and she's utterly…well I don't have to say it, do I?"

"But why…?"

"Personal friend of the MD. We've got no choice!"

"What's the matter with Johnny? Is he coming back?"

"Cancer. He collapsed last week, and he won't be…Oh no, what is the woman doing now? Got to go!" and she rushed back behind her control desk and started fiddling ferociously.

today's tweet from **@sallystoneymoor**
Did you hear me on Radio SWISH today? If not, you can catch it on Listen Again www.swish.co.uk

Wednesday December 14th

The critical path

This time when Gray showed me down to Kit Wyatt's office and ushered me in, it was Kit who asked what I would like to drink. He said to Gray – "And let's have real coffee this time, and some of that special Waitrose almondy Austrian cake thing with marzipan inside it – oh damn, what's it called?"

So even dynamic printers suffer 60-plus memory loss. It's not just woolly-headed women writers.

"Stollen?" said Gray.

I showed Kit my self-publishing to-do list and he scanned it, saying *hmm* and *aah* under his breath, and then, "Do you mind if I write on it?" and when I said "Fine," he got a pencil and jotted down important details that I hadn't thought about, and elaborated on some of the things that I had.

"You don't have a time-line," he said. "This is going to be fun." He got up from his chair and came out from behind his desk and said, "Let's sit over here at my table." He cleared the table on the other side of the room, and got a chair for me and held it out for me to sit in – very polite – and then sat down himself. He smelled amazing. Wendy would have been able to name his yummy after-shave: Wendy knows these things.

He said: "I don't want to take over, but critical path planning is a bit of a passion. And I might be wrong, but I see you more as a creative type. Right?"

I nodded. "But do you really have time?"

"I said – I'd like to do something to apologise for that shocking stag party fiasco. I can't even bear to think about it..." He shuddered. "And I have a window."

"But don't you have Christmas preparations to do?" I said.

He jumped up and reached for the cord to straighten the Venetian blinds, that I hadn't noticed were crooked, and said with his back to me: "My kids are sorting out Christmas. They've done it since Juliet...my wife...since she died." He cleared his throat. "So anyway, they do it all, and I just slot in." He turned round and came and sat down again. "After Christmas we usually go away. But this year I'm staying at home."

He was businesslike and focused. There was no friendly chat, and no smiles. The man is so changeable! You never know where you are with him! We sat side by side in front of my laptop, working on my critical path, the mouse between us on the table (I do like a mouse, not just a trackpad). Twice, we reached for the mouse at the exact same time, and we both pulled back like lightning, as if there was an electric charge between us. Did he feel it, too?

Or did the mouse have a faulty connection?

Unfortunately, he had to go off to lunch with one of his daughters before we'd quite finished, so he insisted I go back tomorrow.

And that was my productive morning.

When I got home, I felt so relieved that I was no longer struggling in the dark on my own, that I opened a bottle of Merlot, and watched the lunchtime edition of *Neighbours* as a private, mini-celebration.

Or did I open the wine and have a drink to calm me down, because when I left Wyatt Printing, I felt a little bit unsettled – OK, completely strung out.

today's tweet from **@sallystoneymoor**
Don't you just love words?…imbroglio, fiasco, oxymoron, ineluctable, ineffable…whatever!

Thursday December 15th
Witty

Another meeting with Kit, to work on my critical path.

They'd decorated the place for Christmas. They must have done it last night. There was a vast Christmas tree in the reception area, tinsel strung round the reception desk, and seasonal pot-pourri in a basket on the coffee table in the waiting area. There were stylish streamers hung all down the corridor, and there was even a six foot Christmas tree in the corner of Kit's office. Plus, Witty's bed had a row of red paper pompons hanging from it, and some rather expensive looking designer perspex snow flake clusters dangling from each end.

"Someone likes Christmas!" I said, as I went in. I walked over to stroke the cat.

"Who wouldn't?" Kit said. "Who couldn't?"

"Hmm..." Should I mention Gus? "It's been a cause of some strife in my house. My husb...my ex loathed it, but it's everything I love! In fact, seeing your tree has reminded me I need to get one organized myself. All this book stuff has made me forget."

"Forget a tree? Shocking. We'll put it at the top of your time-line."

We sat next to each other at his table again. He had done a bit of work on my stuff since yesterday. "These are just *my* thoughts, *my* suggestions – what do you think?" he said.

"Great. Thanks."

All the time we were working I was aware of him, as if he had this force field around him. It was weird. Really weird. Our chairs were close together and one time my knee touched his, and once his foot nudged mine, and one time when I was leaning over, my thigh touched his, and I looked down and saw his firm cyclist's muscles taut beneath his trousers, and I lost track of what I was saying.

So there we were, side by side, close to each other so we could both reach the keyboard and the mouse, and he turned to say something to me and smiled, our faces a few inches apart. Our eyes locked, and I thought he was going to kiss me. But then he turned away and carried on with the planning.

And one time he typed something and turned to me and said: "So what do you think?"

But I was lost in a haze of his warm breath, and his yummy after-shave. I stared at him and said, "Sorry?"

He looked at me steadily. "What do you think about that?"

"About what?"

"Um…" he said, "I have no idea." Then he blushed.

When we'd finally finished the plan, he offered me more coffee and a mince pie with brandy butter, and we chatted about this and that and not very much – so much more relaxed than the other day in my kitchen, and just the kind of free range conversation that is delightful to have with someone new, someone intelligent, someone witty and charming and gorgeous and…gosh, listen to me!

He told me he'd heard me on the radio.

"I don't have you pegged as a *local* radio person," I said.

"I heard it in the warehouse," he said. "I'm a Radio 5 man, myself. Or Radio 4. You were impressive."

I blushed. "Thanks. But I have been on quite a lot. You get used to it."

There was a thump, as Witty jumped off his cat bed onto the floor, and Kit and I looked round in time to see the cat throw up.

I winced. "Hairball?"

Kit jumped up from his chair, saying in a worried voice, "Not again. No, it's not a hairball, I only wish it was. He was doing this all yesterday. Even when nothing came out – he was retching his little guts out. Poor Witty. I'm going to have to take him to the vet. *Now.* Do you mind?"

I got up from my chair. "Of course not. I'll go, and get out of your way." I gathered up my papers and put my laptop in its case, and said, "Thanks ever so much for all your help, I'm much clearer now and…" but Kit wasn't listening. He had picked up his cat and was cradling him gently in his arms.

"I hope he'll be OK," I said.

Kit looked up and gave me a wan smile and said, "Oh Sally, so do I."

today's tweet from **@sallystoneymoor**
What conclusions can you draw from the way someone handles their cat?

This tweet later deleted!

Friday December 16th

Cat stuff

I phoned Kit to ask how Witty was, but the receptionist said he was working at home, and gave me his number. It felt wrong to disturb him at home, so I emailed him.

```
Hi Kit,
I'm just emailing to ask how Witty is. I do hope
the news from the vet is hopeful and they were
able to give him some helpful medication.
Best wishes
Daise
```

And as soon as I'd clicked *Send* I realized that I'd signed it Daise, and not Sally. I'd just been emailing Giovanna – that was the reason.

I got an email back within the hour.

```
Hi Sally/Daise,
The vet ran some tests and it's not looking
good. I am nursing Witty at home. He isn't fit
to come to work.
Thanks for asking.
I hope everything is going well with you. Gray
is getting on with your cover and says he'll
have something to show you in a couple of days,
All best
K
```

Poor Kit. He is obviously crazy about that cat. You get attached to cats in a sotto voce way and only realise how much you like them when you lose them, or when it looks as if you will lose them.

today's tweet from **@sallystoneymoor**
The trouble with having more than one identity is remembering who you are ;-)

Saturday December 17th

Speed-dating again

Richard and Wendy egged each other on and went to speed-dating tonight, together. I went along out of nosiness. It was a toss-up as to whether to go along or to stay at home and decorate my tree, which Richard and I collected this morning.

Both Richard and Wendy appear to be horribly scarred by their encounters with Gary-the-Lad and Three's-not-a-crowd-it's-a-party-Melissa. They both said they were going to be careful this time.

"I'm going to choose someone who looks safe," Wendy said. "And I absolutely won't be going on a second date until I've got the guy's birth data and drawn up his chart. If only I'd done that with Gary, I'd have seen his horrific Grand Cross in fixed signs, with Mars conjunct Uranus square Venus, *and* Mercury opposite Neptune, and I'd have backed right off. I can't believe I was so stupid. It was a reckless hit-back-at-Alan moment. I must have been mad!"

I'd expected it to be a quiet evening as it was so near to Christmas, but we were invaded by a singles walking group called Crag-Hoppers, who had turned up en masse. Pippa was there helping behind the bar again, and with her was my stalker, Glenys Wallis. Glenys gave me a shy smile and a discreet little wave, and I made myself pull back my mouth into some semblance of a grin.

There weren't many people on the in-a-relationship side, I guess because the novelty of getting to know fellow villagers had worn thin, and they were all at home wrapping Christmas presents, or at the Big Band Christmas Music Concert at the church. I had to sit with Billy Bathgate again, who told me in unnecessary detail about another atrocity committed by residents of the Stag Party House: someone was sick in the bin outside Billy Bathgate's shop. Shock! Horror!

I left and went home as soon as I decently could, but not before seeing that Richard and Wendy had each hooked up with people wearing red and green checked shirts. Richard's woman also had on hiking boots and what looked like Dickies combat trousers. That's the way to his heart. And so much safer than pink satin hot pants.

today's tweet from **@sallystoneymoor**
Collective noun for a group of walkers – an amble?

Sunday December 18th

De-briefing

Wendy's man:

She got off with an accountant called Hamish and said, "It's weird how a checked shirt on Gary looked really sexy and on Hamish it looks boring and tame. We're meeting for coffee on Tuesday, in his lunch-hour, at that frowsty café near the chip shop in Bakewell – that café that's stuck in the 1960s. Can you think of anything less promising in terms of romance? But it could be post-modern date-kitsch. Maybe he's got hidden depths."

Has Wendy been reading something other than *Heat*? Post-modern? Kitsch? What's got into her?

Richard's woman is called Debz (yes! apparently with a z!) She has green principles and works at the Environmental Centre, running recycling courses, amongst other things. She apparently wears hiking boots as fashion items. Hmm. Richard is quietly enthusiastic. They were going for a hike this afternoon, even though it was freezing cold and threatening snow. I am agog to know how they got on.

My day was mixed. I brought down the box of tree decorations from the attic, which is good. But when I stuck my hand in the box to get out the lights, I was stung by a wasp. Now my palm is as red and hot as a Christmas ham, and the back of my hand looks inflated. It looks preternaturally fat and young, with no veins or wrinkles or dimples in sight. It is so swollen I am having to type left handed.

today's tweet from **@sallystoneymoor**
Felled by a (very) late summer wasp sting......ouch!

Monday December 19th

Health report

I didn't feel I could email Kit at the weekend about Witty, but I emailed him today and got this reply:

```
Hi Sally,
Poor Witty. We're near the end, I think.
It's nice of you to ask.
Scarlet and Peony (daughters) have come to say goodbye.
K
```

Poor Kit.

Scarlet and Peony? What extravagant names! Was it his arty wife who chose them? Brick and Gray are unusual, too.

I worked this morning, and after lunch I made some of my famous chocolate brownies and sloshed in some brandy I found in the cupboard. Well, why not? It's Christmas.

today's tweet from **@sallystoneymoor**
Yum – fortified brownies.

Tuesday December 20th

A shoulder to cry on

An email from Kit:

```
R.I.P. Witty Wyatt. Much loved. Already much missed.
K
```

I rushed to the gift shop at Hassop Station and bought him a tasteful card. Then I sat in the café and wrote a message and jumped in the car to drive down to his printing works to deliver it, when I thought – *Hang on, I should take him something else, as well as the card!* So I drove home and got the brownies out of the cupboard and opened the tin and chose the four squidgiest ones (i.e. the best) and was going to wrap them in foil but then thought they looked a bit plain, so I pushed them to one side and took off my coat and made my whoop-di-do-this-is-a-special-occasion-chocolate-icing, and plopped a dollop on each of them and quiffed it, and then couldn't wrap them up because the icing would crush, so I put them on foil on my coolest (as in trendiest) plate and carried them out to the car.

Then when I got to the printing works, I felt a fool and left the brownies in the car and went inside with just my card.

Gray was on reception and we had a chat about the progress of the cover. He showed it to me on his computer screen and it looked fab. "You'll have it in your Inbox when you get home. Let me know what you think and whether the layout of the back cover is what you want. Please say if there's anything you want to change."

I assured him I would, and he sent me down the corridor to see his dad, without ringing through.

I knocked on Kit's open door, and went in. Kit was sitting with his head resting on his hand, his elbow on the table. He was staring glumly out of the window. He turned to face me. His hair was mussed up and wild, which combined with his crisp white shirt and his grey suit waistcoat was pretty sexy.

Why was I thinking stuff like that? His cat had just died!

"I'm so sorry," I said. "I bought you a card." I put it down on the desk in front of him.

"Thanks." He tore open the envelope and read the card. "That's nice. Can you stay?"

I sat down and waited for him to speak. He stood my card up on his desk and looked out of the window again. I hadn't noticed before how thick and dark his eyelashes are, nor the small dark scar on his jaw-line.

"I feel so flat," he said. "Daft, isn't it?"

"I wouldn't say so. I know what it's like to lose a cat. It can knock you out."

His arms were outstretched on the desk in front of him now. He has lean hands with nice nails. The room was silent, but down the corridor someone was laughing. Kit was looking at Witty's empty bed. I reached out to touch his hand, but then drew back. My heart was thumping. Could he hear it?

A tiny wisp of tinsel fell rustling from the Christmas tree. I looked back at his hands on his desk, so near to me, so far away, and thought, "Oh, what the heck?" and reached out and laid my hand on one of his, gently, tentatively. I was trembling. He swivelled round and looked into my eyes. A pulse was pounding in my temples. He laid his other hand, warm and firm, on top of mine. *Don't ever move it, Kit.*

"Got you now," he said in a low voice – *that* voice. My knees turned to pudding. I was weak and moist.

He got up and walked round the desk and I got up too, and before you could say self-publishing, he'd rolled me into his arms and pulled me into one delicious slow-mo kiss. And oh boy, can he kiss.

We kept on kissing, and then he sniffed, and I drew away a little. His eyes were wet. "Come here," I said, and held him as tight as I could, breathing in the scent of ink and glue and his after-shave: a heady combination.

But then there were footsteps in the corridor and he pulled away, hurrying towards the window and turning to lean against the sill as Gray came in, carrying two mugs.

"I bought you some coffee," he said. "White, no sugar, Ms Howe? Dad's is black."

"Thanks, kid," said Kit.

"Thank you," I said. "Please call me Sally."

As soon as Gray had gone and was out of earshot again, Kit said: "I've wanted to do that ever since you didn't throw my light at me."

"Bullshit! You tore me to shreds!"

"I was taken aback. You looked so different from how you did on the Trail. Impressive and gorgeous in your maxi-coat, and did anyone ever tell you how sexy you are when you're all riled up? You tug at your hair, and your eyes flash, and your cheeks go pink and–"

"Stop it. You're embarrassing me!"

"You know that Fleetwood Mac 25th anniversary concert? When you trounced out of the room with your long black coat swirling behind you, it reminded me of Stevie Nicks singing Rhiannon."

"I wish you wouldn't." I covered my face with my hands. Was he winding me up? Me like Stevie Nicks? Come on!

"And I wish I felt up to taking you out for a drink."

"It's eleven o'clock in the morning."

"So?"

"But you don't feel like it, do you?"

"Not when I think of Witty."

"Well, let's sit and drink our coffee and you can tell me all about him. How old he was, where he came from, why you called him Witty."

He smiled at me and I smiled at him.

"Oh," I said, "do you like really squidgy chocolate brownies?"

"Very much so. Squidgy is what I like best."

I drove home on remote control. One minute I was turning out of his car park and the next I was pulling up in our drive. I can't believe what happened. *Did* it really happen? Did I kiss a man who wasn't Gus? Do I fancy the pants off a man who isn't Gus? Yes on both counts!

But how does *he* feel? Was it an aberration? A burst of bereavement madness? I've heard of people coming home from funerals and bonking all night as some kind of affirmation of life, but surely that's not what the clinch was about, was it? Oh mercy me, I hope not.

Tweet?

No tweet.

I couldn't possibly tweet what I feel like tweeting.

Wednesday December 21st

Emails

I dreamed about Kit. And I haven't been able to stop thinking about him the whole of the day.

He emailed this afternoon:

```
Hi Daise
Can't concentrate. When I look at your critical
path I see your face.
In a daze
K
p.s. Why Daise?
```

I emailed back:

```
Hi Kit
I would need to see you to explain about Daise.
It's too long for an email.
Daise.
```

And I spent the rest of the day going into my room and checking my email.

Richard called and told me lots of stuff about someone called Debs but I can't remember a thing he said. Do I know this Debs?

I've just checked again and he still hasn't emailed back. It is worse than being a teenager. It is worse than waiting for a literary agent to get back to me.

Am I expected to sleep tonight?

today's (Giovanna-sourced) tweet from **@sallystoneymoor**
Stripy mittens and Turkish Delight – two more reasons to enjoy winter

She writes such tosh.

Thursday December 22nd

Butterflies

I woke up to find another email from Kit. He sent it at 3 a.m.

```
Hi Daise
What are you doing at Christmas?
I am accounted for on C Day and B Day, but am
home in an empty house on the 27th until NY.
Could you, would you, come over and keep me
company?
```

```
Please say yes,
K

Hi Kit
Yes.
Address needed.
Daise
```

My heart is thumping and I am shaking and what am I going to wear?

It is years and years – a lifetime ago – since I felt like this. I have butterflies. I feel sick. Will we go to bed? Will I know what to do with someone who isn't Gus? Will he go off me when he sees me in the nude? How will he react when he finds out I only have one breast? But that is the least of my worries. Oh God!

Wendy rang and rambled on for hours and hours about someone called Hamish. Who the hell is Hamish?

today's tweet from **@sallystoneymoor**
Have you got your Christmas butterflies yet?

Friday December 23rd

Cooking therapy

I still felt shaky this morning, but not as bad as yesterday. I sat at my desk and tried to work out how to write my novel's 'Sexy Complication,' (a development in the story that raises the stakes, makes Jenny's goal clear to the reader, and sets Jenny and Liam at cross-purposes) but it was hopeless: my mind was too full of Kit.

So I gave up and spent the morning making vegetarian goodies for Sam for Christmas – a cashew and mushroom roast, a broccoli and stilton flan, a pile of vegetable samosas – and then I got a text from him:

```
Going to Luke's squat to escape the bloated
consumerist capitalistic crap. See you New Year.
Have a good one. xxx
```

...and I felt like throwing it all at the wall. Bloody vegetarians!

Richard is coming here for Christmas Day and Boxing Day, so he and I can roast the spuds in goose fat and not olive oil, have real beef suet in the forcemeat balls, enjoy our Co-op Free-Range chicken and sausages and bacon in all their carnivorous glory, while picking at the carcase and licking our fingers, without veggie family members looking down on us from the moral high-ground.

In four days I'll see Kit.

today's tweet from **@sallystoneymoor**
Save turkeys! Eat a vegetarian!

Christmas Eve

Three days to go

"Have you noticed that the chemist shop isn't done up for Christmas?" Richard said this morning, when we were in Bakewell getting those last little hitherto-forgotten things. "I wonder why it isn't."

"Maybe they feel the same way about Christmas as Gus. What about the agricultural suppliers?"

"They were tugging a forelock to Christmas. They had a special display of snow shovels and axes."

"Richard, do you think I look like Stevie Nicks?"

"Who the hell is Stevie Nicks?"

In three days I'll see Kit.

today's Giovanna-sourced tweet – where does she get them?
@sallystoneymoor
Flat pack reindeer...bring them on!

Christmas Day

The best and the worst

I Skyped Nina and family in Munich this morning, Daniel in Denver at teatime, and I sent Sam a text saying
Happy Days, love Mum xxx

And have I honestly missed them? Any of them? Really and truly?

No, because I am full up with the dread and the thrill of seeing Kit in two days time.

Later, and calmer:

The best thing about not having a houseful of family here for Christmas is not having to worry about everyone:

- Are they having a nice time?
- Do they like their presents?
- Can we get through the day without any unpleasant spats?

The worst thing is:

- being genuinely pleased with all the hair products that Nina sent me to try on my newly(ish) shorn hair, managing to use the gel in the tube correctly, being delighted with the result, going down to show Richard, and his saying: "Hmm, very interesting. You look just like Camilla Parker-Bowles."

Thanks for nothing, Richard. I am going to Kit's in two days and I need to get my hair right! Oh my God, it is seriously scary!

Afterthought:

I have been reading back through the last few pages and noticed an epidemic of exclamation marks. Bodmyn Corner (my erstwhile creative writing guru) would be horrified, and Spiky Pete would have a coronary. Do I care?

No, because I am going to see Kit in two days time. Whoop-di-doo!

Actually, the best thing about not having family here at Christmas is that I don't have to ask if they mind if I go to see Kit.

Giovanna's fittingly enigmatic tweet for a festive day when I've just watched a programme about retro toys:

today's (Giovanna-sourced) tweet from **@sallystoneymoor**
when did I last think of a Rupert Annual?

Boxing Day

The nether world: that time after Christmas

Most years, and generally speaking, there are two ways of looking at the limbo that stretches from Christmas Day to January 2nd.

1/ a time of retreat from the world in which one can spend time with family, reflect on the past year and make plans for the year ahead, indulge in endless games of Scrabble and comfort television (e.g. *Ballet Shoes*, a bumper episode of *As Time Goes By, A Year with a Community Midwife*) and emerge fulfilled and renewed and buoyed up for the coming fray.

2/ a time of social claustrophobia when you are cooped up inside with the family from dawn to dusk because the weather is crap with a capital C, a time when you suffer endless games of Scrabble and repeats on telly (e.g. *Ballet Shoes*, a bumper episode of *As Time Goes By*, *A Year with a Community Midwife*) and emerge at the end of the week like a rat released from a trap.

But I don't have to worry about any of this, because tomorrow I'm going to see Kit.

Tuesday December 27th

At Kit's

I parked my car and knocked on his front door and he opened it and pulled me in and snogged me before I could even take off my impressive maxi-coat. Oh......oh.

It is 1 a.m. and I am sitting in bed in his spare room. I am so wired that there is not a hope in Hathersage that I will get to sleep, so I thought I might as well write down what happened next.

After the initial snog, he took me into his sitting room and we sat by his fire and opened a bottle of champagne and toasted Christmas, and then he said: "Here's to us."

Then he offered to refill my glass and asked if I'd like to stay the night.

"I just want you to feel able to relax and let go, not worry about the drink-driving issue. I can lend you some of my pyjamas, and you can have a choice of bedroom. There are four apart from mine." Oh wow. Of course I said "Yes," while thinking *Thank God I set up Chewy's automatic cat-feeder for just such an occurrence.* Even so, when we came upstairs later, I was feeling too nervous to do anything other than head for here – the spare bed.

He'd made two dinners – a meaty one and a veggie one – because he didn't know which I'd prefer. This man is *so* considerate. I chose the boeuf bourgignon, followed by a sliver of orange and almond cake, which he served with cream, into which he'd mixed rose water. Extra effort, or what? But who's interested in food?

When are we going to get it together? I can't wait, and at the same time I am really, really nervous. Once we're under the duvet with no clothes on it should be fine. I am worrying about the transition from being fully dressed to being under the duvet and out of sight and just flesh on flesh. *He* looks in good shape, as far as I can tell through his clothes, but I have one breast, and that one points downwards, and I have multiple stretch marks, and I have a squidgy bit just above my hysterectomy scar that never ever goes, no matter how much I weigh.

I need to sleep, or I will look horrendous in the morning (fully dressed.) I am going downstairs to see if Kit has such a thing in his pantry as cocoa.

Wednesday December 28th

Kit

When I went down to Kit's kitchen at 2 a.m. I found him in his dressing gown, leaning against the Aga.

And everything was fine. More than fine. It was amazing.

Sometimes I worry about what I write in this diary and one of those times is now. It is a writer's notebook when all's said and done, and it does occasionally get left around in the common areas at home, and Richard and Wendy and Sam are nosy-nellies, so I'm thinking that it would be unwise to record a blow-by-blow account of what we did, and when we did it, and where we did it, and what was said, even though it would be extremely helpful for times in the future when I need to write passionate love scenes which feature a couple who can't keep their hands off each other.

This morning Kit drove me home. He put "We are young" by Fun on his CD player on repeat and we sang along to it all the way from Froggatt to Stoneymoor. I collected my toothbrush, and clothes for the rest of my stay, and restocked Chewy's feeder, and no-one was there to ask me what I was doing and where I was going and when I was coming back, and what was for tea. And it was wonderful.

Thursday December 29th

Kit and me

We are living in bed.

The only thing I am willing to note here is that Kit has SIX Christmas trees. SIX!

Friday December 30th

Me and Kit

This man is...

Saturday December 31st

Down

For the last four days, Kit has been receiving texts and emails and what-evers on his swanky iPhone from all his kids, which is nice. A close family.

This morning, he was in the shower and I was sitting propped up in bed trying to finish the *Recorder Jumbo New Year General Knowledge Crossword* that we'd been doing together. I was lying back against the soft pillows (with diesel blue Egyptian cotton pillowcases) racking my brain for the capital of Peru, when Kit's bedside phone rang and I picked it up without thinking.

"Hello?"

"Who is this?" said a cross female voice.

"Are you wanting Kit?" I said.

"Who are you?" she screeched. "Yes, I would like to speak to my father."

At that point, Kit rushed out of the en-suite with a chocolate brown towel wrapped round his waist, lunged across the bed, and snatched the receiver from me. I poked him hard in his hairy chest, but he flapped his hand at me to brush me off and got up off the bed and marched back into the bathroom, shutting the door behind him. Fancy his snatching the phone from me! But oh dear, why did I pick it up? I shouldn't have, but I've been so relaxed, so very much at home, it was an unconscious response to a ringing phone.

A muffled, energetic conversation was going on behind the bathroom door, but I couldn't hear any of the words. Kit finished speaking and came out.

"Why the hell did you pick it up? You shouldn't be answering my phone!"

I flinched at his harsh tone of voice. "You're right. I wasn't thinking."

"It's not on! You've really landed me in it now." He finished drying himself, and yanked on his clothes. "Honestly!"

I got out of bed and walked over to him. "Kit. Look at me. I am very sorry. I won't do it again."

"You'd better bloody not," he said, shrugging off my hand, and reaching down to pick up a sock.

For four lovely days and nights, I'd been living in a warm and happy, sexy dream, and now a phone call from the real world had demolished it.

I watched him stomping around the bedroom. He had been so sweet to me, but this explosive abrasiveness about the phone call reminded me of what he was like when we collided on the Trail: mean and aggressive.

I wanted to retreat.

"Kit, I think I ought to go home. Sam will be there, and I'd like to spend New Year's Eve with him as I haven't seen him over Christmas." This was a lie. Sam was staying with friends.

"Whatever you like. Do what you need to do."

JANUARY

Sunday January 1st 2012

Frayed at the edges

"*Six* Christmas trees? *Six?*" Wendy said.

I'd been trying to nail Jenny and Liam's 'Sexy Complication', but Wendy had burst into the house, saying, "Christmas is so claustrophobic! I need to talk to someone I'm not related to!" So there we were in my kitchen.

"Six Christmas trees is a sign!" she said. "You love Christmas! Gus was always a total pain about it, but Kit obviously adores it as much as you do. So–"

"For heavens sake, Wendy. *Loads* of people love Christmas. Weren't you listening to the rest of what I said?"

"So what if his daughter was upset when you answered the phone? All grown-up kids can be difficult when their parents find new partners. Is it going to worry you what Sam thinks about you having a four day bonk-fest with Kit?"

"Sshh, sshh, he'll hear you. He's home. He doesn't know about Kit, so don't you dare go and tell him. In any case it's not relevant now. Kit and I are...oh, I don't know what we are."

"Because of one stupid phone call?"

"It doesn't matter how many bloody Christmas trees he had, nor that he is the most attractive man I've met in years, nor that he was amazing in bed, nor that the time we weren't in bed was sooooo lovely, and I really, really liked him and I thought he really liked me...oh..." I trailed off, caught up in memories of Kit and me and me and Kit, and then I remembered how it ended and said "...but the way he blew up at me. It was out of all proportion. I can see it might be a tiny bit awkward for him if his daughter didn't know I was there, but why was he making such a big deal of it? Was he hiding me from his kids? Did he see me as a bit of fluff to get him through the longeur of the week after Christmas? I should have known it was too good to be true that at this age I could meet a potential–"

"Get real! You don't think you're *that* good in bed, do you? If you were young and luscious and incredibly sexy, maybe he would have thought of you as a bit of skirt. But you're not – you're a tolerably attractive, young-looking 60. Men don't have 60 year olds as bits of fun, not if they are as yummy as Kit Wyatt. Silver foxes like him can scoop up women as young as 30 any time they like." Wendy has her head in the stars and a brain full of planets, but she's horribly good at bringing people back down to earth.

"Maybe he's one of those men who will go for anyone," I said. "Always at it." (Like her Alan.)

Wendy sat up, adjusting her shorts in the crotch, and said, "OK, what was his bed-linen like?"

"Uh?"

"His sheets. What were they like?"

I tried to picture his sheets and got lost. Those four days with Kit were so wonderful: it was like being in love in a Rom-

Com. Lying in bed making jokes, telling each other about our childhoods and our time at Uni, our favourite music, films, books, fonts, talking about our kids, skirting around the stories of our marriages, and getting up for toast and marmite and tea (Yorkshire tea! – a sign!) and getting back into bed and doing things other than talking, and waking up with his arm around me and...

"Sal! Kit's sheets!" said Wendy, making me jump.

"Oh yes. Sheets. Shabby chic. Nice colour, decent cotton, slightly fraying."

"There you are then! He's not a womaniser – if he was, he'd have smart sheets."

Was she right? Or was she just being Wendy and spouting rubbish?

"Well?" she said. "Am I right, or am I right?"

"I think I rushed into things. I *did* rush into things. It's so long since I've felt like that. I think I need to back off a bit, slow down, keep my distance. I mean – the way he reacted! Is he basically a grumpy old sod, when he's not on his best behaviour?"

"You'll come round." She stretched out her leg and smoothed her black tights, and tut-tutted as her nail caught on one of them. Then she said: "I've been wanting to ask you, what's with the lopsided look? Is it a new trend that's passed me by?" She pointed to my chest.

I looked down and put my hand to my chest and realised that I wasn't wearing my falsie. Well, that was no big deal: sometimes I forgot to put it in. Then I realised! "Oh my God! I got dressed in such a hurry yesterday when Penelope or Peony or Poppy, or whatever her name is, phoned, that I forgot to put it in.

Even now, it is sitting in all its pink blancmange glory, on top of Kit's George III chest of drawers."

After she'd gone, I emailed him. It took me three quarters of an hour to decide what to say, and how to say it. It was just like when I used to email my early pieces to the editor of *The Saturday Recorder* – they were three line emails and I spent more time writing them than I did the 750 word pieces I was submitting for publication.

```
Kit,
Thank you for having me to stay. I'm sorry to
bother you, but I left my prosthetic breast in
your bedroom. When would be a convenient time to
call and fetch it? Or would you prefer to leave
it somewhere for me to collect without bothering
you? Maybe in your outside privy?
Sally
```

He replied immediately:

```
What's up with you?
I will be in every night this week after 6. Just
turn up. For God's sake, just turn up!
K
```

My life is on repeat. Last time I had to pluck up the courage to deliver his blasted light. Now I have to pluck up the courage to collect my falsie.

today's tweet from **@sallystoneymoor**
I can't say I relish déjà vu

Monday January 2nd

Bang goes the empty nest

9.a.m. As I write, Richard is unpacking his stuff in the spare room. He is staying here until an affordable rental place comes up. It may be some time.

"Don't worry, Sally, I know you're busy with your self-publishing," he said, "and I've only got two more chapters to proof-read, and when that's done I'm going to keep myself occupied in Gus's shed. I've decided to make myself some furniture for when I get a house. I'm starting with a table."

Hmm, we'll see how long that lasts. We'll see how long it is before he starts barging into my study every half hour, saying, "Can you spare a minute?"

Sam is still in bed. I was amazed and appalled to find him here on New Year's Eve when I got back from Kit's. I'd thought he'd be out with his friends and coming home on Jan 1st. But he said that New Year is yet another cooked-up celebration to keep the masses doped up and quiet. "All that money they spend on fireworks in London? Bread and circuses, Ma."

Yesterday, I asked him when he was going to start looking for a job. "I'm not. I'm trying to bring down the capitalist system, one benefit payment at a time."

"Are you just going to sit around here doing nothing, then?"

"I'm going back to Occupy Sheffield. Strategy week starts on Saturday."

I thought *Thank God for that,* and then felt sad at the realisation that my joy at his return from Europe had been superceded so quickly by irritation.

"I need to tell you something, Sam." I had to get it over with sooner or later, Kit or no Kit.

He looked up. "You're not going to give me a lecture are you?"

At that moment, I spotted Pippa out of the window, walking down the lane with the blessed hounds. At her side, shoulders touching, was my erstwhile stalker, Glenys Wallis. They were looking very chummy. Very chummy indeed. What on earth?

"Ma! You said you wanted to tell me something."

I swivelled round to face Sam. "What? Oh yes. It's about me and Dad. You haven't been home for so long, I really can't remember if you know the full story. I mean, do you know that we've agreed it's over between us, and he's staying in his cabin in the Rockies for keeps?"

"Course I know. He's really cool, isn't he?"

Cool? Cool? That's not the word I would use.

"So we are separated."

"Well, yeah."

"I mean in the marriage sense."

"So?"

"Don't you care? What do you mean – *so*?"

"Well it hardly makes any difference, does it? I mean, you're both past it now. You've fulfilled your genetic imperative and you're finished."

Sometimes I could strangle that boy. Sometimes I could strangle Gus. They are so alike, those two! If we're talking genetics, it's clear to me that I married beneath my gene pool. I am so much more evolved than either of them. I absolutely am not finished. I was very tempted to tell him about Kit and me and the last few days, but I couldn't face his reaction. Anyway, is there any point?

6 p.m. I have watched *Neighbours* and had one glass of Merlot as relaxation initiatives, and I am now going to get my falsie back.

today's tweet from **@sallystoneymoor**
whenever I feel afraid, I whistle a happy tune

Tuesday January 3rd
Home ~~delivery~~ collection

What happened last night:

I knocked on Kit's heavy oak door with the shiny brass printer's devil door knocker, and he opened it immediately as if he'd been standing behind it. He'd obviously heard my car in the drive.

"I've come to collect my falsie."

"Come in, come in, it's bloody freezing," he barked.

I stepped inside and he shut the door and pushed across the bolt at the top, a habit of his I noticed last week. He walked towards the sitting room, but got as far as the early Victorian rustic oak chest (that has three, yes, three, framed photographs of his dead wife Juliet sitting on top) and then he realised I wasn't following him, and he turned round. I was still standing on his vast, thick, door mat.

"Are you coming in?" he said, in a slightly calmer tone than the one he'd used when he'd opened the door.

"I don't want to interrupt your plans, I've just come to collect my–"

"You owe me an explanation!" he shouted. Then he said in a weird falsetto voice: "*Thank you for having me to stay.*" Then in his normal voice: "Your email! What the hell is the matter with you? Did I dream what happened last week? Did I dream those four fantastic days? Were you just using me for sex?"

My mouth dropped open and nothing came out. Was that what he thought? Was that how he felt?

"Well?" he said impatiently.

"I think maybe we should talk," I said in a whisper.

"I think maybe we should."

So I went in and sat by his fire, and took off my coat because it was so toasty in there, and he offered me a drink and I said *Yes,* because it seemed churlish to refuse, and then I said *No,* because I'd already had one and needed to drive home, and then I said *Yes,* because I thought I needed it, and anyway, I knew I could always ring Richard to come and fetch me.

Finally, we were sitting opposite each other – him on his battered but oh-so-classy leather armchair, me opposite him on a squishy sofa.

"Why did you rush off like that?"

"The phone call."

"What? I know you're a writer but I didn't think you were one of those super-sensitive, neurasthenic cissies who snivel at the least bit of upset."

"But I don't understand why my answering the phone made you so angry. Did you think I was being over-familiar? I did it without thinking, and all the time we spent together was so...well...I was so relaxed. I absolutely see, *of course,* that it was over-stepping the mark, but I did apologise."

"Maybe I over-reacted. The thing is...The girls haven't always been easy about...They have tended to be a bit funny about people I've dated before."

"So you were hiding me from them."

"I would just have liked to have managed it differently."

"It left me feeling as if...That you don't want anyone to know about me, about us. That maybe you just see me as a Christmas fling."

"Daise, Daise," he said. "I am smitten with you. I am so smitten with you, I make myself sick. Look – I didn't tell the kids because it was all so hurried. It swept me away. I wasn't thinking straight. And it was Christmas, and the kids, the girls particularly, still miss Juliet at Christmas, so it's always an emotional time. And then there was Witty dying – and you know I told you that it was Juliet and the girls who found Witty when he was tiny, shut up in a cardboard box outside the Co-op at Christmas...and..." He reached out and grabbed my hands, "But of course I intend to tell them."

He leaned over to kiss me, but there was a thudding on his front door and he pulled back. "What the hell?" he said, strangely panicked. Then, "Oh, no. Look, I'm sorry. I think it might be Peony." He leapt up, went towards the door and turned and said "Do you mind awfully leaving now? This isn't the right time to tell her. I need to do it when I am on my own with her."

"What?"

"Get your coat!" he said urgently. "Come on!" He came back and tugged at my sleeve. "You'll have to go out the back and then she won't see you."

"But my car is parked in your drive!"

"I'll make something up. Quick! Here – take your falsie – it's in this bag!"

I took the carrier bag and let him shove me into the kitchen and out of the back door. I was still trying to pull on my coat, when he said, "I'll ring you," and shut the door in my face. So there I was, one minute being called Daise and sweet-talked and about to be kissed, and the next minute shoved ignominiously out of the back door into the cold and the dark.

I picked my way round the back of the house, seething. It's always the same: if someone says something outrageous out of the blue, I am so gobsmacked, I'm unable to think of a rejoinder. And if someone who is obviously upset or panicking urges me to do something, I fall into line without arguing, and only later do I wonder why on earth I agreed to do what they asked.

I reached my car. Good job for Kit that Peony had not boxed me in. She's boxed him in, though. It's probably been like that since Juliet died. Never mind, he's going to tell her now, and everything will be OK when she gets to know me and realises I'm not a man-eater and I'm not after her inheritance.

As for Kit – no-one's perfect, and someone who says they're "smitten" with me can be forgiven for one or two flaws. I do not intend to let him off lightly, however.

today's (Giovanna-sourced) tweet from **@sallystoneymoor**
Daffodils in the supermarket, in tight, dead-looking bunches. It must be January.

Wednesday January 4th

Back to the typeface

9 a.m. There was an email from Kit this morning, apologising for last night. I'd woken up feeling cross, though, so I replied like this:

```
Hi Kit
Thanks for your email. I went along with what
you wanted last night, but don't expect me to do
it again. I am not a parcel of Class A drugs to
```

be welcomed and enjoyed and then hidden and denied when the drug squad arrives.
Best wishes
Sally

I am working hard to complete all my corrections of the manuscript this morning and have resolved not to check my email again until I break off for lunch.

1 p.m.
Dear Daise (or should I call you Coke?)
I guess I can see why you might be annoyed. Can I take you to dinner at Hassop Hall tomorrow night to say sorry?
love
K

Now he's talking. The man knows how to say sorry. I love Hassop Hall, and I've only ever been once. That was with Iain seven years ago. Why is it that only men I'm not married to think of taking me there? But it will be fab.

Now I am going to get on with my work. I need to get the book ready to send to Gray. He has finished the cover – it looks great – and I am paying him to typeset the text.

Richard was helpful on the proof-reading, and Kate (aka Giovanna) has done me proud on that too, and on copy editing. For a woman whose emails never see a capital letter, she is surprisingly hot on punctuation:

hi daise
attached is the ms with all my corrections – thank god for 'track changes' – one way in which microsoft word excels.
general comments – you're mega-fond of brackets. I think you need to check every time you use

```
them to make sure you really need to - also,
what is it with these long lists of adjectives
with ands in between? why don't you use commas
to separate them?
also just realised that all the dialogue is
shown as "hi there fred" said katy (sixty sixes
and ninety nines)
this is the american way of doing it
in the uk it's usually done as 'hi there fred'
said katy (sixes and nines) - just looked thro
loads of books, and this seems to be the case
and you've got the wrong sort of dashes
throughout, and lots of them!!! you need long
bloody dashes not short ones
best observations
love g x
```

Great – proof reading and copy editing, that's today's blog post sorted.

Thursday January 5th

Heaven

11 a.m. Just got back. Kit dropped me off on his way to work. Oh wow. I stayed at his house last night after our romantic dinner at Hassop. He was sooooo sweet. I shall be wallowing in it for the rest of the day.

today's tweet from **@sallystoneymoor**
So exciting to be doing my final edits!

Friday January 6th

Kids, eh?

I realised I should tell all the kids about Kit. I shouldn't have been complaining to him that he hadn't told his kids if I haven't told mine. Some people wait to divulge stuff like this until the family is all together, but it would kind of defeat the object to wait for my funeral (or Gus's.)

I rang Nina this evening. After some gentle chitchat, I launched in: "Sweetheart, there's something I need to tell you. I'm moving on – from Dad."

"Yes. You're carrying on with your writing, and you're publishing your book yourself. Rock on, Mum. If you want help with the PR and marketing, just ask."

"I mean I am seeing someone."

"You're *dating?* How could you do that? Poor Dad!"

Poor Dad?

"Nina! We've been apart for three years! He's the one who left!"

"Presumably he asked you to go with him."

"Maybe, but he prefers to be on his own."

"But he obviously still loves you."

"Obvious?" Obvious to whom? There is no way anyone could know how Gus feels. He never indulges in anything as sordid as communication: he never writes, phones, emails, texts, tweets, blogs or Facebooks.

"I think he's heart-broken," Nina said.

Ridiculous! She knows how things stand. I told her when Gus left.

"Nina! Would you go and live in a cabin in the Rockies with Tim if he asked you, and be happy to never see anyone else?"

"It sounds heavenly. Could we leave the kids with you?"

"Nina!"

"What you do is your own affair – hah! – literally. But don't expect me to welcome this man into the family."

"I have only just started seeing him." This was true – although I had been seeing a lot of him. Well actually, almost all of him. "I know these things take time to get used to," I said.

"You're 60!"

"Yes, and you will be 60 one day and...Oh never mind."

"I'm going to write to Dad and see how he feels."

"Well, good luck with getting a reply."

This whole conversation was so dispiriting, I couldn't face telling Sam today. Nor did I have the heart to ring Daniel in Denver, not that it was the right time of day: he'd be at work. I emailed him instead, and he sent me this reply:

```
Dear Mum,
Thanks for writing, though you didn't need to
tell me you are dating - I know it's all over
between you and Dad.
He's well chilled in his cabin, so as long as
*you're* happy, I'm happy.
Love Dan

Sent from my iPhone
```

Sweet boy.

I should think Gus is chilled in his cabin. He will be snowed up in there for several months, and good luck to him. I am seeing Kit tomorrow, and I need to shave my legs and paint my toe-nails and decide what to wear. Whoop-di-doo!

Having said that, my legs probably don't need shaving. Hair loss on legs is one of the only good things about being 60.

today's tweet from **@sallystoneymoor**
(my) new concept for 2012: getting ready for the weekend. Ooh, it takes me back to watching Ready Steady Go on Friday nights.

Saturday January 7th

No-one is perfect

A great day! Sam left for Sheffield, Richard was busy with something that did not impinge on me, and I saw Kit.

He picked me up late morning, and took me to lunch at Trevor's Green Way cafe in Matlock – yummy food. I know I'm a bloodthirsty carnivore, but if I was rich and I could have Trevor as my resident cook, I'd be happy to give up meat forever, even bacon.

After lunch we drove back to Kit's house and we were halfway upstairs when Gray came through the front door. So we lit the fire, and settled in with the Saturday papers. Gray was not at all surprised to see me in a social setting with his Dad, and after half an hour of slightly hesitant conversation, he relaxed, so Kit's obviously told the kids. It was a very pleasant afternoon, and we did the Jumbo £500 Prize Crossword together, with Gray helping, too.

Eventually, at 4.55 (not that I was checking my watch) Gray left, and I thought "At last!" but then Kit turned on *Radio 5 Live* to listen to rugby. I was gobsmacked, and said "Really?" and he said: "But it's Leicester vs the Wasps! The Aviva premiership!" with such urgent excitement written on his face that I said: "Oh well, in *that* case."

"I'll go into the snug and listen, though. You stay by the fire and watch the telly."

So I got the listings and decided what to watch and looked for the remote control. No joy. I went in the snug, where Kit was shouting obscenities at the rugby match on the small TV in the corner.

"Remote control?" I said.

"It's here. I'll come and switch it on for you. Tell me what you want to watch."

"Just give it to me."

"No trouble." He insisted in coming in and organising the telly and then went back to the snug, taking the remote control with him. What's that about?

I watched an interview with Rose Tremain, and then when it had finished, and he was *still* watching the blessed rugby, I read the paper. Then I wandered round the house admiring the furniture – which is mostly antique but not in a showy way, more of a handed down in the family and slightly battered way. I also counted the number of photographs of Juliet on display, with or without the rest of the family, or Kit, come to that. Total: 23. I wouldn't mind quite so much if she was old. But she will forever be 49, which is something I can never compete with.

Hours later, when the rugby had finished, we had a nice time.

today's tweet from **@sallystoneymoor**
25 down? 16 across? Fun times pitching in with the Saturday crossword

Sunday January 8th

More nice time

More nice time at Kit's house, mostly indoors.

Talking in bed...

Me: "When did you get your tattoo?"

Kit: "I thought you hadn't spotted it."

Me: "It *is* discreet."

Kit: "A couple of years ago I took Gray to London – a bonding trip, father and son. It was after his girlfriend left him for someone else, and he was devastated. We got a bit sozzled, and he wanted a tattoo and he persuaded me to go with him. He's got the same one as me, but on his shoulder. Tattoos aren't really me, you know."

Me: "I like the motto."

Kit: "Juliet would be appalled. But you know – on days like today – I rather like it."

Me (THINKS): Juliet, Schmuliet. She's not here to be appalled, Kit. I'm the one who's here, and I like it.

Isn't it odd how things that you have hitherto disdained suddenly become attractive when you find out that the person you're nuts about has (or does) that thing?

today's tweet from **@sallystoneymoor**
You can find the most surprising things under other peoples' watch straps.

second tweet from **@sallystoneymoor**
Today's motto: One life – live it.

Monday January 9th

Bookshops, books and italics

I had to go to Sheffield for my six-weekly appointment at Pricey Paul's, and while I was there, I popped into Waterstones. It's very funny: I can't pick up a book now without assessing the cover design, checking what font they have used, and looking to see if it has perfect binding or is "sewn limp." (I *love* that phrase!)

I bought Anita Shreve's latest book, just so I could use my *Society of Authors* discount card at the till. And as I was the only customer standing there, I took the opportunity to chat to the guy behind the counter about my new book. He was very helpful. He looked up *Fast Work* on his computerised till, and said it had sold very well, and he was sure they'd be able to stock *They Met on the Bridge,* and I could have a signing there when the book came out. The sticky point was when he asked which wholesaler was handling it. I couldn't answer. I have not yet approached either of the main ones. I'm waiting until I have a proof copy to send them, and then they can see that the book's not rubbish. He said I'd need to send them an AI sheet. I nodded sagely and said "Of course," while not having a clue what he was talking about. As soon as I got home, I looked AI sheets up on the net: they are Advance Information sheets about a soon-to-be-published book. Yay! Another self-publishing blog post.

Richard was in the shed when I got home, muffled up to the eyeballs to keep out the cold, planing something. "How are you getting on with your table?" I asked.

"Very slowly. After you left, a couple of Mormons knocked on the door, and it was half past eleven before I could get out here and start work. I don't have a problem with Mormons as people. My problem is Joseph Smith's magic glasses. There is something worrying about them."

today's tweet from **@sallystoneymoor**
I don't think I'll ever get over the novelty of using my Society of Authors card when I'm buying a book.

Tuesday January 10th

Beleaguered

Richard has already started disturbing my work, and it's driving me insane.

This is a typical morning:

I get out of bed and stumble to the kitchen to get myself tea, and to my study to collect my laptop, with the intention of coming straight back to bed without engaging in any kind of conversation. I am semi-comatose, thick-headed, unable to bear noise or animation of any kind, and in the perfect state for writing fiction, being still in some demi-monde of consciousness.

Unfortunately, Richard is in the kitchen in his boiler suit munching muesli, while looking at furniture-making videos on YouTube on his laptop, while listening to John Humphries grilling an unfortunate MP on the *Today* programme. I try to sneak in and out of the kitchen with only a minimal good-morning, but he leaps upon me and subjects me to a barrage of talk that I am too weak to withstand. As I wait for the teabag to impart some decent colour to the boiling water in my mug, I lean against the worktop and stare at Richard, saying nothing. I do not respond. I am rubbing my eyes and yawning, and giving (without faking) every non-verbal signal known to man that says I am deeply dozy and unavailable for social intercourse.

He is oblivious. He goes on about some geek in Canada who posts on YouTube, who makes amazing wooden jigs for every kind of purpose (what is a jig?) and who has decided that milk bottle crates are the perfect storage device for a workshop and yet it is illegal to take them as they are the property of the dairy and so he has designed and made his own replicas in wood, using a special jig that he designed for the purpose. I, meanwhile, am glassy-eyed and silent, and thinking *SHUT UP SHUT UP SHUT UP.*

As soon as he pauses for breath, I retreat to bed and open my laptop and resume my writing. I have just got into a tasty bit of dialogue, when Richard knocks and comes in and says "Are you writing?" and I say "Yes," and he carries on anyway:

"Because I want tell you something REALLY EXCITING I heard on the news. There is a woman in the North of Scotland with the exact same DNA as the Queen of Sheba."

Oh my God!

today's tweet from **@sallystoneymoor**
I never found the companion that was so companionable
as solitude – Thoreau.

...which is one of Gus's favourite quotes. I never thought it would come to this.

Thursday January 12th

Silver fish

Wendy called to show me her booty from the January sales, including some Union Jack shorts, which looked faded and tattered enough to have been around since the Crimea, not just since the start of the season. I was worried she'd joined the BNP, but she said: "It's fashion! I am so ahead of trend. The Queen's Jubilee and the Olympics are coming up this summer."

I admired the rest of her purchases as much as I could (I wouldn't say her taste and mine overlap very much) and then she wanted to know about Kit.

"There! I knew it would be on again! All that hoo-hah about the stupid phone call – all blown over."

"What about you?" I said. "What happened to that last speed-dating guy you met before Christmas?"

"Horrible Hamish? I met him for a coffee – I told you all about it before Christmas, but you were all *Kit-this* and *Kit-that*, and I know damn well you weren't listening."

"I'm really sorry, Wendy. Tell me now."

"He spent the first half of our non-date telling me about his irritable bowel syndrome, and when I tried to change the subject to his interests, he told me he went to Pilates class so he could work on his pelvic floor exercises."

"Do men *have* pelvic floors?"

"Apparently yes. Not that I really want to know. Anyway, I managed to wheedle his birth details out of him, and when I got home I did his chart, though he was already a no-hoper. His chart was incredibly dull – so many planets in earth! And no hard aspects to give it any spice, not a square or an opposition in sight – not even a minor quincunx or a sesquiquadrate! A complete and utter dud."

"Poor Hamish."

"Internet dating's the way to go. I'm starting with *Flirtbox*, *Fifty Already*, and *Plenty of Silver Fish*. I'm about to set up a date with someone from Sheffield. He says he is young at heart and has a streak of fun running right through him like Blackpool rock. He also looks well hot."

"How can you bear it, Wendy? Doesn't it make you feel weird? Are you going to meet him somewhere public?"

"I'm not an airhead! Course I am. And I want you to be there as back-up to...you know...to sit at another table and make sure...I don't know...I've suggested lunch at Hassop Station Café. Are you up for it?"

"Definitely! It will be fantastic copy and–"

"Bloody writers – everything is fodder for a future novel!"

"And of course I want to make sure you're OK."

"Yeah, yeah."

today's tweet from **@sallystoneymoor**
Anything you say will be taken down and may be used in a novel.

Saturday January 14th

More nice time

Another lovely day spent with Kit.

He picked me up and before we did anything else, we had to call in at his bank to withdraw a chunk of money he was giving to Gray, to buy a second-hand car.

We were standing in the queue together and as we got near the cashier's desk, I stepped to one side and the guy behind said "Hello" to Kit.

The bank clerk who was serving Kit was filling in a form, and asking Kit a list of annoying questions. He said: "And what will you be using the money for?"

Kit turned to me and rolled his eyes, then said to the cashier, "Sex and drugs and rock and roll."

And the guy who knew Kit said, "No change there then," in a loud voice, and laughed. Kit laughed too.

The cashier remained impassive and said: "I'll put it down as leisure activities."

Was it *just* a joke? Does Kit have a dark disreputable side that I don't know about? Am I playing with fire?

It has been overcast for days, but the sun actually came out this afternoon, so we walked up to Curbar Gap. We looked at the view, and then there was then a brief tussle over which direction to take from there. Kit wanted to go along Froggat Edge and I wanted to walk along Curbar. I gave in.

Talking in bed...

Kit: "You know when we first met? When you derailed me on the Trail?"

Me: "You mean when you were really vile to me and–"

Kit: "Let's not get into all that again. As I was saying...when we met on the Trail, did you have a plait? Or am I imagining it?"

Me: "I did. I grew it to make me look authorly."

Kit: "So why did you cut it off?"

Me: "I dreamed Gus said it made me look sturdy and sensible. The kiss of death.

Kit: "He was right about that, if about nothing else. You look soooo much more attractive with your current haircut."

Me: "*If about nothing else*? What does that mean?"

Kit: "Why would any man want to leave you?"

This man says the sweetest things.

today's tweet from **@sallystoneymoor**
The snowdrops in my garden are looking lovely.

Sunday January 15th

Persona non grata

Kit was at some family do at his daughter Scarlet's house in Sheffield. All the kids were going, plus partners. I'm Kit's partner and they all know now, because he's told them, so I'm wondering why I wasn't invited.

I spent the morning trying to write, but Chapter 14 has floored me. Writing is such a mood thing. Sometimes I read through what I've written and I think it sounds great – witty, pithy and smart. The next day I read exactly the same bit and it's banal and boring.

I gave up trying to write the novel and worked on my PR campaign plans instead. e.g. a list of where to send my book in the hopes of getting a review.

I wouldn't mind the pictures of Juliet all over Kit's house if she didn't have such a lovely face – if she had just one flaw, like a big nose, or a horrid neck or flyaway hair or too much lipstick. It does look on some of the photos as if she was prone to over-pluck her eyebrows, though. Maybe I can focus on that.

today's tweet from **@sallystoneymoor**
How are all you writers getting on with the new year 1,000-words-a-day challenge?

Monday January 16th

ISBN

I spent the day wrestling with the ISBN Agency website, finding out how to apply for an ISBN, and then applying for one. This kind of stuff does my head in, but at least it's blog fodder.

I miss Kit. I rang him to ask him to lunch and he said he'd love to see me, but he's got a huge job on at work this week, and can't spare the time till Saturday. Is he cooling off?

today's tweet from **@sallystoneymoor**
"An artist's life has so few rewards." (M*A*S*H)

Thursday January 19th

On His Majesty's Service: an undercover operation

A quiet day. The only thing of note was Richard telling me that he has been to Penrose in Pilsley so many times to examine their furniture without buying anything, that the staff are getting suspicious. Would I pretend to be married to him so he can look like a customer who has brought his wife in to check something out? I said I would, but not today.

today's tweet from **@sallystoneymoor**
Snowdrops, now in frozen flower, poking through the snow.
View media

Saturday January 21st

Location, location, location

I suggested to Kit that we spend the day at my house. I like his house, but the all-pervading presence of Juliet sometimes gets me down. But *he* said we should go to his, because we had the house to ourselves, whereas Richard is at mine, and Wendy is always in and out, and Sam could arrive back home at any time. So I gave in. Then, when we turned into his gate, there was a sugared-almond-violet Fiat 500 parked in the drive, which I recognised as Peony's. He said "Oh hell," and immediately put his car into reverse, shot out of his gate, did a hand-brake turn and sped away.

He explained: "Peony'll be there with her new boyfriend. I can't stand him."

"Does she still have a key?"

"They all have keys. And Juliet hid one in the rockery. That's still there. She couldn't bear the thought that one of them might come home unexpectedly and be locked out. They were teenagers, then, of course."

I took a deep breath and looked out of the window. He was speeding down to the bridge at Calver. "Do you know where you're going?"

He snorted. "I always know where I'm going: Manchester – so you can swan around John Lewis."

"Do I want to go?"

"Women always want to go shopping."

"Pull over, buster, just pull over! There! That lay-by!" He stopped the car. I was incensed. "Let's get a few things straight, 1/ I am not *all* women 2/ I only want to go shopping when I have something I need to buy 3/–"

"You told me that going round John Lewis always calms you, like some woman in some film or other who likes to go to Tiffany's."

"Don't interrupt. 3/ I don't want to go shopping 4/ I didn't need calming until now 5/ Some woman? It's Audrey Hepburn in *Breakfast at Tiffany's* and she went there when she had the mean reds" (even Gus would know that) "6/ Why on earth would you go to Manchester when it's twice as far as Sheffield? and 7/ Did you not consider asking me what I wanted to do?"

He looked shame-faced, and I instantly forgave him. "Sorry," he said. "Where shall we go?" Even then, he didn't say 'Where would *you* like to go?'

"To my house."

When we arrived, Wendy was sitting in Richard's car in the drive with a road atlas on her knee and Richard was locking the front door. I asked her what was going on.

"I came to see you, but now I'm navigating for Richard – he's going to some tool exhibition in the middle of Birmingham. I figured that where there are tools, there'll be men." She saw the quizzical expression on my face. "What? I can read a map! I can chart the bloody heavens, can't I?"

Talking in bed...

Me: "Do my wrinkles bother you?"

Kit: "What are you talking about?"

Me: "I hate being old."

Kit: "When you're looking at the face of an older person you're fond of, you don't see their wrinkles. You see their eyes, and the light behind them, and their smile, and the softness of their cheek."

Analysis...

Good points – "a person you're fond of"

Bad points – 1/ "an *older* person you're fond of" 2/ he didn't deny I had wrinkles.

today's tweet from **@sallystoneymoor**
'Middle age is when you're sitting at home on a Saturday night and the telephone rings and you hope it isn't for you' Ogden Nash

Sunday January 22nd

Sunday supplements

I was reading the books section of *The Recorder* in front of Kit's fire. (Yes, we were back at his house again.) It said that Doris Lessing had sent one of her books to publishers under a pseudonym, as an experiment. The book was repeatedly rejected. When it was eventually published under the pseudonym, it sold about a tenth as many copies as books published under her real name.

"Isn't that amazing?" I said to Kit. "Unknown authors are on a hiding to nothing. If you're part of the literary elite, not only do you never get rejections no matter what the book is like, you also get your books reviewed twice in the same paper – once for the hardback and once for the paperback. What can an unknown author do?"

"Change your name by deed poll to Doris Lessing," he said, getting up to go out. "Back in a minute."

I leaned over to get the remote from his side of the sofa to switch on the telly, but struggled to work it. It's really complicated, compared with ours. Eventually, I got it on and worked out how to get the menu up, and joy and delight! There was a Fred Astaire film on – *Swing Time*. Fred was in the middle of singing *The Way You Look Tonight* to Ginger.

Kit came back into the room and said "You don't want this rubbish on, do you? There's last year's rugby highlights on Sky Sport." Without waiting for an answer, he grabbed the remote and switched channels. I snatched the remote off him and changed channels again and put the TV on mute and glared at him.

"You've lived too long on your own!" I said.

"It was much more restful on my own."

"Is that what you want, then? What you prefer?" I threw the paper down on the floor and got up.

"Don't be daft, Daise. We'll watch whatever you want."

"It's the principle. You can have your wretched rugby on. I've got this on DVD at home. It would just be nice if you asked."

Talking in bed…

Me: "I don't understand why you haven't been snapped up by some woman. It's quite a long time since Juliet died."

Kit: "I was saving myself for you."

Me: "Smarmy thing. Seriously, what's the score?"

Kit: "Women always want me to retire so I am free to go out with them on day trips, go away for weekends, go to the U3A with them, have afternoon tea at garden centres – God preserve me! But I love my work. I don't want to give it up until I am old and doddery and lose my marbles and start insisting everyone uses Comic Sans."

Me: "Not all women want all that stuff."

Kit: "The ones who don't are hard-asses."

Me: "Do you think I'm a hard-ass?"

Kit: "Yours is lovely and soft. Come here."

The picture of Juliet I hate the most is the one Kit has in his bedroom. It's an informal snapshot of her on a beach. She's lying on a towel on her stomach, reading, and she's turning to look at the camera, and smiling.

today's tweet from **@sallystoneymoor**
Sometimes it's hard to know where to go on a cold Sunday in January, although bed is always nice.

Wednesday January 25th

Chaperone

It was Wendy's lunch date. I planned to get to Hassop Station first so I could check out the books, and say hello to Lisa, the manager, and watch for Wendy and her potential new man, and then try to bag a table near to them. The café part of Hassop Station is in the old booking hall and it has a high ceiling and large south facing windows so it's lovely and light, and on dark days, you can imagine you're on the set of *Brief Encounter*. You always see lots of people you know there – it's a tourist honey-trap, but the locals really like it too. Today I saw Pippa and GW (the blonde stalker). They were coming out of the door, as I arrived. They didn't see me: they were in a huddle, giggling, and GW's arm was round Pippa's shoulder. Intriguing.

I managed to get a small table near to Wendy and her man, but the place was heaving, and as soon as I sat down with my soup, another woman put down her tray, asked if she could join me, and took off her anorak.

Meanwhile, Wendy's date, Guy, was spreading out an Ordnance Survey map on the table and saying how excited he was that Wendy lives out here in the Peak District – assuming that it meant she's a keen hiker. Poor sap. He was talking about dry valleys, escarpments, interlocking spurs, and lots of other stuff I remember from Physical Geography lessons. Every couple of minutes his voice got louder with enthusiasm e.g. "And that's a fantastic walk if you want the ultimate thrill of an oxbow lake."

His map took up so much room it covered their lunch, and Wendy was trying to look as if she was listening to him, while trying to forage for her seafood platter under the Peak District.

Poor Wendy. I spotted her scratching behind her knee, which was not a coded message to me: it's what she always does when she is über-bored. She kept looking in my direction and rolling her eyes.

"Do you know that woman?" said the woman at my table.

"No," I said, a Judas. "Why do you ask?"

"She keeps making faces at you. I know the chap she's with. He's a friend. It's their first date – he met her on the internet. He asked me to come along as back-up. He wanted a second opinion on her – I think her name is Wendy."

"Really?" I said insouciantly. (I do like that word.)

"She looks a bit flighty to me. Oh my goodness! I've just seen what she's got on her feet. Those shoes won't stand up to the mud in Monsal Dale and Water-cum-Jolly. Don't you think he has nice hair – so thick – and don't you think he dresses nicely? Practical, but manly – like Alan Titchmarsh."

She gushed on about her friend, Wendy's date, and I began to suspect that she fancied him herself and wished *she* was sitting where Wendy was. Wendy, by contrast, was looking less and less interested. Her eyelids were drooping, and she looked on the point of sleep. I took emergency measures, and dashed out to the loo to ring her up.

"Sorry. Can't talk now," she said. "I'm having a lovely lunch with someone and then we're going for a walk, I mean a hike. Ring you later."

She's a nutcase. Beyond help. Wendy doesn't walk much on pavements, let alone across moors.

I finished my soup and left.

today's tweet from **@sallystoneymoor**
The ISBN for my book arrived! My book is now OFFICIAL. I never thought a string of mere digits could make me feel so excited and so happy.

Saturday January 28th

Gloss

Kit and I have been working hard all week and not seeing each other, but talking every night on the phone, emailing bits and bobs, and then on Saturday he's been driving over and picking me up and we spend the weekend together. Today when he arrived he asked me where I wanted to go and I said

"Sheffield, to the Millennium Gallery, to see that China exhibition."

"Really?" he said. "Sheffield?" He turned to look at me. Then he turned back and started the ignition and said "OK," without enthusiasm.

We went, and I enjoyed it, but he seemed on edge. I wanted to have lunch in the Botanical Gardens, but he wanted to go to a pub, so I agreed. Then I asked him to drive home along London Road so I could go to the Farrow and Ball paint shop. Richard has promised to decorate the hall and landing for me, and I wanted to get a paint card to choose a colour. Not that I can afford F&B. But their colours are always an inspiration.

"Really? Farrow and Ball? You can get one from the shop in Wirksworth." Why was he being so difficult? We were one mile away from this shop, and Wirksworth is half an hour from my house. "OK. If we must," he said. He parked down a side road and said, "You pop in and I'll wait here. There's something on the radio I want to hear."

"What?"

He looked at his watch and said "Er...*Any Answers*."

"I thought you hated listening to the views of the public." (Like Gus.)

"Do I have to account for every minute of my day to you? Just go and get the bloody paint card, then we can go home."

The shine had gone out of the day. He was being really snippy, the opposite of amenable, whatever that is. (Yes, yes, Spiky Pete – I know my vocab is slipping these days. It's too much time spent on publishing, and not enough on writing.)

I got out and slammed the car door on him, and he banged on the window and shouted to me to be more respectful of his car, and I stalked off. As I reached the corner, a sugared-almond-violet Fiat 500 turned into the road and pulled up behind Kit's car. Two glossy young women got out.

Was it Peony and Scarlet, whom I'd still not met? It looked like it, because they went straight to Kit's car to talk to him. I stood on the corner and eyed them up. One was wearing a wool coat with a shawl-look wrap around collar, the other wore a beautifully draped anorak I recognized from the Toast catalogue. (I only ever drool over Toast clothes. I never buy them on account of the price.) They both had on impeccably cut trousers and beautiful, lace-up ankle boots. I stood there dithering on the pavement, expecting Kit to jump out of the car and call me back and introduce us all, but he didn't. He spoke to them through his open car window, so after a minute of hovering, I gave up and went to the paint shop. As I was leaving the shop, the glossy girls arrived and passed me and didn't look at me. One had that thick straight shiny hair, and the other's was soft, gorgeously washed, and a little bit messy and mussy and floppy, altogether perfect. The worst thing about them was their incredibly slender hips, which means that Juliet probably had slender hips as well, so now I feel like a humungous house.

"Kit!" I said, when I got back to the car. "Was that Peony and Scarlet?"

"Yes."

"So why didn't you introduce me?"

"Just do up your seat belt, will you?"

He turned on the ignition and set off, turning on the CD player as he did so. Clapton was singing *Layla*.

"Why didn't you introduce me, Kit?"

"I wasn't in the mood."

I switched off the music and turned to look at him. "What kind of mood is that? Why didn't you introduce me?"

"You're being really querulous today. Let's get home."

"Is that it?"

No reply.

We drove back into Derbyshire in silence. Why didn't he want to introduce me to the girls? Had he even told them about me? Gray knew. But did the girls? Did Brick?

"You haven't told Peony and Scarlet, have you?" I said, as we passed The Chequers. "What about Brick?"

"Gray is cool. I just haven't found the right opportunity to tell the others."

"You promised me you'd tell them weeks ago!"

He reached out and put his hand on my knee. "Come on, Daise, don't be harsh. It's not so easy."

What a lily-livered apology for a man! I'd had enough. Why is he making such a big thing out of telling them? Is he blowing it up out of all proportion? Or does he, as I suspected before, regard me as temporary and so not worth mentioning?

I'd had enough. I didn't want to spend the rest of the day with him. I'd rather be home in my kitchen drinking tea and listening to Richard warble on about scarf joints and band-sawing techniques.

"I'd like to go home," I said. "I have things to do."

"I thought you were going to do me," he said in his best seductive, black treacle voice.

"Get lost. Just take me home."

He took his hand away. "Suits me."

As I got out of his car at my gate, I said "When you start acting like a grown-up, and face up to your kids, let me know." I slammed his car door for the second time today, and marched down my drive.

I stepped inside the house and closed the front door and leaned against it, eyes closed, in an abyss of fury and disappointment.

Someone said "Hello," and I looked up to see a pile of tatty luggage at the bottom of the stairs, and a young woman I didn't know from Eve walking down the hall towards me, holding a plateful of buttered toast. She was naked.

[illegible]

Wednesday, February 1[illegible]

Incommunicado

[illegible]

And [illegible]

[illegible] wants an empty house.

Thank God for self-publishing. Making [illegible] contacting people about the book and [illegible] I can concentrate [illegible] there [illegible] way [illegible] writing. In any case, my nerves [illegible]

FEBRUARY

Wednesday February 1st

Incommunicado

It is four days since I saw Kit. He has not rung. I have not rung. He has not emailed. I have not emailed. Our relationship is in tatters. I am beyond…I was going to write *I am beyond emotion*. But what on earth does that mean? I am a writer and I can't describe how I feel. Pathetic.

And I can't believe what I said to him. It was like an ultimatum. Sally Howe doesn't do ultimatums. She is patient and forbearing (i.e. she grits her teeth while she struggles to see the other person's point of view) and she will do anything to avoid nasty conflict. Hence she has a brother and son who keep boomeranging back to live with her even though she desperately wants an empty house.

Thank God for self-publishing. Making lists and contacting people about the book are both things I can concentrate on, when there's no way I'd be able to do any writing. In any case, my novel is languishing in the wastelands of the second act, after the 'Sexy Complication,' and I'm dithering about what happens next.

Work-wise, I have contacted the managers of four local Waterstones to ask if I can have signings in their stores when the book comes out in May (answer yes). I have emailed six book blogs to ask if they will review the book (two yeses so far.) I have made a list of newspapers and magazines to send copies of the book, in the hope of getting a review.

As long as I'm busy like this, I can banish Kit from my mind, but every night in bed, I replay everything that went on between him and me, and try to work out if I misread his feelings, or misinterpreted the situation, or made more of it than it warranted: have I just been making a fool of myself? Apart from that one time when Gus went away on his very first trip, and Iain fell for me and I *flirted*, just *flirted*, with the idea of an affair with him (let's face it – with Iain I was never engagé) I have not been in this situation since I first met Gus. Yes, I had lots of boyfriends before Gus, but I was a teenager then and only one of them was serious – Stuart Robinson. This thing with Kit makes me feel like a relationship greenhorn. At 60! Pathetic.

I thought I knew how he felt when I was with him, but now we're apart, I am clueless about what went on in his head and what is happening now. All I know is that I don't want to get back into it until I know he is serious, and I know he has sorted it out with his kids.

As if the Kit rift isn't bad enough, as if having Richard and Sam here isn't a humungous drag, I am now playing hostess to a lunatic girlfriend who walks around in the buff. I am not a prude, but it's very discomfiting not knowing when you're going to bump into a bare body on the landing. And it's not just Xanthe! Sam is at it, too.

"It's not naturism, Ma, it's protest nakedism."

"Cover yourself up and *then* tell me what you mean!"

He went away and came back in his towelling bathrobe and said, "We're protesting against the perfect body image portrayed in the media, that's making girls as young as six get anorexia."

"At home? Where no-one can see you? What kind of a protest is that?"

"You and Richard can see us."

"Yes, and I think we've got the message now. Poor Richard. It's much worse for him having a naked nubile woman around every corner than it is for me. He's been terrified to come in from the shed."

"You make it sound as if there's a whole crowd of us here."

"Two unwanted nudists *is* a crowd, Sam."

"I've told you – it's protest nakedism! And we're protesting here, because it's too cold to go out like this at the moment."

"Yes, and too cold inside, so you turn up the heating and it feels like a furnace and it's costing me squillions in oil! I like the house cosy, Sam, but it's been like having the menopause all over again with constant hot flushes!"

"TMI, Ma."

"On the contrary! Not enough information! If you and Xanthe are going to stay here, you can either contribute to the heating costs, or you can get dressed and we'll have the heating on at a sensible temperature. End of story."

There. That told him. Bloody Kit should bring his bloody kids over here and I'd sort them out for him.

today's tweet from **@sallystoneymoor**
February 1st – yay! – The start of a new month always fills me with optimism.

Sometimes my tweets make me want to vomit. And that is one of mine – not one of Giovanna's.

Thursday February 2nd

In the genes

Sam and Xanthe are now fully dressed when they appear in public areas, but I know that as soon as the weather warms up, they'll be stripping off again. In hanging my argument on the cost of the heating, I laid myself wide open to future abuse. Oh dear.

It's so annoying: I am sympathetic to a lot of what Sam thinks and acts upon, just as I am with Gus. The problem is that neither of them knows what *moderation* means. They take everything to ridiculous extremes and I end up wanting to whack them over the head with a pick-axe handle.

today's tweet from **@sallystoneymoor**
This may be February and yes, it's cold, but every day brings us one day closer to summer.

Another sick-making tweet.

Friday February 3rd

Dreams

Seeing Xanthe's firm young flesh when she was sashaying around in the nude made me consider my own ancient body. How could I imagine that I look OK and that Kit could want me on a permanent basis? I must have been mad. Things like this go round and round in my head and make it hard to go to sleep at night, and when I do eventually nod off, I have annoying dreams. I have now dreamed on two consecutive nights that Bruce Forsyth and I were an item. Sometimes one's unconscious can be very disappointing.

A more optimistic thought about my naked body: at least I'm better off than Mrs Mountain. I once overheard her say (in a post office queue debate about public nudity and Page 3 girls) "Mr Mountain has never seen me naked. And he's never said he wanted to, either."

today's tweet from **@sallystoneymoor**
It's crazy how happy I feel when I see the tops of the daffs poking up through the soil.

Saturday February 4th
More dreams

I woke myself up in the night saying "Sam, do as I asked you to do." I also dreamed that I bought two separate brands of tins of condensed milk and when I opened them, one after the other, they were empty. I think this dream means that family life is not what it's cracked up to be. At least Bruce Forsyth was not in evidence.

today's Giovanna-sourced tweet from **@sallystoneymoor**
War horse. My kind of pony.

Sunday February 5th
Quiet Sunday

I wonder what Kit did today.

We woke up to heavy snow. Richard and I went out for a walk on the Trail, and I took my camera so I could take some pictures to put on the blog. My readers seem to like my photographs of local scenes.

As we tramped across the fields to Little Longstone and through a footpath gate, Richard said, "Someone has been round taking all the nuts off these gate fastenings."

"Who on earth would want to do that?" I asked.

"Vandals."

"The nuts will have just dropped off, you fool. You don't get vandals round here."

"You get them everywhere."

"And what kind of vandals would want to take nuts?"

"Specialists."

I miss seeing Kit. I miss him, I miss him, I miss him.

today's tweet from **@sallystoneymoor**
The Monsal Trail under snow and with just a whisper of tourists – my kind of heaven.
View image

Monday February 6th

Dust sheets

Richard is decorating the landing and stairs for me. He says it's a thank you for letting him stay here, but I happen to know that his furniture-making has stalled temporarily because he has bought a band-saw and is waiting for it to be delivered. I also know that he gets freezing cold out there in the shed.

He asked me to find him some dust sheets to cover the carpet. Gus always used to describe dust sheets as namby-pamby arrangements, but Richard is a careful type: when he's making jam he wears a calf-length apron and wellies.

I retreated to bed with my laptop, to work, and when I emerged half an hour later to go to the loo, there he was up a ladder on the landing, with the dust sheet spread out below. Wonderful. I returned to bed.

Twenty minutes later there was a shriek and a bang and I ran out to find the ladder over the stair well with him at the top, and splodges of paint splashed all down the stairs. He'd dropped a fully laden paint-roller. Having spread out a dust sheet at the start, he hadn't thought to move it, as he himself moved.

I didn't shout. I didn't moan. I just said quietly and with impeccable restraint, "What a shame you didn't move the sheet." Then I helped him to scrub the carpet, and we managed to get all the paint off.

"Do I get points for cleaning it off so well?" he asked.

"What? If you'd been using the sheet, there'd have been no need. *And* I helped you. Nil points."

"Are you ill?" he said. "You didn't shout when you came out and saw the paint."

"I'm glad you noticed. I wanted to lay claim to the moral high ground."

This is Sally Howe, on the moral high ground, wishing I was somewhere else with Kit. I wish he was coming with me to see the David Hockney exhibition on Thursday. Still, it might be fun travelling down on the train to London with Wendy. I've said I'll go down Oxford Street with her for a couple of hours, although I really, really don't fancy it. Then I'll go to the exhibition, and we'll meet up later.

I am sick, sick, sick of having Kit living inside my head. Sometimes I want to cut it off so I don't have to think about him any more. Should I be trying to get over him? It's ten days since I slammed his car door on him. He's had plenty of time to talk to his kids and come back and tell me he's sorry for being a wimp and will I take him back and...

today's tweet from **@sallystoneymoor**
Doors and old-fashioned phones – there for slamming. Where would we be without them?

Tuesday February 7th

Blast from the past (spot the cliché)

I check my email all the time in the hopes of getting something from Kit. Today, instead, I got one from Iain. From the sublime to the ridiculous.

```
Hi Sally,
I hope you're surviving February - I remember
how  much you hate it. This is just a shot in
the dark -I was going to see the Hockney
exhibition with my daughter Bec the day after
tomorrow - Thursday - but her boys have gone
down with a really nasty bug and she needs to
stay at home with them. Would you like to have
her ticket? Meet me for lunch at the RIBA,
first? Our tickets are timed for 3.p.m. Let me
know soonest. I'll check my email every half
hour.
Love
Iain
```

Oh my goodness! My ticket is for 4 p.m. I hope Iain's gone by then. I really don't want to meet him. Does he never do anything new? The last time I was going to meet him in London (seven years ago) we were going to go to the RIBA for lunch and go to a gallery, and Bec had some disaster and he had to cancel.

Plus ça change. The man is boring with a capital B. On the other hand, at least his children (i.e. Bec) understand that widowers need to move on and be free to find a new partner, not like some people I could mention. No names, no pack drill.

```
That's a really lovely offer, Iain. Thank you.
But I already have a ticket for Hockney. I hope
you find someone else. Thanks for thinking of
me.
Cheers
Sally
```

Thanks for thinking of me? I sound like a literary agent's rejection letter.

I have counted at least five clichés in this diary entry. I wonder if my relationship problems are doing permanent damage to my ability to string a few sentences together sans clichés.

today's tweet from **@sallystoneymoor**
When someone in my writing group said "Clichés are OK because they are the best way of expressing an idea" I was lost for words.

Wednesday February 8th

An unlikely purchase

Sometimes I wonder about Richard...

He is searching for narrow plastic tubing for a new woodwork project (I didn't ask what) and he's been unable to track any down.

Richard: "Will you and Wendy be going near a plastic tubing emporium, tomorrow?"

"On Oxford Street?" I said. "Not a chance."

"What about the Royal Academy. Is there a gift shop there?"

"Of course."

"Well, they might sell artists' materials – plastic tubing, for example."

"No, Richard. No!"

It's a bummer: I was going to tweet about going to see Hockney tomorrow, but Iain might see it.

today's tweet from **@sallystoneymoor**
You never know who might see your tweets…Twitter is like a roller coaster: exciting and scary.

Thursday February 9th
Hockney rules

9 a.m. East Midlands Railways. It's good to be leaving Derbyshire, where Kit is, even if it is only for the day. The trouble is I am taking my head (which is full of him) with me.

9.15 a.m. This tea is awful! Is each bag half full of sawdust? No. If it was it would have more flavour. It must be stuffed with shredded cotton wool. Why can't they serve Yorkshire Tea?

Midnight: What a day! Will have to write it up tomorrow.

today's tweet from **@sallystoneymoor**
Blown away by Hockney! It makes me want to buy an iPad and have a go.

Friday February 10th

Yesterday

Oxford Street was awful. I trailed after Wendy disconsolately, wishing I was under the duvet at home. Wendy was sweet, trying to buck me up by pulling clothes from the rails not for her, but for me. I, meanwhile, smiled wanly and shook my head. At least we got me some sun glasses to wear for visiting the Royal Academy incognito, in the hopes of avoiding Iain. After she'd realised she wasn't going to distract me by suggesting clothes for me, we started on her own long list of must-haves, but she fell in love with a women's tux in the first five minutes, and blew all her budget on that.

"Where would you like to go, Sal?" she said, as she stroked the vivid pink paper carrier bag containing the tux. "I can't bear to see you so droopy. What can we do to cheer you up?"

"I don't know."

"How about Heal's? You love Heal's. Didn't you say you needed a birthday present for Nina?"

Heal's is a place that is restful and calming with items in the best of taste, just like John Lewis in Sheffield; the merchandise is arranged in displays that don't shout at you, they coax you. But even with a calm brain, I couldn't find anything I liked. When you're feeling down-and-out miserable, even lovely things look lacklustre. After fifteen minutes of picking things up and putting them down again, Wendy steered me up to the first floor café, and sat me down to talk to me about Kit. It was really boring, because I have been round the facts and my feelings so often in the last two weeks that there appears to be no new light to throw on either subject.

"Maybe I shouldn't have said it to him," I said.

"Why *did* you say it? It's not like you at all."

"Because I felt, I feel...I don't know...so strongly about him. I felt we were on the verge of something really serious...you know...long term...and...and...I didn't want to get in any deeper if he was going to end up throwing me over in favour of his kids. I couldn't bear it. Let's not talk about it any more. You say something!"

"Maybe I shouldn't have spent all my money on the tux. It's not like me to buy something brand new and expensive. Richard said he liked my eclectic secondhand wardrobe. Maybe we should have gone to some vintage shops instead of Oxford Street – I'd have got better value for money."

Richard making comments about Wendy's wardrobe? Really?

She went on: "I'm thinking about joining a uniform dating website. They're for anyone who wears a uniform, or for people who like people who do, i.e. me. I *love* firemen! I wouldn't fancy a paramedic, though. If they started to tell me about their work, all the gory details, I'd throw up. Not a good look." She blithered on like this for a while, as I was too glum to talk, and then we ordered a sandwich. She ate hers and then she ate mine because I couldn't face it, and then she went to have coffee with one of her sons, the one who works in the City. I got the tube to Piccadilly.

There's a huge, five storey Waterstones opposite the Royal Academy, so of course I went in to see if they were stocking *Fast Work.* I didn't expect to find it, but there it was on the shelf! One copy. I turned it so the cover faced outwards, and stood back and admired it, but then thought it would look even better on one of the display tables. So I laid it next to Victoria

Hislop's *The Island* on a table labelled *Perennial Favourites*. Good job I was wearing my dark glasses.

The courtyard in front of the Royal Academy was swarming with people and the shop outside the gallery entrance was so crowded I had to push my way up to the ticket-checker. Usually I hate being in crowded places, but even in spite of feeling crap, there was such a happy buzz – so many people excited to be going in to see the pictures, or coming out having loved them – and it was so infectious, it bucked me up a bit.

In the first gallery, the audio-guide prattled on about watercolours, but I was gripped by a wall full of oil paintings of East Yorkshire countryside in the full high colour of summer. It was fabulous! The vivid colours in the paintings were so stunning, it was like getting an injection of joy.

The leaflet I'd picked up talked about Hockney's acute sensitivity to the seasonal changes in nature, as if it was something unusual. This could only have been written by a young Londoner. As if Hockney's sensitivity to the changing seasons is not shared by every single person who lives in the countryside!

When I saw his video of the woods in May, I swooned. I could have sat there watching it until the spring arrives in Goose Lane, and the verges are high with cow parsley. Eventually I dragged myself away, and went out into the shop to find Wendy, who emerged from behind a pillar – with Iain!

He gave me a big hug, and over his shoulder I mouthed silent obscenities at Wendy.

"But why didn't you tell me you had tickets on the same day?" he asked.

"I've been depressed, Iain. I didn't feel up to company – please don't take it personally. I didn't want to spoil your visit."

"Is the self-publishing not going well? Is it February blues?"

"Yes, that's it." I had no intention of telling him about Kit. "But the paintings have really cheered me up," I said, changing the subject. " Aren't they fabulous?"

"Absolutely. He's so prolific! Amazing for someone his age!"

Wendy said: "I told Iain we'd be delighted to go for a meal with him before our train. Where shall we go?"

I dragged her off to the Ladies.

"What were you thinking, Wendy? You know I was trying to avoid him!"

"I'm worried about you, sweetie. I thought you needed your ego boosting. Iain's harmless, and spending an hour with him will remind you that you're perfectly fanciable, and great company, even if Mr Kit Wyatt doesn't appreciate the fact. That man wants his head taking off and screwing on again the right way round."

There was no escape from Iain now, so I gave in gracefully.

Iain knew a good Italian restaurant, and on the way he insisted we went into the bar of a posh hotel for a drink. We sat on low couches arranged around a glass table with lighted candles on it. There were shimmering lights above us, and strands of glittery stuff dangled from the ceiling, reflecting all the lights. A young woman with a neat blonde bob, and wearing a white shirt with a suit waistcoat and a pencil skirt came over to bring us nibbles and take our order. The white shirt with the waistcoat made me think of Kit, and I gave a huge sigh. Iain noticed and reached over and put his hand on mine. "I'm sorry you're feeling so low." He's a nice man. Why didn't I fall in love with *him*?

Wendy had to keep the conversation going for the rest of the evening. I couldn't stop thinking about Kit.

today's tweet from **@sallystoneymoor**
A glass of Sauvignon Blanc for £9? How do people afford to live in London?

Saturday February 11th

Marketing opportunity

Whitney Houston died today. It's so sad.

Apparently, Sony have hiked up the price of her greatest hits from £ 4.99 to £7.99.

If I died, I wonder if my publisher would increase the price of *Fast Work*.

I think not.

today's tweet from **@sallystoneymoor**
Phosphorescent bloom.........snowdrops in full moon

Monday February 13th

Mystery mood

I think Richard may be having a late mid-life crisis after all. For one thing, there's the dust sheet and spilled paint incident, which was so unlike him. Secondly, he's been on a diet for a while and is newly sleek and trim, and he insists he's going to continue, even though his bottom is disappearing and in danger of becoming a non-bottom. Not a good thing in a man or a woman. Bottoms are nice.

For another thing, he's stopped complaining about Sam's boot-cut low-waisted jeans that I gave him in the autumn: he's worn them so much that they now have a rip in them and uncharacteristically, he is still happy to wear them out and about.

Another weirdness is that when people ask him how he is, he no longer says 'Fine' or 'OK', he says, 'I'm rockin'.' (Note the dropped g.) The most unsettling change, however, is his mood. These days it's not just good, it's positively buoyant.

"What's going on, Richard?" I said.

"I have no idea what you're talking about," he said. "Now, when are you going to come to Penrose with me and distract the staff so I can measure an antique, two drawer console table?"

today's tweet from **@sallystoneymoor**
Did you know that in the French Mr Men books, Mr Bouncy was called Monsieur Rebondi?

Tuesday February 14th

Valentines

I got a Valentine card! It was a David Hockney card – a print of *Three Trees near Thixendale, Winter, 2007* (*blank for your message*). Inside the card, the sender had stuck a piece of paper which bore a typed message, *Happy Valentine's Day. Missing you. When am I going to see you again?* The postmark on the envelope was too smudged to read, but I knew who'd sent it – Iain, obviously. I have to admit that it's nice to be wanted, even if it is by the wrong man.

I was sitting there pondering how much simpler my life would be if I liked Iain as much as I like Kit, when the telephone rang. It was Wendy. "Sally, Sally, someone's sent me a Valentine card!"

"It'll be that hiker guy – the one with the huge map."

"It can't be. He lives in Sheffield and the card's hand-delivered. Who can have sent it?"

"Alan?"

"Don't be stupid. He's my husband."

"What's it like?"

"Pink and lacy, and it says *My love is like a red, red rose,* and inside, the person has written *But you are beautiful.*"

"Show me tonight," I said.

The village hall committee had shifted the monthly speed dating night to tonight (for obvious reasons) and I went along with Wendy and Richard because someone called Juan wants to give flamenco classes in the hall and was giving a free taster session. After that, I was coming home.

The demo had already begun when we turned up. As we went in, Mrs Mountain rushed out looking very flushed, and said, "I may start going to his class instead of Pilates. I am going home for a G and T and a cold wet flannel. Then I'll be back."

Pippa was cowering in the porch, due to the decibel levels of the machine-gun-type stamping on the wooden floor of the hall. Even out there in the porch it was louder than a demolition, and sounded a hundred times wilder, as if someone was wreaking random havoc with one of Richard's gorilla bars, or a wrecking ball. There could even have been a riot going on. Wendy mouthed – over the din – a story about Juan holding a class in Ashington Memorial Hall at the same time as a committee meeting in another room, and the committee had to evacuate and squish into a tiny, six foot by six foot ante-room next to the toilets, for an hour and a half, to escape the din.

I watched the demo and was on the point of leaving, when Pippa came up to me and asked for a private word outside.

"Oh thank you, Sally. Thank you. I need to ask you something in the strictest confidence, yes I do." She opened her handbag and took out a greetings card. "Look at this – but please don't let anyone see. It's vital. Vital."

It was a pink lacy Valentine card saying *My love is like a red, red rose,* and inside, the sender had written *But you are beautiful!* In other words, it was identical to the one Wendy got. I looked at Pippa and said, "Well, isn't that lovely? Who do you think it's from?" I didn't ask her why she was showing it to me.

"The reason I'm showing it to you, Sally, is so you can tell me if you think it's from Richard. It was hand-delivered. Is it his handwriting? I wouldn't have said it was, but…"

"No. Definitely not. I would know if it was Richard's. I'm sorry, Pippa."

"Not at all. There is nothing to trouble yourself about. Nothing at all. The thing is, Sally, I am in a relationship with someone else." I gasped, and tried to stifle it, and she went on: "I couldn't bear for poor Richard to be pining for me after so many months, when I am deliriously happy with…No. I couldn't bear it."

"With?"

"No, no. I can't say. I'm sorry. So sorry. Byeee!" and she rushed back into the village hall kitchen to sort out the drinks.

today's tweet from **@sallystoneymoor**
St Valentine has a lot to answer for

Wednesday February 15th

Damp squib

"Listen to this! Listen to this!" said Richard, "I just popped into the post office and Mrs Mountain was quizzing Billy the Kid Bathgate about Valentine cards."

"And?"

"She was showing him a card and asking if he remembered selling one like it. Och, he said, now that would be telling, wouldn't it? Come on, Billy Bathgate, she said, did you or did you not sell a card like this with the red red rose rhyme on it?"

"Mrs Mountain got one as well?"

"So it seems. She stormed out of the shop because Billy the Kid wouldn't spill the beans, so I asked him if he had sold any like Mrs Mountain's, and he said *Och, no. That one didn't sell. I sold all the others, but for some reason you sassenachs in Stoneymoor are blind to the genius of wee Rabbie Burns. So I thought I'd send them as a freebie to the under-appreciated women of the parish.*"

I don't know whether to be pleased or miffed that he doesn't see me as under-appreciated.

today's tweet from **@sallystoneymoor**

"Any fool can tell the truth, but it requires a man of some sense to know how to lie well." Samuel Butler.

Friday February 17th

An email from Kit

```
Hi Sally
Gray has finished all the technical wizardry on
the book cover - bleeds, spine widths, all that
```

stuff - and we need you to check it before we print the first copy for your approval.
Please can you ring the office and arrange a suitable time and day to come in.
Kind regards
Kit Wyatt

www.wyattprinting.com
Wyatt Printing, The Old Ironworks, Rowsley, Derbyshire

An official email in his office format. And he signed it *Kit Wyatt*, not *K*, and Kind Regards.

Misery me.

Well, two can play at that game.

Dear Kit Wyatt
Thanks for your email.
Is a visit strictly necessary for me to see it in person? Couldn't Gray email me the finished cover?
Best wishes
Sally Howe

Hi Sally
We could email it, but colours are dodgy to transmit, as so much depends on the calibration of your computer screen, and I know how very particular you are in your requirements. I'll await your instructions.
Kind regards
Kit Wyatt

www.wyattprinting.com
Wyatt Printing, The Old Ironworks, Rowsley, Derbyshire

Well, my instructions are – tell your kids about me, and get your ass over here pronto.

I know how very particular you are... Is that a dig? Is he getting at me? I'm going to have to go in and face him. I'll have to ask Wendy for advice on what to wear.

today's tweet from **@sallystoneymoor**
Great news! My book cover is ready to be approved! Mega-exciting! Can't wait to see it!

Saturday February 18th
Not happening

"What have you been doing? Has anything happened? Anyone called?" Richard said, when he came in from the shed at lunchtime.

"Nothing ever happens here," I said glumly. This isn't strictly true. What happens is I try to work and family members come and disturb me. What doesn't happen is Kit coming over and whisking me off in his car for a lovely weekend a deux.

At teatime, Daniel rang for his weekly chat. He told me his news and asked me what was going on at Goose Lane and I racked my brains. I said, "Next door's cat came in and was sick on the carpet twice. Two great gobs of it." Is this the woman who once had a flurry of pieces in *The Recorder* – a national broadsheet, no less?

today's tweet from **@sallystoneymoor**
Have you ever wished you were someone else, somewhere else, doing something different?

Monday February 20th

Cupcakes

Sam came into my study today with a nicely arranged tray bearing a mug of coffee and a cupcake.

"Here," he said, "from X. She's baking."

The elevenses from Xanthe are a sop. Since she's stopped wafting around in the nude, she's been monopolising the kitchen. She fills the fridge to bursting with their shopping, takes hours to prepare their exotic vegan meals, and when I go in to sling an omelette in a pan, the cooker top is chocca with pans and sauces, and she has the cheek to say *We can't both work in here, can we Sally?* as if we are students sharing a house. Sometimes I long for the old days, when Sam subsisted on a diet of prawn crackers and Coco Pops.

I sipped my coffee and Sam stood behind me, looking at my laptop screen. Some people have no manners. I closed down the file and swivelled round to face him.

"Do you want something?"

"The eighties has a lot to answer for," he said.

"What are you whittling about?"

"Richard is listening to a tape of Suzanne Vega, and the arrangement is sooo bad." He reached across me and picked up the tiny personal rape alarm that he gave me two years ago, which for some reason was sitting on my desk. He twizzled it in his hand. "You've not had much use out of this, have you?" he said in a disappointed tone.

!!!

today's tweet from **@sallystoneymoor**
When did buns with icing turn into cupcakes? And come to that, when did un-iced buns turn into muffins?

Wednesday February 22nd

Domestic bliss

Our unreliable and recalcitrant central heating system will give us heating or domestic hot water but not both at the same time. The plumber spent six hours trying to fix it today and failed.

He also replaced the shower (which Sam and I thought was fine) because Richard said he needed a micrometer to adjust the water temperature – one millimetre out and he risked scalding in one direction and frostbite in the other. (Who, Richard? A drama queen?)

When Sam got up at noon and showered, he emerged from the bathroom bellowing, "Crap! This new shower is crap! It's like standing under a peeing mouse – all you get is a lukewarm trickle."

I found the same.

Far worse than any of this is that I have to face Kit tomorrow, to OK the book cover.

today's tweet from **@sallystoneymoor**
"A woman is like a tea bag – you can't tell how strong she is until you put her in hot water." Anon.

Thursday February 23rd

Facing Kit

"You've lost weight, haven't you?" said Wendy.

"So?"

"You should wear your indigo jeans and a black polo neck. But maybe not: you'll be too hot today with this freakish global warming – 17 degrees! Do you think you'd be too warm in that V neck angora jumper in ivory, cos it'd make you look really tactile, and he'll be in agony. No – the rock chick look – aim for a Marianne Faithful take on it – she's about your age. Wear the jeans, like I said, and two layered T shirts, sheer ones, and that black jacket with the sleeves pushed up, and those funky feather ear-rings Sam gave you. And a bandanna – yes."

I did what she said, and put on lots of eye make-up as well.

Then I removed the bandanna and jacket, and substituted my scarf with the swallow print, and my coat – the one he liked – but I started to sweat (dammit) so it was back to the jacket and bandanna. Crikey. It's tough trying to look like Stevie Nicks.

Gray was on the reception desk and took me into a small office nearby, and I thought I was going to get away without seeing Kit, which would be both a relief and a huge disappointment. I was dying to see him, and dreading it. Gray showed me the hard copy of the cover, which was lovely, and we were talking about the technology behind the barcode, when the door opened and Kit came in. He was wearing a deep blue shirt, not a white one, and an old white work apron of cotton twill. It looked newly laundered, but it was covered in old ink stains. He looked lean and mean and really, really dishy. My heart was thumping so fast I was worried it would show through my two sheer T shirts.

"Gray," Kit said. "there's a girl in reception asking for you. You'd better see to it. I've told you before not to mix business with your private life. Be quick."

I'd forgotten how his amazing voice always turns me to mush.

When the door closed behind Gray, Kit leaned against it and looked at me, his palms pressed to the door at either side of him.

"Is everything to your satisfaction?" he said.

What did he expect me to say to this? No, everything isn't to my satisfaction!

"The cover is fine, thanks," I said quietly.

"And you? How are you?"

"Fine."

We stared at each other and said nothing. My heart was still thumping. Oh dear. You'd think I'd be past this kind of thing at my age.

"Right then, I'll be..." He was clutching the door knob as if to go, but then he turned back to face me. "You enjoyed the Hockney?"

"How do you...Oh, you saw my tweet! Yes, it was wonderful." *He reads my tweets!*

"I went with Peony. I bought the tickets in January. I'd intended to take..."

The door opened and Gray came in, and Kit did not continue with his sentence. Instead, he said, "OK. I'll leave you in Gray's capable hands. We'll be in touch, I'm sure." And he left.

"How's he got the nerve to tell me to keep my personal life and work life separate?" Gray said. "Honestly!"

"He doesn't look well," I said.

"He's been like a bear with a sore head for weeks."

"Oh."

"Grandad's printing apron is a sure sign. He only wears it when he's fed up."

"Oh."

"Have you two stopped seeing each other?"

"You'd better ask him."

"I did. He told me to mind my own business. Do you mind my asking? Do you know why he's so attached to the font, Helvetica Neue UltraLight?"

"What?"

"He was getting really stroppy on Monday, saying he couldn't find the font on his computer and had I got it on mine, and then when I had, he wanted to come and print something out but he wouldn't let me see what it was. He said – *It's personal.*"

My mind raced. Was the Valentine message printed in that font?

When I got home, I rushed to find the card. How on earth did I miss Kit's clue? I brought it upstairs and it's propped up here on my bedside table.

Now what?

today's tweet from **@sallystoneymoor**
"God made the world round so we would never be able to see too far down the road." Karen Blixen

Friday February 24th

The grey pound

Wendy, Richard and I went to see *The Best Exotic Marigold Hotel* in Sheffield. At last, a film aimed at baby-boomers. At last, a film that acknowledges that people over 60 still want sex. I hope the film makes a packet and encourages more film makers to cater for the older audience. We are still alive and kicking, even if some of us are nursing bruised and battered hearts, and are baffled as to how to proceed.

today's tweet from **@sallystoneymoor**
I loved the Best Exotic Marigold Hotel – so much more than Slumdog Millionnaire for wrinklies.

Monday February 27th

Nagging

```
Hi Sally,
Attached is your latest royalty statement.
Are you well?
Is everything OK? You haven't blogged lately.
You really do need to keep up your web presence.
It's even more important if you're self-publishing.
All best
Donna
```

Oh bog off, Donna.

today's tweet from **@sallystoneymoor**
Are royalty statements the perfect way to blow away writers' block?

Tuesday February 28th

A black day

The Occupy camp has been removed from the forecourt of St Paul's Cathedral. Sam and Xanthe wore head-to-toe black with scarlet armbands, and spent the whole day tweeting.

I felt like doing the same but without the tweeting, but it has nothing to do with Occupy.

I watched the same episode of *Neighbours* twice. *Neighbours* has its charms, especially when your aim is to escape the real world.

today's tweet from **@sallystoneymoor**
Do you see escapism as good or bad?

Wednesday February 29th

Empty day

Is anything nice ever going to happen again?

today's tweet from **@sallystoneymoor**
I came across some new hype for 2012: the concept of 29th Feb as an EXTRA day to do something special

MARCH

Thursday March 1st

Internet dating

"Look at this one," said Wendy, "He's 62 and he calls himself Literato and he says – It's a beautiful early spring day. I can hear a blackbird singing in the garden and I can see a blush of green on the honeysuckle and I should be outside, but I'm trying to plan my future. Would you like to be part of it? Well, Sal, what do you think?"

"I'm not sure that the phrase a blush of green works. I mean, blushes are usually pink…" I trailed off.

Wendy was in my kitchen with her iPad (even Wendy has one now). She'd persuaded me to take 15 minutes break from work and look at *The Cupid Column* website.

"How about this one?" she asked. "Here's what I like – Northern hills, laughing, cinema not theatre, flowers with a scent, Venice, Yorkshire tea, good bread. I've been described as a good lover…"

"Oh, yuk! Fancy having that on your profile! He was doing all right with his hills and his laughing and his tea but – oh dear! I want a good lover, but I don't want one who's prepared to describe himself as such to the whole of the cybersphere! Switch it off! It's not for me, Wendy. Ooh, no. Kit and I might be finished, but I can't do internet dating. It's too much like a cattle market."

"Loosen up, I'm not asking you to register today. I just wanted you to see how it works."

"Maybe Richard should have a go. His last attempt ended in tears. He contacted someone who was advertising in the dating section of the Ad Mag. He'd picked it up to see about some car parts. He rang the woman and before they'd got as far as describing their hobbies, she was listing the equipment she had in her bedroom – shackles, clamps, carabinas, cable ties – and it freaked him out. Poor Richard. He couldn't open his Screwfix catalogue for days."

"I know. He told me. We talk about our dates – share tips." She hurriedly switched off her iPad. "Anyway, must be off. I have a date to go to. You never said what you thought of my outfit. I got it on eBay."

I perused her navy and white striped jumper with a sailor collar, and navy bell-bottomed trousers with three buttons down each hip.

"Very nice." Wendy has so many outfits with a nautical theme, I couldn't think of anything new to say.

"Is it a bit much?" she said. "I'm meeting a guy off the uniform site. Do you think it might be a bit weird for a traffic warden to be walking down the street with a sailor?"

"Traffic warden?"

"I know, I know. But he looked really cute in his picture."

Later:

I just solved a mystery that's puzzled me for years. i.e. why do you sometimes get spare blank pages at the ends of books after the text has finished? Answer: because for litho-printed books, the number of pages in the book has to be divisible by 16. This means that if your text covers 328 pages (as mine does) you are left with 8 spare pages.

I also found out that the pages at the beginning of the book, before the text of the novel starts – the pages covering *About the Author*, other books published, details of the printer, dedications, all that jazz – are called 'prelims.' Does the fact that I find this stuff fascinating mean I'm becoming a self-publishing geek?

today's tweet from **@sallystoneymoor**
How would you describe yourself in just two sentences?

Friday March 2nd
Not a good look

I was sitting in the sunshine on our front patio, drinking coffee, pondering how to write the novel's 'Hook' (a situation that irrevocably binds Jenny and Liam together). I'd been gardening for two hours and I was zonked. I was wearing an ancient, stained, and shapeless mustard-coloured cable jumper of Gus's (that somehow escaped my autumn cull) with 80's jeans that tapered me into the shape of a golf tee. I hadn't washed my hair because I was going to have a shower when I'd finished. I looked appalling. So who decided to call at that very moment?

I heard his car racing down Goose Lane. He swerved into the drive, skidded on the gravel, turned the engine off, leaped out, slammed the door, and charged down the drive towards the patio.

"Game on," he shouted across the lawn.

"Game on?" I said, as he rounded the pile of buddleia prunings on the path. I couldn't stop a gigantic smile from spreading across my chops – it was so lovely that he was coming to see me! "And what's game on supposed to mean, Mr Wyatt?" I was frantically combing my hair with my fingers and tweaking out bits of twig, pulling my sweatshirt down over 'those problem areas' and wishing I was wearing different jeans.

"I've phoned Brick and told him about us and he's fine. Told Gray – well, he knew anyway. Just had coffee with Scarlet and Peony and told them. So – game on." He sat down on the bench opposite, tapping his fingers on the arm of the bench, up and down, up and down.

I couldn't speak. I just sat there looking at him, smiling inanely.

"So," he went on, "can we stop this stupid stand-off? We're not young. We don't have time to waste on striking poses and clinging to entrenched positions and all the rest of that crap. You could develop a dodgy hip next week. I could get cancer the week after that."

Tears of joy and relief filled my eyes. And his voice – oh, his voice.

"What's up?" he said. "It's not all over is it? I did wonder, when you didn't mention my Valentine."

"I thought it was from someone else," I managed to whisper.

"Who?"

"It doesn't matter. I only wanted one from you."

Before I could say anything else, or even wipe my eyes, the front door opened and Sam came out. "Xanthe wants to know if you've got any tahini. What's up with you?"

"Nothing. I've got something in my eye. Come here, Sam. I want to introduce you. Kit – meet Sam. Sam – this is Kit Wyatt, my printer. Well, not my printer, but the printer who's printing my book."

Sam said, "Hi."

Kit stood up to shake his hand and then sat down again.

I said, "And he's also a friend."

Sam said, "OK. Nice to meet you." He turned to me. "Tahini?"

"No. Sorry."

He went back inside.

As soon as the door closed, Kit burst out – "A friend! You told him I was a friend! So I've been in the dog house for a month and you haven't told your kids about me!"

"There was no you and me until five minutes ago."

"There was when Sam came out!"

"Oh, do shut up. It won't be an issue for my kids. Now I know it's game on, as you so elegantly put it, I'll tell them. I want to do it when I'm on my own with Sam. Is that unreasonable?"

"Whatever. It's good to see you, Daise, even if you are looking a bit..." he wrinkled his nose. "So are you going to spend the day with me and come to Fischer's tonight? I've reserved a table and a room and I need to ring and confirm by noon."

Fischer's! This man knows the way to my heart.

Fischer's is in a village five miles away from Stoneymoor. It's an exclusive country house restaurant with rooms. Pop stars doing a gig in Sheffield stay there. Famous actors performing at the Sheffield Lyceum hang out there. Locals go there for a special treat. The ambience and the food and the service are what make it special.

"But you will get changed, won't you? I don't think the ragamuffin look is quite right for Fischer's."

"This is my gardening get-up, you cheeky thing!"

"Oh – almost forgot – I've got something in my car you might like." He jumped up and went to his car and brought back a jiffy bag. I looked inside. It was my book! The approval copy of my beautiful book!

"Thank you! Thank you!" I shrieked. "Isn't it fab? Isn't it, oh, isn't it..."

I stroked it and sniffed it and opened it and flicked it, and put it to my cheek to feel the smoothness and the newness, then I stroked it again and laid it carefully on the patio table on top of the jiffy bag. And then I flung my arms round his neck and kissed him as if I hadn't seen him for weeks. (Which I hadn't.)

"Well, I don't know," he said between kisses. "I tell you it's 'game on' and you sit there as limp as a left-over lettuce leaf, only manage a smile as paltry as PG Tips, and speak in a voice as quiet as a mid-list novel, and then I give you a book and you more or less ravish me. I'll make a note for future reference."

As paltry as PG Tips...even Kit can do similes better than me.

Talking in bed...

Kit: "All that wasted time! Four God-awful weeks! What did you do?"

Me: "I worked. I missed you. I worked. I missed you. I went to the Hockney. You weren't there. I came home. I missed you. I worked. And I watched *Neighbours* twice a day. I always do that when I'm miserable."

Kit: "You're kidding me. That crappy soap the kids were always watching when I got home from work?"

Me: "I'm in very good company. Philip Pullman watches *Neighbours*."

Kit: "I'm not knocking your writing, Daise. I know how good you are. I've just read Fast Work. But I wouldn't say you're in the same league as Philip Pullman."

Me: (THINKS) He read my book! He read my book! And he likes my writing!

Me: (SPEAKING) "You have to realise, Kit, that a writer can learn from any fiction, good or bad. It shows you what mistakes to avoid in your own writing – caricatures, poor plotting, unconvincing dialogue. Watching *Neighbours* is educative. You don't think I watch it for entertainment do you?"

I really haven't known him long enough to tell him the truth: that *Neighbours* is fab, that I love all the stupid plotlines – the amnesia, disputed paternity, blackmail, on-off love affairs, business wars, mistaken identities, manipulative ex-girlfriends, violent ex-boyfriends, people stuck down mine shafts, plane crashes that kill off half the street. And the characters – Paul Robinson, Karl Kennedy, Lucas, Jade – they're like family. One day I'll confess to him, but not just yet.

Me: "What about you? What did you get up to, apart from reading my book? I am so chuffed you read it!"

Kit: "Why not? It's very funny. Hmm, well, apart from that it was work. And cycling. I had to get my endorphins from somewhere. Then Hockney – what a shame we couldn't go together. And work. And cycling. I used to ride along the Trail hoping I'd bump into you – not literally. Once is enough for that kind of caper. But whatever I was doing, Daise, you were always on my mind. You were always on my mind."

Who needs Willie Nelson?

today's tweet from **@sallystoneymoor**
Save the sweet talk – grand gestures do it every time. On second thoughts, I'd like the sweet talk as well.

Saturday March 3rd

Recap

The reports are all true – Fischer's is fab. I loved it all – from the long winding tree-lined drive to the squishy sofa in the lounge that I could hardly get out of after one Bloody Mary, to the private dining room where Kit and I had our dinner. Private dining room!!! I have never eaten at a restaurant in a private dining room before. It sounds so debauched. In fact, the private dining room at Fischer's is called "The Study." It has cosy wallpaper and a dresser with china and old books, and a bookshelf in the corner filled with cookery books. We had crisp white table linen and candles, and our own cute waiter in white shirt and black waistcoat. (Until I met Kit I never realised I had a fetish for men in white shirts with waistcoats.)

The food was good. Kit was raving about the beef. Well, the food would have to be good – the place has a Michelin star. Me, I loved the great big golden surprise treat of being there with Kit, the classy bedroom with the blue and white striped wallpaper and the thick white cotton counterpane, and the view through the leaded windows of the Chatsworth hunting tower peeping out of the trees on the hillside.

And we had those white waffle dressing gowns which I adore – the luxury of it! Ooh, I do lead a sheltered life. I bet Anita Shreve stays in hotels with white waffle dressing gowns all the time. Everything about the place whispered *class* and *comfort*, right down to the handmade tablets of lemon grass soap in the bathroom. We even had real ground coffee from Pollards on the hospitality table in our bedroom. The only thing missing was Yorkshire tea, but I can manage without Yorkshire tea as long as I have Kit. (?)

Talking in bed...

Me: "Does it bother you that I've only got one breast? Does it feel weird?"

Kit: "You still have one that works, don't you?"

Me: "What?"

Kit: "Look, I don't mind. It's just another battle scar. You're here in my arms – that's what matters."

Me (THINKS): Poor Juliet. She may have been beautiful, and will always be 49, but she's a dead 49. I am alive and wrinkly and have only one breast but I'm in bed with Kit. Poor Juliet. It's better to be alive and imperfect than perfect and dead.

today's tweet from **@sallystoneymoor**
No-one in the world can do a better job of being you than you. (Note to self to remember this.)

Monday March 5th

Telling Sam

Sam verbally assaulted me on the landing: "So tell me, Ma, where the hell were you and Richard all weekend? We couldn't find the bottle opener. We had to go down the lane and borrow one from Mrs Mountain and she wanted to rope X and me into organising the young peoples' village events for the sodding Jubilee. As if."

"Richard was away?" (Where?) "Didn't I tell you I was going to Kit's house?"

"But why did you stay over?"

"I told you that he's a friend, Sam, but he's more than that. We're a couple. An item. And, shock, horror, we sleep together."

"At your age?"

"Yes, at my age!"

"Oh, you mean for companionship. Like mates. Well, if that's what you want – cool. So long as you steer clear of the squelchy stuff."

"Listen, Sam. I know you think I've fulfilled my biological imperative and therefore I'm past it, but that's based on the premise that people only have sex in order to have children. I'm damn sure you and Xanthe don't want children." An awful thought struck me. "Do you?"

"Course not. But we're young. People your age having sex is perverted. I mean – how can you even fancy someone when they're as old as you? It's bordering on necrophilia. No offence."

"I'll have you know that the fastest growing incidence of sexually transmitted diseases is in the over-60s."

"Oh, gross. I'm out of here. I don't have to listen to this. It's as bad as listening to X reading out the technical bits from *Fifty Shades of Grey*."

Oh dear, oh dear, oh dear. Why on earth did I mention STDs?

I spent all this morning reading my beautiful book, and I found at least a dozen mistakes – missing quotation marks, a paragraph badly aligned, spelling mistakes, a lower case letter when it should be a capital, etc, etc. It is really weird that you can go through something a zillion times, and mistakes will still elude your eye. I worked like stink, so that by 2 o'clock, I'd sent a corrected PDF of the text to Kit, along with a couple of miscellaneous requests, such as – "Please will you slot in that tree symbol on the title-verso page that shows the paper comes from managed forests?" (I feel like a real publisher when I use terms like title-verso.)

At lunchtime I asked Richard where he'd been all weekend. "Are you leading a secret life, Richard?"

"I was here! I was working in the shed! The only time I went out was to Penrose. Wendy came with me and distracted the staff while I measured a chest of drawers. She's surprisingly good at it. She cornered both of the assistants in the entrance bit by the till and when I'd finished measuring, they were so engrossed in a conversation about clothes, I had trouble hauling her away. She is a card. She does make me laugh."

Hmm. Wendy is expert at distracting anyone from their work.

today's tweet from **@sallystoneymoor**
How come errors only become glaring once they're in print?

Tuesday March 6th

Pippa goes shopping

I woke up today, thinking – *My book is fab. I can't wait for the new approval copy to come.* Then I picked up the imperfect copy from my bedside table to have a little gloat despite its imperfections, because it's my book! And I've done it all on my own! And I am impossibly proud of it! And if I don't stop using exclamation marks my writer's voice will suffer permanent damage!

I worked for three hours solid, and in the middle of the morning went outside, gasping for fresh air, trying to clear my head. It's not just getting it into print, it's all the other new things I'm having to get to grips with now I'm a publisher. And then there are all the annoying people I'm having to deal with, such as Fifi Swallow, a writer whose novels are published by the publisher of *Fast Work*. When her novel came out, she asked if I would interview her on my blog, and I did: I gave her a big splash. Then she brought out a second book and I covered her again. This morning I emailed her and asked her to return the favour, and she responded with a mingy one-line email: "I think I'll pass," as if I was offering her a chocolate biscuit. I think I'll pass?? I think I'll pass?????? What happened to the idea that fellow authors should stick together and be supportive? With an *I think I'll pass* attitude, she'll never get a writing buddie as described in *Mslexia*. I think I'll pass, my…foot.

So there I was in the front garden, ripping up dandelions to get her out of my system, when I heard a voice – "Sall-lee! Coo-ee!" It was Pippa on the lane, walking one of the blessed hounds.

"Hi, Pippa. Have you lost the other dog? Why only one today?"

"Really, Sally. As if I could lose one. And this is Maisie. But you're teasing. You know that the one with this little bit of extra fringe is Maisie. You know. Yes you do."

"So where is Millie?"

"Poor dear Millie has strained one of her hind legs. She has to rest. But oh we do miss her on our walks, don't we Maisie? Yes we do."

"You should borrow Gus's sack barrow and take her out on that," I said as a joke.

"I have a better solution. Yes I do. Look at this!" And she thrust the advert under my nose. A pet stroller. It looked like a mini baby buggy with a Scotch terrier riding in it. "It's arriving this afternoon." She looked at her watch. "I must dash. I'm meeting Glenny-Wenny – I mean Glenys – you know Glenys Wallis? I'm meeting her for lunch. It's a business lunch. That's what it is. Village Hall business. Yes."

I believe you, Pippa. Thousands wouldn't.

today's tweet from **@sallystoneymoor**
"Live fast, die young, and have a good looking corpse" –who said that?

Random!

Wednesday March 7th
Official introduction

I was driving through Rowsley today and couldn't resist calling in to see Kit at work. Gray was on reception and said a warm hello and then, "Go on down. I know you won't be disturbing him. Scar and Pee are there."

And I thought – Damn. If I'd known, I'd have put on some mascara and my better jeans.

I knocked on his door and he called out "Come!" and I opened the door and peered round.

"Daise! Great!" He grabbed my hand and kissed me on the cheek. "The perfect chance to introduce you to my girls!" He was beaming, the girls were scowling. "Girls, this is Sally. And Daise, this is Peony," pointing to the one with the more angular face, "and this is Scarlet, or Scarlie."

"Scarlet, Dad!" said Scarlet, firmly.

And then there was a chasm of silence.

And I was thinking *What the hell do I do next?* Handshakes? Too formal, and out of the question when the girls had their arms rigid and clamped to their sides. Hugs? Definitely not. Big smile? Not a runner, as both of them had their gazes glued to their pretty designer boots.

In the end, I cleared my throat in the hope of getting their attention, and said, "Hi," in a stupid voice that came out ridiculously high, and I waved – a prissy little wave, as if I was polishing a mirror right in front of me.

And Peony said "Scar, we really must…"

"Dash," said Scarlet. "Yes, we must. I've got to deliver…"

"That artwork," said Peony. "She's got to deliver some art work. So Dad, we'll catch up with you another time. OK?"

They were finishing each other's sentences! And so obviously making up an excuse to leave.

They bustled out, and their giggles were all too audible as they scuttled down the corridor. I pictured them nudging each other and saying *Oh my God!* in between their sniggers.

I made no comment to Kit, I just smiled uncertainly at him, and he beamed back and said, "I'm glad that's done. It went well, didn't it?"

today's tweet from **@sallystoneymoor**
Love is blind.

Thursday March 8th

An auspicious date

My book is coming out in May, in time for the holiday season, and I'm hoping to have the launch at Hassop Station, in the Café and the Bookshop, but I was dithering over the date. I mentioned this to Wendy.

"Ooh, elective astrology! I've always wanted to have a go at this! I'll pick you an auspicious date." She took her ephemeris out of her bag and opened it, and then said "Durrrh, I'm going to have to do this at home cos I don't have your birth chart imprinted on my mind."

At teatime she re-appeared on the doorstep, hyperventilating with excitement. "It has to be May 11th – Jupiter is conjunct your moon, it's your Mars return, Uranus is trining your Ascendant, and Saturn is smack on your Sun Mercury conjunction in the 10th house. I've never seen such a lovely line-up. The sky's the limit! Hey, maybe your book will sell so well that your agent will get back on board and sell the film rights. Wow! The Oscars! You'll need someone to hold your hand, so you'll take me, won't you? What shall I wear?"

By the time she left, I was expecting an imminent phone call from Hollywood and a FedEx van screeching to a halt at the gate, bearing first class air tickets to Los Angeles. And then I remembered that the book has not yet been published and no-one but me knows anything about it.

today's tweet from **@sallystoneymoor**
I've blogged some tips on planning book launches for all you first time self-publishers. Check out sallystoneymoor.com
#booklaunches

today's tweet from **@sallystoneymoor**
Have your launch in a bookshop, then introverts can lurk behind bookshelves when the socialising gets too much for them
#booklaunches

today's tweet from **@sallystoneymoor**
ooh, ooh, don't forget you can claim the cost of refreshments (and anything else) against tax. #selfpublishing

Golly, three tweets in one day. I am on fire!

Friday March 9th

Reading matter

Richard and I were both in tonight, sitting by the fire. Sam and Xanthe usually stay in their room in the evening. For this relief much thanks. It's bad enough having her hogging the kitchen and leaving the pans to soak in the sink for days, without her sharing my sitting room and tut-tutting about our bourgeois choice of telly progs.

Not that we were watching the telly tonight. Richard was leafing through his *Screwfix* catalogue while I drooled over the new one from *Toast*. I love this season's linen collarless shirt in cornflower blue, but it's £95, for heaven's sake. When my new book becomes a runaway bestseller rivalling the success of *Fifty Shades,* I shall treat myself to something from *Toast*. In the meantime all I can afford is a hankie, and only then when it's reduced in the sale.

Richard was hankering after something rather different…

"I really miss having an angle iron."

"What's that for?

"Propping things up, scribing along. It's a stalwart lieutenant. It doesn't do much, but what it does, it does very well. Ooh, and look at these spokeshaves – why am I so susceptible to the charms of spokeshaves?"

today's tweet from **@sallystoneymoor**
If my ship came in I'd get a new wardrobe, in both senses of the word.

Saturday March 10th

Spectre at the feast

There I was all week, longing for the weekend so I could spend it with Kit, and what happens? Peony and Scarlet descended after lunch today, and stayed until 8 o'clock. 8 o' clock!

Kit and I came home mid-afternoon from a really nice walk in Bradford Dale and found Peony's car in the drive, and I nipped upstairs to take off my tight jeans, and found the girls in our bedroom with random clothes strewn on the bed. Peony was in platform sandals and a Laura Ashley floaty number, posing in front of the mirror, and Scarlet was sitting on the basket chair, pulling on a pair of thigh high boots to go with her black velvet mini-dress.

When I saw them, my mouth dropped open, and when they saw me, theirs did the same. Who would get their jaws back into operation first?

Scarlet. But her sweet Laura Ashley smile had vanished. She turned to Peony and stage-whispered: "What the hell is she doing here?"

I could have asked her the same question, but instead I blurted out some ridiculous apology (!) and ran out onto the landing, and as I stood there taking deep deep breaths to calm me down, I thought – *Bloody hell, they are in what amounts to my bedroom! I should have been asking them what they were doing in there. And talking about me like that as if I wasn't there! How rude!*

I stood at the top of the stairs for a few minutes, dithering as to whether to go back in the bedroom and ask them to leave, so I could change. I chickened out and went downstairs. Kit was in the kitchen leaning his bum against the Aga in his usual pose, and I went over and snuggled up for a comforting hug. "The girls are here. Did you know?" I said.

"Oh yes – Peony rang and said they might come." They were apparently raiding Juliet's clothes for something to wear to a 1970's fancy dress party. Yep, the wardrobe in Kit's bedroom is still full of Juliet's stuff, and so is the wardrobe in the spare room. She was a woman with a serious clothes habit. I would have liked to have been a woman with a serious clothes habit: I've just never had the money.

Kit had just finished explaining, when Peony and Scarlet bounced in and twirled in front of us and said, "Hey, Dad, what do you reckon?"

"You both look gorgeous. Just like your mother. It's such a shame she can't see you. She'd love it that you're enjoying her clothes so much."

The kettle was whistling, so I ignored them all and made a pot of tea. I put stuff on a tray and carried it into the sitting room, saying to Kit as I left, "Are you coming?" but he was laughing with the gurls (my new spelling for the horrors) and he didn't hear me. Eventually he followed. When I went back in the kitchen to fetch some shortbread, the girls were sitting on the bar stools, sipping wine, their delicate knees crossed. The sight of their long slender legs reminded me that not even my little finger could be described as slender. They were purring over what looked like the family photo albums. Then I saw what they were drinking. They'd opened the bottle of wine that Kit and I bought in Bakewell and were chilling for later – and it was a decent

Sancerre from Hattersley's, not some 2 for £10 stuff from the Co-op. The cheek! I retreated to Kit in the sitting room and told him about the wine, but he said I should leave it: he had another bottle of something in the pantry, and it was so nice to have them there enjoying themselves, wasn't it? I mumbled something inaudible. My only meagre satisfaction – and this was clutching at straws – was that the wine they were drinking couldn't have been properly chilled.

Later, I tried an ice-breaker by asking if they needed any help with alterations, as the dresses seemed a little on the large size, but they ignored my offer completely, as if they were deaf.

They behaved as if I was a ghost, a spectre, an irrelevance. They talked to their father, and never to me, even though I tried to be friendly. There were a lot of dead eyes and looking daggers, but not in an obvious way, so when I pointed it out to Kit tonight, he said, "I think you're imagining it, Daise. I expect it's a bit awkward for you when they're here to get Juliet's clothes and there's so much talk about Juliet, and when she wore something, and where she got it from, and then they get out the photo albums to look at her wearing the dresses. It's bound to make you feel a bit de trop."

He hasn't got *a clue*. The only heartening thing about the whole affair was discovering that Juliet was a size 14, like me, so unless she was seven foot tall, it's unlikely she had slender hips.

Just remembered. Peony did speak to me once. I was in the kitchen, checking on the casserole, and spotted what looked like a tiny Santa hat on top of the dresser. I went over and found a cache of tiny cat costumes. I was cooing over the soft pompoms on a Pierrot one when Peony rushed over and snatched it from me. "Those are personal, family things!" she hissed. She gathered up the clothes and said "They're Witty's. Nothing to do with you!" She left the room as I was saying, "Oh, yes. Poor Witty."

Talking in bed...

Me: "You're frowning. What's the matter?"

Kit: "Just worrying about this awful recession, money, my business. Let's talk about something else."

Me: "OK. Here's something I wanted to ask you...You know incy wincy spider? Do you think it's his actual name?"

Kit: "What?"

Me: "Do you think it's his actual name, like Incy Wincy Spider, with capitals: capital I capital W capital S, like The Artist Formerly Known as Prince? Or is the incy wincy bit just an adjective? You know – like – an incy-wincy spider was climbing up a–"

Kit: "I think it's like a newspaper report: Incy Wincy – *comma* – spider – *comma* – age 43 – *comma* – found climbing up a drainpipe."

I love this man. I can say ridiculous things to him and he responds in kind without missing a beat.

today's tweet from **@sallystoneymoor**
Nostalgia ain't what it used to be.

Sunday March 11th

Who's 'de trop' now?

Kit and I came home from a lovely walk along the river this morning to find Pee and the Scarlet woman staggering around the kitchen with hang-overs the size of Russia. Last night's party was down the road from Kit's house, so they came back to sleep at Kit's. They spent all day loafing around in the public areas, and Kit resisted my suggestion that we should retreat to his bedroom with the weekend papers.

"It would be weird and uncomfortable," he said. "And it's my house. Anyway, they'll be coming upstairs to return all the clothes to the wardrobes."

Ah yes, all those clothes that were strewn all over the furniture in the sitting room. Did they buffalo return them to the wardrobes. They sloped off at teatime leaving a trail of detritus, without bothering to say goodbye to me, and there was I in the kitchen making a meal for the four of us. How long will they go on behaving like spoiled brats? It's so obvious that they are the reason Kit hasn't been snapped up by someone before now. It's got nothing to do with women wanting him to retire and have afternoon tea in garden centres.

today's tweet from **@sallystoneymoor**
Yay! to lazy Sundays, and catching up with home stuff!

Monday March 12th

Busy busy busy

Kit gave me my new pre-release approval copy on Saturday. It is 99.999% perfect and I love it, love it, love it. But I have to send a pre-release copy to the buyers at the wholesalers, Gardners, to persuade them to stock it. I kissed my baby goodbye and posted it with all the bumph (a letter about what a wonderful writer I am, my marketing plan, and an AI sheet) and then I came home and emailed a proposal to Radio 4 *Woman's Hour*, to see if they would consider having me on to talk about the themes in my book. On Nina's advice, I suggested a studio discussion, as I'm not famous enough to warrant a one-to-one interview. I do hope they'll consider it.

Then I rang two local radio stations and arranged for them to interview me in May, and then I started to write a self-publishing blog post about the importance of getting a wholesaler. But the post was so dreary and boring, I scrapped it.

today's tweet from **@sallystoneymoor**
I've got just 1 copy here of my brand new book and I've got to give it to someone in the book trade to read. I can't bear to part with it!

Tuesday March 13th

Worrying behaviour

"What is it you do on the internet?" asked Richard as he wiped the kitchen worktop (pretending to be nonchalant).

I sipped my Earl Grey tea and thought. "A bit of research for publishing purposes, writing my blog, looking things up on Wikipedia, tweeting, looking at books on Amazon. Not much."

He put some crumbs in the bin and turned round to look at me. "What kind of research?"

"Well, yesterday I wanted to know what the theme tune of Captain Pugwash was, because in Chapter 15, Jenny is humming it when she's on the punt in Cambridge. You see, Liam gets in and–"

"Yes, yes. But do you go in chat rooms? Wendy does." He turned back, rinsed the dishcloth under the tap and squeezed it.

"Absolutely not. I go to my study to get away from chat."

He put down the dishcloth and sat down opposite me. "There was a woman in *The Recorder* at the weekend whose husband was posting photographs of himself on the internet. He was posing naked on their sofa, with a digitally enhanced penis."

"What?" I choked and spluttered. "Oh God, the tea's gone down my nose."

"Incredible, isn't it? He'd have been much better off posting photos of his power tools on the net and digitally enhancing the blade on the band-saw."

today's tweet from **@sallystoneymoor**
Proper primroses are out on the grassy bank near our village shop.

Wednesday March 14th

Disclosure

I was meeting Kit today for lunch at Hassop Station and took the opportunity to ask the manager about my book launch. He was lovely; and he said yes. And May 11th is a good date for them as well as for me. Excellent: another thing on my massive list ticked off.

While I was waiting for Kit, I hung around in the bookshop and meandered into the non-fiction section, which I don't usually visit, and found a book called *Love in Later Life: the joys and pitfalls*. I thought it might cover adult children's reactions to their parents' new partners. I picked it up and was flicking through it, and then noticed Pippa a few feet away, engrossed in a book called *From Straight to Gay in Three Easy Steps*.

She looked up and saw me smirking, and probably guessed I could see what she was reading, as she blushed crimson.

"Oh, Sally. Hello! I, um, can you keep a secret? Can you? Oh my, I didn't want to tell anyone yet, but..."

We had a brief disclosure chat, and I said I hoped she'd be very happy. Then she left, and Kit arrived, and I rushed over to tell him the news. But as he has never met either Pippa or Glenny Wenny, and as he's only said a brief "Hello" to Richard on a couple of occasions, he wasn't exactly gripped. So we talked about other things, and I had a lovelylovelylovely time. Not one offspring of either marriage was mentioned; we covered our respective tastes in art, and where we should go on holiday this coming September, and whether either of us could spare the time from our work to go on a US road trip – something that we're both very keen on.

When I got home I rushed to the shed and told Richard the news about Pippa, and he said, "Hmm. How does that make me feel? I'm not sure. Did you have a nice lunch with Kit?" Then he picked up a plane and resumed his work.

I have to say that in writerly terms, this was a mega-disappointing reaction. I had been thinking it would be an interesting plot point for a heterosexual woman to start being gay, and I wanted to know how an ex-partner might feel about it. Maybe I can explore it with Richard later.

today's tweet from **@sallystoneymoor**
Celandines come out in the sun, even sunnier than sunflowers.

Thursday March 15th

Hooray!

Hooray, Richard has gone to stay with a friend in Newcastle until Monday, and tomorrow, Sam and Xanthe are going to see some friends of Xanthe's, who live on an old rusty barge on the Oxford Canal near Cropredy. I'll have an empty house!

today's tweet from **@sallystoneymoor**
Home alone – almost.

Friday March 16th

Solitude

I am in heaven. I am here in the house on my own. It is so long since I was here on my own that I feel like sitting and doing nothing, luxuriating in the peace and quiet and the lack of people wanting to talk to me. Bliss. The only person I have seen so far is Gray, who delivered all the pre-release copies of my book.

Later: I have worked my way down a huge list of dull self-publishing tasks, which included parcelling up 24 copies of the book to send to journalists and local radio presenters, bookshops where I am having signings, and famous authors I like, in the vain hope they will read the book and give me a nice comment to print on the back of the final version (some hope!). Even after all of this, my brain is still perky enough to be able to write. This is what solitude does for a person. Is this why Gus likes it so much?

Later still: Yay! 1,342 words achieved on the current novel. I am on fire!

today's tweet from **@sallystoneymoor**
in bed with cat and laptop in an empty house=perfect conditions for writing. yay! #writing

Saturday March 17th

Persona non grata

This is the first weekend that my house has been empty since Kit and I were an established item, so I invited him over to stay. It felt so nice to have him here, in my kitchen, in my sitting room, in my bedroom, in my bed. Last night we ate at Le Bistro in Bakewell, and this morning we stayed in bed late with the papers. Then we had brunch and went for a bike ride on the Trail. Kit has all the gear – black lycra shorts, a cycling jersey with useful back pockets where he stows a miniscule fold-up rain jacket and his energy gel sachets and a spare inner tube. He wears clip-on shoes, with over-shoes (that make his feet look like a gnome's) and a snazzy streamlined silver helmet. I, on the other hand, go cycling in a kagoule and a sweatshirt, with jeans tucked into my socks at the ankle. His bike is smart and sleek and expensive. Mine is twenty years old and tatty, with the mudguards fixed on with cable ties and a shopping basket on the handlebars. He scorns mudguards, never mind ones held on with cable ties, though sometimes in the winter he uses a crud-catcher. I could see him looking askance at my clothes and my bike and I said, "Are you ashamed to be seen with me?"

"Of course not! But you won't mind if I go at my usual pace, will you, which means I might leave you behind. How about if I wait for you at Miller's Dale?"

Yes, I was miffed. What is it about men and bikes and gear and equipment?

I texted Wendy about it later and she texted back, "What do you expect from a Leo?"

It's a bit of a shock being with a man who cares so much about his clothes. Of course Iain is vain, but Richard has not a clue about style, and Gus's taste is decidedly suspect, plus he couldn't care less what other people think.

We drove with the bikes to Hassop Station and set off from there. I decided to enjoy the ride for its own sake and ignore the fact that Kit and I were supposed to be on the ride together. I shan't be going out with him on another bike ride. What's the point, when after three minutes he's a dot on the horizon?

By the time I got back to Hassop, Kit had already loaded his bike onto the back of his car, pulled on a spare jumper to keep warm, and was chatting to a guy with a bike with strange gears. (Kit told me why they were strange but I wasn't listening.) When we went in the café for a drink and a snack, I noticed Peony and Scarlet sitting at a table in the function room. I pointed them out to Kit and he blanched.

"Look!" I said, "Can you see them over there? I think we should go over – we have to, now they've seen us – it's too awkward not to." I was thinking that the more time I spent with them, the sooner they'd get to realise that I am not after their inheritance, I am not out to replace their mother, and when you get to know me, I'm actually OK.

"Oh, but...but I was enjoying a bit of together-time," he said. "Just you and me."

"Don't give me that guff. If you felt like that, why didn't you cycle with me on the Trail?"

"It's all about pace, Daise. It's not personal. I just can't be comfortable cycling at the speed of a snail."

The cheek!

"Come on Kit, I don't want to stay wicked forever. The only way for things to improve is for them to get to know me." And I marched over in their direction, with Kit trailing behind me. When I reached their table, they looked at me as if I was emitting a nasty odour, and I suddenly lost my nerve and stepped aside and let Kit take over.

"Hi," he said. "I didn't know you two came here. What's going on?"

Scarlet said: "We're on our way home to get some stuff, but Pee was desperate for a caffeine hit."

"Do you mind if we join you?" I said, pulling out a chair.

"Whatever," said Scarlet, with a huge sigh. She took her bag and coat off the chair I was holding, making a huge performance out of it, as if it was a feat as taxing as the Tour de France.

I told Kit what I wanted as a snack and he went off to the counter to get it. I sat with the girls, and tried to think of something to say. Lost for inspiration, I came out with something worthy of a new hairdresser: "Are you off out tonight? Doing anything exciting this weekend? Got any plans?"

This question was met with two sets of perfect lips – both pursed. I looked without flinching or blinking from Peony to Scarlet and back again, making it plain I was expecting an answer.

Peony caved in first.

"So have we got anything exciting planned, Scar?" she said.

"It depends what she means by exciting, Pee."

They looked at each other and smirked, and then after what seemed like forever, Scarlet looked at me and said, "We're certainly not staying in for a *Dad's Army* repeat."

The cheek!

Why did they have to be so nasty? I hate this "she" business.

When Kit came back, he and the gurls chatted normally. Every time I joined in, they ignored what I'd said, or addressed their answer to Kit. Grrrhhh!

today's tweet from **@sallystoneymoor**
Great bike ride out on the Monsal Trail today! 15 whizzy miles!

Back at home, I lit the fire, and while Kit shouted at the rugby on telly, I made a fish pie and an apple crumble, slurping a glass of Sauvignon Blanc and singing along to Fred Astaire while I was cooking. It was so comfortable to have him there in my house. I like his house, and I like being there alone with him, but it's not my house, and Juliet is everywhere, not just in photographs, but in the taste, the furnishings, even the garden. And now my existence as Kit's 'partner' is out in the open, one or other of the kids drops in (because Kit doesn't hide my existence and attempt to keep us apart) and if it's the gurls, it's horrid. So to have him here in my house was magic. We ate in the kitchen, which is so much more friendly than the dining room, and we were just finishing our pudding, and about to go and get comfortable in the sitting room, when the front door slammed and Richard appeared in the doorway.

"Mike had a heart attack!" (Richard has hundreds of friends and they're all called Mike.) "I went with him in the ambulance, and stayed while they got him sorted and rang his wife and told her and he's going to be OK, but oh – give me a drink. I've had a hellish journey home."

So all three of us went and sat by the fire. It seemed mean to banish Richard to his room.

Talking in bed...

Me: "Richard's friend Mike is only 57. Younger than us! It's scary, isn't it?"

Kit: "It's times like this you realise you shouldn't be neglecting your bucket list."

Me: "Bucket list? What's a bucket list?"

Kit: "Haven't you got one? It's the list of things you want to do before you die – before you kick the bucket."

Me: "Oh, I've got one – just without the title. A little list in the front of my Writer's Diary, stuff like going to Venice again, seeing Fleetwood Mac live, visiting the *Neighbours* set in Australia."

Kit: "Seeing Fleetwood Mac live! Really? That's one of mine."

Me: "What else is on yours then?"

Kit: "Number one has to be doing a US road trip."

Me: "Yes! Yes! Why didn't I think of that? I'm definitely adding that to my list!"

Kit: "Maybe we should plan to do it together..."

Sunday March 18th

Scuppered

Kit stayed the night again, but it was a rather subdued night. And there were some strange noises outside in the early hours, which I put down to Baxter's tractor on the lane, but when I stumbled downstairs this morning to switch the kettle on, I found Sam's coat slung over the kitchen chair. He's back! It's so unfair! My first weekend with Kit staying here, and the lodgers who are supposed to be absent come back early. So much for a relaxed and cosy weekend with Kit chez moi. Sometimes I hate my life.

I took tea up to bed for Kit and me, and drew the curtains, and there on the drive was a rusty old caravan. Mamma mia.

Sam and Xanthe stayed in bed till 2. Yes, the caravan is theirs. Sam gave me two spotty cups and saucers (purchased by

Xanthe) as a Mother's Day present. Sweet, but no antidote to the rusty caravan.

All day, Kit and Richard circled oddly and awkwardly around each other when they met in the hall or the kitchen or when heading for the loo. It's not that they are antagonistic to each other: it's just that they seem to have nothing in common apart from the tendency to stay in the loo for extended periods.

Talking in bed...

Me: "I've been thinking about my list, my bucket list. I remembered I want to visit the village where Peter Mayle lived – you know – the guy who wrote *A Year in Provence*. Tell me what's on yours, besides the US road trip."

Kit: "Seeing the final of the Rugby World Cup – it's in England in 2015. Cycling up Mont Ventoux. Surfing on Bondi Beach."

Me: "Hmm, not much overlap, is there? – apart from the road trip and Fleetwood Mac."

Kit: "But Mont Ventoux is in Provence – you could go to see that bloke's village while I tried to get to the top of the mountain. I'd have to get into training for it though."

Me: "Did you say Bondi Beach? We could do a tour of Oz – *Neighbours* for me, Bondi Beach for you. What do you think?"

Kit: "Maybe we should start to make a joint list, a couply list."

today's tweet from **@sallystoneymoor**
Life is what happens to you while you're busy making other plans. (John Lennon)

Monday March 19th

Life is not a jubilee

The caravan was offered to Sam and Xanthe by some friends of theirs before they even got to Cropredy.

"It was like now or never, Ma. We had to make an instant decision as to whether we wanted it. And I knew you'd be cool about having it here – it slots into that turning space at the end of the drive really nicely."

"So you and Xanthe are going to move into it, then?"

"No. It's our *Sod the Jubilee* caravan. There are bound to be loads of people in the village who don't want to have anything to do with the celebrations set up by Mrs Mountain, Pippa, Pippa's woman, and the rest of the old Tories, so X and I are going to organise a set of *Sod the Jubilee* activities and the caravan will be our HQ. It's a couple of months away, so we've got plenty of time to get it sorted. What do you think?"

"I would rather not say, Sam."

AAARRGGGHHH!

today's tweet from **@sallystoneymoor**
Spotted one lonely (and preternaturally early) bluebell in the woods this morning.

Tuesday March 20th

Strange cure

Since Sunday morning, I've been feeling weirdly exhausted, and this morning all of my limbs ached and the whole of my head hurt, so Richard kindly drove me to our GP's Open Surgery.

"I've come across this kind of complaint before in other writers," said Doctor McCullen. He'd checked my blood pressure and looked in my eyes with his little torch thingy and said he could find nothing to account for all of my symptoms. "Have you been under any stress?"

"I've been working very hard – I'm publishing my own book this time – and there are one or two family difficulties" (three unwanted residents and now a caravan; plus two nasty pieces of work in another family home) "Do you think it's psychosomatic?" I said.

"Not psychosomatic as such, though it does occur more with those of an artistic sensibility. It's a physical reaction to the pressure – like a migraine. I once had a patient – in my old practice in Hampstead – who was ill from the moment her book was published until she got her first review."

"What happened if she didn't get a review?"

"If it was necessary, I made sure she did – my brother is the books editor of *The Recorder*."

Wow! "So could you get me a –"

"I'm sorry, it's time to see the next patient. Make sure you get lots of rest, Mrs Howe."

"But..."

I am going back to bed. I may be missing the best spring weather in a century, but at least I have an artistic sensibility. Yah boo, world!

today's tweet from **@sallystoneymoor**
There's a whole bank of wood anemones near Hassop.

today's tweet from **@sallystoneymoor**
I've been walking through a long grey tunnel, freezing cold, and I've stepped through a door into another dimension. Spring – Yay!

Two tweets in one day. And it was effortless! Maybe I'm getting the hang of it.

Wednesday March 21st

Golden Oldies

There was a feature on telly about Engelbert Humperdinck, who is in his 70's now (crikey!) because he is representing the UK in the Eurovision Song Contest. I suppose I should be pleased they have chosen someone so ancient. Perhaps I *would* be pleased if I could take the contest seriously, and if I liked Engelbert Humperdinck in the first place. But actually, it's an across the board *nil points* (to be said in a French accent.)

This evening, Richard and I watched a Yusuf Islam concert on the telly (the man known in a former life – mine and his – as Cat Stevens.) He played sweetly but blandly. I haven't seen him for thirty years and it was a shock: he looked old!

"Just like us," said Richard.

"Rubbish. We don't look that old."

"He's looked after his teeth, though," said Richard, as though that made everything all right.

today's tweet from **@sallystoneymoor**
Could perfect teeth be the answer to eternal youth?

Thursday March 22nd

Consolation

Still feeling crap.

Richard said, "You need something to cheer you up."

"Yes! Like what?"

"I'm not sure what to suggest for you. All I need for perfect happiness is a digging bar and a splitting mall."

today's tweet from **@sallystoneymoor**
I filled the house with daffodils from the garden. Lovely!

Are my tweets becoming nature-obsessed?

Friday March 23rd

What's in a name?

"When am I going to meet Kit?" said Wendy today. "I mean, to get a chance to say more than *Hi* to him in passing. You go on and on about how great he is, but he's a stranger to *me*."

"Do you want to see if he's suitable? Ask him about his prospects?"

"Even Richard says he doesn't really know the guy."

"Richard said that to you? OK. How about if we all go out together for a curry – you, me, Richard and Kit. Now, tell me about the traffic warden."

"He's ancient news. I ditched him. He looked really nice in his photo on the net, but when he turned up on the date, I didn't recognize him. He'd shaved his head. That is so not OK."

"How much notice do you take of men's names?" I said. "I read some research this morning that Kevins, Mandys, Chantals and Justins struggle to get dates on websites. The research said that men called Alexander were clicked on 102% more times than men called Kevin."

"I did know a sexy Kevin once…" She was lost in thought. "Nah – I don't care what they're called, as long as they're fit."

today's tweet from **@sallystoneymoor**
We need to talk about Kevin. Is the film as good as the book?

Saturday March 24th

Uncomfortable

Kit was not keen on eating out with Richard and Wendy, but as Brick came home from London last night and brought a friend along, Kit's house isn't conducive to privacy this weekend, so in the end he agreed to go out. We all went to the Maazi in Matlock. I like the Maazi – they're so friendly there and the food is amazing: it's not the usual curry-house fodder. (I like the white table-cloths, too, and the waiters dressed in Indian costume. They even have a waiter standing at the door to greet you as you go in, which is a really nice touch.)

Richard gave Wendy a lift in his car. When she went out to the loo, I whispered, "Thanks for bringing Wendy. It's very nice of you," and he said "There was no point in both of us forking out on petrol."

There were pockets of discomfort throughout the evening, but there were times of easy laughter too. We talked about:

- modern compared with old fashioned printing processes (Richard and Kit);
- local restaurants (mainly Kit and Wendy);
- walking vs cycling on the Trail and the need for a Trail highway code (K and R, with me abstaining because I still feel cross about Kit leaving me behind on our cycle ride);
- rugby vs football (K and R);
- shopping for clothes (K and W);
- the Jubilee, and Sam and Xanthe's plans for it (all of us);
- adult kids (all of us);
- ideas for my book launch party (all of us.)

Driving home to Kit's house afterwards, Kit said, "Where on earth did you dig up Wendy?"

"What do you mean?"

"I mean – she's a freakish oddball with a seriously challenged fashion IQ."

"But she's so funny!"

"Hmm."

"And I like oddballs."

"Hmm."

"And she's a really loyal friend."

"If you ever make me go out with her again, will you make sure she looks normal and decent and doesn't wear, for example, those appalling Union Jack shorts. Honestly! A woman of her age in shorts over black tights! Give me strength."

"According to Wendy, they're bang on trend, with the Jubilee and the Olympics coming up this summer."

"It's you that's the loyal friend, Daise. The woman's an out and out nutter."

Sometimes if I didn't love him, I'd hate him.

today's tweet from **@sallystoneymoor**
Greeted by a waiter in Indian dress on the pavement, then catching up with friends over dinner. Great Saturday evening. #Maazi #Matlock

Sunday March 25th

Foxed

Kit can't come to my book launch.

Kit can't come to my book launch!

We were talking about the launch at breakfast and he asked me if I'd set the date for it, and I said, "Of course I have. It's in six weeks time. I sorted it out that day we had lunch at Hassop and I found out about Pippa and…Didn't I tell you?"

I am gutted. I thought I'd mentioned it to him, and also that I'd explained how Wendy picked the date for me. Now I know what he thinks of Wendy, I'll keep quiet. I didn't actually think of checking the date with him, because with Gus long gone, I am so used to arranging things without checking with other people first.

But Kit has an unbreakable date. It's the anniversary of Juliet's death, and he and the kids always get together that night for a meal. It's an immutable family tradition.

AAARRGGGHHH.

What the hell is the point of the planets being lined up favourably for May 11th if my right hand man isn't there?

I want him at the launch. I need him at the launch. I need him to stand behind me to give me confidence and welcome people in that amazing voice, and be charming, and open bottles with his fancy-schmantzy corkscrew, and hand out drinks and be altogether charming. Or have I already mentioned the charming bit?

"What time do you think the meal will finish?" I asked.

"I don't know! We're out for an evening meal. What time do they usually finish? It depends when they start, doesn't it?"

"Well, what time does it say in your diary?"

"There isn't a time. There's just a big red box around the day. We never fix the time until…This is stupid. Can't you re-arrange the launch? Now I shan't be able to help!"

"Of course I can't re-arrange it! Anyway, I've had the invitations and the posters printed. You printed them! Didn't you read them before you printed them?"

"I had a big rush job on, so I got Terry to do them for me." Terry is his assistant.

"This is crap," I said. "Crap, crap, crap."

Bloody Juliet!

today's tweet from **@sallystoneymoor**
There are tiny green buds on my hawthorn tree. Not long now till the landscape turns green!

Monday March 26th

Another view

Me: "Richard – what do you think of Wendy's clothes? Her Union Jack shorts for example."

Richard: "Delightful. I think she's delightful."

today's tweet from **@sallystoneymoor**
Jubilee and Olympics approaching fast. What have you got with Union Jacks on?

APRIL

April Fool's Day

Talking in bed circa 3 a.m…

Me (surfacing from sleep, quasi-drugged): "Kit, Kit, Wendy wants me to go on a Senior Citizen day trip to Iceland with her, all inclusive for £10, with a good lunch. Do you think I should go?"

Kit (as if I am not talking gibberish): "What date is it?"

Me: "9th of Feb."

Kit: "Definitely go."

Me: "Why definitely?"

Kit: "It's a vile month, so you should do something to take your mind off it."

This man is perfect for me:

a/ he takes my dreams seriously

b/ he appreciates the horror that is February.

today's tweet from **@sallystoneymoor**

Dreamed of snow.......brrrrr...and I was speaking Icelandic.

Monday April 2nd

Application

A good work day.

I arranged 1/ an interview with the *Derby Evening Telegraph* – the journo is going to do a phone interview with me on Wednesday 2/ an interview with the *Sheffield Telegraph*. Their photographer will come next week, as this week he's busy covering Easter: bonnet competitions and egg hunts and other similar hoop-la.

today's tweet from **@sallystoneymoor**
The promotional train is grinding into gear...Cue the Kate Moss mascara...

Tuesday April 3rd

Work, work, work

Work, work, work.

Self-publishing is not *unpleasant* work, but neither is it *fun* work like writing.

I got my April newsletter from the Society of Authors, advertising some tax talks for writers.

As if I'm lucky enough to be a taxpayer.

today's tweet from **@sallystoneymoor**
I must be the only person in the universe longing for a tax bill.

Wednesday April 4th

More work

We woke up to snow and a power cut, which meant no electric kettle, no electric cooker and no central heating (due to lack of power to the pump). I lit the log-burning stove in the dining room and cooked porridge on there. Just as I was spooning it into the bowl, the lights went on.

Yet more publishing work, including sending out launch invitations to everyone from Pippa to Billy Bathgate to the plumber. Then I had my telephone interview with the journo from the *Derby Evening Telegraph*. I think it went OK.

today's tweet from **@sallystoneymoor**
Sometimes dreams come true, but maybe not the right ones.

Thursday April 5th

Who is Anna?

This morning's job was sending off the rest of my pre-release copies to people I hope will be interested enough to read and comment on the book, such as newspapers and weekly magazines. I've given up hope of getting cover quotes from famous authors like Jilly Cooper, Joanna Trollope or Katie Fforde. (Why have they not replied?) Gosh, it's expensive: a brand new jiffy bag, and £2.48 postage for every parcel.

This afternoon's job was driving around bookshops and libraries and post offices and anywhere that has a suitable notice board for a poster advertising my launch.

Despite being so busy, I was missing Kit.

```
Hi Kit
I am driving past you on the way to Matlock.
Could I pop in and bring a picnic lunch?
Love Daise

V. busy, but yes. 1-ish?
K x
```

I didn't have time to make Kit a specially prepared home-made treat picnic so I splashed out on bought sandwiches – bacon and egg on granary (his favourite) – and a Tarte Citron from the Co-op.

He kissed me when I arrived. Ooh, he smelled lovely, ooh, he was verging on edible in his waistcoat and white shirt with the sleeves rolled up.

"It's a bad week," he said. "One guy off sick and one revving up for paternity leave. His wife's overdue and he can't keep his mind on the job. How about you?"

"My head is exploding! I can't get the photo of my front cover to show up on PubWeb, both the wholesalers are doing a Gus and refusing to communicate with me – despite the fact that I've emailed and phoned, *and* posted them everything I can think of bar the names of my grandchildren. The Amazon ebook contract is doing my head in, and I can't find out how to get in touch with a real live person at Amazon to see if they'll stock my paperback. Do you want more?"

"Oh, you poor thing. Sit down," he said. "Would you like me to help?" He unwrapped the sandwich I'd put on his desk. "Wow! Bacon and egg! Bless you!" He took a bite. "Hmm, I think I know someone who could help you with Amazon. Here, this is his number," he said, writing it down on a post-it for me. "He's a nice guy. Just tell him I sent you. Now what else was there?"

He gave me some suggestions as to how to sort out the other stuff, but was interrupted by his mobile ringing. He checked who was calling and switched off his phone.

"Ring them back if you like – I don't mind," I said.

"No. It was Anna, the last person I want to speak to."

"Who's Anna?"

"No-one. Now, I don't know what we were talking about but I want to tell you something. Listen. You need to keep it in the back of your mind, the whole time. It's this. It will all be worth it. You're a good writer, and your book deserves to be published. And all this stress will be worth it in the end."

But before I could speak, there was a knock on the door and a man in overalls came in. "Sorry, boss. Nightmare! We need you in the print room."

Kit swore, and said "Sorry Daise, I'll have to go." He patted my shoulder and kissed my cheek and rushed off. I packed up and left.

Who is Anna?

today's tweet from **@sallystoneymoor**
Co-op Tarte Citron – not bad, when Nigella's out of town

Good Friday April 6th

The worm turns

I came downstairs for my first mug of tea this morning, put water in the kettle and switched it on, and went to sit in my favourite chair – my carver chair – and it wasn't there. Where on earth was it? Everyone knows it never leaves the kitchen. Everyone knows that if I am in the room, I am the one who sits in it. Everyone in the family knows it is *my* chair. I looked in the sitting room and the dining room but no joy, so I went back to sort out my tea and sat in another chair and fumed. I decided that Xanthe must have taken it up to Sam's room or out to the caravan. The cheek! The bare-faced cheek! Here I am, a single, mature, independent woman with her own home, and yet said home is overrun with uninvited guests, unwelcome lodgers, annoying interlopers. That's why I am a fool. The disappearing chair was just the last irritation in a huge long list of them.

And it's not only Sam and Xanthe – Richard has been here for months, supposedly looking for a house to rent or to buy, and yet houses and estate agents have not been mentioned since he moved in at New Year. He has no intention of finding his own place. It's far too comfortable here. And Sam! The boy is 28, for goodness sakes! Why is he living here on the dole with his girlfriend also on the dole and neither of them giving any sign of looking for work and paying their way? I've had enough. This worm has turned.

I went out in my pyjamas to the shed to find Richard, to tell him I wanted him to move out, and my chair was there, covered in sawdust.

"Why have you got my chair out here? It lives in the kitchen. It's my special chair! You know it is!"

He turned his head a millimetre towards me (he was sanding a joint) and said absentmindedly, "Oh yes, sorry. I meant to take it back. Wendy brought it out. She was telling me about her latest internet date and it was a long story and there was nowhere clean or comfortable for her to sit. She does make me laugh. She's a lot better company than you are these days. You're either stuck in your study being a publisher, or you're out with Kit."

What? I'm his sister, not his wife. It's not in my job description to keep him company.

"Richard, I need to talk to you."

"OK." He went on sanding his joint and then looked up and said, "Can you see some sheets of finest grade glass paper anywhere? I seem to have lost them."

This is what it's like. Someone else's agenda is always more important than mine. "Richard! I need to talk to you. Look at me."

Finally, he turned round and leaned against the work bench with his arms folded. I had his attention. "Speak," he said.

"You were very welcome to stay here at New Year, you know you were, but it was always supposed to be temporary. You've been here for three months, and there are lots of houses available now – to rent or to buy – I've just looked in the paper. I'd like you to find somewhere else to live. I'm asking Sam and Xanthe as well. I want to be on my own."

"But, I –"

"You're very welcome to carry on using the shed. That's fine. But I want the house to myself. So. Think on. The new *Peak Advertiser* is on the kitchen table."

So that told Richard.

Oddly, when I went back inside, Sam was actually up and dressed and eating his breakfast of scrambled tofu. (Yuk.)

When I told him it was time he and Xanthe moved out, he said: "That's fine. It does cramp our style a bit, living here. And it's spring, just about, so yeah. X and I have been talking about it anyway. We'll stick around for our *Sod the Jubilee* blast, and then I think we're heading for Devon. Totnes sounds cool. OK?"

I sank back into my rescued carver chair and frowned at him. "That's two months away. That is not OK."

"How about the end of April?"

I got up and looked at the calendar. "Oh, go on then."

It's weird. I am always surprised that when I summon all my inner strength and assertiveness and stick up for myself, people actually respond – and in a helpful way. Why don't I remember this, instead of spending ages pussyfooting around them because I'm afraid of an almighty and acrimonious blow-up?

today's tweet from **@sallystoneymoor**
Can't-live-without item no. 16: my favourite chair

Saturday April 7th

Oh dear

It was a nice day until teatime. Kit and I worked in his garden clearing winter debris, digging up perennial weeds, turning over the herbaceous border. The only tiny ripple in my smooth clear day was a phone call on Kit's mobile which he would not answer: "Because it's Anna." But he did not tell me who Anna is. Is she an ex? Does she want him back?

So there we were at teatime, all rosy cheeked and healthily tired after our outdoor activity, with Kit still exuding hunkiness in his Aran sweater and his jeans with the rip in the knee (which for some reason looks sexy on him, whereas on Richard it looks faintly ridiculous).

Kit was at the Aga, checking the spaghetti to see if it was al dente, Brick was sprawled on the sofa in the sitting room reading the paper (the sports section, probably) and I was standing with a handful of cutlery wondering how to set the kitchen table when the gurls had left a large box of cosmetics on it with the contents spilling out. There was oceans of it! Most of it was vintage (e.g. Mary Quant) so I guessed it was Juliet's. At this point, Peony burst into the kitchen and said, "Hi, Dad, I've just come to grab a scarf from Mum's wardrobe, I'm going to a party." (This kind of thing happens so often, I don't know a/ why they don't just take Juliet's clothes back to their places b/ what would happen if they crashed in unannounced and caught Kit and me deshabillé on the hearthrug.)

So anyway, one minute I was appraising a Brazen Bronze nail varnish that I was sure I used to have, and the next minute Peony was grabbing my arm and hissing in my ear: "Leave it alone! You have no right! Who do you think you are in my mother's house, touching her things?"

I froze, with the blinking bottle of Brazen Bronze stuck in my hand, as if it was welded there. I turned to look at Kit, and Peony let go of me and flounced out.

"Kit?"I said.

"Hey," he said, turning round, "This spag bol tastes a bit iffy. And I seem to remember the mince was right on its sell-by date. Maybe we should go to the Peacock instead — I've heard the new chef's really good. Come on — call Brick — let's go."

Grrrhhh! I wanted to whack him one! What an utter wimp, using diversionary tactics instead of facing up to his gruesome gurls. Why doesn't he do something about them?

Talking in bed…

Me: "Did you hear what Peony said to me earlier?"

Kit: "I'm not sure. I was cooking."

Me: "You heard. You know you heard. Why don't you care? And Scarlet is just as bad. Why do you let them behave like that? To speak to me like that?"

Kit: "I expect Peony has PMT. She's not a bad girl, you know. She's very affectionate."

Me: "Hmph." (THINKS – being affectionate towards one's father in no way negates being offensive to one's father's paramour. I really like that word: it's such a shame it's fallen out of general use.)

Kit: "I always found it best to ignore bad behaviour and reward the good. Don't forget they lost their mother when they were young. I think we need to cut them a bit of slack. Don't be mean-spirited, Sally. It doesn't suit you. It's not as if your kids are perfect, and *they* have no excuse."

Me: "My kids? What's wrong with my kids? You've only met Sam, as far as I am aware, and he's unfailingly polite."

Kit: "He's a scrounger! A layabout! Why do you put up with him leeching off you and contributing zip? And his girlfriend, Sandra. They're a couple of wasters. My girls are younger than Sam and they've been working and supporting themselves for years."

Me: "You sort out your kids and I'll sort out mine. What Sam does with his life is none of your business. He may be living on the edge, but he's very highly principled and cares deeply about what's important, which is not — surprise, surprise — clothes and make-up and parties. Well, obviously not make-up. And she's called Xanthe, not Sandra. And will you stop hogging the bloody duvet. How do you expect me to get to sleep if I'm freezing cold?"

today's tweet from **@sallystoneymoor**
I don't care if it is corny, I love daffodils at Easter. They're so robust, so bouncy, so yellow, so sunny side up!

Easter Sunday

Family matters

After yesterday, I wanted to ditch Kit's big Easter lunch that he always lays on for his kids. But it was the first time I'd been invited to a Wyatt family do, so it was a big deal. I really have to do my best to get on with his gurls, so I stayed and helped Kit in the kitchen, preparing the veg and the Yorkshire puds, while he was doing whatever it is he does with beef. Our time together in the kitchen was the only nice part of the day.

Talking in bed…

Kit: "Well, I think that was a successful day. The kids seemed on good form. The beef was succulent, and your Yorkshire puddings were a triumph."

Me: "The food? The food? Are you completely blind and deaf to what goes on when your daughters are in the same room as me?"

Kit: "What are you talking about?"

Me: "They ignore me, talk over me, talk about me in the third person."

Kit: "Don't get all writerly on me."

Me: "I mean – they call me "She" when I'm in the same room. Who's *she*? The cat's mother?"

Kit: "You must have misheard them. And you and Brick were in a huddle for ages."

Me: "Brick and Gray are great. I'm talking about the girls."

Kit: "Perhaps they can be a bit cool. But it will wear off in time."

Me: "Wake up and smell the jealousy, Kit! They are utterly obnoxious. They're trying to scare me off."

Kit: "Now you're being paranoid."

Me: "Paranoid, schmaranoid. No wonder you've been on your own since Juliet died. That's probably what happened to Anna."

Kit: "Anna? As if."

today's tweet from **@sallystoneymoor**
Nothing beats a good spring clean in the herbaceous border!

Easter Monday

Home turf

Phew. Finally I am in a land where adult children are respectful to their parents and their parents' friends, a place where twenty-somethings do not behave like petted brats.

This morning was the first frosty breakfast Kit and I have ever had together, and the first time I've left Kit after a weekend with just a peck on the cheek and not a snog. We just said "Bye," without saying when we'd see each other again. It's implicit nowadays that we'll spend the weekends together, but we usually arrange if we're going to meet up during the week.

today's tweet from **@sallystoneymoor**
I've been hooked on hot cross buns since the week after Christmas. How will I live without them now Easter's over?

Tuesday April 10th

Progress

I got through loads of work, probably because I was feeling cross with Kit so I didn't spend time mooning over him, and sending him emails, and then checking my Inbox every five minutes to see if he'd replied.

The best development was the buyer from the wholesaler, Gardners, ringing to say he had considered my proposal and checked how many copies of *Fast Work* they sold when it came out, and that he was happy to stock my new book. The discount terms are horrendous, but what choice do I have? I agreed to 60% discount (which they share with the retailers.)

They pay me £3.20 for a book priced at £7.99, and out of that measly sum I have to pay all my costs – printing, promotion, postage, storage at Kit's warehouse, and packing and delivery of orders by Kit's men to aforementioned wholesaler.

today's tweet from **@sallystoneymoor**
Prof-it: the difference between the amount earned and the amount spent (when this is a negative, profit becomes loss)

today's tweet from **@sallystoneymoor**
all you self-publishers out there – check out my blog sallystoneymoor.com for how to get a wholesaler to stock your book. #selfpublishing

Wednesday April 11th

Taking charge

Another Kit-less day. No word from him to me, nor me to him. I am not fussed, because I am boiling mad.

My launch is only a month away and I have nothing to wear, so when Wendy came round on this morning's Sally-disturbing-mission, I told her that if she would leave me alone today, I'd go clothes-shopping with her in Sheffield on Friday, and she could help me find a new outfit and actually earn her title as my personal stylist.

She said "OK," but as she turned to go, she tossed a distracting flyer at me. It was advertising *Intimate Embrace Tango – Find the Joy of Connection and Powerful Healing in this Compassionate Dance.* Some dance teacher from Matlock, who has just been on a house swap for 6 months in New Mexico, is running classes at Ashington Memorial Hall, and Wendy plans to go. "Look!" she said, "No partner or dance experience necessary. Don't you think it would be an ace way to meet a man? I really fancy what it says: 'listening and moving as one in each other's arms.'"

I followed my usual practice when she disturbs my work: I did not reply, and stared silently at my screen until she'd trundled off to pester Richard in the shed.

today's tweet from **@sallystoneymoor**
I just saw a warning about the tango: it contains highly addictive ingredients...in 7 out of 10 cases it takes over a person's life

Thursday April 12th

Back in old Blighty

Nina and family are home from their year in Munich. I rang up to welcome them back and arranged to go for the weekend later this month. Lovely!

today's tweet from **@sallystoneymoor**
I'm so looking forward to a weekend away...

Maybe that will make Kit sit up and take notice.

Friday April 13th

Mystery gathering

After an early lunch à trois with Richard, Wendy and I set off to Sheffield in her car, but when we got to Mrs Mountain's house at the edge of the village, Wendy had difficulty manoeuvring past all the cars parked outside.

"What on earth's going on?" she said. "Who are all those people milling around? There are two guys over there behind Mrs M's laurel bush, wearing those white boiler suits with hoods — the kind they wear at a crime scene."

Our car was stationary and we were having a good old squizz, when Billy Bathgate came up behind us in his van and started hooting, so we had to zoom off.

The shopping trip was unproductive, so buying a launch outfit is still on my lengthy to-do list.

today's tweet from **@sallystoneymoor**
There's nothing so frustrating as coming home empty-handed from a shopping trip!

Saturday April 14th

Working weekend

Kit was working today and suggested I called in to see him at lunch time. I said I was busy, but then let him persuade me.

"Poor you, having to work on a Saturday," I said. Was he doing it to avoid me, because he knew I was cross with him?

"I never resent time spent at work," he said. "And I didn't mind working Saturdays until you came along. But I have so much to do – get the books straight, do some estimates, work on ads for the *Peak Advertiser* and the *Rural Trader*. It's all advertising and promotion, not real printing, but I've got a couple of guys working on rush jobs in the print room, so it's good to be on hand in case they need me."

And right on cue he was needed.

While he was in the print room, I flicked through a magazine I'd picked up in the bank, having been attracted by the photo of Daniel Craig on the front. As well as a splash about James Bond, there was a classy interior décor feature, with a really nice standard light.

"Look," I said to Kit on his return, "do you like this lamp – here?"

He took the magazine from me and looked at the front cover and said: "Those frigging bankers even have an in-house magazine – they draw you in, then spit you out."

"Do you want to talk about it, Kit?"

"No thanks. I don't have time. See you later?"

I arrived at Kit's house at 5 — the same time as him. The house was freezing cold because the timer of his central heating is on the blink, and his Aga was turned off because the service man had been coming the day before, but hadn't turned up. Kit tossed me a blanket from a chair in the corner of the sitting room and said, "Here, if you want to keep me company while I sort this out, you can snuggle up under that."

He lit the fire and we had an OK evening, but not super-friendly. I am still feeling fed up and stand-offish, and I need him to *know* that I am.

Talking in bed…

Me: "Kit, can I ask you something personal?"

Kit: "You can ask me anything you like. Whether I answer or not is another matter."

Me: "Who is Anna?"

Kit: "Is that all? She's a woman from the bank."

Me: "Did you once have a thing with her?"

Kit: "Good grief, no. She's my loan manager."

Me: "So what did you do to get that first name treatment? No-one at the bank knows who I am."

Kit: "Yes, well, the bank takes notice of anyone they're going to make money out of. Not the rich. It's the borrowers they screw, who give them their profits. And I should frigging know."

Me: "Are you having money troubles?"

Kit: "It'll be fine. I've got it in hand."

today's tweet from **@sallystoneymoor**
A toasty Saturday evening, curled up in front of a log fire

Sunday April 15th

Yet more aggravation

Scarlet dropped in late morning to "borrow" a bottle of wine on the way to a lunch party. We were reading the paper by the fire. She was standing in the doorway, and her eyes alighted on the rug I'd wrapped around me last night. It was still draped on the sofa. She picked it up and went right up to Kit and said in a low voice, but not so low that I couldn't hear: "*She* hasn't been using this, has she? We're really not happy about this, Dad. You know we don't like you having people round here. How many times do we have to tell you it's not appropriate?"

Good grief !!!! ???? Whose house is it?

"If you don't stop letting her use Mum's things," she went on, "we're going to have to take them all away, you know."

Yes! Why don't you do just that? I thought. And then I thought – How on earth does this man ever expect to have a relationship that works, with this kind of thing going on?

And then, at last, Kit said something. "Yes, Scarlet. Maybe that's a good idea. I've been meaning to talk to you and Peony about it for ages."

"What?" she yelped (now with zero attempt at discretion.) "You don't want Mum's things here any more? Don't you love her any more? Are you going to trample all over her memory with a stream of other women? Don't answer that. I'm off."

Oh dear. It is getting really, really tiresome. And it makes me feel so uncomfortable – are second-time-around relationships always like this? But I suppose Kit made a tiny move in the right direction. I wonder if he'll follow through. I won't hold my breath.

Is it worth going on?

today's tweet from **@sallystoneymoor**
Possession isn't nine tenths of the law, it's nine tenths of the problem (John Lennon)

Monday April 16th

What the postmaster saw

"Och, and what on this pretty earth do you think was going on at Mrs Mountain's the other day?" Billy Bathgate whispered conspiratorially as soon as I opened his shop door today.

"Maybe she's had a burglary. There were two guys in those all-over white suit things, who looked like SOCO's." I clocked his blank look and explained: "Scene of Crime Investigating Officers." (It's only thanks to Richard that I know the technical terms.)

"That's not what I saw," he said in tones of...actually I can't describe his tone. It was halfway between awe and horror. It seemed to betray the emotion I had when I saw the first of Pippa's wedding dresses, and the second, and the…

"What did you see?" I asked, intrigued.

"It looked more like a gathering of naturists."

"What?"

"Och, yes! I saw a man and a woman in the nude. The woman could have been Mrs Mountain, but I could be mistaken."

"No! You must have imagined it!"

"Believe me, Mrs H, Mrs Mountain in the nude is not something I would ever want to imagine!"

today's tweet from **@sallystoneymoor**
Remember that old country saying? Ne'er cast a clout till May is out.

Tuesday April 17th

Further sightings

"Have there been any more interesting sightings at Mrs M's?" I said to Billy Bathgate today.

"Yes! I did a stakeout near her house for half an hour when I closed the shop last night and I saw a woman come out of her back door in the nude, carrying a blowlamp."

"Mrs Mountain? It couldn't be."

"Och, I don't know. I was so overcome, I drove away without waiting to see who it was."

today's tweet from **@sallystoneymoor**
The key to good eavesdropping is not getting caught (Lemony Snicket) and it holds good for spying too!

Wednesday April 18th

Bad news

"Mrs Howe? Are you sitting down?" It was Mrs Mountain on the phone. I'd recognise her fruity voice in a howling hurricane. It was 6.15 and I was washing up the tea things. Richard had gone out for a quick bike ride before dark.

"What is it, Mrs Mountain? You're worrying me."

"I'm afraid there's been an accident. Your brother. The ambulance is on its way."

My heart lurched. "Is Richard all right?" Of course he wasn't all right or she wouldn't have called the ambulance. "I'm coming." I slammed down the phone and grabbed the car keys and drove like a bat out of hell down the lane to Mrs M's. Billy Bathgate's van was parked in the gateway nearby, and Mrs Mountain and Billy B were leaning over Richard who was stretched out on the tarmac under a blanket, his head on a floral cushion. I rushed up and knelt down beside him.

"Richard, are you all right?"

"I'll be fine, I've just…hurt my…ow…ow, oh hell, it hurts."

I stayed by his side till the ambulance came and then followed behind to the hospital in Chesterfield. Poor Richard. He's now resting in bed here at home. He has a broken collar bone, extensive bruising, and lots of those evil surface wounds you get when you fall off your bike.

"I'm glad you're…well…still alive," I said. "You have no idea what went through my head when Mrs Mountain rang. Do you feel up to telling me how it happened?"

"I was cycling along past her house, minding my own business, when Billy Bathgate stepped out in front of me – backwards – out of nowhere. That was the odd thing. Why was he stepping out backwards?"

The phone rang. It was Billy B.

"Och, Mrs Howe, I'm ringing to ask how Mr Richard is."

"Very badly hurt. How are you?" I was trying to sound sympathetic but I was as mad as…why can I not do similes?

At that point there was a knock on the front door, so I said goodbye.

It was Mrs Mountain.

"How is your brother? I hope he's comfortable. I brought him a jar of my special honey — harvested last year."

"How kind. I didn't know you kept bees, Mrs Mountain."

"The hives are at the bottom of my garden. Do you know…the Chesterfield Bee Fanciers came last week and told me that…well, I've found something out about bee-keeping recently. Bees often sting you because they get caught in your clothes, so if you want to keep them happy, you tend them in the nude. Two of the visitors stripped off and did me a demonstration. I shan't be following it up."

today's tweet from **@sallystoneymoor**
'Get a bicycle. You will certainly not regret it, if you live.' Mark Twain

Thursday April 19th

Visiting hours

When I went in to see how Richard was this morning, he said he felt as though he'd been kicked by a carthorse, so I gave him some more arnica and suggested he stayed in bed for the day.

When Wendy called, she was horrified by his injuries. She spent all day with him in his room, apart from the time she came out and lambasted me for "not having enough treats in the house for poor Rich when he's been through hell." *Rich? Rich?* Oh yes, and the time when she popped down to Bakewell to fetch him aforementioned treats, which included a copy of Richard's favourite free mag from Midco: *Professional Builder*.

At least having them both ensconced in his bedroom meant I got little disturbance from either of them. Nice.

today's tweet from **@sallystoneymoor**
Every invalid is a prisoner.

Friday April 20th

Paparazzi

Tone, the photographer from *The Sheffield Telegraph* came. I tried to give him directions on the phone because people can never find Goose Lane, but he wasn't having any of it, just kept interrupting me with: "Got my sat-nav, got my sat-nav." I was ready at 4 as we'd agreed, wearing my specially purchased and newly applied High Volume and Definition mascara, and my newly pressed green linen shirt. He turned up an hour late by which time my shirt was creased.

At least my face will look nice in the photo, I thought, as I plodded up to bed later. Then I looked in the bathroom mirror. My High Volume and Definition mascara was still high volume but no longer high definition – all round my eyes was a black gloopy mess. Had it been like that earlier? It could well have been. If it was, I doubt that Tone would have cared. I'll just have to wait till the feature appears in the paper before I can put my mind to rest – or not. I wish I could run away and hide.

today's tweet from **@sallystoneymoor**
Post publicity photo shoot – black eyed and peed off!

Saturday April 21st

At Nina's

It is so wonderful to see Nina and the kids again after so many months. Ellie, Fabian and Liesl are so sweet, and so much fun. When I am away from them for long periods I forget just how much I love being with them, playing with them, talking to them, reading to them, cuddling up in front of the telly with them. Why do I think I need a man?

today's tweet from **@sallystoneymoor**
Never underestimate the joys of spending time with grandchildren

Sunday April 22nd

Great expectations

Talking in bed... circa 6 a.m.

Ellie: "Move up, Fabian, I'm falling out."

Fabian: "Gran, please can we read my book?"

Liesl (toddling into the room): "Gan, Gan. Me in bed."

Me: "Come on, now. There's room for all of us. Snuggle up close. What are we reading first? *The Gruffalo, Alfie gets in First,* or *Thomas the Tank Engine*? (THINKS – please, oh please not *Thomas the Tank Engine*.)

East Midlands Trains, 9 p.m.

I've finished my book (Penelope Lively's *Heat Wave* – very good) and now I can think, because I don't have to listen to two women in the seat opposite, discussing their love-lives. They got off at the last stop – Leicester – thank goodness. I say thank goodness, because it's impossible for me *not* to be gripped by the details of other people's lives. Now they've gone, I can think about me and my life, something that's easier to do at a geographical distance from where the action is.

Nina's kids are so loving and affectionate and interesting and fun, and I had a perfect weekend, with no complications. It was so much more pleasant than my recent weekends in Derbyshire. I love being with Kit, but as soon as the gurls walk in, the mood changes and my happiness crumbles. If they lived on Mars or even in South Africa, I could imagine Kit and me being together in five years time. But as it stands, with them waltzing in and out of the house and doing everything unpleasant bar hissing and booing at me, I wonder what future there is for Kit and me. He is obviously devoted to them. How can he split his loyalties between them and me? How is this going to work?

Maybe I am expecting too much from life. I've had one marriage that worked – at least for me – until we hit retirement and irreconcilable differences; and I had two good careers before I took up this patched-up vocation of writing. I have three great kids and three lovely grandkids. Do I need more? Is it asking too much to expect another happy partnership?

today's tweet from **@sallystoneymoor**
Someone should ban Thomas the Tank Engine, and all his friends. Do those dreadful books make anyone else want to scream?

Monday April 23rd

Image problems

"Coo-eee! Sall-eee! How did you get on with the photographer the other day?"

I was hanging out the washing, and Pippa was walking the blessed hounds down the lane. I strolled over and told her how tedious the photo-shoot had been and how I probably would look like a dog in the photo and the guy wouldn't care.

"Let's face it, I'm just a provincial, past-her-best, 60 year old self-publishing novelist."

"Oh, Sally, I'm sure he didn't think of you like that. No. Not at all. You look so nice and normal these days, with your short wavy hair."

Nice and normal? If Pippa thinks that, I must look appallingly mumsy. I'll have to get some pink streaks and start using hair gel and go for spikes. I'll have to do something!

Pippa asked me if she and Glenys (my erstwhile stalker) could help with the launch: "Glenys is very keen, for some reason." I told her I'd be delighted, and I'd give them a job when the time came.

today's tweet from **@sallystoneymoor**
making waves, but is that a good thing?

Tuesday April 24th

A surprise that is not a surprise

"How is that annoying brother of yours?" said Kit on the phone this morning.

"He's doing OK. What do you mean, *annoying*? And if he's so annoying, why do you care?"

"Nah – he's OK really, he's just scuppered my plans. Well, it's not just him that's–"

"What are you on about, Kit?"

"OK. Here's the thing. I know how stressed you're getting with all your arrangements for your launch – signings, interviews, etc, etc – so I wanted to whisk you away for the weekend to unwind. It was going to be a surprise."

"Oh, that's so lovely!"

"It could have been. But then your brother has his accident, and I'm thinking that if I don't tell you, and I just book flights and a hotel and–"

"Flights? Ooh, Kit, where are we talking about?"

"So there I was, on the verge of booking, and then I realised it wasn't that simple."

"It is, it is, where are we going?"

"OK, Daise, this is what went through my head 1/ Are you doing some book publicity thing this coming weekend that I don't know about? 2/ Can you spare the time – at this point in the proceedings – to go away? 3/ Are you going to tell me that you have to stay home to look after Richard? 4/ I know that you don't like me deciding things without consulting you."

The upshot is that we are going away on Friday! A surprise venue! Wendy is going to come round and make sure Richard is all right. He's finding it hard to manage in the kitchen at the moment, so she said she'd cook his tea for him on the days I am gone.

How exciting. And interesting. It looks as if my weekend at Nina's (away from Kit) has bucked his ideas up a bit.

Oh, and I have told him that in future, surprise weekends are exempt from the need for consultation.

today's tweet from **@sallystoneymoor**
The trouble with (nice) surprises is that you can't look forward to them.

Wednesday April 25th

Wine

I went to John Hattersley Wines in Bakewell to sort out the wine for the launch. I do like them there. They recognize I'm a philistine and a cheapskate and yet they're unfailingly polite, friendly and helpful, whilst trying to educate me (when I ask), in the most subtle, sotto voce way.

today's tweet from **@sallystoneymoor**
Can't afford champagne? Try Prosecco.

Thursday April 26th

Two birds with one stone

Wendy took Richard in her car to view some houses.

I worked. I get so much done with those two out of the way. I completed 'The Hook' that irrevocably binds the protagonist (Jenny) with the antagonist (Liam) and has implications for what happens next.

today's tweet from **@sallystoneymoor**
Yay! Writing fest today – 2,500 words and counting!

Friday April 27th

Excitement!

Packing, but I don't know for where! Kit says the forecast for our destination is warm sunshine and blue skies. Can't wait!

today's tweet from **@sallystoneymoor**
on the way to the airport on a mystery trip. It's so exciting! No-one's ever taken me away for a surprise w/e before.

Talking on the plane...

Me: "You remembered going to Venice from my bucket list!" I kissed his cheek. "Thank you."

Kit: "So, what do you want to do when we get there? You'll have to show me around. I've never been. Juliet always wanted us to go but I couldn't face looking at lots of old paintings in dark crumbling churches."

Me (THINKS): He's going to Venice for the first time with me! Yay!

Kit: "Daise?"

Me: "But I don't like looking at old paintings either. I just like wandering around – it's all so beautiful, and the colours are so amazing. Though I wouldn't mind going to the Peggy Guggenheim – that's modern art."

Kit: "We are so compatible."

We arrived at Marco Polo Aeroporto (listen to me – my Italian is flooding back) at midnight, due to a delayed flight. Once in Venice, we scooted out of the taxi and onto the first vaporetto that was bound for St Marks Square, then I realised it was taking us the long way round. But who cares, really? We saw the magical Square when it was dark and empty and with only three cabinieri standing in the corner. (I am *so* impressed I can retrieve my old vocab.) The moon was shining, and all was silent, and the sound of our suitcases trundling over the stone felt sacrilegious. Looking back at the Piazza as we left, it seemed unreal. The Campanile was like an outlandish out-of-scale hologram projected at the side of the Basilica. (Wendy loves the Basilica, with its exotic Eastern shape and its gold decoration, but it's too ornate for me.)

We only met a sprinkling of people as we walked the midnight streets. It felt as if the place was a present from Kit to me. (Maybe that is *slightly* sloppy, Spiky Pete.) The man at the Hotel Gallini was smiley and welcoming and whispered – "You must be very tired."

today's tweet from **@sallystoneymoor**
Venice is a more perfect place than anyone could imagine.

Saturday April 28th

Venice!

I am sitting in the warm sunshine under a blue sky in our favourite café in San Stefano (we already have a favourite café!) waiting for Paolo (our favourite waiter) to bring me a glass of iced tea. I'm catching up on my writer's journal, while dear Kit has gone back to look for my scarf, which I think I dropped between here and the Rialto bridge. We walked to the Ghetto and back (and looked around it) and my feet are killing me.

We have walked and talked. We've been to the Guggenheim. We have sat in cafés a lot. Kit – surprisingly for a rugby fan – likes people-watching and imagining their backstories as much as I do.

Our hotel is small, quiet, cosy and clean, and it's slap bang next to a canal which gondoliers go up and down. When Kit gets back, we're going on a gondola. My treat. Hang the expense!

today's tweet from **@sallystoneymoor**
my favourite Venice quote – a telegram from Robert Benchley: "Streets full of water. Please advise."

Sunday April 29th

Holiday snapshots

So there we were in bed, our heads on the hard Venetian pillows, our feet aching from pounding the fondamenti, and Kit is telling me he's sorry the gurls have been so difficult, and I'm trying to think of something nice to say about them, when through the open shutters floats the sound of a piano accordion and a gondolier singing *O Solo Mio!* It's so wonderfully corny that Kit and I crack up, and I leap out of bed and run naked to the window to join in. I'm leaning *right out* of the window in the dark, singing, watching the gondola as it reaches the corner and rounds the bend, when Kit booms "O Solo Mio" in my ear and I lurch forwards, and he has to grab me to stop me from falling into the canal below.

"Look at you. Flaunting all you've got for a delighted Venetian public!"

"Don't be daft," I say. "Who can see me down this little side canal?"

"Maybe them," he says, pointing to a middle-aged couple standing with glasses of wine on a balcony at a diagonal from our window. They raise their glasses to us and call out "Buona sera!"

It's Sunday morning in the Piazza San Polo and there's an old lady dressed up in her Sunday best, navy suit, white blouse, high heels, necklace and rings, hairdo. She's trying to stand up from the bench she's sitting on, but she can't, and Kit rushes over to help her. She's surprised and pleased and says "Grazie, grazie." Then she walks to the houses at the edge of the square and rings several door bells, but no-one answers. I guess she's calling on friends. Kit says she's playing Rosy Apple.

Sunday afternoon, a sixty-ish couple are acting suspiciously. He is furtively peeling a poster off the inside wall of a stone archway. The poster is advertising an exhibition at the Guggenheim. The woman is standing guard, checking that no-one is watching. The man manages to get the poster off in one piece and rolls it up and hands it to the woman and says, "I offered to buy you one from the gallery shop." And she laughs and says, "Yes, but this was much more fun, and the exhibition ends tomorrow so we don't have to feel guilty." They laugh together and he puts his arm round her shoulders as they hurry away.

today's tweet from **@sallystoneymoor**
Flying home from Venice, happy and refreshed and ready for publication day (May 11th) of my novel– THEY MET ON THE BRIDGE.

Monday April 30th

Press exposure

I was in Saturday's *Sheffield Telegraph*! Yay! Kit is very impressed.

I don't look too bad, thank goodness. The mascara must have glooped later in the day.

When I got back to my computer, I had three unexpected emails in my Inbox.

Email 1: from Iain

```
Hi Sally
Richard mentioned your book launch in his last
email (poor man - that accident sounds nasty.)
May 11th ? Is that right? I'd love to be with
you on the night! But I'm sure you'll have a
houseful, so could you email me a couple of
suggestions of local B and Bs where the decor
isn't too cottagey/chintzy? I doubt there are
guest houses in Stoneymoor run by minimalists,
but if you could steer clear of the truly kitsch
I'd appreciate it. But it's a small thing. After
all, it's seeing you that's important.
Love
Iain
```

Email 2: from Angelina

Hi Sal-gal,
Have been meaning to get in touch for ages and now the spring is here I really do have itchy feet. Can I stay the night at yours? It'll just be me. I think you know that Archie died in 2009? I think you sent me a card?
I'm thinking of buying a bachelorette pad in your neck of the woods, using my romance-writing nest egg. I might as well splash it around a bit. I need to have some fun, and I thought your part of the world was swinging for people our age. Wotton-under-Edge is sooooh dull these days.
Cheers
Angelina
p.s. I am not writing any more - have started an introductions agency for over 55s.
p.p.s. I think there is something wrong with your answering machine. I've left three messages and have had to resort to email in the end.
p.p.p.s. I shan't be bringing Tiggy. Poor, dear Tiggy died last year after we'd been staying in that pet hotel in Leeds. Now he's in a jar on the mantelpiece next to Archie.

Oh crikey, I thought I'd shaken her off. One bitch queen who refuses to disappear. No, Angelina, there is nothing wrong with my answerphone. It does a wonderful job of screening calls. I've emailed her and told her about my launch, as she didn't think to ask anything at all about me in her email. Plus ça change. And I've sent her the same B&B info as Iain. Hah! If they end up in the same one, she'll keep him busy.

Email 3: from Stuart Robinson!

Dear Sallifer
I can't believe you became a writer. How amazing. I saw the article about you in the paper, and although it's been 40 years and your name has changed, I knew you instantly. Those eyes, and that sweet little wonky ear that STILL sticks out of your hair.
I googled you and found your blog and your email address. I hope I'm not sitting in your spam folder.
I would love to see you, for old time's sake. I am very happily married (second time around – this time, 10 years) and I hope you're happy too.
Would you mind if I came to your launch? Or would it be too weird? I am still in Sheffield, so could easily come over for the evening. But I won't come unless you email me an OK.
Love, as always,
Stuart
p.s. if by any chance you aren't the Sally I know, and/or you have no idea who 'Stuart' is – please ignore this email.

Oh my – Stuart Robinson! My first serious boyfriend. I had completely forgotten he used to call me Sallifer. I've never forgotten him, though. He was so sweet and so funny.

I emailed him: Yes! Do come! Can't wait to see you!

I rang Kit tonight for a chat. He was horrified when I told him about Stuart. "You didn't say he could come, did you?"

"Of course! The more the merrier! It's a hoot. Everyone is crawling out of the woodwork. I even got an email from a dreadful woman I used to go to school with: Angelina Thompson. It's always the same – I am just relaxing into thinking I will never see her again, and she rings up out of the blue and wants to come to stay."

"It's so frustrating that I can't be at your launch," he said. "Quite apart from anything else, I was looking forward to meeting Nina. But I really, *really* don't like the idea of your childhood sweethearts turning up and sweeping you off your feet. You've read those stories about Friends Reunited – all these teenage ex-lovers hooking up and walking out of their marriages. How many other of your exes are coming?"

"Only Iain, a really boring friend of Richard's."

"I don't like the sound of this launch."

"Don't be daft, Kit. I'm not looking for anyone else. I'm with you."

"I hope you *are* with me," he said, and then he paused. "I love you, Daise."

I was gobsmacked, melting, silent.

"Daise? Did you hear me? I love you. I couldn't bear to lose you now."

today's tweet from **@sallystoneymoor**
Blasts from the past! Old friends are arriving like buses, all at once.

MAY

Tuesday May 1st

May Day

No-one tells you that self-publishing will make your head explode. There is so much that's new, and so much to do, and the nearer you get to publication day, the worse it gets. I've been emailing and writing and phoning people for PR purposes, then rushing round bookshops and local gift shops persuading them to stock my book. At first I was nervous and tongue-tied, but most people have been friendly and receptive so these days I skip the five minutes in my car, geeing myself up before I go in. The pretty book cover makes a difference, but the key persuader is that it's set in the Derbyshire Peak District, and lots of the tourists like to read books set locally.

Got to stop. Got guest blog posts to write, and so yep, right on cue, someone is at the front door – probably Wendy, arch-destroyer of concentration.

Later:

"Are you there, Sal?" Wendy said, barging into my study. "Rich is on the phone to the hospital about his follow-up appointment. Poor bunny. A broken collar bone is such a pain – it stops him doing the most basic things – he can't drive, he can't ride a bike, even sex is a challenge."

Something shifted in my brain when she said this, but then she diverted my spluttering, frazzled neurones with a shriek, "Wow! Sal! Your Sam! He's ripped!"

I gave up trying to concentrate and looked up from my screen. She was looking out at the garden, her nose pressed up against the window. Ripped? What was she talking about? "What's he ripped?"

"Ripped as in *He is ripped*. That's what comes of having twin boys – you catch all the slang without realising. I mean ripped as in cor-what-a-body! Strongly defined muscles, all that stuff."

"That's my son you're talking about! Don't be so inappropriate!"

"Me inappropriate?" she spluttered. "Look out here if you want to see inappropriate! It's only Sam and Xanthe, flaunting everything God gave them, in your front garden, along with a load of their mates – phwoar, nice pecs on that one. Blimey! The only thing dressed up is the cupcakes!"

I leapt from my chair and rushed to the window.

Protest nakedism again! I stormed outside and shouted at Sam. "I've had enough! I agreed you could stay till the end of April, and today is the first of May. I've got enough on my plate without having you arrested for indecent exposure. You're moving out today – you and your caravan and all your naked friends."

He opened his mouth to respond, but Xanthe got in first. "OK, Sally. Please don't spoil our May Day picnic. We'll go as soon as we can fix up someone to shift our caravan."

Nice attempt at stalling, Xanthe, but I knew who to call. "I'll ring Baxter now," I said, "and I'll ask him to hitch you up to his Range Rover, and tow you somewhere where people don't think you've got anything to do with me."

Baxter was pleased to help. He came round after tea and towed them to the Greenhills campsite near Ashford in the Water. We'll see what the dyed-in-the-wool caravanners up there make of protest nakedism.

There has been altogether too much public nudity in Stoneymoor recently. I blame Anthony Gormley.

today's tweet from **@sallystoneymoor**
22 million Peak District visitors a year. Someone should buy my book, then!

Wednesday May 2nd

Nightmares

I woke at 5.30 from a horrible dream about my book launch. I got to the bookshop early to sort out last minute stuff and found an eager crowd of guests already there – most of whom I didn't know – and one of them asked me if the printer was bringing the books along later.

"What do you mean?" I said.

"Because there don't seem to be any here."

I couldn't see any either, so I rushed over to speak to Lisa, the bookshop manager, and she said in an uncharacteristically off-hand way (*so* not like her): "No, they've not arrived. But it doesn't matter, because we'd only have sold a handful."

This was not a comfort.

today's tweet from **@sallystoneymoor**
have you ever had a dream come true?

Thursday May 3rd

Emergency shopping

I went shopping with Wendy this morning because I still had nothing to wear for the launch, and the gorgeously beaded satin strapless cocktail dress which Wendy had nabbed for me in the British Heart Foundation charity shop, though beautiful, was a/ too tight for comfort and b/ showed way too much shoulder for Hassop Bookshop, even in the evening. Actually it showed too much shoulder for any occasion. Never mind shoulders, even upper arms are a body part too far for women my age, which the buyer at M&S would do well to note.

Naturally, we started at John Lewis in Sheffield, making our way round all the concessions, but it was very discouraging. I tried on lots of items, but nothing fitted.

"The darts on all of these tops are in the wrong place. What's that about?" I hissed in exasperation.

"Hitch up your bra-straps, woman," said Wendy. "And just be grateful you don't have tea-bag tits like me."

After two hours of frustration and disappointment, Wendy suggested we go to Geisha in Matlock. Geisha in Matlock! Twenty five miles away from where we were in Sheffield! It emerged en route that Geisha had been her intended destination all along. She was desperate to try on some incredibly pricey, legendary super-jeans she'd heard about on her fashionista grapevine which claim to make you look a/ like your daughter and b/ as if you have a supermodel stomach and teensy thighs – hence the price tag.

"I can't understand why you aren't trying some on," she said, coming out of the changing room and screwing herself round to get a better view of her bum. She looked slim with perfect curves, just as always. "What do you think, Sal?"

"Sorry to be a bummer, but you look no better than you usually do i.e. fantastic. I really do hate your guts."

She was aghast. "What? Eighty quid and no improvement whatsoever?"

I shrugged.

"Damn," she said, "I was counting on these for a total body rejuvenation! I need all the help I can get, with a new man in the offing."

"You've got a man?" I said, but then I spotted the most fabulous sheer silk chiffon blouse in a sophisticated smoky grey, and Wendy and her love-life slipped away. I bought the blouse and some über-flattering tailored trousers. The blouse is glamorous and sexy but in a subtle way, and has an integral cami so I don't have to worry about visible underwear. I was actually looking for a jacket, but this blouse clings to me in the right places and skims over the others, and when I am wearing it I feel as if I could seduce Daniel Craig.

At teatime, Nina rang to cry off from the launch. Tim has been told he's on a team-building course with work that weekend, and she obviously can't farm out all three kids.

"Oh and you were right about Dad – you know – when you said he wouldn't write back? I've written three times and I've had two pathetic sentences."

"You're honoured to get that. What did he say?"

"Wish your mother luck from me with her new book. Hope you and the kids are doing well. That was it. My father! Two lousy sentences. What use is he as a grandfather?"

"Did you tell him I was seeing someone?"

"Yes, but you aren't now, are you?"

Why do my kids never listen to me? "I told you before. He's called Kit. He's a widower. And I'm very fond of him."

Fond of him? Fond of him? That sounds as if we sit by the fire in rocking chairs, bringing each other cups of tea and chuckling at pathetic sitcoms on the telly.

"That's nice for you," she said. "I hope you'll still have time left for us. We've seen you once in nine months. You and Dad are –"

"You've been in Munich for a year! Did you expect me to fly out every week? I'm crazy about the kids, and I love you, of course, but I do have a life of my own."

Who is the new man that Wendy wants to impress?

today's tweet from **@sallystoneymoor**
What do you wear when you dress to impress?

Friday May 4th

Shrink-wrapped

They've come! The long-run is printed, shrink-wrapped and stacked, and yesterday afternoon Gray delivered two hundred of them here. Kit has dispatched 50 to the wholesaler, and the other 1750 are at Kit's warehouse, from where they will be shipped, as and when they're needed. So now I don't have to worry about not having any books for the launch which – yay! – is a week today.

today's tweet from **@sallystoneymoor**
Just look at my pile of lovely books! Coming to my launch at Hassop Station Bookshop May 11th 7pm?
View media

Saturday May 5th

Interlude

We had a gurl-free day but I was too limp to make full, unbridled use of their absence. (Nudge, nudge, wink wink.) I took the day off from my stressed-out publisher persona, and sat in Kit's garden in the sunshine, pretending to read the paper, but in reality, dozing.

"Well," said Kit, "This time next week it will all be over." And there was a look of relief in his eyes. Is he worrying about some ex at the launch scooping me up and running away with me, or is he simply fed up with me being preoccupied, snappy and (energy-wise) quasi-dead. He gardened around me, and in the evening we went out to the Maazi and thence to bed.

Talking in bed:

Kit: "When I told you I loved you – last week – on the phone – you didn't respond. Are we on a different page?"

Me: "No, but…"

Kit: "But?"

Me: "But I am not prepared to put up with any more aggravation from Peony and Scarlet and…well…"

Kit: "And?"

Me: "And if you don't do something to rein them in, sort them out, I am not sure if…"

Kit: "Daise. I love you. I will sort them out."

today's tweet from **@sallystoneymoor**
Another Saturday, another yummy meal at the Maazi in Matlock. Still loving those waiters on the pavement!

Sunday May 6th

Never again

I was moaning about the hassle of self-publishing at lunch today with Gray and Kit, and Gray said: "But you know how it all works, now. You could write a book about self-publishing."

My book would contain three words: "DON'T DO IT."

I don't have time for fun, my brain is fried, and I am on my knees with exhaustion.

And anyway – I *don't know* how it works. I have Kit as my printer, thank goodness, and what he doesn't know, Gray knows; and I have the nice man at Gardner's, who has not yet tired of me asking him things. But Amazon, and almost everything else, is still a mystery. I am stumbling through unfamiliar terrain in a dark forest, with no map or torch.

today's tweet from **@sallystoneymoor**
weekend recuperation with roast lamb, rosemary and great conversation

Bank Holiday Monday

?

When Wendy said that thing about sex being a challenge for Richard, who was she thinking he'd be doing it with? He hasn't been on an internet date for months.

today's (Giovanna-sourced) tweet from **@sallystoneymoor**
spotted through a window whilst strolling in Ashford in the Water: a fairy liquid bottle, wearing a Cath Kidston apron!

Only Giovanna would notice that.

Tuesday May 8th

Last minute jobs

A busy day. I have:

- uploaded the Kindle version of the book to the Kindle store on Amazon;
- registered my book on the Public Lending Rights database so that when people borrow it from libraries I get a few pence;
- posted a copy of the book to the British Library at Boston Spa (legally required of all publishers);
- had trouble wrestling the ISBN database into submission, so rung up the agency, where the staff are sweet, polite and patient. Whenever I ring them, I can imagine them covering the phone receiver with their hands and whispering to each other: "It's another one of those over-anxious greenhorn publishers." But they're nice to me, so I don't care;
- rung Gardner's to make sure that the books Kit couriered to them have arrived, as a bookseller emailed that she had been told the book was out of stock.

today's tweet from **@sallystoneymoor**
"My head is bursting with the joy of the unknown." Rumi

Wednesday May 9th

Eternal make-over

The end of an era: Vidal Sassoon has died. We all wanted to have a Vidal Sassoon cut in the 60's. Even Angelina. I hated my wavy fringe, and when a girl at the church youth club told Angelina and me that in heaven you get a new body, I remember saying, "Well, I'm going to have a straight fringe," and Angelina saying, "You ought to have a smaller body, first." Oh dear, she'll be here in a couple of days. I hope I can avoid her at the launch.

I had a radio interview with Aleena Naylor at BBC Radio Derby, who is *so* nice and chatty that I forgot I was on the radio.

today's tweet from **@sallystoneymoor**
"Sometimes I think that not having to worry about your hair anymore is the secret upside of death." Nora Ephron

Thursday May 10th

Two professionals and a delivery driver

Went to Pricey Paul's for a cut and blow. What a pro.

Then to BBC Radio Sheffield for an interview with Rony Robinson. Another pro.

Came home and then drove out again to deliver 100 books to Hassop Bookshop for tomorrow.

today's tweet from **@sallystoneymoor**
Never underestimate what a hairdresser can do for you.

Friday May 11th

D Day

4 a.m. Wake up, having dreamed that my alarm clock did not go off and I was late for the launch (at 7 p.m. ?) Try to go

back to sleep, but there is so much crap churning around in my head that I only manage to doze fitfully (I like that word. I like fretfully too.)

6.30 a.m. There's a knock on my bedroom door and Wendy appears with a mug of tea – Wendy?! She asks me what I would like for breakfast. When I query what she's doing here at this time of day, she says she is "helping Rich." Apparently, he wanted to bring me breakfast in bed but is not up to the challenge of cooking yet, or even carrying a tray, although he is "coming along in other areas." So, what would I like? The full English?

7 a.m. Breakfast in bed. Wendy is wonderful – crispy bacon, and fried egg exactly as I like it. She is also surprising. I had no idea she could a/ get up before 9 a.m. b/ do anything more complicated in the kitchen than defrost an M&S ready meal.

8 a.m. Kit calls in on his way to work to give me a good luck hug, a good luck card, and a huge bunch of tulips from his garden – dark red, deep pink and black. "I'm not being a cheapskate bringing you home-grown. It's because I know you love tulips." He is so right. Melt.

10 a.m. I remember that the best time of day to tweet is 10 a.m. so I tweet details of launch. Ooh, I am so up there with my social media marketing.

10.30 a.m. Iain calls with a bouquet of enormous, blowsy, fragrant pink peonies. He says he was going to buy cornflowers because of their pure clear fabulous blue, and he quoted some Pantone colour (Amparo blue?) and then the actual Pantone number (typical Iain!) "But then," he said, "your old schoolfriend, Angelina, who is staying in the same B&B as me, insisted on tagging along to Darling Buds and persuaded me that the peonies were much more *you*." Then he left, saying he had given her a lift to Bakewell and she was waiting in the Bean and Bag Company café for him to pick her up. Yay! My plan is working! (evil pantomime laugh)

10. 50 a.m. Tweet details of launch, slightly reworded, as Twitter won't allow you to repeat yourself.

11 a.m. More flowers – two bouquets in one delivery – one from Nina – bless her – and one from Daniel. My kids are so sweet. It's the first time Daniel has sent me flowers. Has he finally found a woman? I run out of large vases and resort to a bucket and a watering can – both galvanized. Very *Country Living*. Decide to take them all down to the bookshop later (except Kit's, which are staying in my bedroom.)

11.30. Tweet rehashed details of launch and ask my followers to retweet them.

11.30 – 12.30 p.m. Run around tidying up and fretting, asking Wendy and Richard if they think it will all be all right, then panic about my outfit from Geisha and pull out all my dressy clothes from the wardrobe and try on alternatives.

1 p.m. Kit arrives and tells me to stick with the smoky grey blouse because I look hot in it and then says "Actually, I don't want you to look too hot, so maybe you should wear your linen suit," which throws me into a strop – "So what's wrong with my suit?" and he strokes me (metaphorically and literally) and kisses me, and takes me out for a soothing quiet lunch at the White Lion in Great Longstone. I can't face food but manage two Bloody Marys and a packet of bacon fries.

2 p.m. Kit goes back to work and I feel ill and go to bed and watch last night's *Neighbours* online on my laptop.

4 p.m. Wendy knocks on my bedroom door and brings in a mug of sweet tea and some shortbread biscuits and tells me she is going to do my make-up, so wants me up and showered and sitting in the kitchen in half an hour, and as I am always

complaining that I have half as much hair on my head and the rest of my body as I used to have, she has bought me some false eyelashes as a good luck present.

5.00 p.m. Looking fab and feeling bullet-proof now I am all made up. Wendy is such a sweetie.

5.30 p.m. Put on dungarees so I can take all the flowers to the bookshop and not get my nice clothes messed up. Drive down to Hassop Station to check everything is ready, and forget to take the flowers. There is a big table right inside the door completely covered in my books. It looks wonderful. The café area is set out nicely already. Pippa and Glenys are there and all the bottles of wine and jugs of juice and nibbles are beautifully arranged. Glenys comes over and gives me a big hug and says I look fabulous, and Pippa says my "dressed down look" is very avant-garde. I explain I have not put on my outfit yet, and a wave of relief sweeps over her face. Am just leaving to go home and put on said outfit when Sam and Xanthe roll up with tins full of cupcakes – all decorated expertly with thick icing and *SH!* (for Sally Howe) on the top. How sweet. About to get into car to come home and remember treasure hunt, so rush back and hide book (the treasure and prize) amongst the children's books.

6.20 p.m. Get dressed up and Wendy drives me and Richard to the bookshop. They're going to stand at the door to welcome people, explain about the treasure hunt and give out quiz sheets.

Wendy scurries round to the patio area and reappears hauling a chair behind her. "It's for Richard. So the poor bunny doesn't get tired. He needs to save his strength for later."

There's something fishy going on. What is Wendy up to? I turn to watch them as she drags the chair towards him, and they're laughing as they decide exactly how to position it, and then he sits down and she turns away, and he reaches out and gives her a tiny pat on her bum and I think *What are you doing, Richard?* And I'm waiting for her to whack him one, but she doesn't! She just looks over her shoulder at him and grins. And a thunderbolt strikes! Wendy and Richard are an item! *What??!!*

But I have no time to adjust to this, or to say anything to either of them because beyond them in the car park, the first few punters are getting out of their cars.

What happened next – the actual launch – is a blur dotted with people and images, and remembered moments of bliss, embarrassment and panic, just like my wedding day.

Loads of people came – and that was wonderful. The writing group turned up en masse – Kate Wensley, Duncan, Alicia, Spiky Pete, the two Janets, even the man who writes obscene poems – what's his name? – Florid Trev.

Stuart Robinson, teenage sweetheart, did not come. Had he had a change of heart?

At 7.45 I read out the answers to the quiz and gave the prize of Thorntons Chocolates, and at 8 o'clock did a reading from the book. Then I sat at a desk and signed books. Angelina was the first in the queue, her arm through Iain's. He looked strangely pale. I couldn't tell how he felt about the big A – what was that expression on his face? Sheepish? Secret, delighted anticipation? Mild terror?

Angelina's hair was big, blonde and shoulder length, and stiff with hairspray, her talons were purple and sparkly, and she had on diamante earrings and a black strapless dress, unaware that at 60, a/ black is horribly aging and b/ upper arms and cleavages should not be flaunted when you're a scrawny size 10. Even Twiggy's slim upper arms look less than taut these days.

"Sal-gal! Haven't you done well?" said Angelina. "No-one would ever guess that the book is self-published. Although–" and she picked one up and flicked through it, "the paper is very, very white, a bit stark, and it's quite thick, too, isn't it? What is it? 80 gsm? Oh well, Joe Public won't clock a damn thing. So – do old friends get a freebie?"

"Don't be a tease, Angelina," said Iain. "We're here to support Sally – I'd like two, please. One for me and one for Bec." (His daughter.) "How many are you taking, Angelina?"

The black witch frowned and said "Give me one," between gritted teeth.

As I was signing the books for them, Angelina told me that she and Iain couldn't hang around, as they were going to Sheffield for the evening.

"Yes," said Iain, "and tomorrow, Angelina wants to take me to the Turkish baths there. She wants to show me the glorious Victorian tiling." *Hmm, yes Iain, while dressed only in a towel: Angelina doesn't stop at mentally undressing her men – she does it literally.*

"Come on, sweetie. Let's fly. See you over the weekend, Sal-gal?"

Not if I can help it.

As she dragged him away, he turned and mouthed something over her shoulder at me, but I have no idea what it was.

Spiky Pete was next in the queue. "Who would you like me to dedicate it to?" I said.

"No-one!" he spat out in horror.

I smiled at him. "It's really nice of you to come."

He looked flustered and said, "Oh well – the writing fraternity and all that crap."

"That's sweet," I said. "I know you and I haven't always agreed about things, and I know you're a bit doubtful about the kinds of things I write, but–"

"Sorry, got to go," and he grabbed the book and stepped away in a rush and I watched him pay at the till and then scoot off with a man in a black leather jacket. He held the book out to his friend and the guy shrank away from it with palms up and a grimace, and then they fell about laughing. Let them laugh. Let them scorn. I don't like his writing, either. And at least I've got my writing out in the world, not sitting at home on a MacBookPro.

The rest of the writing group were out and out sweeties and between them they bought about twenty books. Wow.

People had come from Sheffield, having heard me on the radio, and there was a stream of bods I can't remember now, and several people from the village including the usual suspects – Mrs Mountain and Billy Bathgate. Richard and Wendy were at the end of the queue.

"We're going to wait for you in my car," said Wendy. "Take as long as you like. We don't mind, do we Rich? You might get a few more customers. There are a few people still lurking in corners, browsing."

"Well done," said Richard, leaning over and kissing me on the cheek. "I'm proud of you."

They left, and I was sitting there thinking

Richard and Wendy!

and

Richard and Wendy?

and

How long's it been going on?

and

Why didn't I realise?

and other such useless meanderings.

Then I looked round the shop to see if there was anyone else likely to buy a book, and a tall slim man with grey hair in a trendy tweed jacket appeared from behind a shelf and said, "Look at you, Sallifer. Just as gorgeous as ever."

Stuart! Who'd have thought he'd scrub up so well after all these years?

I jumped up and walked round the table and stood in front of him and gazed into his lovely dark eyes, crinkled at the corners, and said, "You came. I was thinking that you'd changed your mind. That you'd got lost. Or maybe that your wife didn't like the idea."

He gazed back into my eyes and said, "Libby? Of course not! She found these for me to give you." He brought his hand round from behind his back and offered me a bunch of sweet peas. "Rang every florist in Sheffield, she did. It's rather early for them. These are from Holland."

"She did?"

"I grow sweet peas, like your Dad used to do. And Libby loves them. Knows all about you and your Dad's sweet peas."

I took the flowers and buried my nose in them. Ooh, they were lovely. I looked up at him again and smiled. "It's so good to see you!" I said. "Stuart Robinson! Just fancy!"

I pulled up a chair for him and we sat down next to the table containing my last six books, and we chatted about old times and then about our partners and families and then about old times again and about my dad always bellowing down the stairs at him when he brought me home: "Robinson? Can you hear me? It's way past bloody midnight. Don't you have a home to go to?"

And after I don't know how long, Stuart said, "Well, I'd better go. I left Libby at her friend's house in Baslow."

We stood up and I put my hand on his arm and said, "Thanks so much for coming. It's been..."

He placed his hand on mine and said, "I wouldn't have missed it for the world," and then I stood on my toes to kiss him, and out of nowhere we were in a full-on-goodbye-clinch, a for-old-times-sake-clinch, a this-might-be-the-last-time-we-see-each-other-clinch, a hasn't-it-been-nice?-clinch, and then suddenly I was aware of him tensing up.

I pulled away. "What's the matter?"

"There's a guy just come in and seen us and looked as if he was going to explode and stormed out the door again. Would it be your guy? Your what's his name? Your Kit?"

"Oh no! He thinks I'm going to run away with you. Stuart, I have to go and try to catch him and tell him it's not how it looks."

"Of course."

"Bye!" I called over my shoulder as I dashed out the door. But Kit's Volvo was already pulling out of the car park and there was no point in trying to chase after him and tell him not to be so stupid.

So I went back and said goodbye properly to Stuart and then thanked Lisa for everything, and walked wearily to Wendy's car, where I found her and Richard sitting in the back seat.

I hadn't the energy to talk to them about their couple-dom. I was on my knees with exhaustion.

"Are you hoping I'm going to drive?" I said.

"No, no," said Wendy, getting out and climbing into the driver's seat. "We didn't know how long you'd be, and it's comfier in the back."

"I'm sure it is."

She took us home.

I'll be talking to her later. And Richard. He's a child in the market-place of romance. He just cannot know what he is letting himself in for.

So now I'm back home, I've rung Kit's mobile and left a message. I've rung his home phone and left a message. I've texted him a long text. I've emailed him. And in every message I've explained that there was nothing in the clinch, and how sorry I am that he didn't stay, and how lovely it was of him to call in, and how had he managed it with the family meal and all?

I have had no response of any kind.

Why is he being so pathetically stupid?

Should I be worried?

today's tweet from **@sallystoneymoor**
thanks so much for supporting me tonight at my book launch you lovely, lovely people. I had a blissful time.

Saturday May 12th
What's up?

Still nothing from Kit. I am beginning to worry. Was he so angry or upset that he crashed his car on the way home?

I dragged myself out of bed this morning and managed to get to Chesterfield Waterstones for my book-signing session at 12 noon. Kit had said he was going to drive me there, which would have been lovely, but obviously that was off. Sweet, sweet Wendy took pity on me. She even, at my request, drove past Kit's house to check his car was there and undamaged (it was), and then she whisked me off to Chesterfield, talking all the way. She mentioned Richard several times, but I wasn't paying attention. I was whittling about Kit. And anyway, if she and Richard are happy, good for them – they're doing better than Kit and me. As she parked the car, she wound up her long stream of consciousness monologue with: "So I can tell that when all his wounds are healed, he's going to be amazing. He is so thorough."

Wendy sat next to me at the desk they'd given me and engaged customers in banter when they ignored me and walked straight past my table. e.g. She said to one, "Come and have a look at this book – it's really romantic," and the woman said, "I'm more into murder, myself," and walked out the door.

Now I am going to crash out in bed with my laptop. I should be working on my novel's 'Swivel' (a crisis point when Jenny is forced to choose between her love for Liam and her new career), but stuff that. I'm going to watch all the episodes of *Neighbours* I've missed this week. Perhaps they will numb my brain and relax me so I can stop worrying about Kit. He must have had some family crisis and had to rush off somewhere unexpected to sort it out. I hope nothing awful has happened to Gray or Brick.

today's tweet from **@sallystoneymoor**
it was so nice to meet you at my book signing in Chesterfield Waterstones you lovely, lovely people

Sunday May 13th
Soldiering on

I slept until 2 a.m. and then got up and checked my email to see if there was anything from Kit, and there wasn't, so I came back to bed. I have another signing today – this time at Waterstones at Meadowhall. It will be Meadow-hell. Wendy is taking me – what a pet she is. She's going shopping while I sit in the store and am ignored. I don't ask for Harry Potter crowds, or even a queue out the door. Just a couple of customers who are friendly would be enough.

today's tweet from **@sallystoneymoor**
Looking forward to meeting you all when you're shopping at Meadowhall today. Don't forget – book-signing at Waterstones,12 noon.

Later:

Still nothing from Kit. I don't want to drive to his house, in case the gurls are there. I am so battered and exhausted, I am in no fit state to cope with them. I will ring him at work tomorrow. This is awful. Awful.

My mind is a blank for blogging or tweeting and I've had to return to Giovanna's list:

today's (Giovanna-sourced) tweet from **@sallystoneymoor**
Moss killer at the top of the shopping list.

Have I used that one of hers before?

Monday May 14th

Fretting – not fitfully, but all of the time

9 a.m. I have just rung Wyatt Printing. The woman who answered the phone (who was she and why wasn't it Gray?) said that Mr Wyatt is not taking calls today. I said, "Please ask him again. Please tell him it's Mrs Howe ringing." She said, "Hold the line, please." Then a couple of minutes later she said, "I'm sorry. Mr Wyatt says he is too busy to speak to you. If there is a problem

concerning your book or an order, can you email the appropriate person? I think he means Terry."

Surely, surely, he can't still be in a strop because I was in a clinch with Stuart.

Can he?

I am going to drive over and confront him at his house tonight, gurls or no gurls.

today's tweet from **@sallystoneymoor**
catch me on Peaks-n-Dales Radio at 2.30 today!

Later:

I've just got back from my interview on *Peaks-n-Dales*. They have a new presenter called Sandra Sheldon. The interview went well.

At the end, she said, "It's a lot of work, Sally. You've had to learn for yourself all the ins and outs of publishing. I mean, most people who self-publish just go down the ebook route, which I understand is fairly easy, but you've had paperbacks printed as well. It's a big achievement. You must be very proud."

I said: "I couldn't have done it without my printers, Wyatt Printing. They were fantastic. Gray Wyatt was so patient, and so professional, and Kit Wyatt is…" and my voice broke, and I grabbed the glass of water on the desk and gulped some down, as I thought – *Kit's more important to me than any book.*

Sandra S broke into my thoughts.

"So, Sally, what advice would you give to any of our listeners who are thinking of following in your footsteps?"

"Go to Wyatt Printing. They'll help you with everything. They're all you need."

Then thankfully it was time for the traffic news before I could embarrass myself by blurting any more stuff out about Kit.

As I left the studio I could hear Sandra S's voice over the speakers saying: "Sounds like a bit of a love story going on there." *Oh my God.*

Now I am going to sort out my eye make-up and put on my "hot" grey blouse and I am going to go and see this man who is more important to me than my book.

today's tweet from **@sallystoneymoor**
I almost talked over the traffic news! Live radio! What an adrenalin burst!

Tuesday May 15th

Kit

I knocked on Kit's door last night and nothing happened. I knocked again: zilch. I grabbed the printer's devil brass door-knocker and knocked and knocked and knocked until finally he came to the door and opened it and said "Cut it out, Daise! I was in the shower!" which was patently true, because his hair was dripping and he was wearing nothing but a skimpy blue towel (and barely that.)

"Come in – go and get yourself a drink while I get dry, can you? There's some wine in the fridge."

"No. I will not go and get myself a drink. I want to know what's going on. You are supposed to love me and yet you have ignored me for three days. Three whole days at a time of enormous stress for me. I have phoned, emailed and texted and I'm probably getting RSI from typing you all these bloody messages. You, meanwhile, have been stone-walling me – mardy and silent. I have explained about Stuart, and you're being utterly ridiculous. I love *you*, you moron!"

He smiled. "Yes, and apparently I'm all you need. Give me a kiss."

"What?"

"You're so sexy when you're mad."

"I've heard that chat-up line before, Kit Wyatt." But I allowed him to pull me against his wet body and kiss me and lead me upstairs and all the rest.

This morning he brought me breakfast in bed, and we went over what had happened in the last few days, and about how I hate my book-signing sessions because no-one knows who I am; and I told him how furious I was that he wouldn't respond when I tried to contact him. And he admitted he had over-reacted on Friday night.

But then he said, "I was already upset when I arrived at the bookshop. You were probably so caught up in the launch stuff, and the famous clinch, come to that, that you didn't realise how early I was. Did you notice? I got there at half past eight. Did you think of that?"

"But the meal. Juliet's meal. You must have eaten ridiculously early."

"Or stormed out of the restaurant."

"You didn't!"

"It was an awful evening. There were two things I was determined not to mention, but there they were, like two massive elephants in the room."

"Elephants?"

"You and the business," he said, and then he noticed my expression, and added "speaking metaphorically, obviously. And when I say *you*, I mean *us*. And elephants has got nothing to do with…but you *know* the expression the elephant in the room!" Hmm, nice recovery, Kit.

"Anyway, we made it as far as dessert, and then Peony, who'd probably had too much wine, she started to have a go," (why was he still making excuses for her?) "and Scarlet, who'd also been knocking it back," (more excuses!) "joined in, and both elephants came roaring out from their hiding place behind the sweet trolley and the end result was out-and-out carnage. And I thought *Why the hell am I sitting here at this table at what is supposed to be a cosy family remembrance of Juliet but is actually a vicious, verbal brawl?* So I left. I drove to Hassop, really churned up, longing to see you, and there you were in another man's arms. It was all too much."

"You daft bat."

"I spent two days fuming and worrying, and then by yesterday I was starting to think I'd over-reacted and felt really, really stupid and felt too embarrassed to–"

"Good job I'm not proud, isn't it? Good job I'm a wanton hussy who goes for what she wants and doesn't care what people think?"

He leaned over to kiss me then, but before he could, the phone rang and Kit Wyatt the businessman picked it up.

There followed a tense interchange that I sussed was with one of the gurls. He switched off the phone and put it down.

The colour had drained from his face and for the first time since I'd met him, he looked old. He leaned back against the pillows and said on a long long sigh, "Bloody hell. Bloody, bloody hell."

"Are you all right?"

No response, except his hand stretching across the bed to hold mine.

"Kit? What is it? What's happened?"

"I could lose the business."

"What? How?"

"That was Peony and Scarlet. To let me know that in the light of what happened the other night, they're blocking the bank loan I need to stop the business from going under."

"But they can't."

"All the kids have a joint share of the business. The loan needs to be renegotiated, and the girls are refusing to sign up for the new one."

"But I don't even get why the bank is on your tail. You're always so busy at work. You're always snowed under."

"It's the price of credit. It's the recession. Anyway, that's not the point. The bank says it has to be done and I need all the kids to sign and they…" He jumped out of bed. "I'll have to go. I need to get this sorted. He hurried towards the en suite, and then rushed back and leaned over the bed and kissed me and said "I love you, Daise. I'm sorry about all the crap. But I need to go. I have to figure out what to do."

And now I am sitting here at home, fretting again.

He loves his business.

He loves his gurls.

He loves me.

Something has got to give.

What is the way out of this mess? If he chooses me, he might lose the business *and* the gurls. If he chooses the gurls, he can keep his business, but he will lose me. I don't like the maths of this conundrum. I don't like them at all. I wish I had a bad habit like biting my nails: it would be such a comfort.

How am I going to keep myself occupied while he sorts this out? I should be working on my novel's 'Dark Moment' ("wherein," Billy Mernit says in *Writing the Romantic Comedy*, "the consequences of the swivel decision yield disaster") but how can I, when I am worrying about how Kit will sort things out? I know how he loves Wyatt Printing. Maybe he'll choose that and his family.

I've sent him a text:

Good luck. I won't pester you with messages. I'll just wait to hear. I love you. Daise. Xxxxxxx

today's tweet from **@sallystoneymoor**
mot du jour: conundrum.

Wednesday May 16th
Quiet as the grave

No phone calls, no texts, no messages. No publishing events to take my mind off things. Even Wendy and Richard are not here. They are house-hunting for Richard. Or is it for both of them?

I have cleaned the house, done all the washing (even those footie shin-guards of Sam's that have been at the bottom of the laundry basket for several years); I've been on my bike on the Trail, tidied my desk, done some weeding, and now I have run out of things to occupy me while I wait to hear from Kit. What's happening? What's going to happen to us? He loves his business. I am not convinced that he loves me more.

today's tweet from **@sallystoneymoor**
The lull after the book launch – the perfect space for spring cleaning.

Thursday May 17th

Home alone

No message from Kit.

I asked Richard today about Wendy. Is he happy?

"OK," he said. "This is how it is. I was sitting alone on a vandalised platform at midnight with the ticket booth closed, and no announcements, waiting for the train of death to arrive, and then Wendy rolled up and opened up the station café. The upshot: I am warm and happy, and I have the most wonderful distraction while I wait – Wendy."

He also said he has found a house and will be moving at the end of the month. Not that it will make much difference. I hardly see him these days: he is either out with Wendy, or they're ensconced in his room.

How strange it is that this is what I always wanted – peace and quiet. I should be careful what I wish for.

today's tweet from **@sallystoneymoor**
When the gods wish to punish us they answer our prayers.

Friday May 18th

Success!

Whoopee! I have been reviewed on two popular book blogs! Both reviews gave my book a 5 star rating. I love these people! I am checking my Amazon ranking hourly to watch for a spike in sales.

No message from Kit.

today's tweet from **@sallystoneymoor**
The cow parsley on my lane is divine – even higher and bushier than last year!

Saturday May 19th

Alone

No message from Kit.

I had another signing today – this time at Sheffield Waterstones. I asked Wendy if she wanted to come, but she and Richard were going to choose some curtains for his new house. So I went alone and had a miserable time. Then I came home and had a miserable time, which was alleviated by a visit from Iain and Angelina, which just shows how miserable I was before they arrived.

They are such an odd couple. He is hung up on good design and clean lines and good taste, and she is blowsy and unsubtle and the opposite of everything he holds dear. Does he like her? Or is he trapped? If it's the latter, why doesn't he just cut short his visit and scurry down south to stay with his daughter Bec?

today's tweet from **@sallystoneymoor**
Do opposites attract?

another tweet from **@sallystoneymoor**
There's nowt so queer as folk.

Sunday May 20th

Quid pro quo

No message from Kit. Has he made his decision? – i.e. to choose everything but me – but hasn't had the guts to tell me? He could take some lessons from Gus, who was entirely straightforward and always kept me informed i.e. "I like being on my own in the wilderness more than I like being with you in Goose Lane."

I was feeling so loose-endish and fed up with my own company, and even bored with whittling about Kit and his business and the future of our relationship, that when Sam and Xanthe called, wanting a bath and to recharge their iPad, I said, "Come in! Come in! How lovely to see you! Would you like to stay to tea?" They were visibly touched.

I made a cashew and apricot risotto (my only vegan dish) and an apple crumble with non-dairy fat. The latter was simply not worth the calories: how do people live without butter?

After tea, we were chatting about my book reviews and my sales, and Xanthe told me about her friend who has self-published an ebook and sold thousands. Apparently, the hot tip for e-book sales is to offer your ebook free for a period so it zooms up the charts, and then you start charging again and people buy it because it is visible i.e. at the top of the charts.

I remember seeing the bit on the Amazon contract that lets you offer your book for free for a bit, but I never ever considered it. Xanthe said it was what all the smart people do, but you need to link it with social marketing as well. I'll have to tweet about it, blog about it, and she said she would get her mum – who apparently has oceans of Facebook friends – to post it on her Facebook page.

And oh, bless her, she offered to help me with the technical side of this – what a sweetie she is! We're going to do it next weekend.

today's tweet from **@sallystoneymoor**
Butter and bacon – two things I can't live without.

Monday May 21st

Captive in the queue

I saw Kit today. No, he didn't ring. No, it wasn't arranged. I was in Matlock and I spotted him in a bakery buying a sandwich. He can go out and buy a bacon and egg on granary, but he can't find the time to contact me!

He looked awful – drawn and haggard and nervy. He was dancing from one foot to the other as he waited in the queue, and I rushed in to ask him what was going on. He barked his order at the girl behind the counter (forgetting to ask for his bacon crispy, which shows how stressed he was) and he handed over his money, and then he turned to me and clutched my arm and said: "I'm so pleased to see you."

"What on earth is up? What's happening?"

He groaned. "You really don't want to know. Better not to ask. It's way too complicated."

"Try me, Kit. Tell me. I want to help. Surely we can share things, can't we? You help me with stuff. Let me help *you*. Isn't that what it's all about?"

"Of course, usually, but on this one you have to trust me. It's better you're not involved. It's better you're completely out of it."

"Why? What's happening?"

"Everything I've ever worked for is on the line – the girls are still holding me to ransom. Unless I hand over my life to them, the business is kaput!" At which point his sandwich was ready and he grabbed it and turned to me and gave a grimace and said, "Catch you later," and rushed away, and all I got to do was open and close my mouth.

Later? When later???

Am I of no importance whatsoever? Why doesn't he discuss things with me and let me help? Why does he charge off and try to sort everything out on his own, when we are supposed to be an item? Why doesn't he realize that freezing me out makes me feel unimportant and irrelevant and…?

today's tweet from **@sallystoneymoor**
Isn't May wonderful? It's my favourite month of the year – the cow parsley, the hawthorn blossom, the fresh new leaves everywhere.

Tuesday May 22nd
Weighed in the balance and found wanting

In the absence of a proper conversation with Kit, what he said yesterday has been going round and round in my head. *'Unless I hand over my life to them…'* i.e. cut *me* out of his life.

It is no contest:

a business that a man has slaved all his life to build up and that he loves to bits, plus the confidence of all of his children

versus

a woman with big hips, only one breast and lots of wrinkles, whom he has known since Christmas, who gives him ultimatums about his kids, and who has a houseful of lodgers.

Correction: used to have a houseful of lodgers.

Tweet? There is no tweet. I can't even think of a sick-making one today.

Wednesday May 23rd

Lubrication

I called in at the shop to get some Smarties to cheer myself up, and Billy Bathgate said "Och, Mrs Howe, just the woman I wanted to see."

I thought he was going to say something nice about my book and I smiled expectantly.

"Mrs Howe, I heard you on the radio last week – you and your printer sound as if you've got a bit of a thing going on!" He wiggled his eyebrows and my insides turned to vinegar. "Congratulations! I was sorting out some old newspapers in the garage when I was listening, and I came across this article and saved it for you." He rummaged around under the counter, and brought out a cutting from the *Guardian* entitled *Sex and the over 60s.*

When I got home, I put the cutting on the kitchen table and squinted at it through the hands I had over my eyes. The first paragraph quoted Helen Gurley-Brown, the creator of *Cosmopolitan,* who was interviewed at the age of 80 and recommended a lubricant called Astroglide: "You be sure that you're all goopy before you get into bed."

Billy bloody Bathgate has overstepped the mark this time. The people in this village! The things I have to put up with!

today's tweet from **@sallystoneymoor**
mots du jour: irony and bathos

Thursday May 24th

Empty

An empty inbox. An empty house. An emptiness in my heart.

The only intrusion in the emptiness was Wendy rushing into my study and asking me to tell her Richard's birth time, so she could draw up his chart. I told her I had no idea. He is older than me. How would I know what time he was born?

"Damn it, Sally! The date and place is not enough. I need the time to find out what his Ascendant is and the exact degree of his moon. It's important. I want to do a composite chart for our relationship. I need to know if these little teething troubles we're having are likely to be ironed out eventually."

So all is not rosy with Wendy and Richard. I am not surprised, but it's a shame, even so.

today's tweet from **@sallystoneymoor**
when does a honeymoon end?

Friday May 25th

A close shave

Still no message from Kit. I am soooo fed up, and I am soooo fed up with recording in here that there is still no message.

Iain popped in and I invited him to stay for coffee, as Angelina wasn't with him. I can take only so much of that woman.

"Isn't it funny – and how nice – that you and Angelina have hit it off?" I said.

He sighed and ruffled his hair, which is showing signs of thinning on top, so there is less to ruffle than seven years ago when I was thinking of – ooh, I can't bear to think that I nearly threw everything over and went off with Iain.

"Actually, Sally, I came round to ask for your help. I don't know how to break it to her gently that I'm not interested. I never *was* interested."

"But why does she think you are?" As if anyone *could* break anything gently to Angelina.

"I have no idea how she got that impression," he said. "When we met over our croissants at the B & B on the first morning, I felt sorry for her and she just latched onto me and–"

"You felt sorry for Angelina? She's a predator!"

"That's a little harsh. She's a lonely widow."

"If you think that, Iain, there is absolutely nothing I can say to help. You're on your own."

today's tweet from **@sallystoneymoor**
Fascinating facts no. 23: After mating, the female black widow spider consumes the male.

Saturday May 26th

Rapprochement

Sam and Xanthe came over last night.

Sam wanted to use my printer to print flyers for their *Sod the Jubilee* events – alternative fun things for people to do instead of the village Jubilee, flag-waving ones.

"Oh Sam, why do you have to do this stuff?"

"Because it is blatantly wrong that someone is the head of state just because of who her father was. You're not a monarchist either!"

"No, I'm not, but–"

"Ma. You have to make a stand about things that are important. *All it takes for evil to triumph is for good men to do nothing.* Edmund Burke."

So I let him get on with it.

Meanwhile, Xanthe showed me how to sort out the ebook freebie thing. And she talked me through what to do later on when I start to charge for it. Now that I no longer have to stomach her protest nakedism and her pile of dirty dishes in the kitchen, I can see why Sam likes her. She's actually quite nice.

today's tweet from **@sallystoneymoor**
Download my new book for free and tell all your friends. Go to my blog and follow the link. Please retweet.

Sunday May 27th

Shock

My ebook is climbing up the best-seller lists – just like Xanthe said it would!

I spent two hours messing about on my computer, and breaking off every ten minutes to check my ranking, and in so doing, developed a thick head. So this afternoon I went up to Curbar Gap for a walk to blow the cobwebs away. It was crowded up there because it was a lovely day, but it did make me feel more relaxed. I love hilltop views of Derbyshire.

On the drive home, a broken down silage trailer was stranded in the middle of the road and the only way back was to go down a side road and past Kit's house. I felt jittery about catching sight of him or the gurls – or Gray or Brick come to that – because the longer it is that I don't hear from him, the more desperate the situation seems to be, and the more unlikely it is that we have a future.

And then I saw it! The estate agent's sign outside his house, with SOLD across it! My feet froze in an involuntary emergency stop, and my legs were shaking so much, I didn't want to start again, because I was worried about being unable to brake as I went down the hill.

I put on the handbrake, and rolled down the window to get some air, and a man with a dog walked by (was it a neighbour of Kit's?) and he called out – as only dog-walking villagers do – "Bad luck! You're too late! It's a lovely house, a great place to live, but it went in two days. He was desperate to sell. Business trouble, I hear. Plus he's leaving the area."

Selling up and leaving Derbyshire? He must be in even bigger trouble than I thought. And yet he hasn't shared the problem with me.

And he is leaving without telling me.

I wish I was dead.

today's tweet from **@sallystoneymoor**
Last chance tonight to download a copy of my book for free. Go for it!

Monday May 28th

Desperation

Desperation.

today's tweet from **@sallystoneymoor**
Yay! My book is soaring up the Amazon ebook bestseller chart!

Tuesday May 29th

The highs and the lows

Is it true? What is Kit *really* doing? Surely he wouldn't leave without telling me. He couldn't. If he does, I have misjudged him completely.

I watched a week's worth of online *Neighbours* back to back this afternoon. I have already seen all the episodes but who the hell cares? It is the only way I can think of to numb my brain.

today's tweet from **@sallystoneymoor**
My book is at Number 2 in the ebook chart! Yay!

As if it matters. As if I care.

Wednesday May 30th

Forgotten date

Nina rang this morning at breakfast to tell me what time she and the kids would be arriving, and I had forgotten they were arriving at all! It's been on the kitchen calendar for weeks but I never wrote it in my *Mslexia* diary, and that's the one I've been living by. I managed – by the skin of my teeth – not to let on to *her*. Then I put down the phone and raced around like crazy, sorting out beds and bedding, retrieving the toy boxes from the attic, erecting the cot that lives in the corner of the spare room, and haring down to the Co-op to stock up on fish fingers, frozen chips and Petit Filous fromage-frais.

Then they were *here,* and the afternoon and evening passed in hugs, Lego, dinosaurs, a trip to the village rec, bathtime, and bedtime stories. They are so sweet! Tell me again why I need a man?

Tomorrow, Nina is visiting her friend Sara in Sheffield and taking Liesl with her and I am taking Ellie and Fabian to the Heights of Abraham, because I apparently promised Fabian last time he was here that I would take him for a ride on the cable-cars.

today's tweet from **@sallystoneymoor**
"Grandchildren are nature's reward for not strangling your teenagers." Anon.

Thursday May 31st

The end of our story?

So there I was, shoving a bottle of diluted orange juice ("without bits, Gran!") into a backpack, and calling to Fabian and Ellie to go for a wee and then get their shoes on, when the phone rang and it was Kit.

"Daise! How are you? What are you doing? Today? Right now? I need to see you!"

My heart was thumping like crazy and I was sweaty and trembly, and I was assessing the tone of his voice and thinking – *YES! He sounds upbeat. He sounds affectionate. He sounds as if things are really, really OK* – and a tide of relief swept over me.

"Daise? Are you there?"

"Yes, yes. It's nice to hear your voice. I thought you'd–"

"Look," he interrupted, "I'm in a hurry, but there's something I want to tell you in person. Today. This morning. Can I come round?"

And I thought – hmmm. He ignores me for days, he tells me nothing. Days – no, weeks! – go by and I hear nothing. I find out by chance that he's sold his house, I think that all is lost and he has scarpered, that he's left me without saying anything, and then completely out of the bloody blue, he rings me up and wants to see me immediately. Well, if he's that keen, he can wait. I have had enough of his cutting me out of the loop, his on-again off-again, run away and hide when things get tough behaviour, all these pathetic strops of his! Right now my grandchildren are here, and they're my priority and he can stuff it.

"No," I said. "Sorry. You can't come round right now. I'm busy."

"What are you doing that's so important? I need to see you."

"That's very nice, Kit. I have been wanting to see you, too. Even just to *hear* from you would have been nice. Unfortunately, now is not convenient. I have a date with Fabian and–"

"Who the hell is Fabian?"

"My grandson."

"Of course! Sorry! But why can't I come round? It'll only take five minutes."

"Look, if it really won't wait, I'll see you in – let's think – forty minutes? At Matlock Bath. Get your ass down there. We're going on the cable-cars to the Heights of Abraham. We'll meet you in the car park."

That was telling him. As I drove down the A6 I was feeling mighty pleased with myself that for once I had set the terms of engagement. Maybe I've grown up a bit in the last few months.

I parked the car and got out and looked around for Kit's red Volvo, but couldn't see it. The place was busy and I didn't want to be queuing for ages so I helped the kids out of the car and we walked to the cable-car station and queued behind a couple with a little boy, and two old ladies. Five minutes later, the old ladies were disappearing up the hill, and I was opening my purse to buy our tickets, and Kit arrived, panting and saying "Let me pay!"

He was red in the face, and sweaty, and my heart flipped over.

Then our cable-car swished down and we had to clamber in as quickly as we could, because the cars slow down, but they don't stop. Kit was on one end of the seat and I was on the other, and Fabian and Ellie were sitting between us. The kids were looking out of the window and oohing and aahing and Kit and I were eating each other up with our eyes, over the tops of their heads.

Eventually, I said, "Fancy meeting you here."

And he blurted out: "It's all done. The house has gone. Someone came along with cash and snapped it up. So now the bank is off my back."

"Kit, that's wonderful." I reached my hand along the back of the seat and squeezed his shoulder. He reciprocated and tickled my neck. "But your house! Your house that you loved so much!"

And the cable-car paused half way up the hill, as it always does (whilst the next lot of people are getting on and off) and it swayed a little bit, and Fabian turned round and said, "Why have we stopped? Is it going to crash?" and then he saw our arms reached out to each other and said "Is Kit your boyfriend?"

And Kit said "Yes."

And Fabian said "Oh." Then, "Oh, look. We're moving again!" and lost interest in Gran's love-life and pointed out some canoes on the river to Ellie.

"It had to be done," said Kit to me. "And the business is saved. Wyatt Printing lives on. I can buy a new house, you can move in, and the kids can sod off – I'm free!"

And before I had time to comment on, or even assimilate the bit about moving in with him, the cable-car swooshed into the summit station, and Kit helped us all to get off.

Fabian and Ellie were holding my hands and tugging me towards the path up the hill, but Kit lunged towards me and hugged me – very awkwardly, I have to say: it is not an easy manoeuvre to lean into a passionate embrace when you are holding two grandchildren by the hands.

And he said: "So that's it. Sorry. Got to go. Already late for signing papers at the bank. But I wanted to tell you myself, face-to-face. Monsal Head Hotel tonight? Fischer's was fully booked. I'll ring later," and before I had time to answer, he'd jumped in the cable-car going down and I was wondering if I was picking my stomach off the floor because of the cable-car ride, or his news. Or because of his arrogant assumptions! It was so, so like him, so typical to assume that I would want to move in with him with absolutely no discussion!

"Come on, let's go to the Woodland Adventure bit," I said to the kids. They could run off some of their exhausting energy while I sat and considered Kit and my future. Damn! I hadn't told him I'd been number 2 on the Amazon ebook ranking.

"Look at me, look at me!" shouted Fabian as he scrambled up the rope net.

"Fantastic!" I shouted, while thinking, *move in with Kit?* All the implications rushed through my head. What would happen when either of the families wanted to stay? What would happen at Christmas, for instance? How could we possibly merge all our children? The dynamics were hard enough now when they were all in separate houses. And the gurls would behave no differently. They would be just as vile. Possibly more vile, now their dad had put his feelings for me on the line and got rid of their family home. Did Kit think we'd be sailing off into the sunset in his new, small, but perfectly formed house, and waving two fingers at the girls as they fled the kingdom? He was mad.

After the playground we did the caves, then a little bit of gold panning, and sifting sand to find gems. They liked the activities, and I liked the space. Everything is so tasteful at the Heights – the lovely views, the high end design. I ought to tell Iain about the shingle roofs.

We had our picnic and the children went on the hillside slide, and then back to the adventure playground, where I sat and thought some more about what I was going to say to Kit tonight.

Had it occurred to him that I love my house as much as he loves/loved his? That I might not want to sell up? That I might be happy with our weekends-only arrangement? No of course not – he had seen everything from his point of view. That's why he'd been silent for two weeks and kept me in the dark while he sorted everything out. It hadn't occurred to him that I might be worried about him…or about us. Did I want a future with a man like that? A man who had to be brought to the wire before he stood up to the manipulations of his daughters? A man with a quick temper who exploded at the tiniest provocation, who went off in a strop rather than face up to things and talk them over and reach agreement? Did I?

Well, no-one is perfect. And I love him. I really love him.

But...how could I be with a person who completely shuts me out when things get tough?

Later:

In the evening, over dinner at the Monsal Head Hotel, I wanted to sort things out. I asked him why he'd done his vanishing act, why he hadn't told me what was going on.

"It was really hurtful, Kit. It still is hurtful. Don't you think I'm important enough to discuss your problems with? Or do you think I'm too stupid to be able to help? Which?"

"You're being stupid, now!" He took both my hands in his. "Of course I want you involved and helping me. Of course you're not dumb. This specific problem was different. It was vital to sort it out alone. I didn't want the kids accusing you of interfering. Selling the house was a huge thing for me, but even more so for them! It's so painful for them, tied up as it is with their memories of Juliet. I wanted it to be plain that it came from me, me alone. If they ever ask me in the future about it, I'll be able to say – hand on heart – that I didn't discuss it with you, didn't see you when I was deciding, didn't even ring you up. I don't want them blaming you. I was considering the future – you and me. I thought I'd explained that in the sandwich shop. Didn't I?

"No. You didn't."

"Do you get it now?"

I nodded. Now I understood, and I forgave him everything.

"Well, we need to find a house," he said.

"I don't think so, Kit."

"What? What are you–"

"Don't look so worried! I see us as permanent. I just wasn't expecting this moving-in-together thing."

"But couples *should* live together!"

"*Should?* Are you still doing *should* at your age? Who cares what's conventional? We need to do what makes *us* happy. Don't you think it works – seeing each other at the weekend, and being apart in the week? It's not just me. You like to concentrate on the business."

"Maybe."

"And the thing is, Kit, just lately I've had my house full of lodgers and I actually like being on my own. I love being with you at weekends, of course. But in the week, I get more done. I can think straight. Or I can think in a dreamlike bendy way which is good for writing. I think the weekend model suits us both."

"Perhaps."

"And another thing. If we move in together now, we could alienate the girls forever. I'm sure they'll eventually come round to the idea of me and you. And in the meantime I will work really hard at learning to shrug off their insults."

"They're not bad girls."

I made no comment on this one. I just went on with what I had planned to say. Gosh, I am grown-up these days. "We can have extended holidays – like the US road trip – and we can each have our own house for now, and maybe when we're both ready to do garden centres and move into sheltered accommodation, we can do that together."

"Oh, God."

"I just mean that it's all about finding a solution for now, not a set-in-stone-forever solution."

I sat back in my chair and took a sip of champagne.

"Have you quite finished, bossy boots?" he said.

"As long as you agree."

"Hey – I forgot to say – well done on your sales! I've been checking your Amazon ranking every day. Well done!"

Talking in bed…

Me: "I've always wanted to wake up here – with this fab, fab view of Monsal Dale. That's two things you've wiped off my list – seeing Venice again, and this."

Kit: "What about our couples list? What shall we put on it? Niagara Falls?"

Me: "Nah."

Kit: "That's a relief! Have you ever seen fire flies?"

Me: "No – I'd like to! What about a humming bird?"

Kit: "Stick it on the list. And a kingfisher."

Me:"It would be nice to see the Northern Lights together."

Kit: "And fly somewhere first class!"

Me: "Oooh, yes! And I saw an advert for a Fleetwood Mac Tour at the weekend. They're coming to Manchester! Next year! Shall we book?"

today's tweet from **@sallystoneymoor**
@kitwyatt43 "You've ruined it for me, you know – being alone." (Finch-Hatton in Out of Africa.)

p.s. Finally, I can get on with writing the end of my novel. I need to put Jenny and Liam out of their misery in the 'Joyful Defeat: Resolution.'

Acknowledgements

We'd like to thank:

Dave Hepworth for all kinds of things, but he'd rather we didn't, so we won't;

Phil Cushway for proof-reading and copy-editing and for his comments, suggestions and support;

Chrissie Poulson, for commenting on an earlier draft, and for all kinds of encouragement;

Billy Mernit, for his immediate warm, affirmative response when we asked for permission to quote from his book, *Writing the Romantic Comedy*;

Ruth Carter, Mary Dalgleish, Karen Fine, Jan Hill and *Wirksworth Writers* for reading and commenting on earlier drafts;

Geoff Fisher of CPI for his patience, advice and professional help beyond the call of duty;

Zoë Hepworth for the lovely cover design and execution;

Peter Sharman, of *Peter Sharman Photography* for the brilliant cover photograph;

Isaac Hepworth for help with the cover layout;

Juliet Arthur of stimula.co.uk for her expert work on the cover - artwork and production;

Liz McGregor for the phrase "tea bag tits;"

And to everyone not already mentioned who put up with moans and groans and expletives and complaints – you know who you are – a big thank you.

Permissions